About the Author

Alex Cherniack is a technical writer from Boston living in Cuenca, Ecuador. A national chess master and a boxing enthusiast, he is also the author of *Chess for Adult Beginners* and *Chess for Advanced Adult Beginners* (available from Amazon).

Black and White and Red All Over

Alex Cherniack

Black and White and Red All Over

Olympia Publishers
London

www.olympiapublishers.com
OLYMPIA PAPERBACK EDITION

Copyright © Alex Cherniack 2023

The right of Alex Cherniack to be identified as author of
this work has been asserted in accordance with sections 77 and 78 of the
Copyright, Designs and Patents Act 1988.

All Rights Reserved

No reproduction, copy or transmission of this publication
may be made without written permission.
No paragraph of this publication may be reproduced,
copied or transmitted save with the written permission of the publisher, or in
accordance with the provisions
of the Copyright Act 1956 (as amended).

Any person who commits any unauthorised act in relation to
this publication may be liable to criminal
prosecution and civil claims for damage.

A CIP catalogue record for this title is
available from the British Library.

ISBN: 978-1-80074-703-6

This is a work of fiction.
Names, characters, places and incidents originate from the writer's imagination.
Any resemblance to actual persons, living or dead, is purely coincidental.

First Published in 2023

**Olympia Publishers
Tallis House
2 Tallis Street
London
EC4Y 0AB**
Printed in Great Britain

CHAPTER ONE

Axel was mystified why the hospital and the cemetery were so close together. Their proximity to each other was morbid. What was a patient to think, knowing that graves were just around the corner? Not that his father ever noticed. He had been brought in at three in the morning for another round of hepatic encephalopathy, which had been so scary that Axel could not sleep. Even with a clearer head his father only saw the outside of the car window towards his ever-increasing doctor appointments, and never saw beyond the traffic lights.

It would be eight years next month since Axel had lived in an apartment next door to his father. His sister had a family and the conventional semblance of a full life, while he had remained a bachelor and a loner. His father's health deteriorated badly after he turned sixty. Years of drinking, smoking, and never exercising had caught up with a vengeance; he needed someone close by to take him to the hospital whenever he needed urgent medical care.

In terms of health, it was hard to imagine how they were related. While his father was struggling with cirrhosis, emphysema, gout, shingles, and lupus, Axel had never suffered from any medical ailment worse than a cold. While not a jock, Axel always made it a point to get in some sort of exercise every day before he went to sleep – he did so because he liked to offset the four dozen bottles of red wine he consumed every month. In contrast, the doctors had ordered his father to stop cold turkey a few years ago.

It was painful to see his father's mind slip away along with his body. The encephalopathy came from his diseased liver, causing ammonia to seep into his brain and cause episodes of dementia. Last week he confidently said that his personal helicopter would pick him up and deliver him to his appointments on time; the week before that he had complained that he could not find his watch, not seeing it on his wrist. All those decades in front of the TV with a scotch and ice in his hands were coming home to roost.

Axel, though, was still here, feeling his childhood drip away. The faucet in the family sink was loose and could not be tightened again. He took frequent walks in the nearby cemetery, his iPod on full blast, walking for the sake of walking while the doctors looked after his father. He walked blithely on by the tombstones, not remotely interested in what names and dates were written there, and kept going until his feet ached. Driving his father home, the only physical contact that still felt good was his foot on the accelerator.

His father's mind, when fully present, was formidable. He used to plough through three to five books a week in every conceivable genre, from science fiction to detective mysteries to physics textbooks to biographies. His bookcase filled three entire walls of a large room. But now his sole intellectual stimulation came from a television set, and it was depressing for Axel to see his engagement with the outside world reduced to a remote control.

He used to be genuinely funny too. He could take the essence of a conversation, break it down into its atomic components, and deftly rearrange them so that they came out as absurd and hilarious. (His mother-in-law asked him why he had ever bothered asking for her daughter's hand in marriage, from whom he later divorced. He replied that he didn't marry her for her hand.) But now the humor was forced and parasitic. It became obvious that he needed the input of others for him to perform his tricks, which he was going to perform, unasked for or not. And the jokes became more and more mean-spirited at someone else's expense, usually Axel's, such as always paying the check at restaurants and wondering aloud on the car ride home why his driver was such a cheapskate.

The duty in taking care of his father was still there, but the joy was gone. What replaced it was an inchoate need to knock something solid to the ground. All the delicate maneuvering and persuasion to keep another's life in order was choking the throttle that had once made the wind race through his hair. It was as if he was stuck in that black and white prelude part of the movie *The Wizard Of Oz*.

Axel still loved playing chess – it was his one ego-boosting mechanism that had survived childhood – but his internal editor had begun to sour his move selection. Long before his games had ended, he was excoriating himself for not playing the best continuation at the board, and not dominating his opponent from beginning to end. Even his wins were tainted; he didn't see the winning move sooner, or he didn't convert his advantage in the shortest number of moves. The computer program on his laptop afterward showed up his carbon-based life form limitations at the chessboard without pity. Paradoxically his expectations increased while his self-confidence withered at the board.

His father kept asking Axel to show him his chess games, even though his mind was becoming too distracted to follow the games beyond the opening. It was heartbreaking to Axel, whose father had taught him how to play. All his father could do now was strain to remember how the pieces moved when a game was shown to him. Axel's appetite for chess was turning sour.

The taste was not yet bitter. Chess allowed Axel a refuge from all the negative feelings that were suffusing his days. He still enjoyed creating a work of art with a challenging adversary across the board, and being kept on his toes. However, all the people he kept seeing in the tournament hall were irritating the hell out of him - deep down, he knew that he needed to find a new outlet.

One spring weekend Axel played in a chess tournament a three-hour drive away and had one of the best results of his life, actually winning more money than his traveling expenses. He returned to find his father's apartment empty. He called his sister and discovered that his father had been placed in a hospice. Axel desperately wanted to hold on to the pleasure of his victory a little longer, but realized that it meant nothing in the grand scheme of things. Even the grand scheme didn't feel that grand at all.

Axel tried seeing a psychologist, but outside of a pair of sympathetic eyes and well-meaning murmurings, the sessions did nothing for him. What only helped was red wine, lots of it. The resulting stupor allowed him to get some sleep, even if it didn't exorcise the gloom. The hangovers were easy to push through at work – all it took was practice.

Work was developing technical specifications at an electrical engineering company; he enjoyed taking raw data and turning it into information that others could use, and the company accepted Axel's character quirks as long as he continued to turn in decent work. After he told his boss that his father was dying, Axel was allowed to take mornings off indefinitely to visit the hospice. He never said a word about his father's condition to his co-workers.

Visits to the hospice were full of regrets and frustrations. The family never had explosive arguments. To blow up meant a loss of control, considered to be as bad as shitting in your pants. Axel's father and mother always said "Fuck you" obliquely, never raising their voices, and when they divorced, they did it smoothly by arbitration, without recriminations. Axel had rarely been physically abused; the few beatings he had received as a kid came from his mother. The most violent thing his father had ever done to him was to throw a drink in his face, and the most violent thing Axel had ever done to his father was to shove him across the room in retaliation, resulting in his being kicked out of the house for a week. It was hard, if not impossible, to apologize for harsh words that had been said, for so few had ever been spoken.

The best Axel could do at the hospice was to thank his father for all the things he had given: teaching him how to play chess and how to drive were the two biggest things Axel could come up with. Giving him life was one thing Axel could not bring himself to express in gratitude. He had never felt like he was eighteen or twenty-one, only a stunted tree in a forest without enough sunlight. Sometimes his father was mentally engaged while lying prostrate on his bed, other times the lights were on but nobody was home. It was difficult to judge which situation felt more uncomfortable.

He opened up bottle after bottle of red wine back at his apartment, giving up any pretense of tasting, and even of consuming. Axel almost wished that they sold wine in intravenous injection packages. Part of him was worried that he would end up as his father, but the dark red velvety cushion that poured into his glass was the only entity in the entire universe on which he could lay his freefalling head.

The days and nights staggered on for the next few weeks. One late afternoon when the nurse was there to administer painkillers his father grasped Axel's hand with a wild look. They shook hands with a surprising force, and his father said "Bye." This, Axel was not prepared to process. He replied: "I've always loved you, Dad," which brought tears to his father's eyes. The nurse gently said she needed to check the vital signs of Axel's father. Axel promised to return in a few hours after dinner. When he returned, his father was asleep. Axel left, remembering with animal clarity the high-pitched, ragged breathing.

At nine o'clock that evening Axel received a call at home from his sister. She said that their father had just passed away in his sleep. He had already drunk much more than a bottle of Chianti to wash down his pasta, but he agreed to meet her and his brother-in-law at the body of their late father. He drove over with a bottle of cognac, because he couldn't think of anything better to do. His sister wept uncontrollably, but Axel was numb and just didn't have any emotional gas in the tank.

The brother-in-law had brought a bottle of premium California cabernet sauvignon, a gift from Axel's father last Christmas. Axel helped polish off the bottle in between toasts that sounded tinny, and consumed a good part of the cognac on his own. Then he drove home, incredibly arriving back at the apartment in one piece. He croaked out a message to his boss, telling him what had happened and to not expect him at work tomorrow, lay down on the bed, closed his eyes, and slept.

When he awoke, a huge hole had opened up in his chest. Nothing much had been said, but so much had happened. Words would have to walk a hundred thousand miles to describe what Axel was feeling now. Within an hour his mother called, asking him if he was OK. *How am I supposed to feel OK?*, he thought, but replied that he was managing. Then she invited him to stay with her for the next couple of days. The prospect of spending another night next to the apartment of a dead man was more than he could stomach, and he quickly agreed.

His sister made all the arrangements and organized the funeral. All Axel had to do was show up. His mother persuaded him to recite the Dylan Thomas poem "Do not go gentle into that good night" at the service; however, the words just felt like vowels and consonants, his dry throat straining to get out what he was obligated to say. Many people attended the funeral offering condolences, but Axel was not in the mood to talk with any of them. Inside a rage that had been gestating for a very long time, having no name nor corporeal form, had hatched. It wanted fresh meat, not consolation.

CHAPTER TWO

Axel was born with a bad temper that must have shone enough in his eyes, and kept would-be attackers away in high school. He was too big to beat up physically, and had never stopped developing his body in the same compulsive way he studied chess, as if it were all part of his routine of brushing his teeth. Ever since the age of sixteen he did a hundred push-ups a day, and spurned bus rides if possible, in favor of five- to ten-mile walks.

In college he would add Nautilus weight training to his routine, compulsively going through circuit after circuit until he could do the maximum weight at each station. He could always push a little more weight above his head, calculate just one move further during a chess game at the board, and glare down just about anybody. Axel's mind and body were fine, but his social skills lagged far behind.

Axel was past thirty, had never had a steady girlfriend, and was still a virgin. His world, for all its earthy absence, was hermetically self-sufficient, and he made it work by sheer bloody-mindedness. He grew up never seeing his father need another human being to make his life complete, and neither did he. Axel made himself believe that what he didn't have, he didn't need.

He loved chess because it was self-contained. It had a thick barrier around first rank, the h-file, the last rank, and the a-file. Nested grid lines from the b, c, d, e, f, and g files and the second to seventh ranks further kept chaos from flooding in, like those air-locked containers inside submarines. The squares created files, ranks, and diagonals that crisscrossed the board; they cut through the light and the dark where white and black pieces slammed into each other as did light and shadow during the day, creating positions that were as unique as fingerprints. Each position had a tilt and a texture that was unlike any other, yet looked familiar in positions he had never seen before.

He was born with a belief that there had to be one set of rules that applied to everything. Once he discovered chess, he did not look any further. He fell in love with the sixty-four contained squares hosting six different pieces that interacted in near infinite ways. He grew to love the yin and yang of the alternately colored squares, and the way the pieces could still move in his head long after the chess set had been put away. Axel became good at chess in a hurry. He learned the moves at eight, was able to beat his father at ten, and became better than most adults he encountered by the age of twelve. He earned his master title when he was nineteen.

The better Axel became at chess, the more he wrote off his classmates as fucking assholes who weren't worth reaching out to. Middle school students found an odd nail sticking out in their midst that was too irresistible to hammer down, and teased him mercilessly. In junior high it switched to bullying, with bizarre streaks of cruelty. Once he was playing three chess games simultaneously in homeroom without looking at any of the boards; someone had taped a sign on his back while he was closing his eyes and concentrating. The sign said: "I am weird." However, confrontations had no interest for him. He didn't have the wit nor the nerve to tell the hormone-infused jerks to fuck off, simply tuning them out and concentrating more on his chess, the game replacing all the validation and variety human company could provide.

Axel wanted to be a professional chess player after graduating university, but inevitably reached the limit of his natural talent no matter how much study he put into the game, and had to find a job.

After bouncing around several temp positions for a while, he finally found a job he enjoyed, in a warehouse for a wine company. The work involved unloading containers of wine cases, stacking them in back of the building in logical order, and doing deliveries as necessary. Axel loved it. He developed a great raunchy comradery with his co-workers, learned how to drive around in the city using someone else's vehicle, and safely lift cases with his legs that weighed between forty and seventy pounds each all day, five days a week. After finishing work, he regularly went to the gym lifting weights to protect his back, and quickly bulked up to two hundred and sixty pounds on an even six-foot frame. He would also knock back entire six-packs of beer in one sitting, having so much fun that he never bothered to understand why he never lost any weight.

Eventually Axel became curious about what was inside the cases he was hauling all day long. He put in for a transfer to the wine company's retail outlet in the city. He started out from being the clueless one to the most experienced salesman in the store. In those five years he learned his way around a wine label, and how to convey that knowledge to customers. It was easy because he loved the products, and the benefits were great. With his wholesale discount he could afford to down a bottle of wine with each dinner, and half a bottle for lunch. The products at hand made all socially anxious moments melt away. He also acquired more firsthand knowledge of the taste of the wines on the shelves, and a bigger vocabulary; all the alcohol he was knocking back was an afterthought.

His boss was cool, and the work was fulfilling, but the pay was lousy. Axel decided to switch careers to technical communication not only because it paid better, but also because the lack of training in the software at one of his early temporary jobs still rankled him. Explanations should be explicit and easy to follow, not inferred and forced to guess. He earned a communications degree at a local university, and had to job hunt on the sly for the next year and a half until an electrical engineering company took a chance and hired him. This was the same company that was employing him seven years later when his father became sick.

Axel had a week off before starting his first writing job, and celebrated for three days straight with a case and a half of wine, totally oblivious to all the corks that were in his trash barrel. He had no idea how dependent on alcohol he had become over his past ten years working in wine stores. His new career was beginning, the years in his former profession about to recede, yet in the background he had grown to need alcohol each day for his weeks to run smoothly.

Axel told himself he was just drinking his fill. He knew he was doing good work in his new profession, and sincerely believed that he was reliably showing up for work each day. But cracks began to show through the veneer. As his father's health increasingly deteriorated, he noticed himself with open magnums of wine during the weeknights to wash down TV-dinners, and was finishing them off to boost the buzz of the music that blared through his stereo headphones.

He called in sick, he realized much later, an average of thirty mornings per year he worked at the company, due to splitting hangovers. A month of sick days was way over the official company limit, and the only way Axel got away with it was because he was still able to meet his deadlines, and because his boss too had health issues that took him out of the office for even longer periods of time. By sheer luck Axel was slipping by in a company that rightly should have fired him years ago. The luck should have run out after his father died.

Axel increased his alcohol intake even more after he returned to work when the bereavement leave was over. He had switched to wines in a box, which held three to six liters of wine per container, and no longer discriminated between white and red to pair with the store-bought food heating in the microwave. His compulsive nature required him to finish the contents of the boxes in at most two sittings, and he kept chugging, the hangovers becoming the new normal. He still did a hundred push-ups every day, and could run a few miles if he absolutely had to, but the booze was saddling him with embarrassing extra body fat.

An unsodden part of Axel rebelled against the nightly compulsion of finishing off the box of wine that now always lay open on his kitchen counter. He symbolically poured out a token amount of wine down the sink drain when he got home to his empty apartment, as if he was squirting out a little liquid from a needle to avoid injecting air bubbles into his bloodstream. But once the first glass had been emptied, some low-pressure system opened up in his brain, and had to be brought up to level no matter how many more glasses were downed. He felt like he was drowning, playing less and less chess.

That summer, the other lone male co-worker in his department was accused of sexual harassment, which made his job hang by a thread. Clannishly sticking together, the five other women in the department closed ranks. One of these women egged on the girl making the complaint, showing her which forms to fill out and what numbers to call. Axel felt menaced, and reduced all talk with the females to a bare minimum. The male co-worker was suspended for a week, and to Axel became his only colleague – the women he mentally demoted to co-workers. Unfortunately, his boss had to take the entire department into account, and preferred an uneasy silence to hard choices that might require shaking up the workplace.

One obnoxious female co-worker would not let it go at that. She was a part-time single mom who upon meeting him blurted out that Axel looked like her ex-husband. On the second day of his male colleague's suspension she strode up to his desk, saying that the woman who helped the girl file the complaint – she was her FRIEND – had done nothing wrong. Axel tersely replied that he didn't want to talk about it. The woman stormed away in a huff.

At the copier on the fourth day of his male colleague's suspension, she came up and said that she did not like the way Axel had been looking at her that morning. She tried to say something else, but he walked away from her in mid-sentence. He would not have another conversation with her for as long as he worked there. His male colleague kept his job, but was afraid to talk to anyone in the rest of the department. Axel was not scared, but coiled and magnetically repulsed, up against a hyper-vigilant gang of five, ready to use whatever came out of his mouth against him. They were priming potential attacks on the other side of the chessboard, while Axel kept all his pawns on the third rank, shuffling his pieces behind the pawns, waiting for his opponents to make the first aggressive moves.

That obnoxious female co-worker made Axel really, really angry. She lazily relied on a preponderance of women in the department, socializing in every cubicle on the floor, and doing the bare minimum required at her job. Axel in turn closed down, and went about making himself so overqualified that his boss would not think twice about letting him go.

Over the next few years, he upgraded his technical skills in courses at local universities, and volunteered for projects that went far beyond the typical clerical upkeep in his position. He also went to professional conferences, visited client sites, and soon was on a first name basis with most of the company's senior managers. Once he knew he had a job there for as long as he wanted, Axel only talked to people in his department when absolutely necessary.

The underlying feelings the alcohol was masking were becoming harder and harder to keep down. The feelings alternated between guilt and anger. Guilt because his higher brain knew that all the self-medication was not a sustainable way to go on, and anger in his lower brain because the feeling was just there, all the time.

As the year drew to a close, Axel grew to hate his reflection in the mirror. His brain knew that his life was mixing less and less gracefully with alcohol, yet his protruding gut craved otherwise. Axel was trying to limit his intake to the good stuff only on weekends. However, quantity for the sake of physically stabilizing his body's internal barometer won out over quality. He did not go so far as to spit in his reflection, but on certain days he came close. He was looking for a future version of himself that he wanted to see that just wasn't there.

The more he looked into his face, the less there was to see. His eyes, nose, mouth, ears, and hair looked as indistinct as the apartment he had been living in. Axel without knowing it had become indifferent to his clothes, his furniture, his food, and his apartment that he cleaned only when he absolutely had to. Going out at night instead of drinking at home became too much of a bother; bright sunny days made him miserable. He had heard all the songs in his music collection many times over, yet continued to listen to them for their reassurance, with plenty of liquid reinforcement.

He remembered during one of his head trips inside his stereo headphones when his father picked him up from college at the end of his junior year; they spent five uncomfortable hours in the car, not knowing what to say to each other. Attempts at conversation dried up after every few minutes. They stopped off for lunch halfway home, and while they were waiting for their food, he abruptly said that everyone had demons, and the best one could do was keep them at bay. Then during dessert, he said just as abruptly not to try and change him; he was who he was. Axel felt that way right now – he was who he was, only becoming more so of less.

He kept seeing all those couples on the street holding hands, and became increasingly pissed off and frustrated. *All those happy people clutching each other and going subliminally broke*, Axel muttered darkly, wishing that for just one week, he could experience life in their shoes. Connecting with people was so overthought and undersexed. *Get your own house in order first*, Axel said to himself, while never getting around to putting up a welcome mat outside his door.

CHAPTER THREE

It was December 30. He was alone yet again in his dirty apartment and he had plowed through a good portion of a three-liter box of Franzia Merlot. The box was less than half full, and there wouldn't be enough for tomorrow night – he had to get another one tomorrow before his supply ran out, Axel was thinking, and then a long-disconnected light bulb finally came on.

The previous week he had re-read Allen Carr's book *The Easy Way To Stop Drinking* with the concept of the deliberate last drink. *Why the hell not*, Axel muttered to himself, what did he have to lose, except another year of the same? At eight o'clock that night Axel poured himself one last glass, gulped it down, and dumped the rest down the drain. Then he went outside, put the empty wine box in the trash can, and hurriedly brushed his teeth before going to sleep.

On New Year's Eve Axel woke up, and suddenly discovered that his entire living space reeked of wine. After opening up all the windows, he used up all the Lysol and air freshener under his sink to wipe down the kitchen and clear away the stale air. He threw out his tablecloth because it was covered in wine stains, and then closed the windows before going to work.

After the office released everyone in mid-afternoon for the holiday, Axel treated himself to an early dinner at a premium steak house, drinking water. Upon returning home, he thoroughly scrubbed all the floors and vacuumed the carpets. Afterwards he walked around for over four hours, leaving all thoughts of chemical enhancement at home. He saw an hour of a Three Stooges marathon on TV, and then turned in well before the fireworks went off.

He woke up one hour before the dawn, and after another aimless, long walk suddenly decided to go to his chess club's traditional New Year's Day tournament. Entering the tournament's unrated section (unofficially the section for those nursing hangovers), he won with a perfect score. He went to sleep early again, and woke up with the satisfaction that he had been able to enjoy an entire day without the need for a glass or ten of red wine.

Chess to him in the following weeks became interesting to him again, even if he wasn't putting in enough study time required to make concrete progress. He played in a few more tournaments, his chess rating remaining steady. Axel had good chess results before, which had always been celebrated with a bottle and a half afterwards. The bottle was for the effort; the extra half was for the result.

But sometime in January he had decided to do the entire year without any more bottles, and beyond. He had done it for the first eighteen years of his life because he hadn't known what he was missing, but now he going for another Year Zero, as if alcohol had never been invented. He knew that ignoring longstanding habits would be far from easy, but vowed that chess and exercise would carry him through.

Axel signed up at the local YMCA, and became a fixture on the Nautilus, Stairmaster, stationary bike, and rowing machines for the next few months. By March he still had not had a drink, and had more energy than he had had in years. But after these workouts he remained mad as hell. The sight of Axel's obnoxious female co-worker continued to make him convulse in anger, and loneliness started creeping in from where he wasn't looking. He had a hole in his life, and was trying to patch it with the only tools he knew, minus a glass in his hand. Lots of feelings that he had anaesthetized with wine he managed to sweat off, but some stubbornly refused to be wiped down with a towel.

Axel belatedly remembered that every time he had tried to live alcohol-free, he had raced back to bottomless containers of wine with open arms. It was the boredom and the frustration that made sober life so mundanely hard; all that wine had made him forget enough of the bad stuff to indulge his imagination at the expense of his needs. Having needs made Axel deeply uncomfortable – they necessitated engagement and negotiation with total strangers – and a potential loss of control, which interfered with his imagination. Every morning he woke up in a panic, feeling like he was slipping further and further behind all his peers.

A bachelor chess player he knew suddenly passing away in April, leaving behind no wife nor kids, combined with not having been on a date in years, made Axel fatalistically decide to see a hooker. He could be hit by a truck anytime, and die never knowing what all the fuss was about. So long had he been out of the game, and so frustrating was it to still see all those couples holding hands during the weekends, that he wanted to know if his body parts worked below his waist.

Axel planned carefully, the Internet making research easy, but his first sexual experience was confusing and painful. The name of the escort he chose was Nancy, from an agency. He called at twelve thirty a.m. on a Saturday night, reaching an operator and requesting an hour-long outcall. After arriving and receiving her donation in an unsealed white envelope, Nancy asked Axel to strip and lie on his bed.

He had worked out the difference between incall and outcall, independent and agency, girlfriend experience and porn star experience; he did not want to haggle, considering only providers with listed prices; and he found escort review sites, declining to see someone with less than ten reviews that were more than a year old. What Axel did not work out were his nerves. His health was fine, his brain knew what he was supposed to do, but unused thickets of synapses were making him perform like an inert blow-up doll.

"What's the matter, Axel?" Nancy asked. She had been touching him all over, concentrating on his genitals for the past fifteen minutes, with less than a full erection to show for it.

"I've never done this before," Axel replied. "I've seen the act many times, but physically I don't quite know what to do."

"Sex isn't physical, baby. It's mental. Lie back, close your eyes, and take ten deep breaths."

Axel did as she asked. He soon became hard enough to have sex for the first time in his life. The first time lasted three minutes. The erection went away, and despite future attempts from Nancy to bring him back, they mutually agreed that nothing more was going to happen. Nancy put her clothes back on after half an hour.

"Sorry, Nancy. I did have a good time," Axel said to her at the door.

"You've never done this before, right?"

"Yes."

"This takes practice. Don't be discouraged from trying it again." Nancy had kind eyes. "And my name is not Nancy, it's Erin." She hugged Axel. "Take care," she said, closing the door behind her.

Contrary to his hopes, he felt more frustrated than ever after the experience. He was socially impotent, even if he was no longer poisoning his insides. Axel afterwards briefly tried blind dates through a singles web site. The encounters were more tense than fun, and Axel never got beyond a third date. When he steeled himself to go out stag on the town at nights, talking was too much foreplay to the sensations he had just purchased. His words came out hurriedly, and he felt so uncomfortable that he could not look at anyone in the eye longer than a blink.

Weeks dragged on, and then the months. Every day started with an overwhelming need to get something done, and ended with ambivalence and ambiguity. His life choices had exploded in complexity. Axel found that he had more flexibility in his choices, and could arrive at them with greater efficiency and precision. The extra time afterwards was exhausting. He could finish his to do lists much more quickly with a clear head, yet did not know what to do with the rest of the day.

Axel decided to stick to what he knew – the chess, the exercise – and miraculously the sobriety took. His one remaining vice was food, and he relegated exercise to a habit that would keep his weight down. He was running in place and not sinking into the ground, yet deep down he felt that something better was out there.

CHAPTER FOUR

During a walk around his neighborhood in July, Axel noticed a boxing gym and put it on his list of new things to try out. Well, almost new. While working in the wine warehouse many years ago, he tried out a boxing class in an adult education course. With the build from his maniacal weightlifting, he looked very intimidating in the ring. After learning the basics in his stance and punching mechanics, he discovered he could hit the bag hard. The instructor told him that he had potential, which might manifest itself after a few years of hard work. But Axel was still in the phase of sucking down entire six-packs of beer after workouts, and nothing came of it.

On an impulse the following day, he entered the boxing gym. The place was packed, filled with the sounds of the rat-a-tat-tat rhythms of combinations being thrown on the punching bags, and the shouted instructions of trainers from just outside the ring. The setting sun through the windows made long narrow shadows of the hanging bags on the floor. Axel's nostrils were struck by the pungent smell of acrid sweat that seemed to have hung in the air for longer than he had been alive. New beads of perspiration constantly formed and dropped to the parquet floor by the second. Some people there looked angry, others looked exhausted, but none looked like they were wasting their time. Some moved really fast, economizing their movements so that they hit without getting hit in return. *Just like chess*, Axel thought, *but out in the open.*

While Axel looked around, the owner came out of his office and introduced himself. "Hi, I'm Ted. How are you doing?" he said, extending his hand. He looked like he was in his early fifties, but if he was in his mid-sixties Axel would not have been surprised. Ted was barrel-chested, about a foot shorter than Axel, but had sharp, darting eyes, and not an ounce of body fat.

"I'm Axel. I'm doing fine." He was startled by how firm Ted's handshake was. "I noticed this place yesterday, and my curiosity got the better of me."

"So did most of the people you see working out now," Ted responded with a grin. "I'd be happy to answer any questions you have."

"I once boxed in my early twenties, but that was so long ago I think I'm going to have to learn all over again. Do you have any introductory classes, and if yes how much do they cost?"

"If you want to try us out for a month, the cost is eighty dollars. That covers group classes, self-guided workouts if you prefer those (the laminated printouts are there on the wall), and time with a trainer on the pads each time you come in."

Axel had made up his mind halfway through the conversation to join. Ted looked him in the eyes, not at the chess pieces, and his handshake was genuine instead of all the limp-wristed introverts Axel had been dealing with forever at chess tournaments. He followed Ted into his office. Ted asked if he had physical issues that might prevent him from boxing. Axel couldn't think of any. Then Ted took a waiver out of a drawer from his desk. Axel recognized the verbiage – it was standard at all the gyms he had gone to in the past – and signed the form. Ted ran Axel's card, giving him the receipt, and they shook hands once again. Axel promised to meet Ted for an appointment the following afternoon at 5:30.

The next day Axel showed up in workout clothes, with an extra T-shirt and a towel. He went through a ten-minute stretching routine and three three-minute rounds of jump rope. Axel's cardio was good enough for the nine minutes of the rope, but his coordination sucked, and he could not go more than ten seconds without the rope catching beneath his feet. It was infuriating. Axel knew how to walk and run, but not chew gum at the same time, because the damn gum was sticking to his shoes when he tried to bounce on and off the ground.

Then Ted put him through half an hour of plyometrics, including the push-ups Axel had done all his life. The push-ups gradually became hard, and then impossible by the time the third set had come around. So many of his muscle groups were being assaulted at the same time that not a single one could directly recover on its own. After a brief respite of practicing his jab and straight right in front of a mirror, the punching bags came next. Axel swore that the double end bag was laughing at him each time one of his many jabs missed. The speed bag was no kinder, the sound never reaching a frequency faster than the slow-to-medium tick of a metronome. The six rounds on the heavy bags ruthlessly sapped away all of Axel's remaining strength.

"So, are you ready for pads?" Ted asked.

You have got to be kidding me, Axel thought, as he struggled to control his ragged breathing. "Sure," he replied. The sun had set; at least the harsh light of the day was out of his eyes.

Ted introduced Axel to Jason, another fit and crusty looking man in middle age who could have been anywhere between forty-five and sixty-five years old. Although his arms were dog tired, Axel managed to land punches at the pads according to Jason's instructions for three rounds. Jason then turned Axel back over to Ted.

"Great," said Ted. "Now finish up with some abs. The routine is posted on the wall by the water fountain."

Axel had done many sit-ups in the past, but the experience did not help him a bit, as his legs and arms felt like they had been through a meat grinder. All of his extremities felt like they weighed a ton each, while his core did not feel any heavier than a feather. He managed to heave his sorry body through the four sets, never wanting to get up from the floor again. When he managed to pry himself into a vertical position, he looked at the wall clock. Only an hour had elapsed.

Axel said goodbye to Ted before leaving.

"Not bad for a rusty guy. You remembered something from all those years ago, I can tell. Your jabs and straight rights looked halfway decent. Those two punches, when thrown well, are over eighty percent of what you need in the ring."

"What's the other twenty percent?" Axel asked.

Ted chuckled. "Something that will take up one hundred and eighty percent of your time in here to get right. The first thing you need to do is get into competitive shape."

"That is quite obvious. Right now, the only person I'm competing against is myself."

"You and everyone here in this gym, friend. Same time

tomorrow?"

"We'll see if my soon to be sore-as-hell muscles will allow it. I'll try."

"Bring your mind, Axel. The body will follow," Ted said. They shook hands, the grip on Ted not as bone crushing as the workout he had just had.

Staggering back to his apartment, Axel had the best hot bath he had soaked in for years. He was too tired to eat, and had just enough energy to brush his teeth. He was asleep within seconds of his head hitting the pillow. Waking up the following morning he remembered Ted's last words.

He tried to bring his mind off the pillow, but his body demanded stationary stillness for the next thousand years. The last time he had done exercise this insane was in his junior year in college, when he did a leg workout in the weight room for two hours. He tried to run up a flight of half a dozen stairs to get out of the room, but his legs involuntarily locked up, and he fell forward onto the top stair, almost chipping a tooth. His body felt just like that in bed, only all over.

He changed the count on his daily hundred push-ups that morning to base one, doing ten girl push-ups instead. He knew that the more he walked during breaks at work that day, the better the soreness would dissipate. Not that Axel minded that much - he was hooked. The sensory experience of the sweat, the syncopated sounds of the gloves on the bags, the whoosh his arms made when they threw punches, and the choreography that had to be mentally processed in real time made him forget all the bubbling hatred that had been eating away at his serenity for so long. He had finally found something to do that was both visceral and cerebral at the same time, filling the minutes instead of watching them pass by, and making him feel that his life was no longer going backwards.

He went back and signed up for three more months. Gradually settling into a boxing training routine, Axel stuck with it every other day in order to both keep his heart pumping and let his muscles recover. He knew he was a long way away from sparring, but that was OK. The boxing workouts were doing an outstanding job on shoving his temper deep under a lid.

The jump roping in his warmups continued to vex him. Every ten seconds of the rope catching under his feet eventually changed to thirty seconds, then to one minute, and then finally at his fifth week at the gym Axel was able to go an entire round of three minutes of continuous jump roping. And then the rope would catch within a minute of the next round. When three rounds finally passed error free, Axel then humbly noticed women boxers around him doing two hundred-plus revolutions a minute; he could only do seventy. "Fast feet, fast hands," Ted would chirp to Axel when he saw that frustrated look in his eyes during the warmup.

After the warmup Axel would do his hundred daily push-ups at the gym if he hadn't done them already at home. Then came the medicine ball, used both on the floor and against the wall. Next came the plyometrics, moving around an imaginary canvas with more jumping up and down that left his feet sore. Axel moved on to arm exercises with light weights in his hands for several repetitions at the rim of the ring before donning hand wraps and trying to hit small, fast bags for half a dozen rounds. The gym had a clock with a bell that went for three minutes, with a break of a minute between rounds. The small bags still mocked Axel, making him miss more than he hit, and on them he easily transplanted the faces of past assholes he had known.

By the time he slipped on a pair of gloves, Axel was good and pissed, and ready for vicarious release. He pounded the heavy bag hard for six more rounds. He breathed heavily and his arms felt like mashed potatoes after two of them, but he was always able to finish six rounds straight with needing a rest. At this point Axel practiced punches in front of a mirror until Jason became available for pads. Then came a core abdominal routine in which Axel took lots of breaks, because by then he was out of energy. All the gas in the tank had been spent, and there would not be any more until a wall of soreness seeped into the marrow of his bones the following day, through which he had to pass before doing the workout all over again.

The first week Axel used disposable plastic gloves and the

common boxing gloves on the gym racks, but the gloves stank so badly of sweat that he quickly bought three pairs of hand wraps and boxing gloves of his own at a sporting goods store. It was the first exercise he had taken up which required personal equipment beyond shorts, T-shirt, and a pair of sneakers. Later he would add a mouth guard, headgear (the common ones at the gym stank too), two extra shirts, a towel, and a water bottle, all of which required a workout bag. Before then all he needed to take to a gym was a knapsack.

After the second month of workouts had ended Axel took stock of his boxing inventory outside of the contents of his bag. Just under six feet with a stocky build, he was one the bigger guys in the gym and could hit hard. However, he never knew he had always been this slow and clumsy, which made him grateful he had never picked a fight with a stranger all these years; he would have been creamed. Guys half his size landed five punches to his one during the rounds with the heavy bag. If that bag was him, Axel wondered, in an actual match they would rack up the points as if they were revolutions of a jump rope on the ground.

Axel signed up for six more months. He started taking group classes; they held between three and twenty people, and usually lasted forty-five minutes. The classes concentrated on specific muscle groups, such as arms, legs, or core, or consisted of prolonged bag drills. Axel ate them all up, because the exhaustion after the classes had ended made him forget how angry he always was. In terms of alcohol consumption, he had dried out, but nothing substantive yet had taken the place of all those bottles and boxes of wine. Only the sweat, and the post-workout aches and pains, were succeeding in filling the cracks. Maybe, Axel hoped, the anger would someday go away.

By October Ted noticed all the work Axel had been putting in, and invited him to join his sparring classes. He deferred, explaining that he didn't yet feel ready. Ted said no problem; they were constantly being offered. In reality, Axel was being an unreasonable perfectionist, imagining that he could expertly land punches on an opponent without being hit in return, the fantasy fueled by the rounds on the heavy bag that didn't hit back. Chess gave off the unscathed illusion of effortlessly calculating several moves ahead to forced wins, but boxing, he was soon to learn, largely consisted of trying to land one quick tactical flurry and moving away, while constantly getting hit.

Axel kept his head above water with boxing workouts every other day and the occasional chess tournament. At work he unofficially acquired the title of senior specifications writer, his boss only giving him the most difficult assignments in the department. Life was becoming OK to Axel again, as long as he did not peer too deep underneath.

CHAPTER FIVE

Axel started becoming reckless at work. He started surfing porn on his work computer during lunch breaks. He was caught and tsk-tsked once by his male colleague, and the IT department could have busted him any day, any time. But the IT department ran amok on the Internet as well, and Axel was never punished.

Just before Halloween, he got into a screaming match with the obnoxious female co-worker over their shared phone which her daughter called every other day. His boss finally had to intervene. He did not want to be forced into a position to fire and hire personnel, so he moved Axel to another desk across the floor among the engineers. The compromise made Axel occasionally hear instead of having to look at the obnoxious female co-worker on a daily basis, and relieved a lot of the pressure.

Axel finally took Ted up on joining one of the monthly sparring classes in November. On a Saturday morning, he did a drill with a husky kid from the local high school, who was about to enter the Golden Gloves. The kid was told that this was Axel's first time, and encouraged him to relax as they traded fixed punch combinations and blocking from a stationary position.

Axel's adrenaline got the better of him, and he snapped off two jabs and a right that bloodied the kid's nose. Ted yelled at the kid to keep his hands up. The kid's good nature evaporated, and he started with a frenzy of combinations that Axel mostly blocked save for one hook that landed with an electric jolt on his jaw. Axel's bubble had officially been popped. It did not hurt that bad; actually, it was scary and fun at the same time.

The following Saturday Axel finally learned why Jason and the other trainers had insisted on bringing his hands immediately back to the face after a punch – leaving them out meant getting clocked in the head. Axel was working with multiple partners of different sizes and styles. They were doing three-punch drills, where one threw a trio of punches and the other started with his trio the moment the third punch had been thrown. The drill could go slowly, or as quickly as a real fight, depending how fast the partner reacted.

Axel learned to cover his body well, but continued to leave the top of his head open for shots. He didn't mind that much because he bought into the notion that the top of the head was the hardest part of the body (and because he was so damn tired after one and a half hours of strenuous drills that he couldn't lift his hands all the way up), but afterwards at home he found himself reaching for the Ibuprofen.

The next Saturday Axel found himself on the ropes inside the ring with every member of the class. For one minute, Ted called up two people to square off in the center and spar at medium to hard intensity, and then return to the ropes so that another pair could go. Axel was called up six times. He wasn't paired with the advanced fighters who had done amateur bouts, but he didn't spar against beginners either. One of his partners had basically one weapon, his right hook, which Axel ran into more than once, and gave him his first black eye. He showed up at the gym during the following week to attaboys.

The final Saturday of the month had Axel doing real sparring alone in a ring with two different opponents for a total of six rounds. He did fine with his first opponent, using his longer reach to land enough punches to bloody another nose, but had much more difficulty with his second opponent, who nailed Axel with a straight right to his cheek in the second round. The punch snapped back his head so hard that he felt tingles up and down his right arm.

"Keep your head down! Imagine you're holding a tennis ball on your neck with your chin!" Ted yelled from outside the ring. Axel recovered enough to block further bombs from his opponent's straight right, but then found himself getting blasted on the other side of his head. Axel was confused by the time their third round started – he was keeping both his hands up high to protect his face, but this opponent circled quickly, and treated his upright hands like goalposts through which he shot soccer balls. He was getting peppered with punches all over.

At this point, Axel remembered a chess maxim about defense – the best one was most often a good offense. He turned into the abuse, walked forward, and managed to push his opponent into a corner. For the rest of the round Axel kept him pressed against the ropes, and got into a grinding war of body punches to minimize his opponent's speed in the open ring. When the bell finally rang, he and his opponent hugged, and Axel looked up to see that the rest of the class had been looking on intently with appreciative nods.

"Not bad," Ted said to Axel afterwards in his office. "You took away your opponent's strength and managed to turn it into a weakness."

"The only thing I remember was a blunt instinct to walk into a buzz saw, and eating extra punches," Axel replied. He felt bruised all over.

Ted laughed. "You have a good appetite for them, Axel. You can't dish them out with taking your fair share. Work out hard this winter, I have a proposition for you. In April I'm going to start a new three-month program of intensive boxing training, followed by a fight finale in front of a large crowd. It's invitation only, and you're in if you want to do it."

Axel smiled wryly. "Paying membership dues so that I can get punched in the face. What's not to like?"

After a long absence, Axel resumed running. He did not have the build for it, something his stocky body reminded him of every other moment, but he forced himself out on the road three days a week. Although never going to break distance records, he could keep going for forty minutes straight. The speed and the distance were not as important as the time spent continuously moving. Jumping rope after a day of running became brutal on his feet, but the extra cardio work let Axel extend his workouts from two hours to three.

He drifted away from the conditioning routines he had started out with upon joining the gym, and started doing more rounds in the ring with the guys he had met at the sparring classes. The sparring without an audience did wonders for Axel; it made him feel more comfortable trading punches with a person in the ring. All the people Axel boxed with were friendly and supportive. They never took hard shots at the areas each had left open, merely tapping them. Axel knew that in April the supportiveness would be replaced with competitiveness, and was grateful for the opportunity to iron out his most glaring boxing flaws before they might truly hurt.

Spring the following year arrived very quickly. Axel looked at himself again in a mirror. His eyes were clear, his weight was back down under two hundred pounds, and his whole body twitched as if ready to explode into motion in all directions. Ted's three-month intensive boxing program was due to start next week. Axel's excitement exceeded his trepidation, no longer caring if that he might be putting the cart in high gear before the horse was ready. *Let the chips fall where they may*, Axel thought to himself. *Or the punches whistle into his face.*

CHAPTER SIX

Push-ups until I puke, Axel grumbled, his lactic acids in his biceps building up to critical mass. He was in the third day of Ted's intensive boxing program with fifty other prospective boxers, and all of them squeezed in together around the ring. They had already done several hundred squats, and run over five miles the past hour. The lactic acids would kick in after a very good night's sleep, and scream at him the day after tomorrow when he came back to do it all over again.

Axel was the old guy. Had he not been working out so hard that winter he would have dropped out panting within minutes. The spring air was still cold and prickled his skin. Even if it took place only six hours a week, the training was brutal. Ted told Alex after the first day that professional boxers did this sort of exercise six hours a day, seven days a week, for months when they prepared for a fight. The people at the foot of the ring suffering with Axel – sweating just as profusely onto the canvas, making the surface really stinky just like the shared boxing gloves – were in their late teens and early twenties, some of them already accomplished amateur fighters.

This world was totally unlike his chess world. The latter had been welded into his psyche since childhood, and directly expanded and contracted according to the amount of study he was able to apply to the game. His mindset inside the sixty-four black and white squares, while still capable of a surprise or two, was mature. In contrast, the single square of the boxing ring appeared as a massive mountain in front of him, totally mysterious and covered in fog; he was at the foot of it, and doing endless amounts of push-ups to climb it.

After three weeks the preliminary workouts eased, and Ted split the participants up into two teams. One different weeknight was dedicated to each team for training, and all met on Saturday for inter-team competitions. Axel could have limited himself to the two mandatory attendance days, but he showed up a third night so that his practice did not fall behind the others. He did want to be shown up drastically in the sparring that was soon to come.

The Saturday workouts cut into Axel's weekend chess tournaments. He decided to play an invitational tournament at his local chess club, meeting on a weeknight outside his personal team's training sessions. Running concurrently with the boxing training, the tournament would meet one weeknight a week for three months. Axel had no burning desire to come in first, because first prize was a few hundred dollars he didn't need, yet he did need a counterweight to all the boxing he was doing.

His competitors in the tournament were long time frenemies. All were surprised at his appearance, and complimented him about how much weight he had lost. At this point his weight was a hundred and ninety-eight pounds, down from his habitual two hundred and thirty-five. Axel sat the board during his games as did a tiger crouched down in a cage, newly aware about how martial chess could be. A devastating tactical or strategical move during a game could be the mental equivalent of a hard punch thrown to the head or to the body. *The mind could hit just as hard as the body*, Axel mused.

His opponents as the tournament progressed were just as tough as he remembered. They knew his feints, favorite pawn formations, and least favorite situations to face during a game. The aggression felt more naked this time around, to become even more intense in the later rounds.

After four weeks, the boxing program participants started sparring. Ted did not put Axel in the ring with the accomplished amateur fighters, but he did pair Axel with other guys in his weight class, with nobody holding back.

His first real taste of boxing was against a lanky six-foot four college student who had a five-inch reach advantage. It was a very long three rounds. Axel could not even get within striking distance without experiencing full combinations all over. The best he could do was approach fully covered like an armadillo curled up in a ball, and wait for his opponent to throw a punch in order to obtain any opening. The best he could do was not get hit so often.

Then there was the short husky guy who was an ironworker. He compensated for lack of reach by his compact and punishing body shots. Going toe to toe against him was dangerous because of his lower center of gravity and sumo wrestler leg strength. Axel stayed in the open ring when he could, sticking and moving. Except when the powerball charged, driving him into the corner and blasting him in the lower quadrants, and making Axel wonder why he had ever taken up boxing. Luckily, this opponent had less stamina than strength, and in the third round he managed to get in a little payback.

Axel had one secret advantage on these younger dynamos: he had given up drinking. On the Saturdays when the sparring became serious, a lot of knuckleheads still partied hard the previous night, and had come in hung over. While the preliminary workouts sweated out a lot of the alcohol, their stomachs were still a little queasy when they took on Axel. Often all it took was one well aimed hook to the ribs to make them double over, to the great amusement of the trainers. Sometimes their shorts did not smell so nice afterwards too.

Axel did not have the luxury of feeling smug. He too was discovering new ways to get hit. He would block a punch and get smacked on the side of his head because he did not bring his hand back to his face in time; he would throw a straight right hand, only to have his opponent slip under it and blast his ribs; he would roll under a hook only to careen into an uppercut; or his hands would just stay in the same place too long and his face would get idly swatted by a pair of floating jabs. The heavy bags swaying on the chains never acted like this.

Despite being slower, Axel found a way to economize his movements and err on the side of caution. He maintained the classical stance of keeping his head down, and his hands up, at all times. It looked stodgy, but did the job in protecting himself. Time had bestowed Axel with modesty and common sense, which the younger boxers had yet to acquire. For example, some of them adopted the non-classical approach of sometimes lowering their hands, but moving their heads constantly. They had to practice to make this perfect, and during their learning curve they received many hard shots.

Eight weeks into the program Ted announced that some of the fights in the finale were going to be posted for the gym's new YouTube channel. However, those fights would only be filmed if both fighters consented in writing. Axel demurred. He confessed to Ted that he was old enough to feel self-conscious, and hadn't even told his family that he doing serious boxing. No problem, said Ted, he could postpone his decision all the way up to the night of the fight.

The more serious the training became, the more his sense of humor grew. He was putting in hundreds of hours of punishing exercise for the payout of six minutes of fighting in front of a crowd, which could be ruined in an instant by an injury during training. Just like a tournament chess game, where hours and hours sometimes went into preparing for an opponent, which the opponent often blithely sidestepped by playing a different opening altogether. Or putting in hours of grinding calculation at the board, all of which could go off a cliff by a careless mistake in the ending due to fatigue. Axel had found another way to be a conquistador of the useless in his life, and it made him laugh.

Other weird parallels in boxing and chess came to Axel. Boxing had six basic punches: the jab, the straight punch from the dominant hand, the hook, the left uppercut, the right uppercut, and the hook from the dominant hand. Chess had six basic pieces as well: the King, the Queen, the Rook, the Bishop, the Knight, and the Pawn. Both competitions were timed, although in chess the clock was more an extra piece than as a signal to rest. A boxer could lose in roughly the same way by taking more punches, the same way a chess player could lose by having an opponent take more pieces. The most important competitive thing boxing and chess shared was that they both demanded self-control and respect for what the opponent could do.

Axel also mused about how chess was different from boxing. Fast hands were good in boxing ("be first" the trainers liked to say); to hesitate was to get hit. However fast hands almost always led to bad and shallow chess, unless it was a blitz game with only five minutes or less on the clock for the entire game. In slow chess, being first to show one's plans on a chessboard was similar to tipping one's hand during a poker game. Unlike boxing, reactions in chess were just as important as actions, if not more so. Zugzwangs (German for "compulsion to move") frequently arose in chess endgames where having the move caused the player to commit hara-kiri, losing the game immediately. Thinking fast and slow, Axel ruminated, not only had different gears, but different gearboxes altogether.

In the chess tournament Axel gave as good as he got, the energy boost from the boxing allowing him to remain feisty and sharp as the games went on late into the night. The time control was forty moves in two hours, followed by one hour for the rest of the moves, for both players. The mental fatigue that ensued in the fifth and sixth hours was why competitive chess at the highest levels was a young man's game, but Axel for this tournament had found a way to turn back the clock on move forty-one.

He played in an uncharacteristically freewheeling style by sacrificing pawns, and even a couple of pieces, for the sake of the initiative in his games. His moves acquired a harder tactical edge when the middlegames began. Such a style, while promising greater rewards, carried proportionately greater risks – he scored some scintillating victories, but had a few embarrassing defeats. Axel's change in style did not translate into greater playing strength. The amount of points he gained as the closing rounds approached would have been the same if he pursued his usually cautious approach with several draws instead.

As much as Axel wanted to push his opponents around on the chessboard as he could in the boxing ring, he was too experienced a player to know that was impossible unless the position allowed it. If the position was equal, no amount of huffing and puffing could change the evaluation. His opponents were just as experienced, and just as unlikely to lose their heads. While boxing had an empty canvas except for two boxers, chess games were chock full of pawns bunched up into chains with their own special rules that limited the desired motions of the pieces. Attempts to force kinetic movement in a chess game yielded more blunders than inspired moves.

The dynamics of a slow chess game changed when time on the clock grew short. To run out of time was the same result as being checkmated, so the pressure to make all the remaining moves in a given time control (often with seconds left) required snap decisions that approached those in boxing. The boxing Axel had been doing had a side benefit of forcing him to use scant time efficiently, and he was never in time pressure during the tournament. However, he blew two won games when he could not exploit his opponents' time pressure. They were blasting out moves from necessity, while he was out of sync by continuing to use slow deliberate calculation. The search for the cleanest win burned up precious minutes, and put Axel in time pressure with his opponents. Then the loser was the player who made the last mistake before time ran out.

In the next to last round Axel scored a crucial victory against the defending club champion. He found himself in a four-way tie for first going into the last round. His final opponent next week was going to be a crafty veteran who had long known how to throw Axel off his rhythm. This master used quasi-legal psychology at and away from the board. In the past he often called his opponents to reschedule games, sometimes an hour before the game was supposed to start.

During games that started on time, he would often arrive twenty to thirty minutes after his clock had been started (in classical tournament games, chess players have one hour to show up and make their first move, or lose by forfeit). Even when this opponent showed up on time, he was notorious for playing bizarrely passive openings that caused many opponents, including Axel, to charge in prematurely and become overextended, resulting in quick losses. This did not bode well. Axel had been playing ultra-energetically throughout the championship because physical energy had been coursing through his veins. Sitting still and waiting for the right moment for battle to begin with this player was going to be hard.

Three weeks before the fight finale, Axel still had not made up his mind if he wanted his boxing match on YouTube. By then Ted's program was nothing but sparring. That Saturday he put Axel in his first inter-team competitive bout, against an ex-college football player named George. The fight was in front of all the participants of the program, each cheering their team member on, in three two-minute rounds. The rounds felt like they were thirty seconds each from all the adrenaline. Both were in fighting shape and not tired at all when the fight ended. Axel was pleased to learn that the trainers gave him the fight on points (he drove George into the ropes more often, and had landed more jabs), and that he was able to help his team.

Three days later in the final round of the chess championship, the nemesis bamboozled him again. Rather, Axel bamboozled himself. His opponent showed up on time, and played a conventional opening. The past did Axel in, as he tried to avenge the psychological tricks that had been played on him before. Overreaching in the game, he offered a pawn sacrifice without sufficient compensation, which was calmly accepted and prosaically converted into a simple win for the other side. He realized that he had nobody to blame but himself for the result, even if his opponent was a dick. The nemesis won the tournament, as the other two who were tied with them drew in the last round. Axel played against his opponent when he should have been playing the position.

It would not be the last time his chess mind and boxing mind did not mesh properly. Boxing continually raced around and stopped suddenly on a flat canvas, whereas chess was continually and tenaciously climbing up mountains made by the mind. Stopping in boxing was tactical, a prelude for an opening to land another punch; whereas in chess, stopping was for strategy, an opportunity to create a foothold for operations much further in the future. Axel in the game had misplaced his frame of reference, going fast when he should have been going slow. He had done so much sparring that he equated going slow with getting hit.

Fast chess was another kettle of fish altogether. There, hand-eye coordination trumped deep thinking, as in boxing. Axel usually lost to the hustlers in the park not because they played better chess, but because they managed their clock better, winning on time forfeit when they were down ridiculous amounts of material. No referee was on hand to stop a blowout in chess; a blitz game ended only when one of the players was checkmated or lost on time, whichever came first. Axel always sought to find the best move with the time available to him, instead of never falling behind on the clock, which is why he never played for money.

Somewhere in between was the golden mean for a perfectly satisfying modern chess game. That meant, however, leaning towards an ever faster beat with shortened time controls. Faster time controls – games with only thirty minutes or fifteen minutes or five minutes or even one minute for all the moves - were the only way organizers could make chess appealing to sponsors, and to Internet audiences. Quick flashy combinations had become the main attraction. As popcorn tactics prevailed, however, deep strategical thinking started to fade away.

Axel grew up with chess at a much slower pace, before computers overpowered grandmasters with their brute ply strength over human imagination. While he could play blitz chess, he preferred more time to choose among possible positions to make the best move, rather than be forced to lurch on instinct before the clock ran out of time. But modern life was not on his side.

After the chess tournament. Axel wondered: was it easier for a chess player to learn how to box, or a boxer to learn how to play serious chess? Chess players who relied on slow-twitch, deliberate thinking would have to pick up the pace of their decision-making processes to learn how to box; boxers who relied on quick-twitch reflexes would need to slow down, and think before they moved. Both had to ascertain a problem and approximate the best possible solution with the resources available. For a boxer, those resources were mostly found in physical conditioning; for a chess player, those resources were mostly found in mental alertness and strong nerves. But physical conditioning was also important for top-flight chess, and mental acuity was a precondition for a disciplined boxer. He sighed. This question had no definitive answer.

CHAPTER SEVEN

Ted's boxing program drew to a close in June, and Axel was relieved. He was tired of coming into the gym with sore muscles, and constantly having to protect his face. He was starting to hate the smell of his sweat-stained gloves and headgear, too, lacquered over with Lysol. But he was also excited about boxing in front of a lot of people. He just wasn't sure if he wanted to have his friends and family watching, and definitely did not want it posted on the Internet.

Axel decided two days before the fight that he would not tell his friends at all, and his family only after the fact. He wanted to have a fight behind him, and make sure he didn't suck, before inviting anyone he knew to watch. He also opted out against having his bout posted to YouTube – what would a prospective employer think of that? Axel's decisions limited Ted to choosing a barrel-chested high school senior named Jim as his opponent, who had the same privacy concerns about college recruitment officers. They were well matched, having sparred with each other several times the past month. Ted was going out of his way to make Axel's first exhibition bout as tension free as possible.

On the night of the fight, Axel drove to the gym with a queasy feeling in his stomach. He had chosen not to eat for several hours, fearing a sudden need to upchuck, and intended to pig out immediately afterwards. His intentions were foiled when he found that his fight was Jim was eleventh on a card of fifteen, and wouldn't go on for another two hours. He relented after the third fight, eating a couple of apples he had brought with him.

Finally, the moment for his fight came. The crowd was large, and the ring seemed to have doubled in size over the last hour. *This is silly*, Axel tried to say to himself, *I've been sparring in this space for well over a year*. However, his throat and chest felt tight when their names were announced, and tighter still when the referee had them touch gloves seconds before the opening bell. The bell sounded shortly afterwards of course. Axel was alone with Jim, in front of many people, without a net.

The tightness disappeared once Axel and Jim exchanged punches. Exhaustion then took the place of the tightness over the next three rounds. During the first round all he could think of was *Oh God, what have I got myself into?* The second round, Axel discovered still more ways to be hit, while people were watching him. After the first minute in the third round, Axel and Jim rapidly burned out the remaining fuel in their tanks, and became exhausted. So, they switched to endorphins, and were still maniacally pounding each other when the closing bell rang, to the cheers of the crowd. Axel and Jim hugged, and later ate pizza slices together while watching the final fights. The training for the fight felt like forever, yet it seemed to be over in a matter of seconds.

Time had exhibited itself to Axel in very strange ways; he might invite chess-player friends to cheer him on if he ever did this again. As he left the gym, his mood lightened a bit to include gratitude for what he had, and for the time left to make what he had a little better. The warehouses of wine he had consumed to deaden himself from the world were receding a little more into the past.

Axel tried to keep the same training regimen for a few weeks after the fight finale, but quickly realized that such a pace was not sustainable. Without a goal at the end, the inevitable "why?" crept in, which killed motivation inside and out. He knew by hanging around the gym that boxers between fights stopped training altogether, and stuffed their faces all day long for weeks on end, before starting up again when there was a new bout on the horizon. Axel's workouts to the gym tapered back within a month to the ones he used when he first visited.

Axel was restless during the summer. While he did his minimal workouts at Ted's gym, the bulk of his time shifted to chess openings, middlegame tactics, and endgame theory from books, despite it all becoming slightly cross-eyed. He could not feel from a book the ramifications on choosing an alternate move in a competitive game.

The river was as deep as it was wide; he was missing something in the fabric of the chess moves he was following, no matter where he concentrated his attention on the board.

To get a fresh perspective, Axel hired a local grandmaster named Garen for chess lessons. Originally from Armenia, he had once played for the national championship there, and retooled himself as a high-level chess coach once he emigrated to the United States. He lived in the next town over with his daughter's family.

Garen emphasized to Axel the very first day they met that if he aspired to a higher title such as International Master or International Grandmaster, he would have to work a whole lot harder. Axel said that he knew that full well, but he just didn't know how. "Welcome to the secrets of the Armenian chess school," Garen replied with a mock sinister chuckle. He asked Axel for the game scores of three hundred of his most recent tournament games. "Be prepared to put in five to ten hours of work each week for the next few months," he said as they parted ways. They met up again for weekly sessions a few days later.

Until he had worked with Garen, Axel had no idea how quickly and cavalierly he had been pushing his pieces over the board. "Did you consider what would have happened had he not exchanged Queens?" "How would your combination have worked had the pawn been on h5 instead of h6?" "When did you realize during this loss that your attack was not going to work?" "What did you think your opponent's plan was at this point of the game?" "Why did you castle on this side of the board with only the h7 pawn as cover?" Garen asked relentlessly during the sessions. He was posing more problems for Axel to solve from his own games than Axel had time work out over the board while the games were actually being played.

Garen gave him hundreds upon hundreds of chess positions to solve, all collected from Armenian chess publications that had never been translated in the west. It would take more than one lifetime to go through them all. Giving him a lopsided grin, Garen said: "I don't expect you to go through all these problems and solve them correctly, only enough of them so that you see chess in a new way. Ultimately, the only person who can get you to the level you want is yourself. All I'm trying to do is give you a new pair of eyes, and show you where you need to go."

It had been a long time since Axel had taken apart his intuition at the chessboard. Where he was today as a chess player was the result of decades of habit and study. Things were what they were because they became that way. To examine it closely was to get out the window of a steadily moving train, rappel down, and re-paint the wheels. It was slow, hard work, and Axel was glad he had no big tournaments on the horizon. Trying to do this and play top-flight opponents at the same time would have led to half-baked concepts at the board, not to mention spectacular crash and burns.

He played in local tournaments during the summer and fall, against opponents he had been facing for decades, playing the same openings with them playing the same replies, with the same sorts of positions cropping up, and obtaining the same middling results. Axel knew deep down that Garen's methods would yield concrete results by next year. That wasn't the problem. The real problem was that chess had ceased to be his only window onto the world. He had put in too much time in another pursuit - boxing - to stick with such monomaniacal study. The two-headed genie could not be put back into the bottle.

While mulling over his dilemma, Axel one morning read an interview with the Soviet chess grandmaster Mark Taimanov, who was also an acclaimed concert pianist. Taimanov said that whenever chess felt stale, he switched to music; and when his music no longer gave him joy, he switched back to chess. Axel decided to switch back actively to boxing, as he had not worked out seriously in Ted's boxing gym for close to six months. The time had come to sweat out the ennui.

CHAPTER EIGHT

Axel went to Ted in his office in December. Ted looked up and grunted, as if he had only left yesterday. "Get back into boxing shape, and then come to me for a talk next month. I'll have a proposition for you."

The jump rope at full speed became an old pain in the ass that he had unexpectedly grown to miss, as did the push-ups, the squats, and hammering that monster truck tire with a sledgehammer. After a long absence, the resumed heavy workouts had a different slanted view, and Axel could imagine new directions for his boxing to go.

He wanted his punches to be faster, but realized that he had a maximum hand speed beyond which he could not surpass. He would therefore have to learn how to punch smarter. He examined his combinations in front of a mirror, noticing arcs and angles in his throws that could be tightened up. *Speed must be a matter of distance and time*, Axel concluded, and closely observed the accomplished boxers in the gym to see what he could imitate.

He saw that their entire bodies always moved in one unit. No flailing arms, no feet wide apart, and no head stuck out like that of a turtle outside of its shell. The punches were extensions of their twisting bodies that naturally generated torque, the arms being the part of the punch that moved last. These mechanics were easy enough to replicate in a stationary position, and could even be duplicated while moving around on a heavy bag, but Axel realized that doing this while crouching in front of another moving opponent was going to be as easy as learning differential calculus. It looked brutal on the knees.

He also observed that the more tired a boxer became in the later rounds of a fight, the more the mechanics broke down, and the more the fight degenerated into a brawl. The difference Axel saw between novice boxers with loads of misplaced energy and accomplished, experienced boxers was as plain as night versus day. The experienced ones simply waited for the fight to come to them, expending as little energy as possible, and watched their opponents wear themselves out as the fight progressed. Then they struck, taking full advantage of the dropped guards and the diminished stamina of their adversaries. An accomplished boxer managed breathing well, fully exhaling after each punch, and gulping in the maximum of oxygen afterwards. They never seemed to pant, no matter how long the fight went on.

Above all, the best boxers in the gym had fantastic footwork. As did champion tennis players with their blistering forehands, their feet always seemed to be planted in the best possible spots when they executed their punches for maximum leverage. The speed and deliberation in their steps helped them out of trouble as often as it guided their opponents into trouble. This skill reminded Axel of a rival's quote about Alexander Alekhine, world chess champion in the 1930s: "I can see the combinations as well as Alekhine, but I cannot get into the same positions."

Axel knew he had much more to learn about boxing than he did about chess. Chess to him was about nailing down the winning details that pushed his experienced opponents over the edge, whereas boxing was still in the contour surveyance stage, his current broadsides missing by a mile. After five weeks he got his conditioning back up to where it had been before the exhibition fight, and then went to Ted's office to see what the proposition was.

"This July we are co-sponsoring a fight night of amateur charity bouts for cancer research," Ted said. "These are sanctioned amateur fights, Axel, not the exhibition fight you did last year. You have to get medical clearance from your doctor, and apply for a boxing permit from the US Amateur Boxing Association. We're trying to get an opponent for one of the participants. He's a big athletic guy new to boxing, and has a family member going through chemotherapy. I've been trying to find an opponent close to his size, and you fit the bill. If you're interested, we'll pay for all the application fees and supply all the equipment – all you have to do is show up and box. Want to do it?"

"How long is the fight going to be?" Axel asked.

"It's US Amateur Boxing Association rules, with three rounds of two minutes each. There will be a certified referee, and three official judges ringside. It won't be here. We've booked a local sporting arena –

several hundred people will be in the crowd."

Axel considered his options. More of the same of what he had been doing, bad: something scary and potentially painful for only six minutes, and it's for a good cause...

"I'll do it," he said.

Ted smiled. "Excellent! His name is Steve, and like many others who are doing this, we are training him from scratch. If possible, can you come to some of these training sessions and work out with him? Come when you can. We'd love it if you could come more often during the last month, and give Steve the sparring practice he needs. Steve's tough enough to take your hits. What he won't have in experience he will more than make up for in motivation."

"OK, here I go again. A rebel without a clue. When's the next training session?"

"This Wednesday at six p.m. Thanks, Axel."

Axel met Steve that Wednesday. He wasn't the biggest person Axel had boxed, but he would prove to be one of the strongest. He was six foot two of solid muscle, an oak tree with thick limbs. (A streamlined version of Axel, only three inches taller.) He was fighting in the charity event for his young boy, who was battling bone marrow cancer. Despite having started boxing a month ago, his drive was obvious within minutes.

Axel and Steve started light sparring. Until now Axel had been able to punch forward and drive back all his opponents, but Steve was so strong he didn't budge; Axel had to move around laterally instead. Steve's jab was good, but his straight right was slow out of the gate, and he did not have a hook yet. Once he learned how to throw his straight right and hook as well as his jab, his height advantage would be difficult to overcome.

The nights that spring at the gym were long and pleasant, even as the sparring grew harder. Steve was introduced to hooks on the side of the head, and Axel was forced to learn how to stick and move for entire rounds. When Axel was tired, the jabs from afar woke him up in a hurry. When Steve was tired, he dropped his hands enough for Axel to deliver a rare power punch that made him move backwards a fraction of an inch.

Axel had his familiar fight jitters as July approached. The event was getting television coverage, as well as donations that exceeded the wildest hopes of the organizers. In June they announced that the venue would be moved to a larger arena in the city that seated fifteen hundred people. Axel boarded what he thought was a bus a few months ago only to find that it was turning into a bullet train, and hoped that he didn't end up looking like the nondescript schmuck being battered around in the ring by the star in a professional wrestling match.

The physical checkup was no problem. Axel's health had always been boringly good; every time he showed up for a physical, the doctor said there was nothing wrong him, and to come back in a couple of years. The doctor did a light version of the full annual physical, cleared Axel within minutes, and sent him on his way with a signed release for the gym. The gym submitted the release with his application to the US Amateur Boxing Association. They fitted Axel and Steve with official trunks, shirts, headgear, and gloves. Their hands would be professionally wrapped at the night of the fight. They could bring their own shoes.

Axel still hated running, but Steve said he was upping his daily runs to ten miles each, which shamed him into hour jogs every other morning. He decided to put in ten rounds on the heavy bag every night as well, something he knew Steve wasn't doing. The intensity of their sparring sessions was by now a close replica of what would occur in front of thousands of people, minus the people. Axel still hadn't decided to tell anyone what he was doing.

Three days before the fight, Axel broke down and decided to tell his mom and his sister. His mother was horrified; his sister was worried too, but they were proud of what he was doing and wished him luck. Everyone at the gym wished Axel luck too, jokingly reminding him to hit Steve back. From a friendly exhibition fight in front of a hundred people to a real amateur fight in front of thousands – what the hell was Axel thinking? He was only going to get an answer to that when the bell rang at the end of the last round.

The fighters were obligated to show up on Saturday afternoon - four hours before the bouts began - for the weigh-in, the hand wraps, a group photoshoot, and an informal chat with the ring announcer so that he had something informative to say about each boxer who stepped into the ring. Seeing Steve, Axel said in mock horror: "Dammit, he showed up!" After a shared laugh and a courteous fist bump, both informally avoided each other in the fighters' locker rooms for the rest of the night.

Axel and Steve easily made the weigh-ins for their weight class, that of heavyweight. They were the ninth fight on a card of eleven bouts, and would not go on for at least two hours. Axel hated the waiting. He changed into his trunks and cleared his head as best he could, jumping rope until sweat poured down his body, and going to the urinal often to empty his skittish bladder.

Finally, his turn came. His hands were wrapped and marked off with an 'X' by a fighting official. He popped in his mouth guard, put on his gloves, and went downstairs to the arena. Jason from the gym was there to give him a last-second warmup on the pads, but Axel was too keyed up to hit them with any controlled power. The sounds coming from the many people in the seats was scary loud. The last fight had finished and the boxers were waiting for a decision from the judges. Axel took off his right glove and made one last dash to the men's room. When he came back, Ted was there to put the glove back on and lead him to the ring. Ted would be joining him in his corner, to Axel's immense relief.

Axel heard his name called, and he went through the door as if he were about to go skydiving. The arena was dark and big, with the ominous presence of a full house. Ted followed him from behind, telling him to go to the blue corner. Ted's corner guy according to the rules immediately put on his headgear. The headgear fit over his head, but not comfortably. Actually, not comfortably at all; it felt like a tourniquet. Better too tight than too loose, Axel reasoned, but it left strafe marks on his skull when he eventually took it off.

Some people had cheered for Axel, but many more cheered for Steve when he came into the arena. As Steve was walking up to the ring, Ted's corner guy said that his opponent had given an interview to a local radio station, which had been picked up by social media and helped sell out tickets to the event. Ted then snarkily added that most of

Steve's fans were here because it wasn't a school night, which made Axel laugh, and relaxed him enough so that he didn't freeze up. Axel took one look up out of the ring, and saw many, many people there, at least fifty rows of them. He then reduced his peripheral vision to that of the ring only.

After Steve had his headgear put on, he met Axel in the center of the ring to hear the fight rules from the referee. *Yes, definitely very motivated*, Axel thought. Steve had the posture and the demeanor of a volcano about to blow. When they touched gloves, Axel knew that the next few minutes were going to be very interesting. They went back to their corners, the bell sounded immediately, and it was on.

Steve crossed the ring with three long strides. Axel stepped to the right in the middle of the third stride, and was able to catch him in the side of the head with a straight right. Steve recovered quickly, rolling under the still outreached hand and hitting Axel with a hard jab. Axel immediately moved into close range with Steve, denying leverage to his opponent, and started in with body shots. Steve took three of them, then shoved Axel back long enough to land two more jabs. Axel backed off some more, crouched into his stance, and started to stick and move, trying to land two punch combinations with one to the body and one to the head.

Axel was successful with this strategy for most of the round, until Steve charged and pushed him into a corner. The last minute of the round was very long, and very loud. Steve clubbed Axel with a thundering Morse code of two jabs and one right, over and over, to the frenzied cheers of Steve's fans. Axel stayed there and was able to block seventy-five percent of Steve's onslaught until the bell sounded.

Between rounds Ted told Axel to walk over to Steve and just belt him in the gut.

Axel did at the beginning of the next round, which made Steve back off. Axel then did his best impersonation of a moving target, using up his entire repertoire of feints and off-balance punches in the second round. He was able to land the classic combination of a jab, straight right, hook, and another straight right during the second minute, and a solid right hook in the third minute that made Steve's knees buckle. However, as Axel feared, the cheers from the crowd transformed Steve into a six-foot six offensive lineman, and the last thirty seconds of the round were a repeat of the previous one. Steve switched up the rhythm of his jabs and straight rights, and Axel this time could only block half of them until the round ended.

The crowd had somehow managed to grow even louder when they returned to their corners. Both Steve and Axel had managed to do damage: Axel's nose was bloody, and Steve's right eye was going to have a mouse under it the following day. For the final round Ted told Axel to concentrate on the body, and if Steve charged again to clinch so that the referee would break them up.

In the final round, it was Axel who did most of the pushing forward, uncorking uppercuts to the midsection alternated with jabs to the head, making Steve hesitate. Both were becoming tired. They clinched twice: Axel once for catching his breath, and Steve once to stop Axel from opening the throttle to a promising streak of hooks and uppercuts. Steve broke off both the clinches with alacrity after the referee told them to, and both times immediately afterward rocked Axel with half a dozen jabs and straight rights. They were the only two punches Steve used, but they were effective. Axel's experience and his hooks in turn were good enough to stop Steve from steamrollering all over him.

The clack of the board sounded for the final thirty seconds of the fight. This time Axel was prepared for the nitrous oxide burst Steve kept in his tank for the final part of a round and managed to stay in the open ring, moving left and right until he was almost dizzy, when the closing bell rang. They hugged, Steve whispering his thanks into Axel's ear. Axel looked out into the audience again. Steve's fans were on their feet cheering wildly, including Steve's son. *Nine minutes of a scary ride for a good cause*, Axel thought as he was finally able to relax – *seems like a fair tradeoff to me.*

The result of the fight according to the point cards of the judges was a draw, the only one of the evening. Axel took the trophy out of the referee's hand and gave it to Steve in the middle of the ring. The whole arena gave both fighters a long ovation, which Axel only wanted to go to Steve. What Steve and his son were going through paled in comparison to Axel's travails. Life hit much harder than any boxer could.

CHAPTER NINE

Just about everything in Axel's life for the next few weeks felt both wired and humdrum. The adrenaline residue of boxing in front of thousands of people made workouts at the gym for a while feel like housecleaning after several cups of coffee. He had all this energy, and nowhere exciting to apply it.

After a month, the buzz wore off, and Axel was ready for serious training again. Peak fitness at all times was impossible, as very few people are able to live on the mountaintop full-time; however, he wanted his base condition of fitness to be much higher, so that if something interesting came along it would not take him that long to prepare.

He signed up for Ted's next intensive three-month boxing program, which started in late September. The physical conditioning at the beginning was a little less exhausting than last year, but not by much. Axel knew what to expect. Having enough time to recover from the last set in order to prepare for the next one, that was another matter. Axel was still the oldest guy in the program; the lactic acid still flowed by the gallons.

This time Ted threw Axel to the wolves. Immediately after the participants were split into teams, Axel found himself in the ring sparring with the most accomplished fighters in the gym, and he had the novel sensation of having opponents pull their punches on him, lest the blows go straight through his skull or ribcage. One memorable Saturday he found himself paired with Ian, a lightweight who was going to the Olympic tryouts next year, and on whom Axel had fifty pounds. The round they fought was absurdly humbling. Ian landed over sixty taps all over his face and torso, and Axel was unable to land a single punch. Ted told Axel to soak up everything he could in a hurry, because soon no one would be pulling their punches for anybody.

Axel was often paired with a manic German guy named Max, who practiced like Rod Laver hit tennis balls: hard and harder. After complaints to Ted, Max toned down the intensity of his hits from one hundred to eighty percent, which from a broadly built six-footer still made Axel dread any drills with him. He got more bruises from his time with Max than from all his other sparring partners combined, and had no choice but to turn up the volume on his own. Max did not take it personally, and seemed to think that this was how normal boxing practice should go. Axel would have hated to see Max actually mad at him.

Halfway through the program, Ted announced that the fight finale was going to be with boxers from other gyms, and to be televised by a local cable TV news program as part of a reality show. Again, Ted announced that participation was voluntary, and that those who wanted to be in it needed to sign waivers agreeing to be filmed. Axel felt comfortable enough in the ring by now to let others see him box, and he signed the waiver.

Axel had no idea who his opponent was going to be for the finale. His pugilistic skills had advanced to the point where he was interchangeable with most of the experienced fighters in the gym. Once he realized that he was going to be hit in a fight no matter what he did, he fatalistically accepted what would be coming, and was determined to poke back as often as he could.

His chess sessions with Garen were much slower going, as his main opponent was his previous stupider self. Somedays Axel was more stupid than usual, and could not solve one of the positions after half an hour. "This sort of stuff, Axel, is as much glandular as cerebral; your synapses have to keep firing no matter what your mood is," Garen would say as Axel frustratingly tried to solve a stubbornly opaque problem. Axel most of the time was able to shake off the heaviness in his head, and find a plausible solution, even if it was not the best one.

With a clock, a chess player could only sink so deep into a position at the board without being forced to look at the time and make a move for practical reasons. Garen's positions had no practical time limit, but came with the harder accountability of getting every move right, in the correct order. Rules of thumb were not good enough. The whole solution had to appear at once, not as some patchwork of mini-sequences of moves pieced together by common sense. Chess at the highest levels was really like that, Garen insisted. World-class players had developed the ability to see sequences of exact moves in bigger chunks, and exclude chaff more efficiently so that the germ of a winning idea appeared clearly and more quickly to them than their opponents.

Axel doubted if this would work for boxing. Just move faster, get in more punches, move away before the opponent could respond, and win a match on points was the modus operandi. Definitely not moving around for prolonged stretches of time, waiting for that killer shot, as on the chessboard. A killer shot could still lose in boxing if the opponent was still standing afterwards, when many lesser shots had landed in the opposite direction before. Short of a knockout, one punch in boxing counted just as much as another as far as the judges were concerned. And Axel was nowhere near yet the level of boxing that involved knockouts.

In the gym, Axel was having too much fun to be worried about knockouts. He concentrated on how to hit his opponents harder, and more often. He actually started to walk into flurries of punches to drive sparring partners into a corner, so that he could transform them into heavy punching bags. To give a hit, it was necessary to take a hit. If they were professional fights, of course, Axel would never have been so generous.

The crowd was not going to be as big in the gym for the finale as it was for the charity amateur bout, but the opponent was definitely going to be much tougher. Despite it being another exhibition fight, Ted told Axel the week before the finale that he had been paired with a boxer from a rival gym with ten amateur bouts to his name. They sat down in his office to watch seven of his future opponent's previous fights on YouTube. He was big as Axel and just as fast, but he was more of a counterpuncher who waited for openings instead of venturing combinations of his own. Ted told Axel to attack, attack, and attack, and not give his opponent a chance to return fire.

At his last sparring session before the bout, Axel was very aggressive in the ring, chasing down his opponents and trying to land as many shots as possible. He was thoroughly winded afterwards. Axel told Ted he would follow his advice to swarm, but he was worried that he might run out of gas by the second round. "Don't worry," Ted said. "With all this sparring you're doing, the extra gas will be there when you need it."

He showed up the night of the finale, champing at the bit and raring to go. Axel's fight was one of the earlier ones, the fifth on a card of twenty. He met his opponent, a friendly looking guy named Joe who still sported a black eye from an eleventh amateur bout he had three days ago. Win or lose, he joked, you can brag that I had a black eye at the end of our fight. Axel laughed, and wished him luck. Cameras were in two of the corners of the ring, but Axel did not pay serious attention to them.

Axel ripped through the pads with Jason during the third fight, and excitedly slipped on his headgear and mouth guard immediately afterwards, even though he wasn't due to go on for more than a few minutes. "Don't kill the guy, Axel!" Jason said over his shoulder as he made his way over to the ring when the fourth fight ended. To Axel's pleasant surprise, Ian, the lightweight going soon to the Olympic trials, was going to be his corner guy. As he stepped into the ring, the only thing Ian said to him was, "Let your fists fly, and trust they'll land."

The bell sounded in the first round. Axel and Joe met in the middle; Joe delivered a nice feint, and caught Axel with a powerful right hook on the jaw. Axel responded by going straight into Joe's personal space and exchanging body shots while their shoulders were pressed together. Joe repeatedly clubbed Axel's left shoulder until the referee told them to break. They broke apart, and then Axel went on an offensive that did not let up until the end of the round. He chased Joe into a corner with a barrage of jabs, and got off half a dozen good one-two combinations until Joe spun himself free. Axel continued to use one-two combinations to force Joe into another corner, and then unloaded his hooks. Joe used his experience to block most of them, but enough got through to force him to clinch. They broke apart again, and Joe tried to get to the open ring, but Axel cut it off and gradually forced him in another corner where he had to fend off jabs, uppercuts and more hooks until the bell rang.

Axel walked back to his corner. He was already quite tired, knowing that he had two more rounds to go. Fuck it, he said to himself. Ian must have read his mind and said, "Fuck your fatigue - keep going. Keep this pace up, and I swear your bout will be the best of the evening. Floor it!"

The second round Joe tried to go on the attack, but Axel fired off a rapid volley of jabs that kept him back. Then Axel launched a powerful series of jabs and straight rights, walking behind each one of them all the way, and Joe was back in the corner. Axel unleashed a jab-right-hook-right, and Joe shelled up; When Axel launched the same combination, Joe shoved his way out onto the ropes. Axel followed him closely, landing repeated ones and twos by walking sideways and matching his location. Joe clinched again. Upon breaking, Axel drove Joe into the one corner he had not yet been driven into, and kept him there with straight rights, uppercuts, and hooks until the bell rang.

Axel walked back to his corner on fumes. He was trusting his second wind to arrive after a minute's rest. Ted came to his corner and told him to switch up the punches so that some landed in Joe's midsection, and to start using more right hooks. Only then did Axel hear the crowd; it was very loud.

Axel's second wind only lasted one minute into the third round, during which he did land some hard body shots and a right hook that made Joe's eyes open wide. There was no way Axel was going to be able to do a fourth round. Fortunately, by then Joe was backpedaling all over the ring. Axel kept charging forward, but not as crisply as he did before, and Joe was able to get in some good jabs and a right. After what felt forever, the closing bell finally rang. Axel and Joe hugged, and the crowd gave both fighters a standing ovation. He walked over to thank Joe's corner men, who bumped fists with him with the same wide eyes Joe had after the right hook.

Axel left the ring, and was immediately met by Ted. He congratulated Axel on a great performance, and said large chunks of his fight were going to be on TV as well as YouTube. Axel thanked Ted for pushing him to his limits and beyond. He was exhilarated and still a little exhausted. He left the gym shortly afterwards, but not before giving a short interview for the cable producer as he caught his breath.

Axel met up with Carli in a hotel room three nights after the fight. He had found her escort website, liked her photos, and called her up with his heart in his mouth earlier that afternoon. She had answered on the fourth ring, and told Axel to be in the hotel parking lot ten minutes before the appointment before calling her number again to receive the room number.

Axel called again and received the hotel room number. Before knocking on her door, he had gone to bathroom for the seventh time that hour. She let him in, and after counting the contents of the unsealed white envelope Axel had left on the dresser, briefly chatted for a few minutes. Then Carli told Axel to undress and lie down on the bed.

Axel had watched twenty minutes of porn on his computer before driving to the hotel, to get himself in the mood. What happened in the hotel room didn't come close to what he had seen on the computer screen. She touched his whole body while giving him French kisses, yet Axel could not get aroused. She then went directly to his genitals and tried to get him hard with oral sex. Nothing was happening.

Carli took a break, and curled up to Axel for a few minutes and chatted to him some more. After half an hour, she resorted to a hand job, and finally succeeded in jerking him off within a minute. The orgasm was short, perfunctory, and not even remotely satisfying. Axel had paid for an hour, but he knew his time here was done, knowing that he would be doing none of the positions he wanted to do in the porn video he had seen. He thanked Carli, gave her a peck on the cheek, and let himself out.

Axel drove back to his apartment not angry at himself, at women, or even at the world in the general, but sad. Sad that fifteen straight years of self-medication had mischanneled his testosterone to the point where he had forgotten how to enjoy himself. Sad that giving up alcohol and taking up strenuous exercise hadn't helped at all here. Sad that he had never developed the machinery to approach intimacy with a member of the opposite sex, and even sadder that calling up a stranger on a website was the only way he currently knew how. Axel had punched his way out of a bad canyon of personal stagnation, but he still had a lot left to learn.

CHAPTER TEN

Axel lay awake on his bed. He had been sober for close to three years. He had just spent Christmas at his sister's house with his sister, mother, brother in law, niece, and nephew, and was back in his apartment. The most interesting present he received under the tree was from his mother, a Lonely Planet travel guide for Berlin.

Axel had casually mentioned for years at family dinners that he had always wanted to visit the German capital. He had a German sounding name, and his sparring experiences with the hard-hitting Max that year had him intrigued what was in the water of that country. Plus, Berlin had the oldest and biggest chessboxing gyms in the world, many of which were open year-round.

Chessboxing popped up on Axel's radar a few months earlier; Max mentioned it after a sparring session, after Axel said he did competitive chess. Intrigued, Axel looked up the history of this strange recent hybrid sport. Chessboxing was first mentioned from the 'Nikopol' trilogy of graphic novels by Enki Bilal, in a book called *Froid Équateur* written in 1992. The Dutch performance artist Iepe Rubingh turned that fiction into reality a decade later, organizing the first chessboxing bout in Berlin 2003, and later the first championships under the auspices of the newly minted European Chessboxing Association. Since then, chessboxing had expanded worldwide with a professional marketing arm, and substantial gyms springing up in London, Los Angeles, New York, and Moscow.

A chessboxing bout consisted of eleven alternating rounds: six rounds of chess and five rounds of boxing. Rounds lasted three minutes for both chess and boxing, with sixty second breaks in between. A chessboxer won in the chess part by checkmating the opponent, having the opponent resign, or having the opponent forfeit on time; winning in the boxing part was accomplished by either knocking out the opponent, having a referee call the fight, or scoring more points from the ringside judges if no decisive result occurred in the chess game. If the chess and boxing parts were both declared draws, then victory would go to the fighter with the Black pieces.

Each fighter's boxing gloves were removed for the chess round, and noise-canceling headphones were provided to block out the sounds from the audience. The time control for the chess was essentially a rapid chess game, where each fighter had nine minutes to finish all the moves of the game. If the referee believed that one of the fighters was stalling during the chess game so as to unilaterally have the fight decided back in the boxing ring, then the referee could step in and compel the fighter to move in ten seconds (just like a ten count in boxing). Once the chess round had ended, the gloves came back on after a sixty second break for more boxing.

Axel drove back home after Christmas dinner, the Berlin travel guide in his front seat, with fantasies of chessboxing buzzing in his head. He rolled the car window down to let in the cold winter air. He knew of course that he would have to become much better at boxing before he ever came near to doing a chessboxing bout. On the bed, his mind spun.

It was much easier for a boxer to learn rapid chess than it was for a chess player to learn boxing. The chess player above all would need not to have his head ripped off, and then retool his chess game for the faster time control. In contrast, all a boxer needed to learn was fast chess. The challenge for both the boxer and the chess player was to adjust the heart rate and focus the mind for the proper discipline, just like the biathlon (skiing and shooting).

Getting off the bed, he decided upon a resolution for the following year: if his body let him, he wanted to box in two to three amateur bouts.

The regional Golden Gloves competition were coming up in a couple of weeks, but Axel didn't feel ready yet. He told Ted so on January 2, yet also told him what he wanted to do that year.

Ted asked if he still had the small yellow boxing record book that the lead judge had handed him after his amateur fight from the charity boxing event. Axel had, and Ted replied that it needed to be renewed each year by paying an annual fee to the US Amateur Boxing Association. That book would need to be presented at all future events to be marked up should he wish to participate in any more amateur bouts. Amateur fights, Ted continued, were constantly being held around the state, and if he really wanted to, Axel could do one every weekend - his current record was zero wins, zero losses, and one draw.

"I'm organizing a Saturday afternoon training session for the boxers who're going to the Golden Gloves - join us! Get a taste now of what real amateur boxing is like. You need to get used to it as often as you can. Don't overthink it and over-train months between fights. You'll always have stifling expectations and bad reflexes."

"I'm over thirty, Ted. I really don't want to get beat up by teenagers."

"Don't worry, Axel – you can handle it."

On Saturday morning, the kids going to the Golden Gloves, like Axel, were still trying to exorcise all the holiday food they had eaten. The push-ups during the group exercises felt like hell, and the squats even worse. Ted was utterly pitiless. He didn't like the sluggishness in the squats, so he made everyone do duck walks and burpees until everyone was on the floor groaning. "I may yet throw up in your gym, Ted," Axel muttered, which made Ted chuckle.

"Do it outside if you must. I just had these mats installed."

After ten rounds on the heavy bags, they all donned headgear and mouth guards, and went straight to sparring. Axel found to his pleasant surprise that he could mostly hold his own. The kids in the lower weight classes were way too fast for him to match punch for punch, but one shot from Axel counted for every five of theirs that landed. For the kids above his own weight class, Axel was able to negate most of their strength and power by getting up close to minimize the power of their outstretched arms. For the kids in his weight class, Axel found still more new ways to get hit, and learned as much as he could.

He would need three days afterward to recover from this afternoon, knowing full well that all his opponents would be back in the gym within two days at most, as if nothing had ever happened. Axel thanked

Ted for the taste, and said that a couple of amateur fights for him this year might not be too difficult. "Of course it's possible, Axel. As my grandfather once said, the difficult is easy – it's the impossible that takes a little longer," Ted replied, slapping Axel on the shoulder.

The year was new, but the days remained short, dark, and confusing. He wasn't lonely that often, but all the exercise did make him horny and frustrated a lot. Connecting with people outside of a boxing ring or a chess tournament continued to be a frustrating experience for Axel, his bunch of wires trying to fuse all at once with another stranger's bunch of wires, with the power turned on.

Axel tried to connect with a few of the women who boxed in the gym, the ones older than the university students. Just about all of them had serious boyfriends, or husbands already, which killed all future conversation dead in the water.

In February he hit it off (socially) with a friendly vivacious girl named Skylar during one of the general group boxing classes. He asked curiously why all her fingernails were painted different colors, and she replied it was a fun thing she had decided to do with a group of her girlfriends. She then jokingly offered to paint all his toenails different colors, whereupon Axel tried to jokingly respond in kind that if she saw his toenails she would run away screaming, immediately biting his tongue afterwards. But Skylar snorted derisively, playfully starting in with combinations of punches around his torso. Axel then snapped out a jab that ended half and inch from her nose, stopping Skylar dead in her tracks and her staring at his fist with startled eyes. Axel then slowly moved his fist forward, tapped her gently on the nose, and grinned. Skylar grinned back.

At an exhibition fight night two weeks later at the gym, they found themselves standing next to each other in the crowd, looking at the all fights together, and talking for over an hour. She was wearing a fur coat, sharing hilarious politically incorrect insults about animal rights activists who thought fur was an abomination. They mostly talked about the styles of the fighters in the exhibition bouts, as both Skyler and Axel had sparred with most of them, and about mixed martial fighting, and how it compared to boxing.

Axel knew better than to talk about chess. *She's ten years younger,* Axel thought to himself, *there's no way she would go out with me.* He was about to throw caution to the winds and ask Skylar out anyway, until a group of her friends found her and whisked her away to meet more of their friends. They hurriedly said goodbye with a friendly fist bump, and that was that.

Axel next ran into Skylar two weeks later in the gym at another group boxing class, sporting an engagement ring, and as friendly as ever. He felt like Pluto with the longest and most distant orbit around the sun, countless satellites just outside Earth's atmosphere running circles inside him. He was on the far rim, and destined to spend most of his time alone. *So be it*, Axel said resignedly. He could not ask more from this pleasant face as much as he could make an aggressive move on the chessboard without the position supporting it.

He had not forgotten Garen and his insanely difficult chess sessions. By this point they were only meeting once a month. Garen would briefly meet Axel at a coffee shop, hand over a batch of problems, and tell Axel to write down his answers with all variations worked out. They would meet again for Axel to hand over his answers, receive feedback from Garen about the quality of his last answers, and collect another batch of problems to solve. Cheating with a computer would not have made the solutions any easier, for Garen wanted all the plausible alternate variations explored, analyzed, and evaluated along with the answers.

Solving Garen's problems made Axel feel quantitively smarter, but the exercises did not immediately translate into tournament success. This type of pondering over a single position for hours at a time did not help one whit in finding the best move in a chess game with a rapid time control. A strong local master had recently confided to Axel that he had stopped studying endgame theory deeply – there just wasn't enough time to work out all the subtleties in an endgame anymore with a sudden death time limit.

Garen himself admitted that the chess world was revolving on its axis much more quickly than before, and that his training methods might have fallen behind the times. He suggested a change of address so that Axel could face tougher and more varied opponents to improve his game, such as New York or Europe. Axel saw the logic of Garen's suggestion, and had the funds to do so, but was not yet ready to live a totally itinerant life of the mind.

Axel persevered in his slow, hard study. He respected chess too much to treat it superficially, and reduce his style to skimming stones lightly over the water. He did not want become so involved in his deep dives that he plunged too low and became too bogged down to swim, but he did want to see more of what was underneath. He wanted a fresh perspective by closing his eyes and seeing greater distances in the dark – the equivalent of going underwater and holding his breath for longer periods of time. It was good for his soul.

CHAPTER ELEVEN

Axel was in decent shape when he asked Ted in late February if an amateur bout was available during the spring.

Ted said one was scheduled in April at Brockton, the birthplace of undefeated heavyweight champion Rocky Marciano. Not only did Ted offer Axel a spot on the card, he promised to be in his corner for the fight too. He then printed out and handed to Axel a training regimen for five days a week, to be repeated each week until the fight, each workout consisting of no less than three hours. Nobody would be checking up on Axel to see if he followed the regimen or not.

Axel chose to do his training in the evenings, from eight p.m. until the gym closed at eleven p.m. He pretty much had the entire gym to himself, save for Lou, a trainer whose shift was so quiet that his main job was to lock up and turn off the lights. Lou said that this was what boxing was all about, the training on one's own and assuming that someone was always watching. Time spent sparring with others was paltry compared to that spent in solitary, active practice. They did some time practicing on the pads, but Axel was primarily there for physical conditioning. The only true measure of his nightly workouts was how exhausted he felt afterwards.

When he slept, he dreamed a few times that he was carrying an older, slower version of himself all over the gym during the workouts. Nobody could take this private "pleasure" away, and Axel worked out harder than he had ever worked out before.

The nights were dark and cold in March, and in the practically deserted gym Axel noticed idiosyncratic details in the décor that would stay with him as training props. He noticed the W.B. Mason clock on the wall above the sign-in sheet that timed most of his warmup exercises, and saw that it was askew ten degrees counterclockwise. He adjusted his head to fit between two strips of masking tape on one of the mirrors that forced him to crouch down, judging the top strip to be three and a half inches long and the bottom one just under two inches. He noticed the vertical placement of the tears in the heavy bags covered up in duct tape. All these strange visual cues, found nowhere else in the world, helped make Axel keep his own internal time in the workouts. They would later serve as reminders during his later fights to help him remember all the hard work he had put in, and not give up.

Axel asked Ted at the end of the month if any of the other fighters in the gym going to the amateur fight needed sparring practice, drawing the cheerful response that plenty of people would love to smash him in the face. For all the fighters going to the event, he was setting up a series of informal sessions on Saturdays, and on every other weeknight, for the next three weeks. Axel thanked Ted caustically; his fists felt as hard as stone, and he was ready for the abuse.

The abuse arrived two nights later. After a short warmup, everyone lined up on the ropes inside the ring, where two would meet in the center for one to three rounds at a time. For the first time ever, he was told with all the fighters to go at it full throttle in a practice. Axel waited between his skirmishes in the center with equal measures of exhilarating excitement and suffocating dread. Many of the fighters were knocked down, and there was blood. He went into the middle half a dozen times, moving with an extra careful defensive crouch thanks to the muscle memory from training between the two lines of masking tape; punches nonetheless did get through, and jolted as from loose power lines.

Axel went full force against the heavy middleweights, cruiserweights, and heavyweights he faced in middle of the ring, with up to twenty fighters around inside the ropes looking on. Axel thought the other people must be as nervous he was when they were waiting for their turns, but they hid their anxiety much better than he did. It took a long time for Axel to realize that what looked really important to him inside the boxing ring was not so important, and often not even noticed at all by others.

When the practice was over after an hour, Axel felt the same hybrid sensations of being drained yet wired as he did after the end of a long hard-fought tournament chess game, but with the additional feeling of his face stinging when he re-emerged into the chilly spring air. Every square centimeter on Axel's arms and torso became pounded and sore, but the air tasted cold and sweet when he exited the gym, as if it were ice cream.

He could think of nothing else for the next two days, making imaginary feints at colleagues who walked at him in the corridors, and bouncing on the balls of his feet when they were walking away. He felt more boxed in than usual driving his car to work, and became insanely impatient when his car was stuck inside a traffic jam. He found himself constantly moving when the rest of the world was standing still.

Two nights later, Axel arrived at the gym for the abuse to begin again. Ted left him in the middle for five rounds this time, leaving Axel totally gassed by the fourth round and struggling to keep his hands up for the fifth. "Your fight in Brockton is only going to have three rounds of three minutes each, Axel, but you should get used to fighting totally exhausted. Some boxers out there can take all of the air out of you in the ring after ninety seconds," he said when he saw Axel wilting.

Axel went to five more of Ted's informal smash fests. Fighters from other local gyms had started turning up, so Axel could not get used to any one particular style, nor brace himself against what to expect against a repeat opponent. Not all of the boxers were of the same weight categories. If a bantamweight was told to mix it up in the middle with a heavyweight, the heavyweight had to pull most of his punches while the bantamweight could hit as hard as he wanted. If the fighters were within fifteen pounds of each other, though, they unapologetically went at it without holding back.

Several accomplished women boxers from the gym were also invited; they were paired against guys too, including Axel. He had no doubt that most of these ladies could knock him on his ass in a street fight, but US Amateur Boxing Association rules forbade men and women from sparring. Therefore, their time together in the center of the ring was the women going full offense and Axel doing nothing but defense. They drew blood when Axel missed a block.

Axel had lost so much weight the last couple of months, he was no longer a heavyweight. He had become a cruiserweight (under two hundred pounds) without consciously trying. His waist size shrank from a thirty-six to a thirty-four to a thirty-two, and Axel knew he was going to need two sets of clothes in the future: one during training, and one outside of training. He could eat whatever he wanted, yet stuck to three square meals of sensible food a day, which in quantity were probably five meals packed into three.

Ted said he had no control over the opponent Axel would meet; he should just show up in the best fighting shape possible and take whatever comes. He also told him to stop training one week before the event so that his body could heal. The intensity Ted was putting him through now would be nothing compared to the intensity at the bout.

The week before the event, Axel stopped. He had done all the necessary physical and reflex work, and all that remained was to show up in Brockton for nine minutes of scary and painful exercise. The duration of the week felt like a month. The soreness and the exhaustion died down, but his apprehension rose to feverish levels. He walked constantly in vain to slow down the thoughts racing through his head. All the work he had put into preparing for the fight had felt so seamless and perfect – the actual fight, no matter how he imagined it otherwise, would be broken and imperfect all over.

Axel decided not to describe this bout to his friends and family until afterwards as a fait accompli. He drove down for the event in a van with Ted, all of the other fighters from the gym who were going to fight, and the gym trainers Jason and Lou. Axel easily made his weigh-in for the cruiserweight at one hundred and ninety pounds, and turned over his small yellow boxing record book over to an official at the welcome desk, not needing to undergo another physical from a doctor because his last amateur fight was under a year ago. He changed into his trunks, covering himself up with sweatpants and a sweatshirt. Axel had his hands wrapped professionally again, marked with an 'X' on each fist. Then he waited in the locker room.

Ted later swung by and told him his fight was seventh on a card of fifteen bouts. His opponent was a twenty-seven-year-old guy from Dorchester who had weighed in at a hundred and eight-eight pounds, and had an amateur record of four wins and two losses. He was in another locker room; they would not be meeting until walked up to each other nose to nose in the center of the ring. Ted would be in one of the corners waiting for him just before the fight was to begin. He told Axel to think tough thoughts, and then went up into the arena to be in the corner for one of the earlier bouts.

Axel waited some more. He had been chatting with the gym trainers and the other fighters in the locker room on one level, but on another level, he felt totally alone. The anxiety of being in a new venue was doing its best to drain the strength out of his legs. He struggled to remember the off-kilter wall clock, the precise length of the masking tape strips, and the duct tape pattern on his favorite punching bag in the gym, hoping that they would be sufficient anchors for what he was about to do. After another hour, Jason from the gym said his fight would be soon, and held up some pads so that Axel could warm up. Stripping off his sweatshirt and sweatpants, he put on his gloves and did a minute on the pads. He filled out his last minutes in the locker room doing push-ups, until a boxing official stuck his head in, and said it was show time.

The crowd was larger than the exhibition fights at the gym, but smaller than at the charity boxing event, and it was partisan. His opponent's name, he found out from the ring announcer, was Brendan. Brendan was an inch taller with chiseled shoulders that were covered with tattoos, but with slightly shorter arms attached to them. Several of Brendan's friends were in the audience, and Axel had his first experience of being booed. Ted told him in the corner before the opening bell to keep his hands up at all times, to stay in the open ring as often as he could, and to try to have some fun. All those weeks of hard preparation, and it had suddenly come down to this...

The bell sounded, and Axel pushed out from his corner. He started bouncing on his feet, and waited for his opponent to come to him, which he did immediately. Axel with beginner's luck timed his opening volley perfectly, shooting out a jab the moment his left toes hit landed on the canvas, and nailed his opponent straight in the nose. The toes of his other foot touched the canvas, and he immediately launched a right straight without thinking, which landed into his opponent's mid-section. Axel then fired off a hook that found its way to side of the head, and wheeled away before his opponent could retaliate. *A good way to start*, Axel thought, *let's keep it going.*

Brendan recovered quickly, turned to face Axel, and charged. *I'm going to get hit no matter what*, Axel muttered to himself above the din of the crowd, *time to get it over with.* He rocked on his heels in a full crouch, with his hands held high, and waited for the onslaught, which came with unnerving speed. His opponent flicked off a quick jab, which was a set up for a straight right. Axel could tell by the way the tattoos moved in his shoulders that the hard right was also going to be a set up for some hooks his opponent was dying to unleash. So, Axel turned in to take the straight right with his shoulder (*there's my first hit – ouch*) to set up a hook of his own. He raised the arm as he was still moving forward, and launched it straight into the headgear where his opponent's left ear was. He hadn't been hit back, so Axel continued with an unanswered right uppercut, then turned his hand over and kept going with a straight right, left hook, and another straight right. The referee stepped in and told Axel to go to a neutral corner while he gave a standing eight count to his opponent.

Brendan passed the eight count, and Axel remembered Ted's advice to stay in the open ring. He moved to the left and right, applying ladders of jabs to the head and body to keep his adversary from doing damage. His opponent tried to charge twice more, but Axel than switched to his straight rights to stop him in his tracks, stepped into his jabs and rights to force backward movement, and then resumed his ladder jabs while moving to the left and right until the bell for the end of the first round sounded.

In the corner, Ted looked at Axel with blank bemusement, as he gave him water. "Keep doing what you're doing," was all he said in the break between rounds.

The second round started. Brendan was rocking sideways as he walked forwards, primed to unload hooks from the get-go. Axel turned his stance sideways, and resumed bouncing on the balls of his feet as his opponent moved in close. Axel saw a tattoo on the left shoulder start to dip, and started to roll towards his left. A foot away with the distance closing in fast, Axel rolled under a tremendous whooshing sound above, popped back up, turned to see his opponent's head completely undefended, and then went to town. With all his strength Axel threw a left hook, two straight rights, another left hook, and a right hook, sensing his opponent's knees wobble. The referee stepped in again and declared the fight over.

Only five minutes had elapsed since he had stepped into the ring. Axel was dazed: he had managed to drive in the fast lane without crashing his car. Having his hand raised by the referee afterwards as the winner's mattered little to him, the sounds from the crowd mattering even less. He was more immediately worried about his opponent, and went to see him in his corner to see if he was all right. Brendan was still shaking too many cobwebs out of his head to give him an affirmative answer, but his trainer assured Axel he was OK, and congratulated him on a good fight.

Axel after changing into his street clothes hung around the arena to watch the final fights, cheering his fellow gym fighters and continuing to marvel at how they seemed to manage to control their nerves so much better. He was inordinately pleased to have his official amateur boxing record book returned to him, notched with a win. *No one will ever be able to take this away from me*, Axel said to himself with quiet pride.

CHAPTER TWELVE

The fighters, trainers, and Ted stopped off at a sports bar on the way back to celebrate. Axel still didn't like being around the smell of alcohol, but did not want to be unsociable. He hung out at a large table in back with them drinking pitchers while he sipped ginger-ale. Beer was an old demon to Axel, a beverage somewhat deprecated by all the wine that flooded in afterwards, but a potent trap all the same that never stopped trying to re-ingratiate itself as his long-lost best friend. The celebrating became loud and raucous, and some of the beer inevitably spilled on Axel's clothes; even a little spilled into his ginger-ale. The ginger-ale he was quietly drinking tasted increasingly sweet and cloying while those around him were loudly enjoying themselves.

None of the other people at the table ever pressured him, but Axel had such a good fight, and had come so far from the day he walked into Ted's gym a couple of years ago, that he impulsively took a swallow from the beer glass of the person sitting next to him.

He immediately regretted it – *Christ, it was Budweiser*!

The same Budweiser he blindly chugged down the first month of his freshman year of college, the Budweiser that made him throw up so much and so often that his roommate requested a transfer the following semester, the Budweiser that gave him splitting hangovers for the next eight semesters, the Budweiser that washed down all those whole pizzas and made him feel bloated and undesirable to the opposite sex, and the Budweiser that made him clean up all the vomit on the floor which didn't make the bucket by his bed.

Like some perverse time-machine, the taste of the beer instantly teleported him back to those golden years that were cheap pyrite at best. He hurriedly excused himself from the table saying that he needed some air, and walked around the parking lot where the van was until the others were ready to leave, cursing his punctured state of mind and loss of self-control.

The next couple of weeks were lousy for Axel, when he should have been feeling at the top of the world. That stupid gulp had made him lose a lot of confidence in his subsequent choices for the next few weeks.

He entered a chess tournament the next Saturday morning, and lost to two middle schoolers by moving his pieces out of sync to the time control. In one of the games he moved too slowly and lost on time, and in the other he moved too quickly and blundered his Queen straight out of the opening. He withdrew from the tournament in disgust, but not before losing fifty rating points.

Then at the gym the following week he impulsively jumped into a sparring session without warming up properly. He practically ran into a tremendous right hand from his partner that snapped his neck back so hard that his shoulder tingled afterwards, and he was afraid that he might have whiplash.

Eventually, Axel stopped hyperventilating from drinking that beer, and he never got whiplash. He could still recall the taste of the hops in his mouth at will, but had no need to wash it down with some more of the same. He had accomplished so much in the other column which did not involve alcohol that the craving for another drink had nowhere to go, and faded away.

He subsequently entered another chess tournament, and thrashed one of the kids he had lost to so thoroughly that he barely needed more than a minute. The tingling in his shoulder, he learned later from a visit to his doctor, was called a stinger brought on by a pinched nerve in the neck, and caused by the head being jolted suddenly to the side. The stinger occurred from the cumulative effects of all the heavy sparring he went through to prepare for the fight, and would go away after his body had fully rested.

Yet Axel never forgot the mini-tailspin that sip of beer had caused. That insidiously pleasant taste he would bring to the forefront of his mind whenever he felt his future spirits sagging. To become really good at doing something, he now knew more clearly than ever, meant both saying goodbye to the past, and no longer taking its phone calls.

CHAPTER THIRTEEN

The workouts at the gym Axel gradually reduced to maintenance mode, showing up only three nights a week for group exercise classes – nothing more. He decided to immerse himself in chess again. He did Garen's homework assignments twice a month, up from once a month.

Axel was not a good enough chess player to be invited to international closed tournaments; however, he was strong enough to enter the open sections of big chess festivals, where professional grandmasters often played. A big one called the World Open took place over the Fourth of July holiday weekend in Philadelphia, which Axel decided to enter again after several years. The open section had nine rounds spaced out over five days; the prize fund, while paltry compared to professional golf or tennis, was substantial for chess, and drew some of the strongest players in the world.

He had first played here as a teenager in the scholastic side event, when he went with a chaperoned group from two local schools - they gave out huge trophies then. Axel managed to win one for third best placed junior that was bigger than all his previous scholastic trophies combined, one that he fit with great difficulty into the car trunk for the drive home. The next time was after he had finished his junior year of college, shortly after he had earned his master's title – he had a par result, which was well out of the money. The tournament venue had seemed so huge then.

Later, after having entered the work force, he returned a few times more, and was struck by how intellectually rich but monetarily poor most of the participants were. The ones who actually depended on the money looked like they were stuck in that depressing 1970s movie *They Shoot Horses, Don't They?* about a danceathon set in the Great Depression – it made him appreciate chess as a hobby only, and the virtues of steady W2 forms.

This time Axel was here to test the effectiveness of Garen's training. He had prepared hard, as hard as he did for boxing, and wanted to see how the work he had put in the past three months would pan out. The time control was classical, with two hours for the first forty moves, and one hour for the remaining moves.

In the first round he was paired with a much lower-rated high school freshman, his chess dad in tow hovering over his shoulder. Axel could smell the chess dad's aftershave, and was really annoyed by his presence, until the first original position was reached where he could block him out by concentrating on the game. His opponent played well until he dropped a pawn in the early middlegame, whereupon Axel converted his extra material relatively easily.

In the second round he faced a visiting Indian master rated only a few points lower. The game started quietly and became an early endgame, with all the pieces exchanged off save for a Rook and Bishop for Axel and a Rook and Knight for his opponent. Axel successfully used the superiority of the long-range Bishop over the short-stepping Knight to enter a pure Rook endgame a pawn up. Rook endings though were notoriously hard to play perfectly – even world champions were known to screw them up – and Axel made a crucial inaccuracy that his opponent exploited to escape with a draw. In the postmortem he and his opponent found a more promising continuation for Axel. It would have been very difficult to find over the board, and even there his opponent had good drawing chances, so he did not feel so bad.

In the third round he played a strong master from Iowa. The game was sharp from its opening moves, his opponent sacrificing a piece for two pawns and an attack. Axel buckled down and found a counter sacrifice of the exchange, which restored rough material parity but broke his opponent's attack and passed the initiative over to him. The moves to and from the sacrifice and counter sacrifice ate up a lot of time, and both players hurried their later moves to meet the first time control. Fortunately for Axel, his opponent walked into a Knight fork of his King and Queen during the time scramble, and immediately resigned.

In the fourth round Axel was paired way up against a visiting grandmaster from Britain who was currently ranked number nineteen in the world. The game took place between a special section behind the ropes where the top ten boards were played, the moves being broadcast over the Internet. Axel knew he had a very tough customer on his hands, but games like these were why he came to the tournament, and he resolved to give it his all.

The game evolved into a dense layer cake of interlocking pieces and potential pawn breaks that threatened to explode into a volcano of tactics. Axel held his own until move thirty-five, when he blinked and blundered a piece, resigning shortly afterwards. His brain felt like it had done four hours at the Nautilus weight circuit station of his college days, each station set at the maximum weight.

The round schedule was two rounds a day for the next four days, with the final round on the fifth day. Axel went to sleep in his hotel room after his loss, and managed to sleep eight hours straight, but he woke up just as tired as when he had turned out the light. The cumulative effect of all his mental exertions would weigh him down even more as the tournament went on.

In the fifth round Axel was paired up again against an international master from Poland. He made an idiotic mistake in the opening and lost the exchange (his Rook for his opponent's Bishop). However, Axel dug in his heels and resolved to make the conversion of his opponent's extra material as difficult as humanly possible. He turned both pawn structures into irregular messes, where sneaky tactical counterplay could flourish, and computer-like accuracy was required from his opponent. The energy of Axel's pieces fed on the unnatural pawn structures, and he was able to force a perpetual check to obtain a draw, to the enormous annoyance of his opponent.

In the sixth round Axel was paired against a strong teenager from California, the current US Junior Champion. The fatigue must have been getting to his opponent too, for he played the opening quickly, and mixed up the move order of a sharp variation from the Ruy Lopez. Axel was paying attention, and played a sharp disruptive sacrifice that forced a quick win. It was a rare gift in such a strong tournament, and Axel said so when he accepted his opponent's embarrassed resignation.

Axel went back to his hotel room with a large block of time on his hands. All he could do was mindlessly watch hours of the Cartoon Network and reruns of *Law and Order* until it was time to go to sleep.

He woke up even more tired than the morning before.

In the seventh round Axel found himself back behind the ropes, paired against a grandmaster from New York City. His opponent quickly exchanged off most of the pieces in an equal position, expecting to outplay Axel in the endgame. The game went down to the wire. In the final sudden death time control the position was still equal, the minutes dwindling down to seconds for both players. His opponent's tenacity paid off, as with fifty-five seconds left, Axel made a critical error moving his King back one square diagonally, instead of moving it straight back which would have maintained the balance. His opponent jumped on the blunder, exploiting the extra tempo and promoted his pawn to a Queen one move ahead of Axel. He checkmated Axel with eleven seconds left on his clock. Six hours the battle had lasted, and ultimately it had been decided in a blitz game.

Axel had but little time to wolf down a hamburger after his loss, and hurry to the board before the eighth round started. His opponent was one of the best woman players in the country, somewhere in playing strength between an international master and an international grandmaster. Her style was positional, for which Axel was profoundly grateful – he was still too frazzled from his last game to get into a tactical slugfest and expend his dwindled energy in calculation. Not that such a game was easier to play. The positional weapons she chose to use on the board were heavy and blunt in nature instead of sharp and jagged, and would have done just as much damage had not Axel managed to remain alert. They agreed to a draw halfway into the second time control.

Axel slogged his way back to his room after eleven hours of virtual head butting. His brain had the consistency of oatmeal, the temperature of which was lukewarm at best. The last round started early next morning, and he had to wake up extra early so that he could check out of the hotel. He had shallow pounding dreams for the next six hours, then wrenched himself out of bed and stuck his head under an ice-cold shower for ten minutes. After checking out he checked his bags at the customer courtesy desk, had two slices of toast and four cups of coffee for breakfast, and made his way to the tournament hall for the last round.

In the ninth round he waited forty minutes for his disheveled opponent to show up, a master from Connecticut. Axel would have won a bet by guessing that he had woken up only minutes before. His opponent drank lots of coffee at the board to get himself through the next couple of hours. Axel was in no mood for another long game, and played one of the sharpest lines in opening theory against his opponent's Sicilian Defense: win or lose, he wanted the game to be over with quickly. His opponent fell into a murderous attack, and Axel finished off the tournament on a high note with a win in under twenty-five moves.

Only then did Axel look at the tournament cross table to see if he had won any money. This was a longstanding habit of Axel's at big open tournaments, looking at the cross table only once the last round had finished. He hated playing chess with the tournament standings in the back of his mind; they were only a distraction. Having no practical chance of winning money for the top ten finish places – the competition was way too strong – he sometimes was able to win several hundred dollars for first or second place in his specific rating bracket. Alas, four players close to Axel's rating had outperformed even more and finished a point higher, claiming that prize money for their own.

Axel didn't care; he had stopped coming to this event with any expectation of winning money a long time ago. He was totally chessed out, yet satisfied with his play. He stood his ground against tough opponents for the money he had paid, even gaining a couple of rating points in the process. Studying all the time, forever becoming smarter in his own mind, had little value if it didn't run into a reality check every once in a while. Axel did not do this reality check every year, because with a full-time job it was just as exhausting for his mind as training for a boxing match was exhausting for his body.

Several die-hard chess players organized a private blitz tournament after the last round had ended, but Axel was not interested. If he saw another chess piece, he was going to barf.

CHAPTER FOURTEEN

The pendulum swung in the other direction, and Axel wanted to do another amateur fight. Ted said one was coming up next month in late August. Axel resumed working out at the gym five nights a week, enjoying the cool night air and the reassuring thuds he administered on the punching bags.

On Saturdays he showed up at ten in the morning, just before weekend classes began, where some sort of "pick-up" sparring had developed over the past few months. Boxers of all levels of ability assembled from the gym and from other local gyms: even professionals occasionally dropped by to get in an informal workout. The sparring sessions were unsupervised; the boxers were trusted to control themselves in the ring if one of them looked like they were getting hurt.

At the beginning of August, Ted organized another series of smash fests on alternating weeknights. Sixteen fighters were lined up on the ropes of the ring, and Axel strangely thought about chess. *Sixteen pawns, one square in the middle, how do you make pawn chains...? Four pawns to each side of the ring; if only you split up the ring, you'd have two classic pawn centers facing each other...*

Axel's musings abruptly ended the moment he was thrown in the middle with a hard-punching southpaw from another gym. They did three fairly painful rounds, yet Axel still had chess on his mind. *I'm opening with 1. d4, and he's always playing the Dutch Defense with 1...f5 because his lead hand is forever poised to crash into the right half of my center.* Later he sparred with a tall guy, and Axel kept thinking about fianchettoed Bishops striking from afar as he scrambled away from his opponent's long-range bombs. Having a continuous stream of chessboard thoughts while getting hit made the rounds go by shorter, and the blows sting a little less.

Axel had been through this meat grinder before, so the reflexes needed for an amateur fight came back to him within two weeks. He did another week anyway just to dot imaginary i's and cross speculative t's, until seven days before the fight arrived, when Ted ordered him to stop training. The fight was going to be in the next town over, not far from the gym. Ted was going to be his corner man again, telling Axel to show up two hours before the doors opened to the general public.

This time Axel felt confident enough that he wouldn't suck, so he told his friends and family where he going to be. His mother nearly fainted when he finally told her about the last amateur fight, and he was ninety-nine percent sure she would not be there. His sister had small children, and was especially sensitive to exposing them to violence, so he was ninety-five percent sure they were not going to be there either. The chess-player friends he told though were excited (and secretly, he was sure, were going to take pictures to use as future blackmail material). Many said they would be there for the fight. Axel hoped that he would be able to hear them above the crowd noise and his nerves.

Axel turned over his boxing record book when he arrived at the venue, successfully made his weigh-in for cruiserweight, had his hands professionally wrapped and marked with an 'X', and waited for hours in the locker room. Ted came by and said that his fight was tenth in a card of seventeen bouts. His opponent was a twenty-two-year-old from a local gym, had weighed in at one hundred and eighty-five pounds, and was fighting his first amateur fight. Ted knew nothing about him, and told Axel to come out of the first round cautiously and restrict himself to the basics; he would work out a strategy for him on the fly for the latter two rounds. As Ted left to help one of the other gym fighters in an early bout, he squeezed Axel on the shoulder and told him to hang loose.

Axel warmed up on the pads with Jason when the seventh fight ended, and skipped rope afterwards until he was called out to the ring by a boxing official. The crowd was slightly smaller than the last amateur event, and Axel was able to see three of his friends standing up from their seats, cheering him on. Axel smiled, and then grinned at them tightly when he saw their phones raised high set to record. Future blackmail was on their agenda, definitely.

The name of Axel's opponent was Jared. He had a tapered build with a two-inch height advantage. Touching gloves with him in the center of ring, Axel sensed a strange centrifugal movement in his hips, and had a weird sense of déjà vu as the opening bell rang.

Axel stuck to the basics, approaching sideways and bouncing on the balls of his feet, but was put off at the stance of his opponent who moved toward him. Jared was sideways, but not bouncing on the balls of his feet – instead he was rocking his head from side to side in an exaggerated fashion, as if his upper torso was the sliding weight part of a metronome. He was jerking left to right across the canvas in a forward fashion, like a demented robot with Tourette's Syndrome.

Axel found out quickly when they met there was a method to Jared's apparent madness, as his head suddenly jerked to one side and reappeared, accompanied with a crashing hook to Axel's head. Axel instinctively moved back to see three more forward leaning sideways bobs of his opponent's head, and then suddenly feel both his sides hit with a pair of hooks to both sides of his rib cage, and then another hook to the other side of his head. "Circle to the left and fire jabs!" he heard Ted yell.

Axel did so, but not before receiving one more hook to both the head and the body. More annoyed than hurt for taking six unanswered punches, he now saw his adversary as a really challenging double-ended bag to hit. He threw four jabs, all of them missing. Axel remembered to stick to the basics, bringing his hands back immediately and moving to the left, but that rocking head in front of him was making it hard to concentrate.

Axel's opponent promptly squared off the ring and didn't allow any more circling to the left. A new flurry of hooks followed. However, the element of surprise was gone and Axel suddenly visualized himself on a balance ball, developing a sideways motion that roughly synchronized to the manic sideways rocking of Jared's head, and allowing Axel to block most of the hooks. Three hooks though got through, and Axel knew he was going to lose this round on points if he didn't land a punch soon.

He tried to throw a left hook of his own, and felt his glove smash into the glove of his opponent's. For that one brief moment of contact Axel knew his opponent was relatively stationary, so he stepped to the right and immediately fired a straight right hand into Jared's shoulder. His opponent backed off and tried to circle to his right, but Axel then followed up with a jab delivered out of his sight and at a forty-five-degree angle, and felt a satisfying thud. Turning to face his opponent he found that he was going to draw blood from the opposing nose.

Jared quickly got out of range. Axel, however, was able to back Jared into a corner. He was finally penned in enough to make Axel think about throwing combinations, but then the bell sounded to end the round.

He walked back to his corner, bewildered.

"What crazy oscillating electrical circuit did they plug him into, Ted? Maybe I should wait until he gets dizzy from all that rocking and starts hitting himself."

Ted chuckled. "This is why I keep telling you guys to move your head. He does it quite well. But he doesn't move his entire body with his head. That makes him off balance just after he moves all the way out to the side, and just before he moves back in again to deliver the punch with his torque. When you don't see his head, crouch, plant your feet, and clip his midsection that's still in your field of vision. He'll slow down after a couple of those, and then you'll have a heavy bag you can pound instead of that double-ended bag you keep missing."

It was seconds out before the next round started, and suddenly Axel remembered why his opponent gave him a sense of déjà vu. Many years ago at an amateur team championship he encountered a chess player his teammates had dubbed "The Pecker." This person rocked back and forth in his chair like he was Woody Woodpecker during his games. When he had a winning position, he would rock forwards and backwards ever more manically. He eventually lost a game; while his opponent converted his advantage, the pecking movement slowed down, and then totally stopped pecking when he resigned. *OK mister sideways pecker*, Axel said to himself as the second round started, *time to slow you down.*

Jared approached with the same sideways forward rocking movement, and Axel was prepared. As the head jerked to the right, he planted his feet and fired a quick jab that nailed the left obliques of his opponent's abdomen. The head quickly crossed of his vision towards the other side, and Axel stepped forward to deliver a right to the opposite obliques. Then he saw all of his opponent in the same frame.

Without thinking, Axel landed a right uppercut, twisted back slightly, and threw all his strength into a right hook that knocked down his opponent. Jared was able to get back up, but he did not pass the referee's standing eight count, and Axel was awarded the fight. They hugged, and Axel complimented Jared on the strength of his hooks. "Yours are pretty good too, man," he graciously replied.

Ted smiled and said as Axel returned to his corner: "A few more of these, and you might actually look like you know what you're doing." Axel picked up his boxing record book before changing into his street clothes, and high fived his friends waiting for him outside the locker room. We have video, they said; you are going to be a star.

One of his friends posted a video file of the boxing match to his chess club's blog the following morning. The post received over a hundred comments the following week, half of them expressing surprise, the other half clamoring for more information on Axel. The cat was out of the bag, but he had grown sick of living in that bag. The furor eventually died down after a month.

Axel never heard anything from his co-workers, because he had never told them. After several years of doing his job, he had become so used for being taken for granted that he was only showing up there to pick up a paycheck, a paycheck that according to his financial advisor he needed less and less. Also, he had also become so irritated by the cubicle mannerisms of his neighboring cubicle dwellers that to tune them out was easier than having to talk with them. He did still like one or two people there, and kept chatting with them, but not about chess and boxing.

He received a strange phone call the following month from the president of the United States Chess Federation, asking for permission to disclose his contact information to a reputable organization – they wanted to send Axel a registered letter. Intrigued, he consented. The following weekend Axel signed for a packet at his door, and opened it.

The packet contained the New York Athletic Association's amateur boxing rules and regulations, a doctor's waiver form, a booklet describing the rules of chess, another booklet describing the rules of chessboxing, a form for a criminal background check, and a press release that described the formation of a newly sanctioned body in the state of New York to hold chessboxing bouts. Attached just inside the paper clip holding all the paper together was a business card. The name on the business card was Vyacheslav Molotov, president of the New York Chessboxing Association. On the back of the card was written in a bold upward slant: *Call me!*

There were too many official forms in the package for it to be a practical joke, so Axel took the rest of the day formulating questions in his head that he wanted answered, and called that night. He heard in a faint Slavic accent: "Hello, you've reached Vy. I can't come to the phone right now, so leave a message." Axel left his name and number at the beep, and hung up. Within seconds his phone rang. He picked up and said:

"Hello?"

"Hi, is this Axel?"

"Speaking."

"Hey Axel, this is Vy Molotov from the New York Chessboxing Association. Great, you got my package. Do you have a few minutes to talk?"

"Sure."

"We're going to be holding our inaugural chessboxing event in Brooklyn on December 30, and I need fresh bodies. Do you know what chessboxing is?"

"I read about it online last year, and I read your booklet. How many rounds of chess and boxing will you have?"

"We want to make it official, so it's going to be six rounds of chess and five rounds of boxing. You're more than qualified in the chess part, and I've seen all three of your amateur boxing bouts. You can handle yourself in the ring too. Interested in being on the card?"

"Uh Vy, I've only had three amateur bouts, and how did you see the second one? As far as I know, it wasn't even filmed."

Vyacheslav laughed. "I saw that from a cellphone video of an ex-girlfriend of the boxer you knocked out. She posted it on her Facebook page. Man, you pounded the shit out of him!"

"It's still only three bouts under my belt. Is three going to be enough for the regulations you have to follow?"

"This sport is so young, Axel, you only need one. All the bouts are going to be for charity, so I can't pay you as I can a professional fighter. However, you'd be a trailblazer, and a great draw to bring in the crowds. I'd love to have you. Please think about it - you have a spot if you want it."

"Let me sleep on it, Vy. When do you need an answer?"

"Can you tell me yes or no by next week? Marketing something so new takes a long time, and the bigger my head start the better."

"I'll call you in a couple of days, I promise. When's a good time to call you?"

"Anytime."

"Thanks, Vy. I'll call you soon."

"Thank you too, Axel. Take care."

Axel hung up. In a couple of weeks, it would be Labor Day. What did he want to do with the rest of the year? What did he want to do with the rest of his life? He loved chess, but with a mature kind of love, with well-defined ups and downs, and with an ever-diminishing sense of accomplishment. He was growing to love boxing as well, even if it frequently scared the hell out of him. The two strands could be woven together into a new kind of DNA, a new life in a brave new world.

He aimlessly walked around his town in the dog days of August, the steps he was taking eventually taking shape as a backup for the great running jump he was about to make. He called up Vyacheslav the following week, and said he'd do it.

CHAPTER FIFTEEN

After Axel hung up with Vyacheslav, he knew that he had to invent a new sort of training.

The chess needed to be sped up, broken up, and put back together for the rapid game part of the chessboxing match. Axel confirmed in the chessboxing rules pamphlet that he would be playing six three-minute rounds of chess outside the ring. The game would have nine minutes total for each player, with up to six enforced breaks should the match go the distance. A single chess round would be a mere chunk of a game that was to be continued later. This was counterintuitive to Axel, who was used to playing entire chess games in a single sitting.

Another wrinkle was that the referee during a chess round could force one of the players to move within ten seconds. If the referee did not know much about chess, he could inadvertently affect the course of the match by forcing a quick move in a complex position. Axel could only hope that the referee inside the ring knew more about chess than the rules; if not, some bullet (less than one minute for the entire game) chess training might be useful.

Then there was developing the ability to think clearly at the chessboard after getting hit by a punch. Axel had won many chess games at parties while being totally shitfaced, but this was different. To develop a carefully thought-out strategic plan from the opening, and then systematically realize it in the middlegame and endgame, would be counterproductive. The operative chess tools in a chessboxing match were going to be tactics, tactics, and more tactics. Not that Axel had to discard all his chess knowledge distilled from decades of slow practice, but he was going to have to start doing wind sprints in his calculation drills, decide which opening setups to burn into his active memory, and put heavier focus on the shinier aspects of the position.

The boxing part was much more straightforward: learn to how to box for five three-minute rounds instead of three, and to up his boxing game a lot. Axel knew he was a better chess player than most amateurs, so his opponent would likely concentrate on knocking him out instead trying to checkmate him. The primary training focus on the match was going to be boxing; he trusted that the chess (with a couple of minor performance tweaks) would take care of itself.

Axel went to the gym the following afternoon, and told Ted what he was going to do. "Can't help you with the chess, Axel, but I can definitely help you train how to box for five rounds. You get a little more time for strategy, and feeling out your opponent before going in for the kill. Start running a lot more," Ted said. "Do you want to do my three-month intensive program again? It starts in two weeks. I'll put you in the fast lane." Axel said yes, actually looking forward to three more months of hard sparring.

Axel started serious running again, at first two miles at a fast jog, then gradually adding distance, four times a week. He did not have a runner's build, and knew that he would never be doing marathons. He settled on moving for no less than sixty minutes, instead of distance. He sweat profusely after each run, and his legs felt like lead the following day.

He had to renew his membership with the United States Amateur Boxing association, which meant taking another physical in the last week of August. The doctor glanced at Axel, and after scanning his bloodwork and urine tests, cleared him to fight within a minute. An extra copy of the doctor's report was sent to the New York Chessboxing Association, along with a copy of his boxing record book and United States Chess Federation card (it had Axel's membership number from which the organizers could look up his current rating). Vyacheslav called a few days later to say that his paperwork was all set – all he had left to do was show up on December 29 for the weigh-in, and to choose a charity for which to fight.

Ted's boxing program began the Tuesday night after Labor Day. As promised, it had a much harder edge to Axel this time around. The first two weeks had the usual boot camp, but after those workouts had finished Ted told Axel to stick around for an extra hour of sparring. Sparring while exhausted was what training for bouts with extra rounds was all about, Ted explained, and he threw Axel in with fresh fighters who had not done the grueling two-hour workouts beforehand. The first week was brutal, but in the second week Axel was able to finish the sparring without panting up a lung. The after-training sessions were for three rounds only; Ted promised to make them longer as the program went on.

After the participants had been split up into teams, Axel found himself doing bouts for team points three Saturdays out of four. During the second month, Ted made it a five-rounder against Dave, a fellow boxer from the gym with a dozen amateur fights under his belt. Ted explained to Axel and Dave that punches landed in the fourth and fifth rounds would count more than the first three rounds.

Axel and Dave touched gloves and squared off, and the opening bell rang. Having five rounds in which to work made Axel pace himself, and deliberately examine the punches thrown at him. Dave had a tremendous hook which he tried to set up with misdirection, using long series of jabs and feinted uppercuts. If the guard went down, Axel knew from previous painful experience, the hook came in with the force of a freight train. So, he mostly worked inside, getting in some good body shots, and forcing several clinches. After a clinch, he began to notice that Dave had a habit of dropping his left.

Axel marched into volleys of punches for three rounds, walking in while throwing his straight right the most often, forcing repeated clinches, and holding back on his left hook. He was trying to get Dave used to the idea that the only money punch he was going to use was the right hand. He knew that one good surprise hook alone would not be enough to win the bout, and bided his time trying to think of a follow-up he could use. Dave was stymied from launching his favorite punch, but had good defense, and reacted well to the changing ring dynamics. Axel waited.

Finally, one minute in the fourth round, Axel saw the missing piece. Both fighters had become tired, and cracks in their boxing stance were beginning to show. When Axel was tired, he tended to look down when he charged, missing follow-ups because he was looking down –

this was pointed out to him in the corner at the end of the third round. When Dave was tired, Axel now saw, he forgot to move back diagonally when hit, moving straight back instead, which set himself up for an uppercut. The pieces fell into place. Axel again walked into Dave's punches, forcing Dave back and causing a clinch. Immediately after they broke apart, Axel crashed a surprise left hook into his opponent's head, and followed up with a right uppercut when Dave was still in range by moving straight back.

Doubly stunned, Dave moved towards Axel trying to set up another clinch. Axel allowed it, but this time when they broke apart reversed the order of the punches, starting with the right uppercut and ending with the left hook. His opponent now wobbly, Axel fired off another quick left hook and a straight right to the mid-section before circling away – he didn't do more because he did not think that this was the proper setting for hurting his opponent. It was a training bout with no record at stake.

The rest of the fight was uneventful. Axel continued to be extra careful in keeping up his left guard so as not to be clobbered by Dave's hook, and trading jabs while moving around the ring for the rest of the fourth round. In the final round, Axel applied persistent pressure by continually advancing, forcing an opening, striking, and moving away before a counter shot could follow. Dave did not try anything ambitious. Axel landed a dozen more punches in the fifth round, and because of the bombs he had landed in the previous round, was awarded the fight on points.

Ted complimented Axel's control afterwards, but said he could have been much more aggressive in the final two rounds: "Dave is a big boy. He's had plenty of amateur fights, and can take the abuse. Don't be afraid to go for it if you smell blood. You have to trust that the referee will stop the fight before it becomes ugly. That means you have to trust yourself too, Axel, and let your fists go without thinking about the consequences – don't hold back next time." Ted added if he saw any more hesitation in Axel's next five-round fight at the gym, he would deduct points from Axel, and give them to his opponent.

CHAPTER SIXTEEN

Axel needed to work on his reflexes in chess too, for the fast time control. Not far from where he lived was a park where chess hustlers played all comers for money. They did not play as much chess as they perfected their clock management for games that lasted five minutes, three minutes, two minutes, and even one minute to each player for all their moves. Despite Axel's superior chess knowledge, he almost always lost money when he played in the park, and only played there a few times a year when he was bored.

The chess hustlers always used the same method against Axel. First, they would get ahead on the clock at the expense of their position. It took time to develop an advantage, making Axel fall behind on the clock. Then they would hang on for dear life in losing positions, in some instances playing on even though down a Queen and Rook, for it took precious seconds to convert an advantage. Finally, they would call Axel on the clock and win the game on forfeit, even if they only had a pawn left. Theoretically the pawn could queen through all the extra opposing pieces, and checkmate the opposing King, even though it was ludicrously unlikely. The money didn't bother Axel as much as he hated winning and losing chess games this way. In this format, resigning a game no longer meant any sense, nor did the point of playing good moves.

Nonetheless, Axel decided to play a lot more blitz chess in the park to improve his hand and eye coordination with the clock. The pace would be similar to that of the chessboxing bout. He didn't expect to learn much about chess, but he hoped to be able to channel his threats on the board onto leaner, meaner torpedo tubes. On Saturday afternoons, after boxing practice had ended, he went to the park with forty dollars to blow.

He played with Willie, a person he had seen there for over a decade. Willie was a frequently homeless ex-con with a cheerful disposition, and reflexes that would have put a lioness on the Serengeti to shame. At first, he tried to get five-minute to one-minute odds, fatuously citing Axel's strength. "Nice try, Willie," Axel replied, holding up two twenty-dollar bills. Axel insisted on a dozen two-minute to two-minute games (considering how close that time control would approximate the conditions in New York), and promised twenty dollars no matter what the results of games would be. He added that an extra twenty dollars would go to Willie if he managed to win the majority of the contests.

Willie agreed, and Axel found out anew the limit of his chess prowess in a fast time control. None of the openings Willie played were conventional, and followed a mysterious logic that had been developed sui generis in the park. It took Axel thirty seconds to see the flaws in the setups while Willie moved instantly, which proved to be a fatal disadvantage as the moves went on and time grew scarcer. The only moves Willie played were easier to find than Axel's optimal moves to close out a winning advantage, and Axel forfeited on time in won positions three games in a row.

Axel then tried another approach, playing moves to match Willie on the remaining time instead of digging an extra few seconds to find the best move. He didn't need to scramble anymore in the final phase of the game, but the moves he bashed out with Willie didn't feel like chess; they felt more like patty cake. He drew two games, lost one, and then won two games in a row.

"Four more games," Axel said, and Willie nodded. *There must be some middle ground,* Axel thought, between sinking down amid the weeds and losing on time, and mindlessly skimming rocks on the surface of the water. He knew the Soviet chess champion Mikhail Botvinnik's suggestion that he should concentrate on tactics when it was his turn, and focus on strategy when it was his opponent's. The trouble was Willie moved so fast that it was all tactics, and did not give enough time in the allotted two minutes to form a plan that was both cogent and timely. It felt like the first sparring Axel had ever done, all nerves and jagged energy, all the while forgetting to breathe.

Axel that day could not solve his problems at the board; the score of the final four games was one win, one draw, and two losses. Willie received the forty dollars with gratitude, and welcomed a rematch under the same terms, anytime. Axel thanked Willie for the games, and said to expect him one week from today.

Axel's progress in the boxing gym had been so slow and steady, Ted said to him after a practice that he needed a jolt. The following Saturday Axel was excused from a portion of the group drills, and was told to spar exclusively for three rounds with a middleweight boxer Ted said was visiting from another gym. Axel had never seen him before.

The middleweight's name was Lars, and he hit like a heavyweight. Before Axel could feel out his opponent's style Lars had thundered in two jabs, a straight right, and a hook that dropped him. Axel got back up, and saw that there were still two minutes and fifty seconds left in the round. He approached Lars crouching and covering himself up to the hilt, only to be clocked by another right hook and a left uppercut that made him see stars. *Getting hit by this guy hurts*, Axel thought, and he decided to settle for at least one punch on this guy before the round ended. He was not successful. Lars slipped, ducked, and blocked with such supple dexterity that Axel saw the counterpunches crash into his head in slow motion, and was powerless to stop them.

Mercifully the first round finally ended. Only six minutes left. Jason came by and asked Axel if he was all right. Axel nodded, and asked Jason for ideas. With one eye towards Ted looking out of his office, Jason shook his head, and told him to do the best he could. During the second round Axel tried to move around the ring more, but Lars was faster and tagged him with repeated whack-a-mole swats. He came close to hitting Lars once with thirty seconds left in the round; he took a jerky step to the right and threw the fastest jab he had thrown in his life. Even that did not work. Lars ducked in time, and to add insult to injury, ripped off two stinging jabs of his own before circling away. The bell rang, ending the second round.

Three minutes left. Jason was waiting for him in his corner to give him water. Axel looked up and noticed that the entire gym was crowded around the ropes, watching the action in the ring. Jason suggested mixing things up to keep Lars guessing. "Why not?" Axel replied. "Nothing else is working!" The bell sounded for the last round.

Lars stuck out his gloves to touch as they approached. After touching gloves, Axel quickly retracted his into his fighting stance and floored all the gas left in his tank. He started to throw his combinations in reverse order (hook, right, jab), suddenly switch tempo in mid-step (charge, throw an empty jab, and charge again), and even throw the same punch six times in a row. Yet he still could not land one single goddamn shot on Lars. However, Axel did not get hit as often, and he swore he could see Lars smile slightly at him through his mouthpiece.

The bell rang. Axel and Lars hugged, and they heard the muffled sound of the other boxers applauding through their gloves. Lars had opened a deep cut on Axel's right eye. Ted came out to tell Axel to have Jason tend to that eye, and then to see him in his office - his practice was done for the day. Lars went on to work with the other experienced boxers in the gym, but with not nearly as much ferocity.

Axel plopped down in the chair in front of Ted's desk. He was going to hurt like hell tomorrow. "That Lars guy is a hell of a fighter, Ted. What's his amateur record?"

"I have a confession to make, Axel. His name isn't Lars, it's Leonard Villes. He is a professional, with a record of fourteen and one, and is currently ranked number eleven in the WBC rankings. You did quite well, since I told him not to go easy on you."

Axel's battered eye opened wide. "Well, if that were a real fight, I think Lars won it quite handily. Why did you unleash him on the likes of me?"

"Lenny's trainer and I go way back. He mentioned to me that Lenny had gone a long time between fights, and needed some serious practice so that his skills didn't erode. I told him of your chessboxing bout at the end of the year, and how you had been plateauing. We figured an intense couple of rounds would be good for both of you. Am I right?"

"I think you want me to draw a couple of lessons from this, Ted. Am I right?"

"You are. What did you learn today?"

"That there is no such thing as coasting some of the time when it comes to training. It's all stop and jerk, and pushing myself further every day. If I ever forget that, a thousand Leonard Villes will be there to smack some sense into me."

"Yeah, that's pretty much it. I just want to add that if you can improve your hand speed, and concentrate on being in the moment, you will have time to mix up your game, and save a fight if it's going against you." Ted tilted his head. "You were way overmatched, but you didn't give up; you tried something different when you were getting hammered six ways from Sunday. You even made Lenny smile. Believe you me, that's an accomplishment – he's always been a cranky bastard."

"How many more surprises do you have for me before I fight in New York?" Axel asked with a grimace.

Ted laughed. "As many as you can handle, friend. You start getting complacent again, I have so many more forks for you to stick into toasters."

"What the hell happened to you?" Willie asked a tired Axel in amazement, as he sat in front of him in the park, a few hours later.

"A little practice hitting the boxing bags, Willie – the bags hit back much harder than usual today."

"Man, I should put up a couple of them 'round where I'm living right now," Willie chuckled. "Same deal as last week?"

Axel held up forty dollars. "Five games. Let's go."

The games started off fast and furious. Axel tried to speed up his hands, to translate the sudden jolts and shocks of his boxing rounds into attacking plans he could use in his positions with Willie. The first three games were hard, but Axel did not fall behind on the clock, and the results were one win, one loss, and one draw. With each game he could feel the mental wall grow softer, allowing him glimpses beyond.

In the fourth game, the seconds of the clock began to slow down. His brain acquired the extra dimension of hovering over the board, instead of breathlessly moving in and around the pieces. The result was an easy win. In the fifth game, Axel felt that he had all the time in the world to calculate a long forcing variation, yet when he pressed his clock, he found that only seven seconds had elapsed. The variation led to a winning advantage, yet he carelessly lost it in the blink of an eye and the result was a draw.

Axel handed over twenty dollars for the five game mini-match, which he won with a score of two wins, two draws, and one loss. Willie, wanting the extra twenty dollars, asked to play more. Axel was in a generous mood – losing twenty dollars was easier than getting the shit kicked out of him by "Lars" – and agreed.

They played ten more games. In some of the games, Axel was able to mentally stretch out the time, and think reflectively instead of reflexively. In other games, the mental picture in his head remained cold and hard, and he could barely think more than two moves ahead so as not to fall behind on the clock. Reflexes or reflection, it always seemed to be one or the other. Axel wanted to look for even better moves amid the sounds of the pieces being moved, but the clock did not allow it.

Still, Axel kept his head and scored six wins, two losses, and two draws. Willie lost the last three games quickly, and held up his hands in a surrender gesture. Axel give him the twenty dollars anyway because he liked Willie, and because playing chess for a living in a park was so damn hard.

"Thanks for the games, Willie. I need more experience at this time control. At the end of the year I'm doing a chessboxing bout in New York, and –"

"Whoa, dude. You're going to do this with boxing? You're even more batshit crazy than me!"

Axel flashed him a devil-may-care grin. He hadn't given out one of those in a very long time. "Why not? Much sooner than later I'm going to become too old to do it. I'd rather have a face full of bruises and cuts with no regrets than the other way around."

"When and where, Axel? I'll make the trip to see it."

"Thanks. It's on December 30 in New York somewhere. I'll be back for a few more matches before then, and can tell you more."

"Come back anytime for practice. I can't wait to tell the others I'm helping a chessboxer train."

Axel gave him another crazy grin. Today had turned out to be a very good day.

CHAPTER SEVENTEEN

Axel found nothing online on how to train for a chessboxing fight – not even a blog post. He looked around in his apartment, searching for tools at his disposal. He had a heavy boxing bag ten feet away from his desk, and his desk had a laptop connected to the Internet. It was enough, Axel decided – he would make this up as he went along.

He set on his desk a portable boxing timer to eleven three-minute rounds, with a one-minute break between the rounds. He also set up a chess program on his laptop for a game with nine minutes for himself and the computer opponent. Opening a water bottle on the desk, Axel then changed into shorts and a T-shirt, wrapped his hands, ensured a clear path from the desk to the heavy bag, and put his boxing gloves by the heavy bag. With one hand he started the boxing timer, and the other he started the chess game on his laptop.

The bell on the boxing timer rang, and the chess program instantly played out a move on the screen. He played against the chess program until he heard the boxing timer ring. He then paused the game, walked over to the heavy bag, and slipped on his boxing gloves to wait for the timer to ring again. When it rang again, he hit the bag as hard and as fast as he could until the round ended. Off came the gloves, and Axel strode back to the desk with the laptop where the bottle of water was waiting for him. He sipped on the water while he waited for the next ring of the boxing timer, after which he resumed the chess game on the laptop. Three more minutes of the chess game, the boxing timer rang again, and the game was paused while the gloves came back on.

And so on until there was a decisive result in the chess game. The chess program when set up to maximum strength was unbeatable, even for grandmasters, so Axel adjusted the settings of the playing strength to more closely match his own. After six rounds of chess and boxing, he noticed how much more difficult it was to remain tactically sharp in the game when he was breathing heavily, as if he was in bad time pressure.

To his regret, Garen's deep thinking exercises would have to be put on hold – fists were going to fly, as were the pieces with less than ten minutes for each player in the game. Axel wasn't aiming to play professional-grade chess in New York – he only wanted to keep enough of his wits about him at the chessboard without forfeiting on time, while getting hammered in the boxing ring. Instead, his chess training was going to be solving many tactical combination exercises from books and websites, as quickly as possible.

If his opponent was a weak chess player, then Axel could rely on his experience and superior knowledge of strategy to outplay him. But only if his opponent was a weak boxer, and Axel knew that was too much to hope for. He was probably going to be paired with a seasoned fighter with much more boxing experience, and less chess expertise. Then tactics would become crucial, for chess in its most reflexive form was nothing but tactics. There would be no place for quiet reflection between five brutal rounds of boxing.

Vycheslav excitedly called Axel again in late October with more details about his chessboxing bout in New York. He was going to be fighting in the Barclays Center in Brooklyn; the bout was going to be filmed for an ESPN special to be broadcast next year.

"Have you decided on a charity yet?"

"Yes, the Red Cross. A few years ago, the apartment building of a friend of mine burned down. They gave him a debit card with enough money on it to purchase most of the stuff in his current apartment." The friend since had moved to New York; *maybe I could get in touch with him again*, Axel thought.

"Great, great!" Vycheslav replied. "Axel, would you be available for a brief interview on camera in early December? We want to include it for a DVD of this event. If you are, I'll mail you a release form for the interview later this week. I'll also send you a basic bio form and questionnaire – can you please fill them out and return that to me soon? It's for the press release."

"No problem, Vy."

"Thanks. Also, at the weigh-in on December 29, would you be willing to do a small photo shoot with the other chessboxers in the event? It will only take an hour."

"Sure. I'm training hard for this, and will show up ready to go."

"Just what I wanted to hear! I'll talk to you again shortly, and will be able to tell you who your opponent is going to be."

"Thanks, Vy. I'll talk to you later."

A package by registered mail from Vycheslav arrived for Axel next week. Inside, he found a release form to sign for the interview, a biographical questionnaire to fill out, and another statement to sign that his share of all the proceeds from the event would go to his designated charity, The Red Cross. He filled out the questionnaire, signed the forms, and returned them the following day.

Axel's training went on as the weather grew colder and the days became shorter. The lazy drawn-out sunshine in which he made the decision to chessbox was a distant memory. Taking its place was a cold, hard path of intense discomfort and fatigue. He always seemed to be waking up in the dark, and taking longer periods of time to warm up before his workouts. The very air Axel breathed nipped him at every turn.

The path went steeply upwards as the temperature dropped even further. He was sparring five rounds at a time by early October. At first, he had only one sparring partner for all the rounds, but then Ted mixed it up by putting in anywhere from two to five different partners, all of them fresh and ready to go. Axel received no quarter. "The harder it is here, the easier it will be there," Ted said as Axel sprawled on his chair in the corner gasping between rounds. Axel could only grunt in reply.

He played blitz chess with Willie six more Saturday afternoons in the park, before the weather became too frigid to play there. His speed had improved to the point where he was actually able to make Willie forfeit on time in some of the games. Despite the concentrated study Axel had put into tactics, his opponent had a quicksilver ability to find the best riposte within seconds, and was no passive punching bag. By

November, Axel was consistently winning seventy-five percent of the games. He considered his blitz games to be training, not gambling, and paid the full amount to Willie no matter how many more games he won.

"Got a sister in Florida. I'm going there for the next six months soon," Willie said the week before Halloween. "I'll make the trip to New York to see you though, because I've always wanted to see how well a chess master plays before and after a scuffle. You feeling ready?"

"I don't really feel ready. A better word is prepared," Axel replied. "In the boxing part, I'll be prepared. As for the chess part... well, you know as well as me it only takes one small mistake to wreck an entire game. You can never fully prepare for that, only constantly stay vigilant."

"A punch is easier?"

"Punches to the head all start to feel the same after a while. Mucking up a chess position, however, carries a special kind of pain. I've always hated wrecking even a small portion of one. Feeling tired, or being preoccupied about being hit, should not be an excuse."

"I can't wait to see who'll you be fighting. Will it be a chess player or a boxer?" Willie asked.

"Yes," Axel answered.

Next week Vycheslav called to confirm if Axel was still going to fight as a cruiserweight. Axel said yes, and then was told that his opponent's name was Wojtek Zolutski. A fellow cruiserweight, Zolutski was from Camden, New Jersey, twenty-six years old, and had ten amateur fights with a record of seven and three. He also had a US chess federation rating of 1900, which made him slightly weaker than a candidate master.

"I out-rate him by three hundred points in chess, Vy. He's going to try and knock me out. Or at least hit me so hard in the first boxing round that I won't be able to think straight in the remaining chess game," Axel said.

"He can hit, I won't lie to you about that," Vycheslav replied. "But you can hit too."

"We'll see. This interview you want me to do in about a month. Am I doing it in New York, or is a camera crew coming here?"

"Could you come to New York? I'd put you up in a hotel room for the night. We'll finally meet, and I can give you a tour of our offices, where you can chat with our referees. Ask them anything you want about how they interpret the rules: what they call in the boxing ring, what they call in the chess part of the bout, anything you want to know."

"Sounds good – just give me a week's notice, and I can take the day off from work. I usually dress in blue jeans and T-shirts. Is that OK for the interview, or do you want me to show up in something more formal?"

"I don't expect a three-piece suit, but please don't show up as a slob. Slacks, dress shirt, and nice-looking shoes should be enough." Vycheslav added: "You can find a couple of Zolutski's fights on YouTube prettily easily. Not many fighters have his name."

"Me neither. I have a weird sounding name too."

Vycheslav laughed. "Me three. I'll call you just before Thanksgiving for the time and place of the interview. Continue to train hard, and I look forward to meeting you."

"Me too, Vy. See you soon."

Upon hanging up, a little edge of Axel's apprehension melted away. He now had a definite name to attach to his previously theoretical opponent.

CHAPTER EIGHTEEN

Axel quickly looked up his upcoming opponent online. Zolutski in his three amateur fights (two wins, one loss) on YouTube looked to be about six foot one, with a stocky build. He moved fast and well in the boxing ring, using a quick fluid jab and excellent head movement in lieu of standing his ground and going toe to toe with his opponents.

When given a chance, his straight rights landed hard, as evidenced in one of his online victories – a pair of them caused the referee to stop the fight instantly in his favor. He could also reload and repeat his hooks quickly, as shown in his other victory, where he unleashed a volley of four unanswered hooks. In his one online loss he put too much body English into a hook that missed, causing him to lose his balance and stumble into a crushing uppercut from his opponent.

Zolutski looked like he was going to be a tough customer in the boxing rounds. Axel would show Ted the YouTube fights, and ask for strategies. And since he now had a mental picture of who he was up against, he could start to train with more pinpointed focus.

Next Axel looked up his opponent's chess games in the public online databases. He found only twenty (grandmasters had all their competitive games listed, which were in the hundreds if not thousands; Axel himself had one hundred and fifty of his games on there). The openings themselves were limited to 1. Nf3 when Zolutski played with White, the Pirc Defense with Black when his opponent played 1. e4, and the King's Indian Defense with Black when his opponent played 1. d4.

Axel had faced those openings many times over, and could prepare specialized lines for them all within an hour. The games dated back only five years, which made him wonder if his opponent had only taken up the game in his late teens. If that was true, then Axel felt confident he would be in little danger at the chessboard. But that would need further research. His friend in New York might be able to give him more details.

Ted looked at Zolutski's online fights with Axel in his office. "You can take him, Axel. He has a fast jab that earns him a lot of points with the judges, and his power punches look like they really hurt, but I don't see much in between. It's either perimeter shots, or punch hard up close. See how he came in here and got tagged by that hook? Or –" Ted sped up the video a minute. "– here. You probably saw this, too. He put too much into that hook walking in and threw himself off balance, setting himself for that devastating counter. You have more gears than him. You can switch things up and alternate your tempo. I saw you do that with Lenny, although it didn't help you much. On this Zolutski guy, it'll work."

"How should I train for him specifically?"

"Interval training, lots of it. From now on, I want you to spar with only the middleweights and heavyweights we have in the gym. Against the heavyweights I want you to move more than you hit, and with the middleweights I want you to hit more than you move. You'll be alternating between the partners in the different weight classes each round."

"Do you want me to increase my running?"

"Same amount of running, but again, mix it up. Fast dashes for a minute, slow jog for a minute, normal clip another minute. Stop using the elevator in buildings, and run up and down the stairs. Randomize the speed in segments as you're running up the floors. Come to think of it, that's what now you're going to be doing here for an extra thirty minutes before each practice, and on the bags too. I'll find a trainer in the crankiest mood that day to tell you when to switch speeds. It's much more effective than a friendly face recommending you on when to speed up and when to slow down."

"You guys here are so kind," Axel noted sardonically.

"Hey, we aim to please."

Axel called his New York chess-player friend. He asked if he had ever run into Zolutski in local tournaments, or had faced him across the board.

"Yeah, I saw that hulk last year in the under 2000 rating section of the New York Open. He really stuck out. One slightly built Asian kid after another, interspersed with portly middle-aged guys smoking pipes, and then all of a sudden there's this big guy with a linebacker build. Weird name too, Wojtek Zolutski. I've never played him. Why do you ask?" one of his friends asked.

"I'm going to be doing a chessboxing bout with him next month at the Barclays Center."

"Get out! When?"

"December 30. I'm trying to get intel on his chess game."

"I'll ask around, Axel, but I don't think you have much to worry about the chess. In the game I glanced at, he was getting creamed by a sixth grader. You need to be more worried about his fists."

"I know. Please let me know if you come across a bunch of his game scores. The more recent the better."

"If I can find out his handle on the Internet Chess Club, I know an admin command that will call up what he's played on there, and will email you the games. Holy shit, you're really doing this! When are tickets going on sale?"

"Soon. You should be able to find details by now with a Google search. You'll probably be able to buy tickets at the door, too."

"I'm coming, and so are a lot of chess players here. You have no idea how many people want to see you get punched in the face. I mean that in a good way."

"Oh, come on. That last game we played in Connecticut? You had me so busted that even after blundering a piece away you still had enough for a draw."

"Did you really have to remind me about that? I'm bringing my co-workers too."

"Think I should better quit when I'm ahead. If you find any games, can you please send them to me ASAP?"

"'Of course, Axel. Good luck."

As November drew to a close, Axel grew to truly hate running in the morning. His limbs felt brittle and clunky. His breath showed in plumes, and he felt like a car engine with no oil, spewing smoke. But he persevered.

He showed up thirty minutes early to Ted's group practice sessions to have a trainer tell him to execute time shifts during his interval training. He moved fast, faster, and slow for both running drills and bag drills. Sometimes the trainer told him to immediately stop hitting the bag and rush over to the mat for a footwork drill, and vice versa. His sense of rhythm was initially confused and the joints in his limbs screamed out in pain, but after a few minutes a refined sense of equilibrium developed in him, and he became able to follow any command to speed up or slow down in stride.

When Ted's boxing practice officially began for the group, Axel found that the sudden time shifts he could now execute at will had made him a very dangerous opponent. He actually pulled a couple of punches in his sparring sessions with some of the heavyweights he was paired against because they were open for such long periods of time, and with the middleweights they no longer had as many free shots as before.

Ted asked Axel if he wanted to do a special exhibition fight at the gym three days before Thanksgiving.

"Against who?"

"Don't worry, Axel, I'm not going to pair you with someone who can potentially give you an injury before your fight. This opponent is special. His name is Wayne, and he struggles with Parkinson's Disease. Wayne is a private client of one of our trainers here. The work ethic I've seen him put into boxing this past year puts everyone else's here to shame, including yours. It will be one round, two rounds tops. Pull all your punches, and don't block any of his. Interested?"

"Sure. Should I slip any of his punches?"

"Wayne will throw at most thirty punches per round, and he's a welterweight – you'll live. Please let all but one or two of them land. If it looks plausible, can you take a knee on the canvas as well?"

"OK. When should I show up on fight night?"

"It will be the first fight on the card, so show up at six thirty. Thanks for doing this!" Ted added: "Do you want me to tell the crowd what you're doing at the end of the year?"

"I don't want to take anything away from Wayne, so no."

Just before Axel was leaving for the exhibition fight, Vycheslav called with the ESPN interview details. They wanted him to show up at their New York broadcasting studio at one the following Tuesday afternoon, the interview starting at one thirty and lasting half an hour. Vycheslav gave him the address over the phone (promising to email it too), and who to ask for when he got there. He would meet Axel at the studio, and afterwards take him to the New York Chessboxing Association offices, where he could talk to the referees and have his questions answered. Then spend a night at the hotel Vycheslav had arranged, and return home the following day.

"Sounds good, Vy. I'm looking forward to attaching a face to your voice."

"Same here, Axel. See you soon."

Shortly after he arrived at the gym, he met Wayne. Wayne was one of the most charming people Axel had yet met in the world of boxing. He had a firm handshake, a steady gaze, an infectious laugh, and categorically refused to feel sorry for himself about the cards he had been dealt. If he was afraid of how he might look boxing in front of people, he hid it well. Axel warmly wished him luck.

In the first round Wayne moved well despite his tremors and shuffled straight up to Axel. Axel hovered in front of him in a small semi-circle, in a full crouch and with his body turned away, but with his hands six inches away from the sides of his head. Wayne promptly shot off a jab and Axel bent down so that it hit the top of his head. Axel returned with a straight right deliberately aimed wide, and returned it to his stance deliberately slowly so that Wayne had time for an uppercut that caught him flush on the chin. Axel overreacted covering his head leaving his mid-section open, allowing Wayne to deliver a hook to his ribs. None of the punches hurt.

The crowd was at first confused, but quickly caught on, and wildly cheered on Wayne. Axel stayed close and threw twenty pulled punches over the next two minutes, being careful not to let his punch count exceed his opponent's. Wayne landed two dozen more punches, and was clearly enjoying himself. When the bell rang, the crowd was on their feet.

Axel saw Wayne shaking in his corner during the break, caught his gaze, and raised his eyebrows at him as if to ask if he wanted to do another round. Wayne's eyes said *hell yes*. The bell rang, and Axel came out throwing a pair of hooks and a pair of uppercuts with all his strength in the open air. They made a whoosh. He then marched up to Wayne, slowed down, and resumed the same hovering stance with his gloves away from his head. Wayne got off fifteen more punches, but was starting to tire. So, a minute and a half into the round Axel threw a hook from five feet away and overextended, leaving his head wide open. Wayne fired off a left, right, hook, and another right, making Axel take a knee. He waved his arms to the referee, signaling that he wanted to end the fight.

The cheering lasted a full five minutes. Axel bearhugged Wayne, wishing him a wonderful holiday season, and Wayne's trainer in turn bearhugged Axel.

"Thank you so much," Ted said, giving a hug of his own as Axel was leaving. "You just earned three free months membership at the gym."

"The look in Wayne's eyes was reward enough," Axel replied. "But I'll take the three months, thanks."

"Are you going to be allowed to have a trainer in your corner for the boxing rounds in your chessboxing match? Maybe I can persuade one of my guys to go up to New York with you."

"I honestly don't know, Ted. I think the chessboxers are on their own during the match. I'm going there for a taped interview next week - it's for a DVD they want to sell afterwards - and to talk with the officials who will be judging and refereeing the matches. I can give you an answer when I come back."

"OK. Keep up your running during the holiday weekend. You know what Rocky said to Adrian: to others it's Thanksgiving, but to me it's Thursday."

"Happy Thursday, Ted."

"Happy Thursday, Axel."

CHAPTER NINETEEN

Axel celebrated Thursday that week with his mother and a few family friends of his late father. He didn't tell anyone at the table where he was going to be on December 30, and could only occasionally jump into the conversation with pertinent comments of his own. But the food was good, as was the company.

He obtained permission from his boss to take next Tuesday and Wednesday off from work. The address of the ESPN New York studio had arrived in an email from Vyacheslav, along with a PDF visitor's pass to print out and present to building security, and the confirmation reservation number to his hotel.

On early Tuesday morning Axel hopped on a bus, arriving at the Port Authority Bus Terminal just before noon. He was wearing black loafers, black slacks, a white dress shirt, and a navy-blue sports jacket. He would ask at the studio if they wanted him to wear the tie carried inside his jacket pocket.

Axel arrived at the studio at a quarter to one. Upon showing his visitor's pass, he was escorted to a room where he was given a rudimentary layer of makeup for the camera lights. Afterwards he was led to a waiting room, where an assistant was waiting. The assistant welcomed Axel and gave a list of the questions that were going to be asked, adding that the interview should not last longer than half an hour. She left Axel alone so that he could peruse the questions, most of which were the same he had answered and mailed in for the press release. Someone would come in soon to take him to the studio taping. He did not have to wear the tie.

Fifteen minutes later he heard a knock on the door, and opening it saw a crooked finger from the same assistant to follow her to the studio. Two men were in the studio waiting for him. One met him at the door. He introduced himself as Les, and he was going to be the interviewer; he had a precise voice that projected well, which Axel knew came from years of practice.

Les led Axel to a table where another man was already sitting, wearing a suit with the New York State Chessboxing Association logo emblazoned in the front. He had a wiry build and friendly black eyes, and Axel guessed who he was immediately.

"Hello, Vy. It's great to finally meet you."

"You too, Axel." They shook hands, and Vyacheslav looked him over with an approving glance. "You have indeed been training hard."

"The real test is going to be Christmas dinner. The office parties with the millions of calories I can pass up, but my sister's Swiss chocolates that she leaves out by the pound and loads me up with on the ride home, those are so hard to resist."

"You can indulge a little. You look like you have a couple of pounds of spare for the weight class."

"Guys, you have no idea how much food I can inhale in a single sitting."

Both Les and Vyacheslav chuckled.

"Yes, I do, Axel. I've hung out with boxers just after a weigh-in," Les said. "I won't throw you any curveballs. What Vy asked you in the questionnaire, that's pretty much what I'm going to be asking you. Let me set you up with a microphone." Les fitted Axel with a small black device. "Say testing 1, 2, 3."

"Testing 1, 2, 3."

"Hold up." Les fiddled with the placement of the mike near Axel's collar. "Once more."

"Testing 1, 2, 3."

"Perfect. Good to go?"

"Let's do it."

For the next twenty-five minutes Axel answered questions on when he started playing chess, when he started boxing, why he took up chessboxing, and what he thought his chances were against his opponent. On the last question, he answered that he had no idea what to expect, but had done all the parts of chessboxing, and was excited to try it as a whole new experience. When asked about his choice of charity, he replied that The Red Cross was a godsend to his friend after all his possessions had burned to the ground. Axel hoped that he came across with a semblance of coherence.

"Great interview, Axel!" Vyacheslav said after the taping ended. He laid out a group of photos on a nearby desk. "Which of these photos of you do you want on the website?"

Axel pointed to the one on the far right. "That one. I didn't sound like a boob, did I?"

"Not at all," Les answered. "Some of the other guys we've talked to needed half a dozen takes. One take with you, and we're done. Good job."

"Les is probably going to be our ring announcer – ninety percent probability," Vyacheslav said. "Let's get out of here. Our offices are a short taxi ride away."

"Good luck, Axel," Les said.

"Thanks, Les, I'll see you in a month." Axel followed Vycheslav out into the street.

The New York Chessboxing Association offices were at a walk-up office in Hell's Kitchen. The offices had four large rooms, with enough space for a heavy punching bag and a table with three chess sets. The corners were crammed with boxing gear and chess clocks; one of the walls was covered with boxing affiliation certificates and merchandising posters. Axel and Vyacheslav arrived just after three in the afternoon – the place hummed with activity.

"Axel, this is Bob Jeffries. He is going to be the referee for your weight division," Vyacheslav said, introducing a rugged, solidly built man, instantly identifiable as an ex-boxer, with closely cropped gray hair and piercing blue eyes. "Ask Bob anything you want to know," he added while going off to answer a call on his cellphone.

"Hi, Bob."

"Hi, Axel," Bob replied. "I've been told you're an actual chess master. My chess rating is only about 1600, but I've had over fifty amateur fights. What do you want to know?"

"Are there any amateur boxing rules that are unique in the state of New York?"

"As in different from your state? Nope, we're an affiliate of the US Amateur Boxing Association. What's legal here is the same thing as what is legal there."

"What happens if either my opponent or I play an illegal chess move?"

"The move is retracted. I also have the discretion to punish the player with a time penalty, and to disqualify you if you make three illegal moves in the game. We might give allowances if the fighter is a novice chess player, but with your rating, Axel, I give you fair warning: if you make an illegal move, I'm docking you at least a minute."

"Does the time control for the chess game have an increment? That is, an extra five or ten seconds on the clock after each move?"

"We have to fit ten bouts on the card for the evening, so don't expect much of an increment, if any at all. We won't be giving more than one second per move. You'll know for sure on the day of the weigh-in."

"Can you declare a draw if one of the players is quickly moving the pieces in a dead draw to win on time?"

"Yes, especially if there is an obviously drawn position on the board."

"What is the most time a player can practically take for deciding upon a move?"

"Good question. It depends on the position. If a player has only one legal move for example, I have the right to tap the player, point to the board, and start counting to ten with my hands, just like in boxing. If the player does not make the move by the count of ten, he forfeits. If the position is complicated, I'll give you all the time you need to choose your move carefully."

"Can we drink water in between the boxing rounds at the chess table?"

"Yes."

"One more question, Bob. Are we allowed to have trainers give us boxing instructions in our corners?"

"Sorry, you and your opponent are on your own. If the boxing part becomes too one-sided, you know full well that I will be stopping the bout."

"Thanks, Bob. This is going to be interesting."

"You're welcome, Axel. For you and me both."

Axel spent the rest of the day trying out the equipment at the office. He played a few blitz games against one of the employees in the office wearing the headphones that he would be using in the arena to block out the noise from the crowd. He whacked the heavy bag with the boxing gloves that would be issued to him for the fight. He also tried on his boxing shorts, shirt, and headgear to make sure they fit – all these were put into a box with Axel's name on it. Axel was to provide his own shoes and mouth guard.

Vyacheslav dropped off Axel at his hotel in lower Manhattan later that evening. He told him to email his preferred song for the entrance music, along with a backup song if that was not available. He would be in touch in a couple of weeks to finalize his lodging information, as well as where and when to show up for his weigh-in.

At the weigh-in he would be issued a laminated pass that would allow him entry to the locker room in the Barclays Center. On the day of the fight, he had to show up two hours before the doors opened. All the details would be both emailed and sent via registered mail. Vycheslav then warmly embraced Axel, wishing him a happy holiday before he left in a taxi.

In his hotel room Axel called his New York chess-player friend again, and asked if he had found out any more about the chess abilities of Wojtek Zolutski. His friend said: "I found a couple dozen of his games on the Internet Chess Club. His openings are lazy. He always plays the King's Indian Defense setup with Black, and the King's Indian Attack setup with White. Against 1. e4 he plays – surprise, surprise – the Pirc Defense, which is but a slightly modified version of the King's Indian Defense. Do you want me to email the games to you?"

"No thanks, preparing against him in the chess part will be easy. But I already know what he's going to do. He's going to play a quiet slow game with long pawn chains to draw out the chess rounds, so that he can maximize his time in the boxing rounds to win the bout."

They talked about meeting up that night, but his friend had a prior engagement. He did promise to come on December 30.

"I still can't believe you're doing this, Axel. What are you trying to prove?"

"Ask me again next year."

CHAPTER TWENTY

Axel and Ted had come to an agreement that he would not be participating in the program's finale fight night, but continued to show up at Ted's boxing program practices for the sparring. The week before Christmas, Ted took Axel aside and said that he was ready. On December 23, he ordered Axel to stop working out in his gym, and all other gyms. He told him to show up one more time after the holiday before heading out to New York. Axel agreed; he had taken December 28 to January 2 off from work, and would have plenty of time to drop by.

Before Axel knew it, he was wrapping presents on Christmas Eve. Vyacheslav earlier that day had mailed to him event and lodging information. The address for the weigh-in was in Williamsburg. His hotel was eight blocks away, within walking distance of the Barclays Center. Vy also sent him half a dozen tickets to hand out to family and friends.

Axel didn't think any of his relatives would be interested, and started thinking to whom he could offer the tickets: Willie (if he could be found; Willie left his sister's number in Florida for him before he went south), his New York chess-playing friend who gave him the chess intel on Zolutski, and maybe a person or two at Ted's gym if they were going to be in New York that week. That was it. If any of them had friends, the extra tickets would go to the plus one's. But he would give his family first pick tomorrow just in case.

On Christmas, Axel told his family what he was going to do in New York within the week. They were speechless for a couple of minutes. His mother was predictably horrified; his sister and niece felt really queasy about what he was doing; but his brother-in-law and nephew thought it was one of the coolest things that they had ever heard. None of them could go; they had made other plans. While expected, it was still a little sad for Axel. His other family members were busy living their lives, which had diverged far away from his bachelor path and weird hobbies.

Told to stay out of the gym, Axel started playing lots of online blitz chess after Christmas. He played several dozen games every day, with two minutes for each player. He varied time controls with one second increment, a five second increment, or no increment at all. Axel preferred having an increment – they stopped players with losing positions to rush out nonsense moves in order to have their opponents lose on time – but was prepared to play without one. Zolutski's openings were easy to prepare against, and only took a few hours.

Three days after Christmas, Axel dropped by Ted's gym. The gym was deserted the last week of December, but would swell again soon with people starting their New Year resolutions. Axel offered Ted a ticket; however, Ted had a life too and couldn't tear himself away from family obligations this time of year. He did say that if Axel left him two tickets, he could almost certainly find two friends of the gym who would make the trip to New York and cheer him on.

Ted had found one more fight of Zolutski's that a colleague in the tri-state area sent him, and showed it to Axel in his office. "The fight is from a month ago. It confirms what I thought about your opponent – he doesn't like prolonged trench warfare. It you get inside, stay there for more than a few punches, get out, and then mix up the pace of the fight while continuing to meet him toe to toe again for prolonged periods of time, you'll be fine. You feel ready?"

"I'm anxious, of course. But I don't think I'll embarrass myself in the boxing ring."

"You stopped being able to embarrass yourself months ago. How are you dealing with the anxiety?"

"I've been playing a lot of chess games online with fast time controls. At times dragging the pieces around quickly on the screen feel like boxing, and calms me down."

"Huh, that's a new one. Whatever works, I guess."

"I guess too. I've never done this before."

"You find any useful training techniques out of this, write a book about it. I don't think readers will find it boring."

"Um… what category, Ted? Physical fitness or science fiction?"

Ted smiled cryptically. "Let's do one more set of pads for the road."

The gym was deserted except for one other boxer practicing in front of the mirror. Axel put on plastic disposable globes and a stinky pair of common boxing gloves from the racks. Ted set up the pads, told Axel what punches to throw, and said not to look at the display time of the round clock. The instructions were punch fast, faster, and insanely fast. Axel kept up, hearing the sound of many bells in the background. When they finished, Axel was drenched in sweat, and only then looked at the wall clock. They had going at it for over an hour.

After Axel had put away the boxing gear, he and Ted walked together to the door where they hugged. As they said their goodbyes, Ted suddenly leaned in close, and told him something that would stick in his head for the next several months.

"Every day we write the book, friend. You don't have to settle for reading it. Make your book any category you want, and give it any ending you want, too."

CHAPTER TWENTY-ONE

Early next morning, Axel left for New York. The time of the weigh-in was at three o'clock that afternoon. He knew that he would easily make the weight for the cruiserweight division, but postponed eating all day, just to be irrationally sure. He arrived in Manhattan at lunchtime, still having to commute to Brooklyn. In place of lunch, he bought takeout and stuffed it in the middle of one of his bags. Axel planned to scarf down his meal the moment he stepped off the scale.

He had no luck getting hold of Willie. His sister in Florida said on the phone that he was supposed to show up at her doorstep a month ago, but didn't, and had no idea where he was. She talked like this had happened before, so Axel did not pry and thanked her for her time. However, his chess-player friend in New York was around, who gratefully accepted the remaining tickets Axel had on hand. Axel called him when he arrived in town, and said that he would arrange to leave the tickets at the Will Call window in his name. He hoped that someone would show up from Ted's gym to use the rest.

Axel checked into his hotel, and then walked over to the address of the weigh-in with his amateur boxing book, an extra copy of his doctor's certificate, and lunch inside his knapsack. He arrived at a quarter to three with his stomach growling. He was one of the first to arrive, and was spotted by Vyacheslav immediately. His paperwork was processed in short order. Vyacheslav then led Axel to a room with a scale and three boxing officials. After weighing in at a hundred and ninety-two pounds, Vyacheslav gave him an entry pass to the arena for the following day.

"Wojtek should be arriving soon. Can you stick around for the photo shoot? It's going to be upstairs, and shouldn't take more than an hour."

"Sure," Axel replied with a tight face. He was clutching his lunch in his hands.

"Haven't eaten today yet, have we?" Vyacheslav asked with a knowing laugh. "Go on, eat your lunch at that table over there. We're all going upstairs at four."

As Axel finished off his lunch, he noticed Wojtek Zolutski checking in and presenting his paperwork. There, at last, was his opponent in the flesh, the focal point of all his training the past three months. He was an even six feet tall and powerfully built. The sleeves of his jacket strained against his broad shoulders. He came out from the weighing room with his arena entry pass, and quickly walked over to sit down at the table next to Axel's with a bag that smelled of chicken parmesan. He tore open the bag.

"Breakfast for you too, huh?" Axel asked.

He grinned. "Breakfast of champions, man." He looked at Axel more closely, and with a gleam in his eye stuck out his hand. "Hello, Axel, oh-mortal-enemy-of-mine. I'm Wojtek," he said.

They shook hands in a mutually tight grip. Axel said: "Nice to finally meet you too, oh-lethal-adversary-I-finally-get-to-meet-in-person. What was your weigh-in weight?"

"Hundred and ninety-eight. And you?"

"Hundred and ninety-two."

Wojtek nodded and said in between bites of his meal: "I could have made it a lot lower. Why the hell did they schedule this just after Christmas?"

"It was probably the only night they could get at the Barclays Center."

"Yeah, you're probably right." Wojtek had demolished his sandwich in three bites, and was wiping his mouth. "Your chess game intimidates me, Mr. Axel. You must know where I am going to be concentrating my efforts."

"I do. May the best man win," Axel said extending his fist.

"May the best man win," Wojtek replied with a broad smile. They bumped calloused fists.

"What charity are you fighting for, Wojtek?"

"Something I believe in very strongly – the Wounded Warrior Project. In 2010 my brother Andrzej came back from a tour of duty in Afghanistan really fucked up and needing a lot of help. These guys returned our phone calls within minutes, and followed through on every promise they made to get my brother back on his feet. What's yours?"

"The Red Cross," Axel answered, and told him of his friend's apartment fire wiping out all his belongings a few years ago, and how they helped restock his new home.

"Oh man, life kicks harder in the balls than anything you and I can throw," Wojtek said.

"Amen."

They went on to chat about who had the best chances of winning the upcoming US Chess Championship, and other stuff, until they heard Vyacheslav asking for all the fighters to go upstairs for the photo shoot.

The photo shoot consisted of individual photos of each of the fighters, faux-fierce poses of opponents in their boxing stances glaring into each other's eyes (some of them genuinely did not seem to like each other – Axel and Wojtek just looked stern), and one big group photograph with the New York Chessboxing Association logo in the background. In all, ten scheduled fights had been approved by the New York Athletic Commission that afternoon – all the chess clocks as a result would be having a one second increment.

Vyacheslav told the gathering to show up at the Barclays Center tomorrow by seven thirty p.m., reminding them to bring their passes, shoes, and mouth guards. Everything else would be given at the venue, the gloves and headgear waiting for them at the ring in their corners. The fight order on the card would be posted in the locker rooms. He warmly thanked them all for coming, and told them to get a good night's sleep. He would see them tomorrow to make some history.

Before leaving, Axel caught up with Vyacheslav, held up the extra entry tickets, and asked if he could leave them at the Will Call window to be picked up by his chess-player friend, the name written down on a slip of paper. Vyacheslav said no problem; he would take care of it. Outside a block away, Axel briefly locked eyes with Wojtek when they were on opposite sides of the street. They gave each other a friendly yet terse nod. *We'll know each other up close and personal really soon*, the gesture seemed to say.

It was dark by the time Axel returned to the hotel. He went straight to sleep. He woke up at two in the morning, and decided for the hell of it to walk to the Barclays Center, walk eleven circuits (one for each round) around it, and walk back. The streets were quiet; the air was still and cold. His head was flooded with thoughts during his walk, which Axel acknowledged and left on the street by the time he returned to the hotel. He then went back to sleep.

Axel woke up at six a.m. ravenously hungry. He went to the hotel restaurant as it was just opening, and downed five cups of cold cereal with a big mug of hot tea. He no longer drank coffee the day of a fight. The first and only time he did so, his apprehension together with the coffee made him want to pee badly minutes before his fight started, and he never forgot how undignified it felt to hold his dick with his hand wraps.

He went back to his room, and caught up on the sleep he was going to lose tonight from all the post-event exhilaration and relief. He woke up again at noon. He took two bananas from the hotel morning buffet, deciding that they were going to be his last meal before the fight.

Axel wished that the afternoon would simply vanish so that he could step into the next room and start his chessboxing bout. But there were still six hours to kill. So, he stayed in his room and watched TV indiscriminately while struggling to keep his surging nerves down. Finally, evening arrived. He took a hot twenty-minute shower, got dressed, packed his mouth guard, shoes, and entry pass in his knapsack, and walked over to the Barclays Center.

Axel arrived at the arena at seven. He showed his entry pass to the desk just inside the only open entrance, where he was given a box with his trunks and directed to the locker room of the blue-corner fighters. He changed into his boxing clothes, had his hands wrapped in plaster and marked with an 'X', and then waited. The fighting card order was posted at seven forty-five. He was scheduled to fight third.

Since the fights officially started at eight thirty, he probably would not be in the ring until ten. To pass the time, Axel jumped rope and did eleven ceremonial clap push-ups (again one for each round). He turned on his phone, which had been off since the night before. On it were messages wishing him luck from his sister, Ted, Jason, and Lou from the gym, and his chess-playing friend in New York. He listened to them all three times over, and another hour slipped by.

Axel was ruminating that it been four years to the day since he'd had his last drink when one of the boxing officials told him that the second fight was winding down, and that it was time to get ready. Axel nodded, slipped in his mouth guard, and bounced over to the door to the walkway that would lead to the ring. *Nothing left to do but jump out of the plane*, he said to himself. The official heard a notification inside his earpiece a few minutes later and then motioned with his head for Axel to go.

The tunnel was ten feet long. At the end was another official with a flashlight, who waved it for Axel to follow. His entry music played as he walked the extra three hundred feet to the ring. To Axel's intense annoyance the song *Thunderstruck* was playing, instead of the AC/DC song *Heatseeker* which he'd requested in his email. The annoyance turned out to be a blessing in disguise, for it masked how loud the crowd was, and initially filtered out the surroundings.

Axel looked up and saw a chess table with a pair of headphones in each chair, a boxing ring ten feet away to the right, an elevated shelf just outside the blue corner holding his boxing gloves and headgear, and Bob Jeffries the referee in front of him, who he had met earlier that month. Bob nodded, told Axel to show his mouth guard, and gestured him to stand by the chess table. Wojtek was scheduled to come out next. It was only then Axel noticed how loud the arena was, but he didn't look up. He was staring at the chess pieces to center himself, and kept his breath steady.

Wojtek came out within a minute to the entry music of a song (Axel recognized it but couldn't quite place the name) by the group Disturbed. He too was checked out by Bob, who then took a White and Black pawn from the board, put one of them in each of his fists behind his back, and extended them to Wojtek telling him to choose. Wojtek chose the fist with the White pawn. He then gestured Wojtek to sit at the side of the table with the White pieces, and Axel at the side with the Black pieces.

Axel and Wojtek gave each other a quick nod. This was happening so quickly...

Bob told them to follow his instructions and to protect themselves at all times, and to go to a neutral corner in the event of a knockdown. He gestured to Axel and Wojtek to touch hand wraps. When they did, Bob then said to put on their headphones, and he started Wojtek's clock.

CHAPTER TWENTY-TWO

Wojtek opened with 1. Nf3. Axel responded with 1...d5. When the next move was 2. g3, Axel knew that it was going to be a King's Indian Attack and quickly moved his pieces into a London Defensive System setup with 2...Nf6, 3...Bf5, 4...c6, 5...h6, and 6...e6. Wojtek completed his opening setup with 3. Bg2, 4. 0-0, 5. d3, and 6. Nbd2. Then he played the passive move 7. a3, which said that he was not going to continue aggressively and place any of his pieces beyond the third rank. He was going to draw out the chess game in a slow positional contest and do his damage in the boxing rounds.

Axel kept up with his opponent on the clock as the game left the opening phase and started in the middlegame. He had a solid space advantage, and had the makings of a solid plan to convert it into a material one. Yet he could hear his heart pound under the headphones. He knew he had been dropped in the eye of the hurricane, and that all hell was going to break loose after the referee paused the game after three minutes. It was going to be a lot louder, too. Nothing else to do but meet it head on, and dance.

Three minutes later Bob tapped both players on the shoulders and stopped the clock. He signaled them to take off their headphones and pointed to the boxing ring. When the headphones came off, the sounds of the crowd jolted Axel and his feet immediately started twitching. Bob pointed Axel towards the blue corner, and Wojtek towards the red corner.

In a large wall display in back of the boxing ring, Axel saw the position that had just been stopped, with the clock times for both White and Black. Below was a timer that ticked off the remaining seconds before they had to box. Axel quickly put on his gloves and headgear, and was in the ring within thirty-five seconds, his opponent within forty. *Five seconds earlier*, Axel thought – *this is a good sign*. Both bounced on the balls of their feet for the rest of the minute, each bounce making the visceral part of the contest more and more real.

The bell sounded for the second round. Axel and Wojtek met in the middle and touched gloves, and it was on. Wojtek leaned in and flicked off a couple of jabs that landed but did not particularly hurt, and moved quickly away from a right hook of Axel's. Wojtek did most of the moving around the ring, throwing a few more jabs to test Axel's reflexes more than anything else. Axel waited patiently for Wojtek to strike, watching his opponent's gloves like a hawk. He didn't mind if no serious boxing action occurred this round; it would give him more time to develop his small advantage in the chess game.

In the second minute, Wojtek's onslaught began. He feinted a jab, then followed it up with a real jab and a hard right, both of which Axel managed to block. Then something about Wojtek's shoulder dipping made Axel instinctively roll under, avoiding a hook that went above his head. Coming back up he stuck out a right hand, which caught Wojtek clean in the chest. His opponent backed off immediately, confirming Ted's prediction that he didn't like trading punches toe to toe. Axel immediately pursued, but he didn't straighten out his balance in time. Wojtek clipped him with a hard hook to his right ear, and it hurt. Axel reverted to defense against the jabs for the rest of the round. Wojtek came in five more times throwing twenty strong punches, of which all but two were parried: a hook to his ribcage and a right that nailed him between the eyes. Yes, Wojtek could hit, but so far Axel was not seeing stars.

The bell sounded. Within a minute both were back at the chess table; the headphones ended the sounds of the crowd as suddenly as they had begun. His opponent's passive strategy ignored thematic pawn breaks that might have freed his game. Axel used his moves in round three to make sure those pawn breaks would never happen without loss of material, crystallizing his space advantage. In round five he planned to start prying open squares in Wojtek's pawn chain so that his pieces could break into the position.

Bob stopped the game, and the players headed back to the boxing ring. This time Axel resolved to mix up the pace of the fight to see how Wojtek reacted to sudden tempo changes. The sound of the crowd was no longer jolting, but energizing.

When the bell sounded, Axel raced over to Wojtek and snapped off two jabs and a right that forced him into a corner. Wojtek defended well, and spun out before Axel could land any more. This time, Axel kept his balance straight and bounced straight towards his opponent. He was trying to square off the ring and put Wojtek in another corner. His opponent was rattled, throwing a hook that was not supported by the rest of his body, and Axel landed his first good punch of the bout with an uppercut that snapped back Wojtek's head. His opponent clinched.

After Bob broke them apart, Wojtek resumed his circling around the ring and fast jab approach. He went in for the ground assault a few times more that Axel was largely able to parry. Axel didn't mind if this was all that happened for the rest of the round – he had the upper hand in the chess game. But for the sake of variety, Axel charged with just thirty seconds left into the round. He managed to maneuver Wojtek in the corner long enough to deliver four body shots, two hard hooks to the shoulders and a right that caused a cut above his opponent's left eye. The bell ended on a sour note when Wojtek exploited Axel's slightly lowered guard to land a hook on the same right ear two rounds ago. That one really stung.

The bell sounded and the players returned to the chess game for round five. Axel's attack was beginning to bear fruit. Few of Wojtek's pieces had advanced beyond the fourth rank, and were starting to trip over each other. He had a gaping hole on his h3 square, where Axel planted a Knight that was defended by his Queen and Bishop, and which threatened to infiltrate from the same square once the Knight moved away. Axel had also opened up a large time advantage on the clock: he had six and a half minutes left, while his opponent only had two and a half minutes. He was sure that Wojtek would be very aggressive the next round.

In round six, the battle came to Axel in a hurry. Wojtek raced across the ring and started quick volleys, throwing seven jabs in a row, Axel knew a power right would come the moment he tried to move. So, he moved into the jabs, eating two painful ones, and shot off a right hook to the side followed by a left uppercut to the gut to make Wojtek back off. Axel then alternated between charging into more punches and hanging back waiting for the punches for the round, trying to be random about it. He knew that if he could get through this round, Wojtek's position would become critical at the chessboard. The voluntary taking of the punches confused Wojtek, and made him hesitate about going all in. He came close to pushing Axel in the corner a couple times, but Axel always clinched, and bounced back into the center of the ring once Bob had broken them up. The bell ended for the round surprisingly quickly.

In round seven at the chess game, Axel was drawing blood. He had won a pawn, while maintaining an overwhelming positional advantage. Wojtek's King was boxed in and seriously menaced, and would be facing checkmating threats once Axel managed to bring up one of his Rooks in reserve. Wojtek took two minutes on one of his moves, drawing a warning from Bob, which left him with only thirty seconds for the rest of the game when the round ended. Even with a one second increment after each move, he was going to have precious little time. Axel knew the next boxing round was going to be war.

Round eight started, and Axel decided that the best defense was a good offense. He met Wojtek in the middle of the ring, and without preamble both started wailing on each other. Axel knew that White's position was not going to survive round nine, and only needed to get through this round to win the match.

Wojtek might not have liked going toe to toe and getting hit by a lot of counterpunches, but he didn't have a choice. Axel though had the choice of making Wojtek fight in a style he didn't like. When his opponent charged, he charged too, causing clinches and the round to tick away; when his opponent didn't charge, he moved off and no punches were thrown, causing the round to tick away. Axel exulted as the bell ended. The chess game was going to resume.

In round nine, Wojtek's clock ran out of time as he faced an inevitable mate in four. He grinned, tipped over the king for dramatic effect, and congratulated Axel on a great match. Only then did Axel look out into the crowd. The arena was huge, but it wasn't close to being filled to capacity – well over half the sections were covered in a black felt for the benefit of the cameras. There could not have been over one thousand people in the audience, a bit of a letdown from the cast of thousands in a blockbuster film that Axel had imagined. The crowd though was great, and had cheered way above its weight class.

Axel was met just outside the ring by his New York chess-player friend and his buddies, who clapped him on the back and said how awesome that had been. They joked that he might become their new bodyguard when they played belligerent chess hustlers in the park. Axel laughed, and said that he would try to meet up with them at a restaurant before going home.

When he was halfway to the locker room, he ran into a smiling face that looked familiar to him. Three steps away, Axel suddenly recognized who it was. It was Max, that maniacally hard-hitting German guy he had sparred with in Ted's gym last year.

"Sehr gut!" Max exclaimed as he slapped Axel heartily on the shoulder. Axel winced, and wondered if Max had ever had an off switch.

"Thanks, Max. How did you know I was fighting tonight?"

"From Ted. I visited his gym this morning. When I told him that I had moved to New York and was heading back that day he offered me the tickets, and here I am. This is my friend Gunther," he said, introducing an even bigger, burlier version of himself.

"Hallo, Axel, most impressive!" Gunther said. He chest bumped Axel which made him lose his breath, and Axel thought he had just crashed a Viking raiding party. "Your boxing is not bad, and wow, you can play chess."

"Thanks, Gunther. Do you play?"

"My tactics are OK, but I do not have the strategy that players of your rating have."

"You were a total python in that game, squeezing the life out of your opponent's position. It was very pleasant to see," Max said. "Let me know if you are ever planning to visit Berlin sometime. I'm friends with some chessboxers there who would love to hang out with you."

"Do you have a card with your number on it?" Axel asked impulsively.

"Ja, ja – hier." Max dug out his card and thrust it under Axel's left plaster hand wrap. "We'll let you go now. Fantastic to see you doing so well! Keep in touch," he said enthusiastically shaking his hand and slapping his other shoulder, making Axel wince again.

Gunther put an arm around his neck, and for an awful moment Axel thought he was going to get head-butted. But the arm had been put around his neck with affection, and it turned into a hug instead.

Axel smiled back at them, turned around, and had just about reached the locker room. when he heard in his right ear: "Great match, Axel! Can you please come with me for a few minutes? We want you to give a brief post-bout interview." It was Vyacheslav.

"Sure." Wojtek was being asked questions in front of a camera when they arrived at a small studio upstairs. Axel waited, taking in the view of the next chessboxing match outside the window. This sport looked really cool from an elevated vantage point. He did a man-hug with Wojtek as they traded places in the studio.

In the interview Axel felt at ease, and was able to describe his fight strategy coherently along with enough wonky chess details from the game to make both the interviewer and Vyacheslav happy.

"You did yourself and this organization proud," Vyacheslav said, as Axel stood to go. He handed back Axel's boxing record book. The chessboxing bout had counted as an amateur boxing match, and Axel's record was now three wins, one draw, and no losses. "I'm doing another one of these next June, and you are one of the first people I am going to call."

"Thanks, Vy. I really enjoyed himself."

"Have a great New Year, Axel. You're going to have a hard time topping this for your next resolution."

"Ain't that the truth."

CHAPTER TWENTY-THREE

When Axel finished his goodbyes with Vyacheslav, he changed into his street clothes and hung around to look at two more of the matches. He looked at his watch and noticed that it was eleven thirty. *Good lord, the last fight won't go on until two in the morning*, he thought, and wondered if any spectators would be left in the audience.

Then he suddenly felt hungry – he had only had a couple of bananas over twelve hours ago. He called up his chess-player friend, and asked if they wanted a quick bite in some diner. His friend said he was just turning in, and asked if he could take a raincheck. No problem, Axel said, they'd catch up some other time. Axel realized that the flip side of telling so few people in advance what he was going to do was that it was hard to celebrate with company afterwards.

Axel walked back to his hotel with light feet, and decided to go to bed hungry. He also decided to check out after waking up and having breakfast. He'd had enough of crowds and preferred to celebrate the night back home contemplating even crazier resolutions for the following year. These resolutions were going to include at least two more chessboxing bouts during the next twelve months.

Upon his return, he called his family and friends, telling them how he did, receiving enthusiastic if not baffled congratulations that made him feel adrift. At 12.01 a.m. in the new year Axel found himself alone in his apartment. He realized he was as alone as ever, and that was OK. Finding the best move in a chess game, or landing a good punch in a boxing match, kept him young. Happiness was too complicated. He did wish though he didn't feel so physically isolated, so one of his resolutions included having a sex life.

A few nights later he screwed up the courage again to call up a hooker whose pictures he liked on an escort site. She told him to show up outside a local hotel, and to call again to get the room number. Axel called again, and there was no answer. He called again six more times, until all he heard on the phone was an answering machine. He drove back to his apartment in a warped and frustrated mood.

A week later Axel tried again and called another hooker whose online pictures he liked. He left his number on her answering machine, and waited for a reply. None came after two weeks of waiting. Axel was ready to write off the purchase of sexual experiences for life until she called on a Thursday night, all super accommodating and willing to meet within an hour. With a misguided sense of doing what he set out to do, Axel went to the rendezvous only to find that the woman behind the opened door was not the same one in the pictures. He told her so in the hallway. She impatiently asked if he was coming in or not. Axel flatly said no, turned his back, and walked away.

Axel firmly crossed this resolution off his list for the rest of the year. It hadn't lasted long, this broad yearning to connect with someone, before it soured and transformed back into the well-paved routes of improving what he already knew. Soon he would be back in the gym, or hunched over the chessboard solving ever more challenging problems, far away from any semblance of dating. He resolved instead to go further in chessboxing than he had gone before, rather than futilely try to develop a new spoke on his social wheel.

The DVD of the chessboxing event arrived from Vyacheslav the following day. Looking at it, Axel concluded that he didn't look like such a dweeb. He played a solid chess game, and appeared halfway competent in the boxing ring. The other matches had better boxing, but the chess games had more errors in them.

Axel returned to Ted's gym in mid-January, and saw one of the speed bags in the corner replaced with a chess table and clock. Ted put a hand on his shoulder from behind.

He said: "Welcome back, Axel. After what you did in New York, I figured what the hell, let's try something new here. The chessboxing bout is on YouTube, if you didn't already know. I showed it to some of the new members in the gym, and they were interested in taking up chessboxing. You want to coach in some experimental classes? If they take off, you won't have to pay membership dues anymore."

"Do you know how good they are at chess?"

"No idea, I'm not even sure some of them know the rules. But they want to do it."

"Um, the chess part of it, sure, I can coach that. The boxing part I'll leave to you."

"Deal." Ted looked around the gym and said: "Go ahead, do your workout. If I see any of the guys who showed interest around here tonight, I'll point you out to them so you can get acquainted."

Axel was an hour into his workout, when a strapping young man introduced himself during the one-minute break in between the rounds. His name was John, and said he was a junior at a local high school who was both on the football and chess teams. He saw Axel's video on YouTube. Could they play a chess game sometime?

"How about now?" Axel asked in turn, pointing to the chess set in the corner. "No time like the present."

John nodded. They went over to the chess table. Axel sighed when he noticed that the Queens were not on their own colors. He rotated the board so that the lower right corner was on a white square, and then reset the pieces. Axel asked John what color he wanted, and John replied they should play two games: one with White, and one with Black.

"How much time do you want on the clock?" Axel asked. He gave John the White pieces.

"Five minutes, no increment." They bumped fists, and Axel started John's clock.

John moved way too slowly, and found himself in time pressure by the fifteenth move. The game was still equal, but if he didn't pick up the pace of his moves he was going to forfeit before he saw move thirty. On the twenty-second move he had seconds left and hung his Queen, resigning immediately.

Axel said: "If you do chessboxing, John, you are only going to have nine minutes for the entire game, and your sitting time is going to be broken up into six different sessions of three minutes each. Try to imagine a game in ninety-second bursts while never falling behind on the clock. Don't worry, you'll have plenty of practice to get it right."

John nodded. "One more game."

The next game John played the Sicilian Defense at a quicker pace, but he fell into difficulties straight out of the opening. Axel played a side variation ideal for fast time controls, which allowed him to quickly develop and mobilize all his pieces. John had to keep the position closed and defend patiently, where he would have had excellent chances, but he allowed Axel to sacrifice a Knight and open up the center, and his King quickly perished.

"You have to play well too," Axel said dryly.

John laughed. "I'm addicted, man. I took up boxing two weeks ago, and I love how every muscle in my body feels like it's been through a meat grinder afterwards. Ted has been kicking my ass worse than all my football coaches combined."

"Wait till you start sparring. You're going to hate Ted even more."

"Heh, heh, heh. How long have you been playing chess, Axel?"

"Twenty-five years. You?"

"I started in the eighth grade, and have hated and loved the game ever since. I can play for hours and hours, and have played in a bunch of tournaments. I feel like I'm going to die in every game. Sometimes, I get so disgusted with myself that I never want to see another chess piece as long as I live."

"Fear and loathing, I love it! Welcome to the brotherhood," Axel said with a smile and an outstretched fist. They bumped fists again.

"I think I might have a student," Axel said to Ted in his office once he had changed back into his street clothes.

"Who, John? Yeah, I saw you playing with him. Was he any good?"

"He's played in some tournaments – his chess game isn't bad at all. He just needs to recalibrate his timing for blitz chess, which isn't hard to do."

"I've seen quite a few of the guys playing chess on that table over the past week, Axel. Can I put up an informal sign-up sheet for your services? There's more than a little interest here in chessboxing, I can feel it. If I can get half a dozen of them, maybe I can organize a class with you."

"OK, Ted. Why the hell not?"

Two other guys approached Axel for chess games the next time he was at the gym. A sign-up sheet for a chessboxing class went up later that week.

The next time Axel was in the gym, he saw that nine people had signed up. Ted asked what additional equipment would be needed, and when would be a good night for Axel to organize chessboxing workouts. He replied five more chess sets and clocks, a couple of tactics problem books, and Friday night for people to meet. Ted ordered the equipment, and told Axel to pick out the books, for which he would be reimbursed.

"Let's have the first class during the second week of March. I'm making attendance at one of my sparring classes the boxing pre-requisite for the chessboxing class. Four Saturdays are between now and then. People who want to do this will have four chances to qualify. What chess pre-requisite do you want to set, Axel?" Ted asked.

"The ability to play a game of chess without making an illegal move is the biggest one," Axel responded. "Beyond that I'm not too picky."

"Be pickier. The class might balloon to forty people with such an easy requirement, and I don't want to spend the money on twenty chess clocks."

"All right. Let me think up a group of problems to solve that you can set up on the board for the guys who want to join. They'll be very basic checkmates in one or two moves, but they'll distinguish those who learned the moves yesterday from those who have played complete games. Those who can solve half of them within ten minutes are in, or if you want to keep the class size further down, make solving at least eighty percent the pre-requisite."

"Sounds good. Can you get the problems to me before Saturday? I'll show them to anyone who wants to join then."

"I'll think up the problems tonight, and email them to you tomorrow."

Axel had already thought out the problems in his head by the time he had arrived back at his apartment. On his laptop he created a dozen sophomore positions to solve - such as back rank mate, smothered mate, various forms of double attacks, and zugzwang - and saved them in a document. He woke up early the following morning, double-checked the skill level of the problems, and emailed them to Ted.

The following week Axel was in the gym, he saw that the sign-up sheet for the chessboxing class had grown to sixteen names. Ted said he was going to take down the sheet soon, and create a waiting list if more than twenty people signed up. "I have five clocks and sets for the class. Half are going to be in ring sparring, and half are going to be playing speed chess against each other," Ted said.

"The guys who signed up, can they spar? And how did they do on the problems?"

"Six are definitely in, including John, who you met. Three of them ripped through your problems in under two minutes. They also went through a sparring class, and are at various levels of boxing ability. Some will be able to do straight sparring by the time the class starts; others I'll let them do three-punch drills. I'm not sure they'll be able to do five rounds in the ring, so maybe we can do abbreviated matches of four rounds of chess and three rounds of boxing."

"OK."

"I've turned down five, either for being unsportsmanlike assholes in the sparring class or being unable to solve half of your problems in under ten minutes. I'd say you set the skill level of your problems just right."

"Good. So is the class still set to go three weeks from now?"

"Yes. We have a quorum, and more should be coming. At this rate we should have between twelve and fifteen potential chessboxers to train. Get your chess lessons ready. Oh, I almost forgot. You ran into Max in New York, didn't you?"

"Yes, I did. How is he?"

"Max is doing well in New York. He called me when he found out about this class through word of mouth. He said you met his friend

Gunther, who was impressed with your performance. He just started studying at a local university, and is very interested in joining the class."

"Did he solve the chess problems OK?"

"Just over half. But he's an accomplished boxer from Berlin, like Max."

"God, that Gunther guy scared the crap out of me. He seemed nice, but so stoked and high on life he looked like he brushed his teeth in the stratosphere every morning."

"Good, I'll make him practice with you." Ted laughed when he saw the expression in Axel's eyes. "Buck up and embrace your fears, Axel. It's taken you far, and will continue to take you farther."

CHAPTER TWENTY-FOUR

Axel prepared a basic chess course over the next few weeks. He had created such courses before for private students. They were designed so that tougher versions of the problems could be swapped in and given to the more advanced participants. He didn't plan to talk a lot; most of the lessons, such as they were, would be his commentary on the boxers' chess moves while they were being played.

The dreaded meeting with Gunther occurred on the first Saturday morning of March. Axel was finishing up his workout, and noticed him out of the corner of his eye. In daylight he looked like a bounding muscle-bound puppy with massive paws, smashing heavy bags as if they were toy furniture. He was six foot three, and weighed well over two hundred pounds, but had very little if any body fat on him.

His eyes lit up when he saw Axel in the gym, and covered the twenty feet between them in five bouncing steps. He moved extraordinarily quickly for a big guy. "Axel! How good to see you! Want to do a mini-match?" he asked, pointing with one glove to the chessboard and another to the empty boxing ring.

Might as well get this over with, Axel thought. "How about three rounds of chess and two rounds of light sparring?"

"Fantastic! How much time for each player?"

"How much are you used to when you play blitz chess, Gunther? I'll gear the time control accordingly."

"I'm used to three-minute with a two second time delay."

"OK, how about five minutes with a two second increment? That should come close to what you're used to over three rounds."

Gunther punched his hands together through the gloves, making a startling loud clapping sound. "Let's do it, dude."

They left their gloves in their perspective corners and walked over to the table. After setting up the clock, Axel took a White pawn and a Black pawn and cupped them behind his back. He put a pawn in each fist, and held his fists out to Gunther, beckoning him to choose. Gunther chose the left fist and Axel opened it, revealing a White pawn.

Axel sat behind the Black pieces, and said: "Light sparring, OK? You have at least ten kilos on me."

Gunther nodded vigorously. "Ja, ja. Ready?"

Axel nodded apprehensively. "Good luck," he said. He waited for the round clock in the gym to ring, and then he started Gunther's clock.

"Good luck," Gunther said. They bumped fists, and the match was on.

After two minutes, Gunther walked into a checkmate on the thirteenth move. "Well, that was embarrassing," he said sheepishly.

"That was a warmup, Gunther. Let's do another one."

"OK. Thanks, Axel."

"No problem." He reset the clocks, and waited for the opening bell to go off for the next round. Then he started Gunther's clock again.

Gunther played more carefully, and only had a slight disadvantage when the bell ended the chess round. He was still in the game when Axel stopped the clocks. They strode over to the boxing ring to slip on their gloves during the one-minute break. *I really don't think this is going to be fun*, Axel said to himself, *but I'd rather find out how tough he is sooner rather than later*. Ted said he would be sparring with Gunther regularly in the chessboxing class, which would either make Axel a much better boxer, or kill him.

The bell sounded for the boxing round, and they touched gloves in the center of the ring. Gunther proved to be very fast, and landed two jabs and a right before Axel could get into his full stance. Once his hands were up, he enjoyed some moderate success in blocking Gunther's punches and landing a few jabs of his own. Then out of nowhere a hook exploded just above his right ear, and dropped him to the canvas.

Gunther asked Axel while he got back up if he wanted him to tone it down. Axel shook his head, and said: "I need to get used to this, Gunther, let's keep going." Gunther nodded, and continued to pepper him with swift jabs for the rest of the round. Axel watched Gunther's potential hooks like a hawk, and moved away before they could be unloaded. The bell sounded without Axel landing any decent punches.

Back at the chessboard, Gunther lost a piece but was able to obtain two pawns for it. The slight disadvantage had turned into a winning advantage, albeit one that would require several more moves to fully convert. Axel stopped the clock to the chess round with an inward grimace – another boxing round was to come. It was only three more minutes, though, and then he could return to this winning chess position.

Gunther picked up the pace in the next boxing round. Axel found himself jammed into a corner trying to fend off hooks. He blocked half a dozen of them, and they still hurt, but eventually had the satisfaction of delivering a solid right uppercut and left hook combination that made Gunther back up enough for him to scoot back into the open ring. Belatedly he realized that going toe to toe with this big guy was a losing game, and started moving around, trying to stick in a few punches and dart away. Unfortunately, Gunther was fast, and Axel could not go in without getting swatted half the time. The bell went off to Axel's great relief, and they returned to the chessboard.

Their chessboxing match finished anticlimactically. Axel ground down Gunther in a long endgame, finally checkmating him with a King and two Bishops against his bare King. Each player had no more than thirty seconds on their clocks when Axel delivered checkmate.

Gunther smiled and said: "Great match, Axel! I thoroughly enjoyed it."

"Me too, Gunther. Tell me, how heavy were you going at me in the ring? Fifty percent? Seventy-five percent? Ninety percent? I need to know for future reference."

"I would say... eighty-five percent. You handled yourself pretty well. I think I have more than fifteen kilos on you, Axel, and that is an unfair advantage in boxing."

"Well, one thousand rating points is an unfair advantage in chess as well, Gunther. Hopefully we can find someone in your weight class who can give you a close game."

"One can dream... thanks, again. I'm really looking forward to this chessboxing class. Up your boxing training, Axel. I want a rematch with you, no holds barred."

"We're going to need a medic standing by if that ever happens,"

Axel replied. They both burst out laughing.

Axel checked in with his financial advisor again, who confirmed that if he maintained his current expenses, he could take the next five years off work without any discomfort, and even retire to a place where the cost of living was low. He didn't really spend a lot. The discretionary money gave him options, and more freedom to speak his mind should he ever find himself in a situation at work where push came to shove.

As if on cue, the obnoxious female co-worker walked into in his cubicle the following Thursday morning with two female witnesses. She rambled on saying that their silence had gone on long enough, and that he was behaving unprofessionally. Axel cut her off in mid-sentence by growling, "Fuck you, get out of my face," and the obnoxious female co-worker shut up. One of the witnesses looked indignant and started to say something, whereupon Axel gave her a withering stare and said: "Fuck you, get out of my cubicle." They scurried away.

He was summoned by his boss to a conference room later that afternoon with a person from HR. His boss said that he had no problems with Axel's work, and asked him what was going on. The person from HR though interrupted, and didn't allow Axel to answer. She was saying that profanity in the office was not acceptable, and was telling him to sign a piece of paper that officially put him on warning. Without thinking he stood up and said: "Fuck you, I quit," and walked out the door before either of them could reply.

When Axel arrived home, the vice-president of engineering called him and said that his resignation was not accepted, and could he please come in tomorrow at nine a.m. to his office. He had always respected the vice-president, and agreed.

The next morning the vice-president asked what was wrong; over eight years had gone by in the company without a single incident. Axel replied that he did not feel secure in his predominantly female department. The vice-president nodded, and then asked if he would consider transferring to a division in another building. This division consisted entirely of field service engineers who had long appreciated his work; he could start with a clean slate there.

Axel asked if he could sleep on it. The vice-president said sure, but added that if he returned the swearing would not go unpunished – Axel was going to be suspended for at least a week without pay. Axel liked him; this person did not sway in the wind, and believed that actions had consequences. He accepted his transfer then and there, since he knew who he was going to be working with, and liked them. The vice-president told him to show up at the new building in two weeks after he had cooled off. Axel was now officially on a leave of absence.

Before he went home, Axel told his sole male colleague the news, and then went over to his old boss's office before he went home to make peace. He apologized for swearing at him. The swearing was really directed at the HR person (indirectly, at that female clique), and he just happened to be in the same room. His old boss accepted the apology, saying he was happy that Axel was still in the company, and wished him luck in the new position.

He then asked when his next chessboxing bout was going to be, taking out a DVD of the New York event out of his desk drawer. He said that pretty much every department manager had seen it. Axel was floored; he really had not been that alone at work all these years. He promised to let him know, and they hugged. He then walked out, completely ignoring the female co-workers. They were dead to him.

CHAPTER TWENTY-FIVE

Axel suddenly had two free weeks on his hands. On a whim he looked up flights to Berlin; several were available the next few days, and didn't cost that much. He looked up hotels with vacancies, finding that they didn't cost that much either. He telephoned Max.

"Hi, Max, this is Axel."

"Hello, Axel. Gunther told me of your little match. What's up?"

"I was planning a quick visit to Berlin next week. Will any of your chessboxing friends be around?"

"Ja, they should. Tell me the days you are going to be there."

Axel told him. "Is that going to be enough notice? I can postpone if they need more time."

"Let me make a few calls, Axel, and I'll call you back. It should be fine."

Max called back an hour later. "No problem, Axel. They'll be happy to show you around. Tell me your email address, I'll send you their names and contact information."

Axel told Max his email address, and thanked him. "I'll send pictures."

"I want selfies. Especially of your face after their workouts."

"Why am I not surprised?"

Axel booked the plane tickets on Lufthansa, and a three-night stay in a hotel near Zoo Station. Shortly afterwards Max emailed the names of his friends, along with their emails and phone numbers. He assured him that they all spoke excellent English. Axel noted with amusement that two more of his friends were also named Gunther. There was also a Franz, and a Wolfgang. He emailed all of them his flight information and his hotel address, and promised to call them the moment he landed.

He then called Ted, told him where he was going, and promised to be back in time for the first chessboxing class. An hour later Max's friend Wolfgang emailed back, telling Axel to call him when he arrived, and to pack his boxing shoes, gym trunks, hand wraps, and mouth guard if he really wanted to have some fun. Axel replied that he would. The day after tomorrow he was on a plane.

Axel landed in Berlin on a Thursday afternoon. It was cold, but no colder than back home. He was amazed how organized the public transportation system was. The train times were clearly displayed in the station, all of them arriving exactly on time. Usually after a transatlantic fight he was so tired that he just threw money at a taxi to arrive at the hotel, but here the U-Bahn ran straight up to the airport and deposited him one block away from the check-in desk without the need of heavy thinking.

Axel called Wolfgang after he had checked in. He was feeling loose and reckless. He had kept up his boxing training routine right up before his trip, and was ready for whatever Max's friends might throw at him. Wolfgang said he would pick him up at his hotel in two hours.

Wolfgang knocked on his door as the sun was setting. Axel opened the door to a compact man in his early twenties, who if he boxed would probably fight in the middleweight division. But Wolfgang was a friend of Max's, and of course he boxed. His aquiline nose was crooked, and he had the telltale cauliflower ears of one who had spent many hours in the ring. His eyes were friendly, and he had a ready smile.

"Axel!" Wolfgang said, shaking hands with a firm grip. "Max told me good things about you. Did you bring your boxing gear?"

"I did, except for the gloves."

"No problem, the gym has plenty of those. Do a light workout your first visit to shake off the plane ride, and then maybe we can go a couple of rounds in the next few days."

"Maybe we could. But do you often box guys with an extra twenty kilos on you?"

Wolfgang's smile widened, showing two missing teeth. "What do you think, Herr Axel?"

"I think you do it all the time."

"I earn money on the side as a professional sparring partner, and will box with anybody. Max directed me to a couple of your videos on YouTube. You'll be fun to work with."

"How long have you known Max?"

"Since Gymnasium. That's where I met Gunther G, Gunther Z, and Franz too. We were all classmates who were in the boxing club. You'll meet them soon."

"Do you guys play chess too?"

"We all play a little, but Gunther B - that's who you sparred with back in the States, Max told me all about it - likes chess the most, and you dispatched him fairly easily. You can probably wipe the chessboard with all of us."

"Yes, but you can probably hit me hard enough so that I forget how the pieces move."

"We'll see."

Wolfgang took Axel to a small restaurant in Alexanderplatz, where they had a small meal of bockwurst and pretzels. Axel stuck to mineral water, while Wolfgang downed a large beer stein. Wolfgang's day job was a CAD designer at a local architectural firm; he worked out at the gym they were about to go to five nights a week. He also hung out at a local cafe to play chess most weekends. "I like the game, but I'm not that good," he admitted. Gunther G though was a candidate master (only a hundred rating points below Axel), while Gunther Z and Franz were strong club players. They all said that they would try to drop in at the gym tonight.

After the meal they left the restaurant and walked around the block to the gym. The gym was in the lower level of an industrial office complex. Wolfgang followed Axel's eyes as he noticed an auto body shop next door, and said: "Yes, very fitting, isn't it?" Axel nodded as they entered. The familiar acrid smell of stale sweat filled his nostrils. They signed in at the entry desk, and while Axel was a guest of Wolfgang's and did not have to pay anything, he did have to fill out an obligatory waiver. Not that it mattered that day, he had brought his workout bag for a light workout only.

The gym was slightly larger than Ted's, with the usual boxing bags and weight stations, as well as a small area off to the right with a demonstration board and chess sets with clocks on seven wooden tables. The gym had two boxing rings instead of one; both the rings had blood on the canvas that no amount of elbow grease could scrub away. Wolfgang said the one on the right was used for chessboxing, while the other one was used for boxing only. Twenty people were working out on the heavy bags; four were playing speed chess. Axel saw a sturdy plastic table with chess sets and clocks underneath one of the corners of the chessboxing ring, and asked if they put it inside the ring during matches.

"For official matches yes, but not for practice matches," Wolfgang said. "Magnetic sets that can be easily removed are used during the workouts, and a couple of guys supervised by the referee move the table in and out of the ring for the exhibition bouts. We only have one minute to move the board between the rounds, and it's easy to jostle the pieces and muck up the halted position. When it's quiet and we don't have enough people to move the tables, we just switch between the rings."

"A little bit of race car pit mechanics is involved, isn't it?" Axel replied. "Being next door to an auto body shop seems even more appropriate."

Wolfgang chuckled. "The locker rooms are over there."

Axel changed, and came out to do his light workout. He jumped rope for six rounds, did one hundred clap push-ups, went through his abs routine, practiced his form in front of a wall mirror, then borrowed a pair of gloves from the gym to hit the various bags. After about an hour, Wolfgang tapped him on the shoulder with a pair of pads in his other hand.

"While you were working out, Gunther G – our candidate master – called and said he should be here in half an hour. He just wants to play chess tonight. Franz also called, and said he'll be here an hour after that. When you're ready, let's do some pad work. That'll kill the time for Gunther G. After your chess with him, maybe you can do some light sparring with Franz. You two are in the same weight class."

"Sounds good, Wolfgang," Axel replied. "Next round?"

Wolfgang nodded, and Axel spent the next two minutes pounding the crap out of their hundred-kilo heavy bag, which left him in a fine sheen of sweat. He walked over to where Wolfgang was waiting, pads in hand. Unlike Ted, Wolfgang did not call out specific punches, but just held up a pad and beckoned Axel to throw. Axel was crisp the first two rounds, but afterwards fatigue set in, and he became slower in getting his gloves back to his fighting stance. Wolfgang started whacking him hard with the pads where his guard was down during the third and fourth rounds.

"Not bad, Axel, but it could be better. After a few rounds you're leaving your glove a few centimeters below your right ear, and your left elbow high in front of your ribcage. That might be good enough against Gunther G and Franz, but with Gunther Z it will be painful. Ah, I see Gunther G signing in. Let's do two more rounds, and then you can switch to chess."

Axel nodded, and during the fifth round took care to cover the areas Wolfgang mentioned. He thought he was doing well in the sixth round too, until Wolfgang cracked an uppercut under his chin before he could land a hook, then whipped out a jab between the gloves in front of his head once he was back in his fighting stance, thudding his forehead and leaving echoes.

Wolfgang grinned.

"Don't take that personally, Axel. That was to remind you that disaster can strike anytime, no matter how prepared you think you are."

"I learn that in every other chess game."

"I'm sure you do. One more minute to go."

Axel practiced extreme defensive boxing the last minute, darting out of range after each punch. Wolfgang though moved effortlessly with him, remaining in striking distance with each step, even though he was only holding up boxing pads. The minute was very long, but it finally ended, and they bumped fists glove to pad.

"Hallo, Gunther, wie geht's? Das ist Herr Axel von den Vereinigten Staaten," Axel heard in back while he was putting away the gloves. When he turned around, he saw Wolfgang standing next to a burly, solidly built man in his twenties about three inches shorter than Axel. The man looked at him, smiled, and held out his hand.

"Hallo Axel, my name is Gunther. I saw your chessboxing video. Quite good, quite good."

They shook hands. Axel asked: "Hi, Gunther. You are Gunther G?"

"Yes. My full name is Gunther Grunwald. Another Gunther you will meet soon. His name is Gunther Zellbacker. The Gunther you met back home, his name is Gunther Becker."

"How do you address each other when you are all in the same room?"

"G, Z, and B, respectively," Wolfgang answered with a guffaw. He gestured with his head to the corner in the right. "The chess tables are over there."

Gunther G asked Axel his rating as they sat down opposite each other at one of the chess tables. 2250 on his best days, Axel admitted, adding that he rarely had the chance to make it go higher by playing strong opponents on a regular basis. Gunther G replied that he was a current personal high rating of 2100. "Good, these games should be competitive," Axel said, starting his opponent's clock. The time control was set to three minutes for each player, with a two second increment.

Gunther G followed opening theory closely, playing main lines for both White and Black that had been analyzed to move fifteen and beyond. It was a welcome relief for Axel, who studied opening theory closely but rarely had the chance to follow play it out over the board, because his lazy opponents at home kept leaving it at the earliest available opportunity. He had played in Europe before, and noted that the chess players here more closely followed the forms - i.e. published analysis - rather than in the States, where they left well-trodden paths as soon as possible, preferring to bushwhack in the margins.

The two second increment kept both players from running out the other's clock on time. Gunther (like Axel and unlike the hustlers who played blitz chess for a living) actually resigned lost positions. Axel hated playing against people who masochistically played on until they were checkmated; they wasted everyone's time.

They played a dozen games over the next hour, sharing heavily analyzed and sharply contested positions in the Open Sicilian, King's Indian Defense, Ruy Lopez, and Slav Defense. Gunther's style was that of an attacker who sacrificed material often and Axel's style was positionally aggressive, so plenty of tactics appeared in all the games. In the end, Axel finished plus two. None of the games had any outright blunders, a refreshing change from the blitz chess he played back in the States.

"It was a pleasure playing you, Axel," Gunther said. "I had a large dinner ninety minutes ago, so I really shouldn't box tonight. But next time you're here, let's do a couple of rounds of chessboxing. It should be fun."

"The pleasure was mine, Gunther. I've been on a plane for over seven hours, and shouldn't really box either until I'm used to your time zone and your gym. But yes, let's do it in a couple of days. I agree, it will be fun."

By this time, Franz had arrived and had changed into his workout clothes. Wolfgang introduced them. Franz was in Axel's weight class and of the same height, but the equal weight was squeezed into different places; he had huge shoulders and long tapering arms, as well as monster thighs and an impossibly narrow waist. He looked like a G.I. Joe doll.

"Hallo, Axel. It's good to meet you," he said cordially.

"It's good to meet you too, Franz. I'm not really up for sparring tonight, but can we do some drills?"

"Ja, no problem. What drills did you have in mind?"

"Oh, I don't know. Practice blocks against jabs, standing inside a tire and trading body shots, maybe even a three-punch drill."

"What is the three-punch drill, Axel?"

"One of the boxers throws three uncontested punches, the other throws three punches the moment after the third punch is thrown, and then they keep switching."

"All right. Let's do the three-punch drill for a couple of rounds. In that ring on the left."

Axel and Franz made their way over to the ring. As they stepped in, Wolfgang said: "Axel, I just got off the phone with Gunther Z. He sends his regrets, but he can't make it tonight. He'd like to meet you later this week, if that is possible. Can you come in tomorrow or Saturday?"

"I'd like to sleep off this time zone difference thoroughly before doing any real boxing. Is Saturday all right?"

"Sure. Let's do ten in the morning. That's when the gym opens, and the two rings will be ours."

"OK."

The bell sounded, and Axel gestured Franz to begin. He opened with three hard jabs to the head that were successfully blocked. Axel answered with a jab to the head, a jab to the body, and another jab to the head: the jab to the mid-section landed. Franz threw a jab and two rights immediately afterwards, the initial jab landing and the remaining punches blocked. Axel threw a jab, then moved to the right and landed an uppercut to the ribs, and followed with a right hook that Franz rolled under. The combinations then became more creative with both moving all over the ring. When the bell rang, Franz threw two straight rights that landed, and ended with a jab that fell in dead air.

In the next round Axel went first. He threw a jab, then suddenly went low and tagged Franz with two slapping body shots. He did his best to move away afterwards, but not before Franz nailed him with an overhead right on his forehead. Having two more punches left before it was Axel's turn, he launched a hard jab and a straight right, walking forward as he did so. Axel blocked the jab and slipped the right, and was able to land a triple jab into Franz's ribs. This round was more toe to toe; all they needed was a tire in which to put both their left feet.

Wolfgang and Gunther from the ropes exhorted Franz to speed it up, so the final two rounds whizzed by in a flurry of quick jabs, straight rights, and hooks delivered while going in and circling away off to the side. Franz's best combination occurred in the third round, when he did an excellent feint with his jab and crashed a right and left hook into Axel's head when his guard was lowered. Axel's best moment happened in the fourth round, when he was able to back Franz on the ropes, put his knee in between his legs, and deliver a stinging pair of uppercuts to the body followed by a left hook to the head.

Axel signaled at the end of the fourth round that he was done. He and Franz hugged, and he shook hands with Gunther on his way to the locker room. After changing back into his street clothes, he sought out Wolfgang, who was at the sign-in desk. He said that all the guys would be able to meet him on Saturday morning.

"Here is a card with the gym's address if you need to find it again. You and Franz are evenly matched, and you are probably a good match for G too," Wolfgang said. "Z you will find is a serious challenge. His fights with B here are legendary."

"Is he a heavyweight too like B?"

"Yes. Give or take five kilos, they are almost carbon copies of each other. We joke that they were fraternal twins separated at birth."

"That's something to look forward to, Wolfgang. I bit the bullet back home, and managed a few rounds with B, so I have some idea what to expect."

"Good. You should be able to hold your own, Axel."

"Only one way to find out. Are you going to be here to join us on Saturday?"

"I'll try… no, no, I'll be here. I'll see you on Saturday, and until then, enjoy Berlin!"

CHAPTER TWENTY-SIX

Axel went back to his hotel and turned in. On Friday he wandered around Museum Island, briefly visiting the antiquities in the Pergamon museum but mostly walking up and down the banks of the Spree River, where he enjoyed the shifting views of the city center.

Axel woke up early on Saturday morning. He did a full regimen of push-ups and squats in his hotel room, then went for a short run. After a shower, a quick breakfast, and lying down on his bed for several minutes of contemplation, he found himself in front of the chess boxing gym at five minutes to ten. Finding the door locked, he knocked. Wolfgang opened the door thirty seconds later.

"Hallo, Axel. All the guys are here. Get changed and let's go," he said with a zest in his eyes that Axel simply did not see in any of his countrymen back home.

On his way to the locker room he saw Franz and Gunther G working out on the speed bags; they nodded hello. Behind them he caught a glimpse of a big blonde guy partially obscured by the heavy bag, who was banging the crap out of it. *Pay no attention to that man behind the curtain*, Axel thought with dark whimsy.

After Axel came out in his boxing clothes, Wolfgang introduced him to Gunther Z. As expected, Z looked formidable. Compared to B, this Gunther looked slightly shorter (about six foot one) and a little heavier, but the extra weight was all muscle. He had the build of a jaguar. Axel could only hope that this one moved a little slower.

"So, do I call you Z for today?" Axel asked.

He smiled impishly. "Might as well. Wolfgang wants to be sadistic and have you play against G for the chess and against me in the ring during all the rounds, but you're a friend of Max's, and we don't want to create any international incidents." His smile widened. "We were thinking of a round-robin with you, me, G, and Franz. Four rounds chess, three rounds boxing. We have the place to ourselves, and can use both the rings. What do you say?"

"Let's do it. Where are the sets and clocks going to be?"

Wolfgang answered for Z: "Let's use the magnetic sets in the center of the ring. I'll help you take them and clocks off for the boxing rounds so that they don't get knocked over."

"And the time control?"

Wolfgang asked G and Franz if they wanted increments; when they shook their heads as did Z, he answered: "Six minutes each, no time increment. That's enough time for all the boxing rounds, but the final chess round will end early."

Axel said that was fine. Wolfgang set up the chess sets and clocks inside the rings, while Axel and the others warmed up on the bags for a couple of rounds. The matches were ready to begin by ten thirty. Axel's first match was against G, and Z would be taking on Franz. As Axel walked towards the right boxing ring, he took out his phone and handed it to Wolfgang, asking him to take pictures when he could – they were for Max.

"Of course, Axel. What are friends for?"

Axel picked G's closed fist with the White pawn, and had the White pieces for the match. Wolfgang set the round clock to begin in ten seconds. Both were sitting cross-legged on the canvas on opposite sides of the board. The bell went off and Axel's clock was started. He thought for a few seconds, and then chose 1. d4 for his first move. G chose the Benko Gambit, which Axel declined by playing 5. b6 and giving the pawn back. The game was about to enter the middlegame when the bell sounded. Axel took the chess set and stray pieces to one side, and Franz took the paused clock to the other. When they were putting on their gloves Wolfgang came by and took the chess set and clock off the ring.

The boxing round started. Axel and G met in the middle, and touched gloves. Since he had a three-inch height advantage, Axel circled around and used his longer reach to jab G in a wide semi-circle. G tried to come in closer and land punches, but throughout the round all he was able to do was eat more jabs with a few straight rights from

Axel, who kept a safe distance. G's one good punch started out as an odd-looking movement in the distance that with two quick steps suddenly closed the gap quickly enough to land a solid right hook on Axel's shoulder. The bell sounded, ending the round.

As Axel and G went back to their corners to take off their gloves, Wolfgang had enough time to put the chess sets and clock back on the sides of the ring. They put the chess set back in the center of the ring with twenty seconds to spare, and sat down again to start the next chess round. The bell rang and the chess game resumed. The middlegame grew increasingly complex: G started a rash attack on the Kingside, where Axel left a Knight and a Rook to defend his King while throwing all his other pieces on the Queenside to break through into the seventh rank there. The round ended, the result of the chess battle being able to go either way.

Axel stuck to his long-range strategy the next boxing round, and was able to keep his opponent from advancing. The more determined G's approaches became, the less stable his footing looked and more openings appeared in his stance. Axel was wary, realizing that it could be a trick, so he kept a healthy distance. G might be winning boxing points due to his greater aggression, but Axel had two more opponents to go. The bell rang, and they switched back to chess.

The chessboxing match ended that very round. Axel made substantial progress infiltrating the seventh rank and had won a piece and a pawn with the promise of more, but G's attack on the Kingside made enough inroads to force a perpetual check. If G did not have this perpetual check forcing a draw, Axel would have easily won with his extra material.

"Good match, G," Axel said, acquiescing to the draw and stopping the clock. "You made the most of your activity on the Kingside."

"Good thing too," G replied. "If I had one move less, you would have wiped out my remaining pieces in the endgame."

They looked over to the other ring, and found that the match there had ended already. Z won in the second round, Wolfgang said, with a tremendous hook that dropped Franz and forced him to cry uncle. Franz was OK, though, and ready to face Axel for the next match.

The chessboxers took a ten-minute break to rest and hydrate. When they returned to the boxing rings, the chess sets with the clocks were ready. Franz sat down across the board from Axel, sporting a cut above his right eye.

The bell sounded. Franz had chosen the White pieces, and opened with 1. b4 – the Sokolsky Opening, informally called the Orangutan. It didn't promise much of an advantage in a tournament game, but this was a speed game and it was easy to find the successive opening moves. Axel replied with a set-up that guaranteed easy equality. Franz played quickly and opened up a time advantage over Axel, but small cracks were beginning to show in White's position by the time the round ended.

Axel had done drills with Franz already, and had some idea what to expect when the boxing round began. Franz's right hooks were dangerous, which he liked to set up with feints from his jab. During the entire round, when the jab come out, Axel moved back diagonally to the right away from any potential hook first, and asked questions later. He also circled constantly to the right, so that Franz could not throw his favorite punch. The round was uneventful, with both only landing a few token punches, and the bell rang. Axel would consider trying to roll under that mighty hook later in the bout.

In the next chess round, any pretense of a White advantage disappeared by move fifteen. Franz was overextended on the Queenside, while Axel had a sturdy unassailable center that was making the movement of his pieces behind the pawns more fluid. Axel had one target already, the advanced b-pawn that Franz had moved to start the game, and was working on developing another by pushing his f-pawn down to the fifth, and then the sixth rank, in order to punch holes in the opposite castled King position. The bell rang again, and Axel knew that he should have his second weakness soon - he would be able to win material by alternating attacks between the weaknesses. He had pulled closer to Franz in time, too.

During the next boxing round, Axel's attention lapsed and he got clobbered by one of Franz's right hooks, and knew that he was going to have a black eye the following day. More annoyed than hurt, he threw caution to the winds and went straight into his opponent's face, landing a couple of stinging jab-uppercut combinations before another one of those damn right hooks thudded into his shoulder. Axel suddenly veered off right, leaving his left arm up in an arc, and catching Franz in a strong left hook to the head as he pursued. That was enough excitement for Axel during the round, so he went back to his conservative stance, concentrating on jabs and straight rights while circling around for an opening. Franz was unable to land any more heavy punches.

In the next to last chess round, Axel had pried open outposts for his pieces on both sides of the board while developing a lasting initiative, and Franz was forced to play defense. His opponent had to parry against six direct tactical threats in a row. Finding only moves in a slow tournament chess game was difficult enough, and harder still in a blitz game. Franz was saved by the bell, but his position was critical, and no longer had his initial time advantage. Both players would have less than ninety seconds each to finish the chess game in the final round.

The last boxing round began. Axel decided to tempt fate and try to roll under that terrible right hook. He saw the jab feints again from Franz one minute into the round, and prepared to go for it the next time one appeared. Axel's best boxing moment of the day occurred during the start of the second minute when he started rolling the moment Franz's left shoulder moved; he completed his roll, and came up with an uppercut that slammed into his opponent's undefended face. He followed with a right cross that forced Franz's knee to the canvas. Axel went to a neutral corner while Franz got back on his feet. Thirty seconds were left in the round when fighting resumed. Franz backpedaled, and Axel was content to shadow his movements in the ring when the bell rang.

The game could still go either way in the last chess round, because the limited remaining time could cause massive blunders. Luckily for Axel, Franz cracked first. He dropped a pawn in a difficult position, then a piece, and finally his Queen in short order. He had ten seconds left, while Axel had thirty, and he was almost certainly going to forfeit before Axel could deliver checkmate. Franz tipped his King, acknowledging the inevitable.

"This is just not my day, Axel. Great cross."

"Thanks. Those right hooks of yours hurt like a bastard."

"I need another punch or two to complement it, and then they will hurt even more," Franz said, smiling ruefully.

They looked over to see how the other match went. Surprisingly, Z had lost. G had survived two boxing rounds with the big man, and then won the chess part when Z's clock ran out of time on move twenty-five.

"Guys, one more match, and then we go to lunch," Wolfgang said.

After another ten-minute break with lots of water, Axel stepped into the ring with Z. He was resolved to get through this match the same way he ripped off a Band-Aid. Just rip it off on the count of one, instead of weighing all those pros and cons, and listening to his usual agonizing self-commentary along the way. If he could last three rounds of boxing, his chances of winning the match on the chessboard were better than fair.

CHAPTER TWENTY-SEVEN

Axel picked Gunther Z's closed fist with the Black pawn. The bell sounded after they set up their pieces. Z opened with 1. e4. Axel answered with 1...e5, and when the game turned into the Classical Four Knight's Defense, chose to go on the early offensive by playing the Rubinstein Variation with 4...Nd4. The main line of the variation involved sacrificing a pawn for the sake of quicker piece development after 5. Bc4 Bc5, but Z was flustered, and played the passive 5. d3. Axel had full equality by move eight, and the initiative by move thirteen when the round ended.

The boxing round started. Axel continued his move first, think later approach, by going straight into Z's personal space, launching hooks to the body and uppercuts to the chin. He stayed as close as possible to his opponent, not allowing him to uncoil and strike with full leverage. The strategy worked for two minutes, until Z shoved him back and cracked his head with a jab, right, hook, and another right. Undeterred, Axel moved into the pain and attacked at close range. The round ended before Z could unleash another barrage of punches in the open ring.

The next chess round began, and Axel could hear his ears ringing. He kept his head down and charged ahead full steam in the chess game. Ten moves later he had won a pawn, while Z's pieces were uncoordinated and vulnerable to being picked off. Axel was satisfied with his position when the bell rang again. The times on the clock were equal, but the game would probably be his two rounds from now. He was telling himself as he put on his gloves on that Z would come at him hard next round, and then Axel told his brain to shut up, and just do it.

The bell rang, and Z copied Axel's playbook by pressing close and punching hard. Although Axel covered himself and tried to stand his ground, Z continued to walk forward, and with his heavier weight pushed him into the ropes. Axel knew that staying here would become painful very quickly and tried to move off to the side, yet ferocious hooks kept him penned in as if he was trapped inside an electric fence. He judged which hook from Z hurt most, and decided the left ones hurt less, so he moved stage left into two shuddering hooks, and wrenched himself free into the open.

Z was on him immediately, and forced Axel into a corner. Phone booth boxing time. While scary to look at from the outside, Axel had learned from many hours of training in Ted's gym that it was the attacker who was more open to shots at close range. Blocking took less energy and less distance for the arms to cross over and cover the body. If the defender kept his composure, the attacker inevitably left openings for counter shots.

Z tried using his shoulder to immobilize his opponent against the post, but Axel dug deep and fiercely socked Z in the gut with repeated uppercuts and hooks. Z released his shoulder, and was immediately met with a straight right into the chest and a hook into the neck. Z's greater weight still kept Axel in the corner, but he didn't mind. He was content to stay in this place for the rest of the round, because he was landing more short sharp blows than Z, which prevented his opponent from winding up for that colossal punch to finish him off.

Z suddenly released all his pressure in the corner, causing Axel to surge forward and temporarily lose his balance. A right hook and left hook crashed into his ribs and head respectively, making Axel dizzy. He jumped back into the ropes, and came back on the bounce with a straight right that nailed Z in the bridge of his nose. Not seeking an engraved invitation for more, Axel finally darted free. One-minute left. Z went straight at Axel again, and Axel circled around into the open spaces shaking his head clear. Z expertly squared off the ring, and limited Axel's maneuvering options. They exchanged sharp combinations of jabs and rights when the bell finally rang.

Axel hoped to finish Z off back at the chessboard, but it was not to be. His opponent defended stubbornly, and while Axel's position was much better by the time the bell rang again, it was not yet won. He put the gloves back on, and steeled himself to finish this.

Back in the ring, Axel approached Z with all the concentration he could muster. The hook that had landed into his right side the round before still stung, and his face hurt all over. All that ringing from the bell was giving him a headache too. *You are what you do,* he randomly thought, as he forced himself forward. Something in the glint of Z's eyes coupled with a freeze frame in the rotation of his body told Axel a massive right was coming. He guessed correctly. He leaned into the blow with all his torque, and then uncoiled with a hook that rocked Z sideways.

Axel tried to follow that up, but Z immediately clinched. They broke apart, and Z resumed his strategy of shoving Axel into the ropes. Axel shoved back more aggressively than he had in the last two rounds, and was able to move off to the right, but not before a loping hook landed on his nose causing it to bleed profusely. Wolfgang appeared. He stopped the boxing clock, and stanched the blood several seconds later. After thanking Wolfgang, Axel looked at the time.

One minute was left in the round, and another random thought popped up in Axel's head: *if I had sixty seconds left to live, how would I spend it? In the fray,* he silently answered, and the boxing part of the chessboxing match ended as it began with Axel getting in Z's face and inside his arms. The bell rang as Z shelled up against five consecutive punches from Axel.

In the final chess round, the game went down to the wire. To Axel's irritation, his nose began to bleed again, and dripped on his side of the board. He stopped the clock to pick up the affected pieces and wipe the blood away, apologizing to Z. "No problem," he replied. Each player by this point had twenty seconds left, and the game devolved into a time scramble, the kind Axel had played against Willie many times in the park. Z had not had such a partner, and inexorably fell behind on time, forfeiting while Axel still had ten seconds on the clock. The final position needed another dozen moves to fully convert into a win.

Z smiled ear to ear and gave Axel a big bear hug, the kind B had given him in New York. "Great match, Axel!"

"Thanks, Z – I need an aspirin."

"Ja, me too," he said with a laugh.

They looked over to see G and Franz at the ropes, asking who won. Axel said he won due to time, and added: "The result could have easily gone the other way if there was an increment."

"Against G maybe, but not against Axel. This position is lost," Z said. "How did you guys do?"

They entered the ring. Franz said: "I finally didn't suck in boxing, and was able to convince G to stop in the second round from a good uppercut."

Axel asked: "What time is it?"

"Twelve thirty," Wolfgang said, entering the ring as well.

"My God, it's only been two hours! It feels like I've been here all week," Axel said.

"You have the pictures to prove it, friend," Wolfgang replied, holding up Axel's phone with a smirk. "Max is going to love these. A few more with you together?"

Axel stood arm in arm with his fellow chessboxers behind the chess set and clock in the middle of the ring, as Wolfgang took their pictures from the phone. They were definitely a colorful bunch. Axel had a bloody nose and the beginnings of a shiner under his left eye; Franz had a deep cut over his right eye; G had a nasty bruise on his forehead; and Z had a scarlet mark right between his eyebrows. But they were all smiling with a wild look in their eyes, as if they just base jumped from the Berlin Telecom Tower.

"Perfect! Email these to us, Axel, or I will be forced to hunt you down and kill you," Wolfgang said cheerfully. "Where do you want to go to lunch? It's our treat."

CHAPTER TWENTY-EIGHT

Axel walked with the others around the block to a local Biergarten, and partook in the bratwurst, but not the beer. The boxing, the bratwurst, and the beer made all his German friends want to take naps after lunch. They said goodbyes with lots of sloppy hugs to go around, Axel promising to email them the pictures from the gym. After the others had gone, he had unstructured free time for the rest of the day in Berlin, the kind of time he never truly knew how to occupy. He was scheduled to fly back early tomorrow.

After dropping off his gym bag at the hotel, Axel decided to return to Museum Island. He went to the Neues Museum, viewing the famous bust of the Egyptian queen Nefertiti, and feeling certain that she must be on a chess set somewhere. Then he visited the Alte Nationalgalerie. While looking at the pictures, he re-encountered a problem that had vexed him in museums for years: which was more important in a gallery, the caption describing the artist and the picture, or the picture itself? Axel shook his head, and told himself to get a grip – maybe he had been hit on the noggin too many times that morning.

It was dusk when Axel left the museums. He walked towards the Reichstag along the river, and noticed a ticket office for a cruise ship nearby. He bought a ticket for a cruise that left two hours later, had a light meal at the first restaurant he found, and killed the remaining time before the ship left by sitting on a bench. He stared at the river running under the lights of the city. The river reflected each light differently each time he blinked. Axel continued staring until all he could see was the moving water.

The cruise lasted two hours. Axel appreciated the extra bite of cold air off the water – it braced and cauterized. He was one of the few people outside on the deck; everyone else huddled inside. He asked a woman on the same side of the boat as him to take his picture. She agreed, somehow making the most of the night flash features of his phone. After an hour, the weather became too cold even for them, and they joined the rest of the group, ordering coffee and sitting down at the same table.

"Hi, I'm Axel."

"Hello, my name is Margrit," she replied in a French accent. She had a pleasant voice. They shook hands across the table. "What happened to your face?"

"Boxing, with two Gunthers and a Franz." Axel told her about his chessboxing bouts.

"Sounds like fun. Did you win?"

"I guess I did. My final score was two wins and a draw; everyone else lost at least one match."

"And why did you do this?"

"The same reason a mountain climber gave when he saw Mt. Everest – it was there."

"Yes, but mountains don't punch back."

Axel had no snappy answer for that, so he changed the subject. "Your accent sounds French. Are you visiting from France?"

"No, from Belgium. I've been traveling around India for the past three weeks, and stopped off to see Berlin for a few days before returning home."

"Neat. Where did you go in India?"

"Jodhpur, near Pakistan. Some amazing palaces and temples are there. The temperature was a welcome relief to Europe this time of year."

"I should visit more places outside of Europe. All those Catholic cathedrals start to look the same after a while."

She giggled. Axel impulsively asked: "Would you like to have dinner with me?"

Magrit tilted her head and looked at Axel for a long moment. She had nice eyes too. "Sure. Where do you want to go?"

"I want to use my credit card once for dinner while here, so someplace nice. Dinner will be on me."

"No, I will be paying for half."

"Deal."

When the ship returned, they randomly picked a direction from the dock, and kept going straight. They walked past the Opera House. Margrit had been in Berlin since Wednesday, and they compared sightseeing notes. Eventually, they settled on a restaurant near the Gendarmenmarkt. The menu was only in German.

"It's Berlin. They'll speak either English or French," Axel said.

"They'll speak English better than you, and French better than me," Magrit replied.

"No doubt."

They both ordered asparagus and potato soup, followed by schnitzel. Margrit had a glass of Riesling, while Axel had mineral water. While they waited for their food to arrive, Axel showed her the boxing pictures Wolfgang had taken on his phone that morning. She scrolled through them, laughing and shaking her head while doing so.

"You and your friends are crazy. Why are you drinking water, by the way? I imagined boxers, even those who play chess, as beer guzzlers."

"I don't handle alcohol well."

"That's OK. Plenty of other vices are out there to go around."

The food arrived, which was excellent. Margrit talked about her trip to Jodhpur during the next two hours. She loved the thousands of blue houses in the city center: from the Mehrangarh Fort, the whole area looked like a big mosaic. The thing she hated the most was the harassment she received from the men on the busses – they just walked up from the rear to sit in an adjacent seat, and groped her. "And they were probably vegetarians, whose religion didn't allow them to drink or smoke. Go figure," she said.

Margrit was returning to Belgium tomorrow to start work again on Monday. She surprised Axel during the strudel and coffee by mentioning that she had a four-year-old daughter back home, currently being looked after by her grandmother. Axel liked her even more; she was just as independent as he was. Axel briefly considered asking for her email, but dropped it. This was going to be a catch-and-release experience. He was going to enjoy a nice moment for what it was, and not make himself miserable by retroactively considering what might have been. He asked what present she brought back for her daughter from India.

"None," she said.

"None?"

"Nothing. My daughter needs to learn that nothing is handed to you in life. If she wants nice things, she is going to have to earn the money herself in order to buy them."

"Interesting. I spoil my nephew and niece rotten by always bringing back souvenirs from my travels, no matter how much space the stuff takes up in my suitcase. But then again, I am not responsible for raising them."

Margrit nodded. "So, what are you bringing back from this Berlin trip for your niece and nephew?"

The question stopped Axel in his tracks. "Wow, until you asked, I didn't think of bringing them anything." He held up his phone with the boxing photos. "This trip was for me."

"You'll find new vices, I'm sure."

Axel and Margrit split the check, and he walked her to the entrance of her hotel. They said their goodbyes just outside the lobby, Axel not expecting a kiss and Margrit not offering one. He gently squeezed her shoulder wishing her a safe trip home, turned around, and didn't look back. The meal was one of Axel's most pleasant dates in memory, even if it wasn't really a date. He had taken about ten steps when he heard other footsteps right behind. He turned around to see Margrit. Before he could say anything, she threw her arms around his neck and gave him a long kiss. They disentangled after a few seconds. Then she smiled, and turned around to go into her hotel. It was her turn not to look back.

CHAPTER TWENTY-NINE

Axel woke up before dawn to catch a six a.m. flight back home. He was going to miss this city. The sun was coming up as the plane left the runway, and the receding view from his window made him smile. He flew back in a small world. Axel knew that he could always close his eyes and teleport back here in an instant, and happily relive yesterday over and over again for many years.

Axel at his apartment copied his photos from his phone onto his laptop, and emailed them to Max and his chessboxing friends. He thought about sending them to Ted and Vyacheslav too, but something held him back. Axel had always been that way: keep information in reserve, so that he would have something to say should the banter ever run dry.

He went to Ted's gym the next day. Ted raised his eyebrows at the purplish black eye, and asked how he liked his trip. Axel replied that he had a blast. Ted told him that the chessboxing class was still on a week from Friday. Six more interested people had passed the pre-requisites, for a total of twelve; a few more might join the next couple of days. Also, someone might come from the local newspaper to write a feature article.

"Has anyone in Gunther B's weight class had joined yet?" Axel asked. He really did not want to be the only one sparring with him.

"Not yet," Ted replied, and he saw the alarm in Axel's eyes. "Cheer up, I'm going to teach you a few new tricks. Do nothing but practice hooks and uppercuts on the resistance elastic bands for today."

Axel had worked with the bands for a round or two in the past, but never for twelve rounds straight – it left him in a sopping, sweaty mess.

"Good," Ted said. Now work with Jason for six more rounds on the pads. He is going to hold the pads much higher and wider than you're used to."

Axel was forced to step in and use all the torque the height in his frame could provide, and was dog-tired after the workout. Ted smirked at seeing Axel stumble to the locker, and said for the next two weeks to increase the rounds on the elastic bands to fifteen, or add three rounds of moving a fifty-pound weight over and around his head like a halo.

He'd had the same homework from Garen for over three months, so that week Axel buckled down and finally finished it, mailing back the answers to Garen with his apologies for the tardiness, asking for more problems. They arrived two days later with a note saying it was OK; life often got in the way, and to finish these when he could.

When Monday rolled around, he actually looked forward to returning to his new job in the company. The vice-president was right: the time away cooling off was good for him. It made Axel appreciate what he truly had.

Axel drove to the new building, far away from the obnoxious female co-workers. The requirements of the new position were easy to pick up. He got along with his new boss and cubicle colleagues so well that he was amazed how he had put up with all that bullshit the last couple of years, thankful he had only blown his stack twice.

He showed up at the gym on Friday night for the inaugural chessboxing class. Thirteen people, including Axel and John, were there. Most of the people there looked like college students. Ted must have put up a flyer at some local university. And there was B, somehow not looking as scary after his visit to Berlin. Ted put everyone through a group workout for half an hour, and Axel gave a mini-lecture on chess tactics for fifteen minutes. Then the chessboxers broke up into two groups: one for speed chess, and the other for boxing. Axel stayed at the chess tables for most of the rest of the class.

After an hour, Axel obtained a fair gauge of the chessboxing strength of the class. John and most of the college students played the best speed chess, but were new to boxing and would be continuing to do drills in the ring for at least a month. The best boxers tended to play the slowest chess; they were trying to leverage the care and dedication they put into their boxing into chess, yet didn't know the game well enough to keep up on the clock.

After an hour of offering advice during the blitz games at the chess tables, Axel heard the call from Ted to get in the ring and spar a few rounds with B. Three rounds, nothing heavy. Axel had learned that for some countries, "heavy" had the same variability as "medium" for how people liked their steaks cooked, and knew that "heavy" for B meant pulling back only after an opponent had been dropped to the ground.

The bell rang. Axel and B met in the middle and touched gloves. Axel jumped back immediately out of range afterwards; he had learned his lesson from last time. B liked to get ahead on points early in a bout and then hold them over his opponent for the rest of the bout.

Axel kept to an asynchronous rhythm during the round, following a randomized teletype rhyme "Duck, duck, goose, goose, duck, duck, goose, duck, goose...", and hoping that it would prevent B from setting, planting, and throwing a punch. The strategy worked beautifully the first round. He found that the irregular time rhythms created awkward angles for B, and openings in which Axel was able to land lots of punches.

During the break, Ted went over to B's corner and said something to him. During the next round B started throwing different-as-telegraphed punches in mid-air near Axel that threw off his rhythm, and allowed B to connect with lots of combinations. Axel resumed his usual conservative stance and approach, but B had more ballast, and the momentum was his. When the bell rang the amount of punches landed between the two rounds was even.

Ted came over to Axel during the next break, and said: "Not a bad strategy the first round, and it's been tried before. However, once the surprise value is gone, those openings you enjoyed tend to disappear. Gunther in the second round did the micro equivalent of squaring off the ring by limiting your ring vision, and with your off-balance approach he got the drop on you more often. I know he is a big, fast, and strong guy, but everyone is vulnerable at the sides and the corners. Practice those hooks and uppercuts you've been doing on the elastic bands, and on the extended pad targets you've been doing with Jason. They'll make him back off, believe me."

The bell rang for the third round. Axel saw B approach, and instead of previously jostling his rhythm for an opening, imagined himself skeet shooting. B was four feet away and closing. Axel saw himself back at the elastic band station and launched a right hook that nailed his opponent's ear after his next step, stunning him in mid-step. Axel quickly closed the distance and fired off a left uppercut that managed to clip B's other ear.

He tempered his further hooks and uppercuts with mid-range jabs and rights and by staying as close as possible to B, not allowing him to use his leverage. When B shoved him away, Axel succeeded in snapping off a quick hook to dissuade him from following up with a power combination. It wasn't a perfect round, as B did have some excellent feints and fast straight rights that slammed into Axel's torso where he was not looking, but it was a satisfying one. Axel would never be afraid to step in the ring with B again.

"Good practice, Axel. Same time next week?" B asked.

"Same time next week," Axel replied. They slammed both their gloves together in the ring with gusto.

Axel looked for new ideas on chessboxing on YouTube. Not many of them could be found. The boxing in the bouts was professional level, yet the chess never rose above that of a local amateur weekend tournament. The Mexican boxing maxim "Kill the body, kill the head," seemed to be the overarching strategy over chess finesse, so Axel continued his boxing training in earnest, while working on chess in his spare time.

He grew to despise the elastic resistance bands during his workouts, but became grateful for what they did for his hand speed after the soreness had faded away. Just like running with the weights on his ankles until two weeks before a fight, and then without, his feet feeling like they suddenly had wings. He also used a short elastic band to tie around his ankles when practicing in front of the wall mirror, which straightened out imbalances in his stance when he moved in wide arcs.

He played John in blitz chess two more nights at the gym the following week before the next chessboxing class. Axel by now had ascertained his rating to be about 1700, which was slightly above average for all tournament players in the United States; in the chessboxing class, he was in the top four.

John had a good positional ground game, but became confused when Axel unbalanced the dynamics of the struggle. Axel would introduce sacrifices, or make "ugly" moves which screwed up his pawn structure yet gave him open lines and plenty of piece activity as compensation. John wanted the positions to be enveloped in structural logic, to always be safe and steady – he soon learned that a determined opponent could muddy the waters at will.

With only a few minutes to finish the games, John frequently lost on time trying to solve the long series of improvised problems posed for him at the board.

"Ted will teach you to always box moving forward, and I'm saying to you right now apply that approach in the chess part too," Axel told John. "If you want to win."

"But if I give away a pawn in the opening, that will be one less pawn to use in the endgame," John complained.

"The great Siegbert Tarrasch once said: 'Before the endgame, the gods have placed the middlegame.' Sometimes pawns just get in the way, and holding on to extra pawns worsens the position. That was true when the time controls were slow, and it's even truer now, especially between rounds where you are getting smacked in the head. Did you ever hear of kung-fu chess?"

"No."

"It's a computer online game, and one of the goofiest variants of chess. While the computer keeps time for the game, you can move your pieces without any regard to waiting for your opponent's turns. The first one to legally capture the opposing King wins. Weirdly, checks don't exist. Neither are pieces fixed to squares because of threats. Get your ahead around that when you finally start sparring, and try to apply that in your chess game during the bout."

John closed his eyes, furrowed his brow, and shook his head violently trying to make sense of what Axel had just said. "You are fucking up my head, Master Po," John said, opening his eyes.

Axel gave him a Cheshire Cat smile. "All in good time, grasshopper. All in good time."

CHAPTER THIRTY

At the next chessboxing class, Axel found that two more people had joined. "I'm going to cap the class at twenty," Ted told him when he arrived. "How long do you want this class to go?"

"I really haven't thought that far ahead. Maybe until the summer, if people keep showing up."

Ted asked before the group workout began how many people wanted to do a chessboxing bout. Ten hands shot up. Therefore, it was decided that the first hour would be devoted to the workout and drills, and the remaining hour would be for the participants who wanted to do the chessboxing bouts. Those who weren't doing the bouts could study problems with the chess tactics books, or do more boxing drills with each other.

Five clocks were soon started for the chessboxing bouts, synchronized with the gym round clocks. The bouts were set for four rounds chess and three rounds sparring/boxing drills – each player received six minutes, with no increment. John was paired against one of the college kids; four other college kids were paired against each other; two experienced middleweights were squared off; and B was matched with one of the cruiserweights with strict instructions to go light on the sparring.

The first round ended with most of the chess games roughly equal. For the boxing round, four of the matches took place in corners of the ring while one took place in an empty space just outside the ring. John and the college kids did three-punch drills, the middleweights went full at it, and B reluctantly pulled most of his punches. The boxing round ended with one of the middleweights drawing blood from the other. In the third round, John to Axel's satisfaction sacrificed a piece for an initiative, and quickly had his opponent on his heels. The other games were still in the maneuvering phase.

In the fourth round, the first decisive result occurred when the bloodied middleweight was bloodied again and threw in the towel. In the fifth round, two of the college kids tried to agree to a "grandmaster draw" (the kind of draw that reflects more on the lack of energy of the players than on the actual position), but Axel stepped in and insisted that they play on. John had a fierce attack, and definite checkmating possibilities.

In the sixth round, the two other college students were just going through the motions in the ring, causing a pissed-off Ted to halt their match and tell them not to come back next week if they weren't prepared to bleed; B and the cruiserweight, to their credit, were working up a sweat.

In the final chess round John finished off his game with panache, hunting his opponent's King with a long series of checks and finally checkmating him in the center of the board. The other two college students wanted to declare a draw between themselves again and Axel relented, since more than thirty moves had been played. The game between B and the cruiserweight ended in a time scramble, which B won after his opponent walked into a checkmate with seconds remaining on his clock.

The class still had half an hour left. While Axel, the cruiserweight, and B bashed each other in the ring, the others (except the two college kids Ted had yelled at) played another chessboxing bout without referees, and thoroughly enjoyed it. Before they left for the night, Ted asked if any of them would object to being filmed, and having videos of their bouts posted to YouTube. None minded. Ted said to Axel as he was leaving that twenty people would probably be showing up each Friday by the end of the month, and that he would order more chess equipment. The strange chessboxing seed Ted and Axel had planted was beginning to bloom.

Vyacheslav called Axel on Sunday night. ESPN was going to air a one-hour program on the December 30 event that Wednesday, at eleven p.m. He had seen an early cut at the studio, and Axel had a lot of screen time. When asked, Vy said he was doing fine. He was trying to put together another chessboxing event that summer in New York, with Russia sending a delegation. Axel could definitely be part of the card if he wanted to – he would send news soon.

Axel told Ted and his family about the ESPN program. His mother had no interest in seeing her son get hit, but his sister was interested. She invited Axel over to her house to watch the show with her family.

His boxing really did not look half bad, even though it looked that he was improvising in half the rounds – he missed having a trainer in the corner to set him straight. His brother-in-law looked at Axel curiously when the end credits rolled, and said to him: "I just don't have a clue what to get you for Christmas, man." His niece cringed at the boxing rounds, while his nephew thought it was one of the neatest things he had ever seen.

Axel's sister asked him to stay after the rest of her family had gone to bed; she wanted to talk to him. She said: "You have way too much free time on your hands, Axel. When was the last time you went out on a date?"

Axel thought of his last night in Berlin, and decided that it didn't really count as a date. "A long time. Why do you ask?"

His sister bit her lip, and thought about she wanted to say for about a minute, finally asking: "Would you be interested if I set you up with someone I know?"

"C'mon, sis. What woman in her right mind would want to go out with me?"

"More out there than you think. So many guys are bland ice-cream flavors like vanilla, chocolate, or strawberry. Your flavor is somewhere between Rocky Mountain Road, Pineapple, and Mint Chocolate Chip. Lots of women would be interested."

"So they all say. I'm interesting for a couple of dates, and maybe a third, but beyond that my calls are rarely returned, and then I get the inevitable 'I'm not ready for a relationship right now.' Thanks, but no thanks."

"OK, OK. But Axel… please know that I love you and always will, but… sooner or later you are going to be too old to do this, and I'm afraid you're going to end up alone."

Axel was suddenly furious, but he kept his temper under the lid and his voice even.

"News flash, little sister. I might be alone, but I'm far from old, and don't need a woman to make me happy. The very worst roommates I've had in my life, without exception, were females. They didn't know how to share common space, constantly accessorizing it without any concern to my private boundaries, and slammed my living habits. They are even worse at work, starting arguments that I was not allowed to respond to without being reported to management. Their company is vastly overrated. I need it like a fish needs a fucking bicycle."

His sister was too stunned to reply. Axel hissed: "What, no snappy comeback? I didn't think so. Toodles." He walked out and slammed the door.

His sister called the next day, and they tentatively patched things up.

Ted emailed him on Thursday that he had thirty people now interested in the chessboxing class (pending their attendance at a sparring class and going through the chess problems), and that a local television station was going to do a piece on them soon, but this did not cheer up Axel. *Chess and boxing were NOT a waste of time*, he kept saying to himself, no matter what his sister implied.

Axel started each morning colossally pissed off for the next month. In general, whenever he felt good about himself, he was able to recall something that made him angrier than ever. He continued to remember so many dismissive jerks that never went away, his father only being one of them. He resolved to re-sublimate them all in front of a chessboard and in a boxing ring – they only truly remained in the background when he had a chance to combine the two together.

CHAPTER THIRTY-ONE

In the next few chessboxing classes, twenty people started showing up. Despite the extra sets and clocks Ted had bought, a new problem arose: not enough space for the tables. A temporary solution was found where the practice chess games were played on the ground, and the boxing took place in blocks of spaces around the ring. Ted quickly found extra foldable tables to deal with the overflow – the boxing could be done in the parking lot if necessary.

Axel joined the others in the physical workout, then concentrated on the chess for the rest of the class. He went through his prepared lessons. He went over basic tactical themes, how to do basic checkmates against the bare King with seconds left on the clock, and how to prepare opening repertoires that were easy to put together and remember. When refereeing, he confined his interventions to pointing out illegal moves and deciding if positions were equal enough to be declared drawn.

The pressure was off Axel to spar with B every week; three of the new arrivals were experienced heavyweights who could give B a challenge in the ring, and were closer to his chess ability. However, Ted did not let him off the hook entirely. If the class was over, and if an odd number of cruiserweight and heavyweight boxers wanted to do more sparring, he was shanghaied into making the number even.

John and the college students who played the best chess had graduated from drills, and moved on to actual sparring. They had a while to go before they could do amateur fights, but Axel knew it was only a matter of time before his perfect chessboxing record would be history. He was at peace with that, and happy at what he and Ted had started.

In the first week of April, a local television news crew arrived and filmed the class, along with interviews of Ted, Axel, and a few of the chessboxers. The reporter said that the piece would air next Tuesday.

Ted was over the moon, because the story would net his gym several new members, and pretty much everyone in the class was happy to be on local TV will all the incipient bragging rights.

Axel though was ambivalent. He had long hated being the center of attention. He still hadn't figured out which elements mattered the most to him from chessboxing: the training, the competition, the anger-suppression, or the fame.

After the news story aired, Ted had sixty people clamoring to join the chessboxing class. He wanted to expand, and asked Axel for advice in how to proceed.

"We can definitely start charging money for this, but I don't have the space to handle more than twenty people for one night," he said to Axel in his office. "How much longer do you want to run the Friday class?"

"I could do it until the summer," Axel replied. "But I don't want to be doing classes more than one night a week. Between my job and my own training and this class, I want some time off to recharge."

"If I started paying you, Axel, would that change your mind? The salary would not be meager from all the new members who joined the gym."

Axel thought for a minute before he answered. "All this is happening pretty fast. My reasons for doing chessboxing, I haven't fully figured them out yet, and I'd like to slow down a little and get my bearings." He stopped, and gave Ted an embarrassed smile. "Sorry, not making much sense. I get it, you want to strike while the iron is hot."

"You're making a lot of sense. More than you think you are making."

"Thanks... OK. This current class, how about we cap it at twenty and run it until June? I like Friday nights. It's a fun way to end my work week. Maybe we can end the class with some sort of exhibition fight night before the college kids leave in the summer."

"Yeah, we could do that."

"And the others who want to join, what nights did you have in mind?"

It was Ted's turn to think for a while before replying. "Oh, that's a good question. My three-month program is starting up in a few weeks, and that always takes place on Tuesdays, Thursdays, and Saturdays. The extra chessboxing classes would have to be on Monday or Wednesday nights."

"If you can find trainers for the boxing part those nights, I might be able to find some local chessplayers who can help out with the speed chess part. I'd have to ask around first before I can promise anything."

"The boxing trainers will be no problem. But can you do the chess part on the other nights for the first few weeks – I'll pay you, as I'm going to be paying you for the Friday class – while you're training the chess teachers? I want to do this right."

Axel nodded. "As do I. Are you going to start off with one extra night, or two?"

"Fuck it, we're doing three nights a week. Just this afternoon I walked into my office to ten more phone messages from people wanting to chessbox. I love having these problems."

Axel and Ted agreed on a salary, and new sign-up sheets went up for chessboxing classes on Monday and Wednesday, to start within a week. They agreed on a structure of the Monday nights for beginners, Wednesday nights for intermediates, and Friday nights for the advanced chessboxers. Tuition would be charged for newcomers in the Monday and Wednesday night classes, while the existing participants in the Friday classes were grandfathered in as free. Axel tailored his chess problem pre-requisites for the different levels accordingly.

Axel only had one candidate in mind for the job of chess trainer. He found him the following evening where the snow was melting, and green shoots had begun to stick up through the ground.

"Hey, Willie, how have you been?"

"Doing OK, Axel." Willie had brushed off armfuls of slush from a table in the park, and set up his chess set and clock. Two other hardy people had done the same. "Sorry I missed you in New York. I went on a bender that started just after Thanksgiving, and it didn't end until a few weeks ago. How did you do?"

"I won, but not because of the boxing. I fought well enough in the ring to stretch out the chess game, where I won in the ninth round."

"Awesome."

"I'm here because of the chessboxing, actually. I started a chessboxing class with the owner of a local gym, and it's proved to be wildly popular. The one class a night has turned into three, and I cannot do all the classes. Would you be interested in coaching chessboxers in blitz chess two nights a week? You'd get paid."

"How much?"

Axel told him the rate he was getting for Friday night, and said he should be able to get the same for him on Monday and Wednesday. "It would be four hours a week, at night, so it shouldn't clash with your gig here. You'd be teaching them basic tactics, time management, and whatever else you think is appropriate for blitz chess. Before you can start you need to meet Ted, the owner, as he is the one who'd be paying you. What do you say?"

"I'm interested. Is Ted in his office right now?"

Axel called Ted, and told him about Willie. Ted said he would be happy to talk with him if they could make it there by eight p.m. After hanging up, Axel looked at his watch. It was seven thirty p.m. He turned to Willie and asked: "Ready for your interview?"

A short taxi ride later, Axel introduced Willie to Ted. They spent fifteen minutes talking behind closed doors. Ted came out afterwards first with a nod to Axel, followed by Willie with a grin on his face.

Ted said: "If your schedule allows, Axel, can you do the first couple of Mondays and Wednesdays with Willie? Willie will get paid no matter what."

"Sure, take it out of my salary if you need to. Thanks, Ted, I appreciate this. Willie helped me with clock management for my New York chessboxing bout."

"Yes, he did mention that. Do you mind if I borrow Willie for another half hour or so? I want to give him a tour of the gym, and introduce him to the trainers he is going to be working with."

After Willie's orientation was over, he and Axel took a taxi ride back to the park.

"I hope this works out, Willie."

"Me too, man. Ted seems really cool."

"He is. We're going to be doing the first two Mondays and Wednesdays in tandem, and then you're solo. Gear your advice for beginners on Mondays and intermediate players on Wednesdays."

"Understood. When's your next chessboxing bout?"

"No idea. I want to get back to regular training the next few months, and then seriously ramp it up for the summer. Maybe sometime in the fall."

The extra chessboxing classes started the following week. Ted made the pre-requisites different than those on Friday. The beginners had to solve ten basic checkmate-in-one problems and attend a one-hour introductory boxing class. The intermediate players had to score seventy-five percent or better on problems involving harder checkmates in two or three moves, and pass an individual evaluation session from the trainers. Both classes were packed, and all of the participants had a lot of fun, but Willie never showed up.

Axel was disappointed, and so was Ted. Axel went to the park on Thursday, asking the other chess hustlers there if Willie had been there the past week.

One of them said: "Sorry, Axel, Willie got arrested for loitering. He couldn't pay the fine, so he's been sitting in jail."

"Do you know which jail?"

After receiving a vague answer, Axel found the jail a few hours later at the local police station. The desk sergeant confirmed he was there, and Axel offered to pay his fine. One hundred dollars later Willie emerged in the lobby. He started to say something, but Axel cut him short.

"Show up next Monday, or don't bother showing up at all."

Willie opened and closed his mouth without a sound. Axel walked away.

He called Ted, and told him what happened. He agreed to give Willie one more chance, but asked Axel to stay on for three Mondays and Wednesdays instead of two, and to look for a backup. Axel agreed.

On Friday Axel asked John if he was interested in being a chess trainer for the chessboxing classes on the other nights. John said he wasn't sure. Axel said that was all right, and to think about it over the next few weeks. In truth, he could have trained the chessboxers for all three nights. But he did not need the money, and wanted the time for his individual workouts, be they in chess or boxing.

Next Monday Axel arrived at the gym, and found to his relief that Willie was already there. One of the trainers said that he had shown up an hour early. Axel nodded to Willie when he arrived, and sat back while he gave advice and refereed over the chess part of the chessboxing matches. The matches in the beginner class had light boxing drills in place of sparring, and many illegal moves in the games that had to be flagged and penalized with time off from the clocks. Willie did an excellent job performing these duties, and Axel told him so after the class had ended.

"Good work, Willie. Remember to gear up the level of instruction for Wednesday."

"OK, Axel. Thanks again for getting me out."

"You can thank me by doing what you're doing without any more drama. I'll be around within shouting distance the next two weeks if you need help, but I think you'll be fine."

The chessboxing bouts in the Wednesday intermediate class had a different set of issues. The boxing part of the matches was designed to be more intense, which a lot did not understand viscerally – many first-time participants discovered the shock of getting hit in the ring, and finding out that it actually hurt. Some took it personally, and overtly carried over their fights over to the chessboard. It turned out that Willie had the perfect background for defusing the conflicts, as he had witnessed countless arguments in the park between those who played for money. "Work it out in the ring, not here!" he barked, and they all meekly obeyed.

The following Monday and Wednesday nights Axel simply told Willie that he was going to be working out in the gym, and to grab him if he needed him. Axel completed his workout without interruption, and he was confident that Ted's staffing needs in regards to chess had been met. John had come back with a reply after the first week saying that he could be a chess trainer as needed; Axel told him to talk to Ted.

Ted said after the Friday class that Willie was going to work out fine. He was pleased to have John onboard too. "I introduced John to Willie on Wednesday afternoon, and they seemed to get along well. I know the nights are going to become warmer soon. Willie has my number, and if he'd rather hustle in the park on a certain night, I know who to call. Thanks for your help in setting up these classes. They've done wonders for my membership numbers."

"You're welcome. I can still do Friday nights, right?"

"Of course. John can fill in if you can't." Ted added: "So when's your next chessboxing bout?"

CHAPTER THIRTY-TWO

Vyacheslav called Axel in late April; another chessboxing bout was going to take place at the Hofstra Arena in Long Island on June 30. A group of chessboxers from Moscow was coming – the competition in both the chess and the boxing would be much stiffer. Was Axel in? As before, the proceeds would go to charity.

"Can I sleep on it, Vy? I never like making snap decisions over the phone."

"Sure. You'd be close to the main event. Not many people in this country have your skillset in chess and boxing."

"Yes, but so do many in Russia, and I don't want to make a fool of myself."

"That won't happen at all, Axel. Have some faith, man."

"Faith in chessboxing is more swagger than self-confidence, Vy, and I've never had much swagger."

"Bullshit. Faith in this sport comes from skill and discipline, and you have that in spades. Give me an answer by the end of the month. I'll be able to swing your travel and hotel expenses."

"OK, I'll talk to you soon. Good night."

"Good night."

Axel realized that he would be without his chess to fall back upon. The Russian chessplayers he had faced in tournaments were very tough opponents, and their boxers he had seen on TV looked formidable. If the last chessboxing match was like climbing the hill of a local park, this one was going be like climbing K2.

He told Ted and Garen of his invitation. Ted told him he was developing one of the craziest corkscrew boxing careers he had ever seen, and said that for a little money he could obtain some sparring partners to get him ready for the fight. Garen did a double-take, and asked what chessboxing was. When Axel told him the rules, he offered to line Axel up with some titled players (international masters and grandmasters) as speed chess partners for a fee.

Axel looked up his portfolio online. Upon finding that he was having a very good year, he redeemed shares from his best performing stocks and deposited the proceeds in his bank account. What else was money for, if not to fund quixotic windmill tilting? The money in place a few days later, he called back Vyacheslav, and heard himself saying he'd do it.

Vy said: "Great! I am going to pair you with a Russian – you'll probably get a FIDE master." FIDE masters varied in strength from a weak expert to a weak grandmaster. From Russia, it was going to fall into the extremity of a weak grandmaster.

"When will I know who my opponent is?"

"I'll be able to tell you in June. That's when the Russians have to send me their roster. And relax, Axel, you'll be facing a fellow cruiserweight who's an amateur, not a pro. The Russians are sending dossiers on all their chessboxers to me next month with their amateur records. All the information I receive on your opponent I'll pass onto you."

"I don't know, Vy, it's going to be hard for me to get Survivor songs out of my head."

Vyacheslav laughed. "Make *Eye of The Tiger* your earworm song, and you'll be fine."

Axel started his training in earnest, while staying on to advise at Friday's chessboxing class. He was glad the chessboxing classes were available, but they were not going to get Axel to the level he needed to be. After settling the payment details, Ted said that his sparring partners would be available in two weeks. B was delighted about Axel's new bout, and promised to help him out whenever he could.

As for chess, blitz games with Willie or the college kids in the chessboxing class were not going to be good enough. A few extra seconds on the clock could not salvage a lost position against a Russian master. He needed to get his head kicked in repeatedly over the chessboard from very strong players in order to get used to his future adversary. Upon agreeing to a price, Garen promised to have such a group ready for Axel as early as next week.

Axel showed up at Garen's apartment for an informal blitz tournament the following weekend, and found two grandmasters, three international masters, and five strong local masters. The local masters Axel had known and competed against for decades, while the international masters and grandmasters were friends of Garen's who had stopped playing in tournaments to work regular jobs. These titled players were getting an appearance fee under the table.

It was humbling for Axel to find that he was the lowest rated player in the event. He hadn't been the lowest rated player in a chess event for as long as he could remember. He started with a goal to finish with a fifty percent score, but lost his first five games in a row. He then hoped that would not finish in last place. Alas, even this was denied to him, and he finished the tournament at the bottom with three draws and seven losses. Losing in chess always sucked for Axel, and it tasted really vile when he had to swallow large doses of it in a single sitting.

This was what he had wanted from Garen though, and he thanked him and all the other players for the necessary lessons while they hung out after the tournament.

"I've heard rumors that you can retire soon, Axel," one of the grandmasters told him. "You were smart to quit chess early, and put in enough time in the rat race so that you can get out before your hair turns white. Me, I have so little in Social Security it's not funny. I've had my fun, but now I'm destined to work in a damn office until I keel over."

"Me too," another grandmaster said. "There's so little money in chess once you get married. The kids come, and then the wife wants a house for them, and before you know it, you're waking up and going to sleep on a treadmill. I like what you're doing with your chess talent – and you do have talent, Axel, we just happen to be extra harsh teachers – you're taking your ability, and leveraging it with another discipline that few people can do as well together."

"If there's any country that can produce such people, it's Russia," Axel replied. "In the United States, I am in the top one percentile of all chess players – there, I'm lucky if I can be a candidate master."

All the players in the room nodded in agreement. Axel continued: "Russians are pretty fierce boxers too. I'm really apprehensive."

Garen said: "I've been researching Russian chessboxers out of curiosity. I've looked at several from the Moscow club who are sending the fighters, and a lot of them are not very good chess players. Most of them would not have even scored a single draw today. Don't underrate yourself on the chess part; you can do damage."

"Yeah, Axel, get out all the kinks you can beforehand," one of the masters said. "If your ego can take it, get hammered here over the chessboard early and often. I think you'll find to your pleasant surprise that your Russian opponent will be hitting with a foam hammer."

Garen took a straw poll, and asked if there was any interest in holding another tournament at his apartment. Enough people agreed for another competition three weeks later. As Axel was leaving, he paid Garen for the next event and asked if he should do any special preparation other than the homework assignments he was already doing.

"Not really. I expected you to get killed today, and you're probably going to get killed again three weeks from now. There's no Socratic teaching value to these tournaments, Axel, they are more about immersion. Just jump into the water, and try to swim. Hopefully, you'll come out good enough for your fight."

"Any specific suggestions when I feel like I'm drowning?"

Garen smiled. "As best you can, forget the previous game where you bombed, and concentrate on the new game as if you were back at the start of the tournament. But you handle adversity pretty well – even during your last loss you played out the game to the bitter end. I just don't have a clue to tell you how to do that when your face is getting smashed in, too."

CHAPTER THIRTY-THREE

During the next Friday chessboxing class Ted asked him if he was available on late Saturday afternoon, and to bring cash.

"I'm not going to get mugged, am I?" Axel asked, half in jest.

Ted cackled evilly. "Be prepared for two hours of hard exercise, and feeling like ground beef afterwards. I'm assembling three guys for you; think of them as klieg lights on your boxing style. Of the three, we'll choose which one kicked your ass the worst, and you can work with him the next couple of months. OK?"

"Not really, but I'll show up."

"Half the battle, friend. But in this case, I'm afraid that is only going to be good enough for twenty five-percent at best."

Ted called Axel at home later that night. He told him the time to arrive on Saturday, and how much cash to bring. On Saturday afternoon, Axel arrived at the gym just as it was closing and gave the money to Ted, not feeling that scared. The shredding he had received from the players at Garen's tournament still stung, and acted as an inner bubble. He fatalistically believed that he could always retreat to that pain should the pain in the ring become too much. But deep down he knew that he was going down the garden path again, with lots and lots of thorns.

The gym closed, and Axel after finishing his warmup found himself alone at the side of the ring with Ted and three guys. One of them was B, who nodded a greeting. The other two were Axel's height, and Ted introduced them to Axel as Tim and Mike. Tim looked like a bodybuilder, with bulging biceps and impressively wide quads, but still appeared to be a cruiserweight like Axel. Mike was a heavyweight like B, with the build of a sumo wrestler.

Ted said to Axel: "I gave these guys your money already. I told them you were going up against a boxer from Russia in late June, and that you needed toughening up. I also told them the one who beats you up the worst today gets the privilege of beating you up more for the next two months while getting paid for it." Everyone in the gym laughed. "You're going to do nine rounds in a stretch, alternating between Gunther, Tim, and Mike each round for a total of three rounds against each of them. I'll give you a fifteen-minute break, and then you're going to do it again. Are we clear?"

"Like stained glass."

"Good. Who do you want to fight first? You pick the order."

Axel asked for a pen and a piece of paper. He wrote down a number, turning the number face down. Then he asked: "Guys, pick a number between one and a hundred."

The three looked at each other, and shrugged. B picked twenty-four, Tim picked forty-three, and Mike picked seventy-five. Axel turned over the page, where he had written ninety-nine. "OK. Mike, Tim, and Gunther, in that order. God help me, let's go."

Axel and Mike gloved up, put their mouth guards in and headgear on, and waited fifteen seconds for the bell to start. The booming sound of the canvas below Mike's bouncing feet did not bode well. The bell rang, and Axel realized within the first minute that Mike's favorite punches were body shots – his forearms rapidly became sore keeping his ribcage safe from all the blocking. He briefly tried going toe to toe against Mike, but his opponent had such phenomenal lower body strength that one pulse from his hips pushed him back several inches. Axel knew then and there that he was going to have to stick and move for all of his rounds against Mike – he would be mauled in clinches. Axel was able to emerge from the round largely unscathed, save for a shot in the final seconds that landed and stung on his left cheek.

One minute of rest, and then Tim started against Axel. Tim's strategy Axel divined within seconds: smash mouth. Axel received vicious jabs straight on his mouth guard and on the bridge of his nose, followed by a cross that would have wrenched his eyeball from his socket had he not jerked back in time. Instead the cross glanced on his eyebrow, causing a small cut. Tim re-combined the punches again and again with frightening speed. Ted called out from the corner "Move your head!" and Axel did not need to be asked twice. He spent the rest of the round bobbing his head from side to side and staying within close range to Tim, minimizing as much as possible shots to the head. He got off one good right that landed flush into Tim's jaw when the bell rang. Some sort of body attack was going to have to be used in later rounds to make Tim back off – this opponent was quick, and not the least bit shy in wanting to rearrange Axel's face.

One minute of rest, and then three minutes with B. His opponent came out of the ring unabashedly swinging haymakers. Axel slipped most of them and thought he was going to be on the ropes for the whole round, when suddenly B stopped and switched to a conservative stick and move strategy while staying in the middle of the ring. Two minutes later, B switched gears and went back to haymaker mode. *Friggin chessboxers*, Axel thought, *they always want to mess with my head*. The round ended with an even amount of punches landed by both sides.

One minute of rest, and Axel was up against Mike again. Axel successfully moved around the ring faster than Mike could square it off for the first minute and a half, until he stayed one split second too long in the same place and found himself funneled into a corner. Thirty seconds of body shots made Axel realize he would not last much longer in this place. He forced himself free back into the open ring at the price of a stiff jab and hook to the head. "Remember your interval training, Axel!" he heard Ted say. While he couldn't physically push Mike back, he did manage to use enough different tempos in his step to keep his adversary guessing and exploit openings to keep the round competitive. Still, in pounds per square inch of the landed punches, Mike came out the clear winner of the round.

Sixty seconds later, Axel was facing Tim. *I have to do something different this round*, Axel said to himself, as they met in the middle of the ring. He aimed for the gut. Despite receiving painful shots to the head, he did have the satisfaction of landing some crunching blows to Tim's mid-section. He even forced his opponent to clinch in the corner after a barrage of body shots. But there was little time for gloating. After they broke from the clinch, Tim fired off a combination that made Axel drop a knee to the canvas – he had seen none of the punches coming. "Stay with him and keep inside his arms, Axel," Ted said from outside the ring. Axel followed the instructions as best he could for the final minute, yet Tim made Axel see blood again with a few more lightning fast combinations to his face before the bell rang.

The blood Axel was seeing was the cut above his eyebrow, which was becoming a big cut. Ted extended the round break while he tended to the cut and bandaged it. "It's not going to get any easier, is it Ted?" Axel asked. Ted shook his head without the hint of a smile.

The round started against B. Axel by now actually looked forward to the rounds with him. The devil he knew went back to haymakers, hoping to build upon the dropped knee with Tim. Axel refused to oblige, and like a turtle retracted his neck almost completely inside his shell. He boxed conservatively, limiting his openings and punching only when he saw a clear shot. It wasn't an exciting boxing round, but it was technically precise, and helped Axel regain his bearings.

A sixty second break, and Axel was in the ring against Mike. They met in the middle, and then Axel with all his strength launched a jab and right walking in to push back Mike an inch, which totally surprised his opponent. *Just wanted to do it once*, he silently said to Mike, *to see if you actually can go backwards*. Axel went back to circling sideways, flicking off jabs and leaning in with harder punches when the distance between them became too close. Axel tried to push back Mike once more, suddenly charging in after a jab, and managed to stop his forward movement, but nothing more. Axel didn't do it again, but realized that it was worth doing again in a later round.

The bell rang, and sixty seconds later Axel was up against Tim, who had proved to be too fast for headhunting. Concentrating on the mid-section did work, but came at a high price. He decided upon a middle course with head-body-head approaches. The first minute Axel suffered. He leaned in to deliver a hook to the ribs but didn't cover his head fully, which Tim exploited with a sudden pivot and a straight right into his eye that was almost certainly going to give him a shiner. But in the second minute Axel launched a jab to the mid-section backed up with a massive right hook thrown in the air that Tim ran into when he evaded it, forcing another clinch. Axel was expecting an aggressive charge afterwards, but was relieved to find that he had finally made his opponent hesitate a little. Tim limited himself to sticking and moving while he shook off that hook to the head. The round ended.

Sixty seconds later, Axel faced B in the ring. *What are you going to throw at me now, old friend...* Axel soon found out that it was everything but the kitchen sink. B was relentless, chasing Axel all over the ring and driving him into the corners for most of the round. Phone booth boxing time again. Axel countered with some well-placed jabs, and moved his head as best he could in the cramped quarters. He was content to sit there in the corner for most of the round letting B expend most of the energy. It wasn't comfortable, but Axel was going to be fighting nine more rounds to B's three, and needed to conserve energy. The bell rang, and finally Axel could breathe again for more than a minute.

Ted asked Axel how he was doing during the fifteen-minute break.

"You know that joke about the guy who jumps off the roof of the Empire State Building? As he passes the fiftieth floor, he says: 'Well so far, so good.' So far, so good, Ted."

Ted roared with laughter. "Glad you still have a sense of humor, Axel. How's your energy level? Are you tired?"

"Not yet, but I'm sure it will be a factor in the rounds to come."

"Yes, it will. You know how pros are able to do this for hours and hours? Great conditioning of course, but also their mindset. To them, there is no difference whatsoever between conditioning, training, and sparring – it's only one continuous zone of boxing. If you can get into that zone, you'll be astonished how long you can go, and how much abuse you can take."

"I'll give it a shot. I would say it's all downhill from here, but even then, that is going to be brutal on the knees."

"And on the face, and on the arms, and on the head, and on the ribs, and on…"

"You're such a great motivator, Ted."

"Hey, I aim to please. They don't."

Axel geared up for another nine-round cycle of sparring – no, boxing. While most of the uncertainty was gone about what to expect (except from B – he was doing a great job mixing it up), the worry about having enough gas in the tank for the rest of the rounds weighed heavily on him. He hoped that at the end he would still be boxing, instead of trying to stay alive.

During the last five minutes of his break, Axel conjured up an image he had read about in a book many years ago. It was from a Kansas farmer who in 1928 had managed to look up into the funnel of a tornado, and lived to tell about it. The center of the funnel had a circular opening about a hundred feet in diameter. The opening extended out above, while at the center rotating clouds illuminated by constant flashes of lightning zigzagged from side to side. From the lower rim small tornadoes constantly formed and broke away, which writhed their way down to the end of the funnel and made screaming, hissing sounds. *Let's box these damn tornadoes as they came down*, Axel said to himself – what the heck did he have to lose?

The image miraculously held for the next seven rounds. Axel traded blows with Mike, Tim, and B for thirty more minutes, imagining that they were Tasmanian devils that could be tamed. Whenever he felt tired, he swept himself into the whirling wind and installed himself into the necessary movements to keep them at bay. Unfortunately for Axel, the tornadoes eventually blew away, and he found himself exhausted with two more rounds to go against Tim and B.

During his last round with Tim, he had to dig deep. Tim used the fatigue to start going for the body as well, and Axel's only had enough energy to counterattack the body shots with head shots. He was feeling the air go out of him like a punctured balloon. Axel was able to land some punches, but at a 1:3 ratio, and it was all he could do to hang on until the bell rang.

Sixty more seconds – at this point they felt like ten – and Axel faced off against B for the final sparring round. Ted yelled: "The finish line is in sight, Axel – do it!" when the bell rang. Axel tried his level best to follow Ted's advice, but he was expending the last of his energy with tired legs on what felt like rotten, spongy floor boards. Still, he kept moving and punching against B, even though his landing/receiving ratio was even worse this round, at about 1:4. He was wondering why time couldn't be sped up at will until he heard the bell, and the boxing that felt like sparring again was finally over.

Axel and B hugged, with B propping up Axel a bit in the embrace.

"I think you're ready for that Russkie," B said, affectionately. Tim and Mike were applauding from the ring. Ted beckoned Axel to the corner with his medical kit – B had managed to open up another cut on Axel's right cheek. After fixing the cut, Ted too gave Axel a big hug.

"How are you feeling?" Ted asked.

"I'm going to eat whatever I want for the next two days," Axel replied. "How messed up is my face now, Ted? It feels numb."

"Well, buddy, all your co-workers will be cutting a wide berth when they see you next week. Try not to get freaked out the next time you look in a mirror."

B, Tim, and Mike came around to say their goodbyes.

"Thanks guys, you gave me my money's worth, and then some," Axel said, sticking out his hand.

Mike snorted, and said: "Get over here, man." He caught Axel in a bear hug, lifting him and making him wince. After putting him down, he said: "This chessboxing fight, it's only six rounds of boxing, right? As far as conditioning goes, you're ready."

Tim bumped fists, and said: "You are mentally tough, friend. Nine out of ten guys would have crumbled after fifteen minutes. I liked how you were able to use more than one style to get through us."

"What worked with you would not have worked with Mike, and would not have worked with Gunther also," Axel replied. He turned to B and said, "You confused the hell out of me all afternoon, Gunther. I couldn't guess what was coming next."

"Life is more fun with surprises," B replied with a grin. They shook hands.

"Gentlemen, thanks for coming in. I will talk with Axel, and we'll decide who his main sparring partner will be for the next two months. Great job," Ted said. "Axel, hang with me a while in my office."

"Want a beer?" Ted asked Axel after the guys had said goodnight and left.

"Honestly, a beer right now would put me straight to sleep. I'll get a grape soda from the vending machine."

Drinks in hand, Ted asked Axel who gave him the most problems in sparring that afternoon.

"I'd have to say Tim. He was the only one who made me take a knee to the canvas. He's fast as hell."

Ted nodded, and said: "What did you think of Mike and Gunther?"

"Mike can do a lot of damage; however, for the most part I was able to defend by circling around in the ring out of his reach. It was relatively easy to form a plan against him. Gunther was crafty, but I've grown accustomed to boxing with him, and the fear factor is less strong. Tim gave me the most stomach-churning moments."

"How about alternating between Gunther and Tim? They'll be happy with half the money. You'll get used to Tim in the next few weeks, but Gunther proved that he can adapt round to round, and that is a quality I want you to develop as best you can. You will probably have a hard time finding out in advance the style of your opponent, and you need to expect the unexpected."

Axel thought for a moment, and nodded. "To expecting the unexpected," he said, raising his grape soda.

CHAPTER THIRTY-FOUR

Ted said he would arrange a sparring schedule with Tim and B for the next two months. Axel went home, soaked in a bathtub for hours, dried off, and looked at himself in the mirror. *Holy shit*, he said to himself, gazing upon the reflection. He had bruises under and over his eyes, scratches on his cheeks and forehead, and varying shades of discoloration all over his shoulders and torso.

On Monday Axel went to work. Minutes after settling into his cubicle, he heard his boss exclaim from behind: "What the fuck happened to you?" Axel told him. His boss chuckled, and then insisted upon a selfie together. "You are a fruitcake, Axel," he said, adding that he was keeping the picture to show at future performance reviews with the other people who reported to him.

Axel did feel not like working out that week, and contented himself to long walks at the crack of dawn. When he showed up at the chessboxing class on Friday night, he sparred several rounds, and it felt like nothing. At the end of the class, Ted took Axel and B aside and asked what were two good days for them to spar at the gym.

Ted said: "The best times are Saturday afternoons and weeknights after eight o'clock when the classes have finished. Otherwise, you are going to have to share the ring with other guys. An hour in the ring should be plenty. I've talked to Tim, and he said he can do Mondays, Wednesdays, and Saturdays."

"Wednesday nights," Axel said. "And Saturday afternoons."

"Fine. Wednesdays and Saturdays are good," B said.

Axel looked at B. "How about Wednesday at eight fifteen p.m. and Saturday at three p.m.?"

B nodded. Ted said he would confirm with Tim.

"Can I leave the money with you, Ted? I want them to get paid up front."

"Sure. Gunther, come to the office on those days before you head towards the lockers. If I'm not in on Wednesday, ask for Lou. He'll give you and Tim envelopes. I'll be here on Saturdays." He asked Axel: "Do you want another week to recover?"

"Nope. I'll sleep when I'm dead. Starting next Wednesday is OK."

B said: "Many thanks for helping out a starving student. You will be rewarded in heaven, brother."

"Not pulled down first from a cross, I hope."

Axel dropped off a lump sum of cash for Ted to dispense, and went back to his running and weight training. In the following weeks, Axel learned hard lessons in the ring from Tim and B. On Saturdays Ted would go to the opposing corner during the round breaks and say something to them that would result in nasty new ways for Axel to get dropped to the canvas. Tim would suddenly fight like Mike, and B would suddenly fight like Tim, not letting Axel's brain relax inside rutted patterns. He knew that Ted was getting him ready for the unknown, but during the sessions he truly hated Ted's guts.

The next invitational blitz tournament rolled around; Axel arrived at Garen's apartment on a Sunday afternoon to face three grandmasters, five international masters, and two local masters. Once again, Axel was the weakest link. His goal for the tournament was to score at least one win. "Try to have some fun today, Axel," Garen told him, looking at his latest black eye. "The only part of you that will become bruised here is your self-esteem."

Axel lost all his games again to the grandmasters. He did, however, manage one win and four draws with the international masters, and won both his games against the local masters for a fifty percent score. While that score did not win any prize money, fifty percent had been his goal in the last tournament, and it vastly exceeded his measly goal of one win for the day. Axel the perfectionist wished he could have won every game, but a short conversation with Garen afterwards set him straight.

"Stop being so binary, Axel," Garen said. "The opposite of a win is not a loss. It's about playing well with the skills you have, or playing badly. You hung tough today, fighting hard in all your games, and finished ahead of four higher rated players in the standings. Quite unlike the last tournament, where you essentially packed it in after your fifth loss in a row."

"I guess," Axel said.

"Well, I know," Garen retorted. He continued: "Deep down you knew that you weren't going to finish first. Trying not to finish last is just as delusional. A win, a loss, a draw… all those are only numbers on a wallchart. Prize money is just another number further removed. Play the best move you can in front of you with each turn until the game is over, and the results you want will follow."

"You sound very much like my boxing trainer. He told me that there was no real difference in the gym between conditioning, training, and sparring – there was, and is, only boxing. Everything outside of that was incidental."

"The Zen of chess and boxing," Garen mused. "You want to pay for one more tournament?"

"Do you think it would help?"

"I do. You went from last place to the middle of the pack in the space of a few weeks. Keep doing what you're doing. I dare say you might finish with a plus score next time."

"I can dream. OK, tell me how much money you need and make the arrangements."

Garen arranged another tournament to take place in three weeks. He also suggested that Axel start timing himself in his current homework assignment. It might spur him to flex his concentration in focused bursts.

The following week was May. A familiar packet arrived from Vyacheslav, asking for a doctor's note, his chess/boxing credentials, a biographical questionnaire, and the name of his charity where he wanted the proceeds donated.

The most valuable part of the packet were brief dossiers on the chessboxers from Moscow. The Russians were sending ten, and Axel eagerly looked at the information on the three cruiserweights. One cruiserweight was named Yuri Stepanovich Kozlov; he was twenty-nine years old, stood at an even six feet, and weighed one hundred and ninety-eight pounds; his FIDE rating was 2275; and his amateur boxing record was fifteen wins, two losses, and one draw. The name of the other cruiserweight was Vladimir Evgenievich Kuznetsov; he was thirty-one, six foot two, and weighed one hundred and ninety-three pounds; his FIDE rating was 2335; and his amateur boxing record was seven wins with one loss.

Axel called Vyacheslav, and asked him if he knew yet which cruiserweight he was fighting.

"I can't give you an answer yet. It's either Kuznetsov or Kozlov," Vy said.

"What information have you sent the Russians about me?"

"I sent them a copy of your existing amateur boxing record and the links to your posted fights last year. Your chess profile is well documented online. The president of the chessboxing club in Moscow was excited to have you on the card."

"It's nice to be noticed. When do you want me there for the weigh-in?"

"June 30, I'll send you the address of the exact location by Memorial Day. Also, can you please come to the same ESPN studio in about a month for an interview? It's for the DVD. I'll cover the cost of the hotel."

"Sure. Is this going to covered on ESPN again?"

"Probably, I've been negotiating with them since March. I'll keep you informed."

"Thanks, Vy. See you soon."

"See you, Axel. I'll know soon who you're fighting. Train hard."

Axel sent Vyacheslav his doctor's note, biographical questionnaire, copy of his amateur boxing book, the name of his desired charity (the Red Cross), and his desired entry music song (*E-Pro* by Beck). He also made two copies of the pictures of Kozlov and Kuznetsov, taping them on the wall next to his heavy punching bag and above his laptop on the desk.

He threw himself back into the running with the weights on his ankles, the punishing chess problems from Garen, and getting clobbered in the sparring sessions with Tim and Gunther. May flew by; the self-flagellation was paying dividends. Nobody but B could threaten Axel in the ring during the Friday chessboxing class, and Willie was having a hard time winning one game against him in marathon blitz sessions. He relished being able to under-promise and over-deliver.

CHAPTER THIRTY-FIVE

Just before Memorial Day, another registered envelope arrived with more definite information. The address of the weigh-in and subsequent photo shoot was enclosed; Axel's presence was requested in ESPN's New York studios on June 2; and most importantly, the identity of his opponent was now official – Yuri Kozlov. Axel would be fighting him in the bout just before the main event.

Axel took a closer look at Kozlov. From the photo in the dossier he looked like a real brawler, with arms of corded muscle. His nose was crooked, and his eyes had scar tissue. His chess games online were those of a solid master, played in a positionally aggressive style. He was going to be a challenge.

Axel immediately told Ted about Kozlov. A few days later at the Friday chessboxing class, Ted said that he had checked with his sources, but came up blank. B overheard the conversation, and asked Axel to scan and email the picture to him. He would forward the picture to his friends in Berlin. If Kozlov had fought in Germany, Wolfgang would dig up and share any relevant data. Axel thanked B warmly. Then they sparred for six ferocious rounds.

Axel upon returning home emailed Kozlov's data to B, and then called Garen.

"What is his full name?"

"Yuri Stepanovich Kozlov. He has sixty games online."

"I'll take a look. Are we still on for the blitz tournament this Sunday?"

"Yes."

"OK. I'll give you some intel then."

"Thanks, Garen. See you Sunday."

Kozlov's games were buzzing in Axel's head when he arrived at the blitz tournament. This time there were two grandmasters, six international masters, and two masters. Garen promised to share his research after the tournament. With Kozlov still on his mind, Axel started his clock in the first round against one of the grandmasters.

The grandmaster obtained an advantage early in the opening, holding it throughout the middlegame and early endgame, but Axel defended stubbornly. He managed to throw up roadblock after roadblock to the grandmaster's path to victory, putting his opponent in time pressure. Attempt after attempt to put the game away was rebuffed, with no sign of Axel being worn down. The grandmaster finally offered him a draw when they both had twenty seconds left on their clocks. The draw was galvanizing.

Axel managed two more draws against two of the international masters, and then won against one of the masters. He was plus one (a point over a fifty percent score), something he never believed was possible two months ago. The next game brought Axel down to earth, when he was crushed by one of the international masters. But he bounced back with a win against an international master (plus one), and another against the other master (plus two).

Three games left. He played the fifth international master, and had a winning ending, but overlooked an ingenious combination from his opponent that put him in stalemate and allowed him to escape with a draw. Still plus two. Against the final international master Axel played out the game almost to the bare Kings. He ran out of time but his opponent had insufficient mating material, which was an automatic draw. Mission accomplished – no matter what happened in his final game, Axel would finish the tournament with a plus score.

In the final round, Axel had White against the other grandmaster. Imagining Kozlov sitting across from him, he impulsively played the Scotch Opening, an opening he never used in serious tournaments. He remembered enough of the theory to keep him in the game, which turned out to be extraordinarily complex. Interlocking bunches of pieces protected each other from veiled threats coming in all directions. Axel was vividly processing everything about the new game that was being made with each successive press of the clock. The late afternoon sun streamed through the windows, and he was happy. Suddenly his opponent made a slip, and Axel picked off his Queen before he could exhale. His opponent slapped the side of his head with a sound of disgust and immediately resigned. Plus three.

Garen tapped him on the shoulder and gave him the prize money for tying for first place.

"All this fun, and I get paid for it too?" Axel asked merrily. He gave the money back to Garen. "Payment for your research on Kozlov. How should I take on the guy?"

"Step into my office," Garen replied, motioning to his kitchen. One grandmaster and one international master were already there, playing out Kozlov's games. Garen introduced Axel to Dima, the grandmaster he had drawn and with whom he had tied for first, and Zoltan, the international master who had crushed him. Both were marking up printouts of Kozlov's game scores. Garen gave them equal portions of Axel's prize money.

"A donation from Axel for your services. What do you of think of Kozlov so far?"

"A solid player with some chinks in his armor," Zoltan said. "As I'm sure you've been doing, Axel, I'm concentrating on the losses."

"And I'm looking at the draws," Dima said. "Playing over the game scores in my head, Kozlov rarely seems to go for it. He only treads where the potential result is clear-cut and dried. I've marked up four games that follow this course. Look at the moves I've underlined in the games when you get home. He could have chosen other much more promising moves."

"Look at this position," Zoltan said pointing at the board on the kitchen table. "Kozlov's opponent offered a piece for an initiative. It was an unsound sacrifice, yet Kozlov declined it. The resulting position would have been uncomfortable, but with a few accurate moves it's clearly won –" Dima and Garen nodded "– there's nothing the opponent could have done to prevent a losing ending. Later in the game, when presented with a similar offer of material, Kozlov backed off again, and this time quickly found himself in a box where he was checkmated. He lost five other games this way, I marked up those for you."

Garen said: "The bottom line is that your opponent doesn't like having his hair mussed up. Go for unbalanced, sharp, tactical positions, and he'll take the path of least resistance by retreating into his comfort zone."

"I've only been looking at his openings, thanks," Axel said. "I'll add your markups, and try to come up with a coordinated game plan."

"Study lots of games from attacking players," Dima said. "Turn your mind into a flying scalpel."

Garen said: "I've looked at his wins. He has good technique. Kozlov's chess strengths are maximizing his chances in double-edged positions while minimizing the risks. It's a good practical approach. But every game is special, and that cookie cutter approach only goes so far."

"As I said, a solid chess player you can make blink. You're on your own for the boxing – man, this guy looks mean," Zoltan said, looking at a picture that Axel had brought to the tournament and was now lying next to the chessboard. "You have a lot of guts getting in the ring with him."

"Please make your chessboxing career brief, Axel. It wouldn't be good for my reputation if one of my students ended up drooling all the time," Garen said.

Zoltan gave Axel his cell phone number, offering to play some additional training games with him before the bout. Before he could awkwardly ask him for a fee, Axel said he would take Zoltan up on his offer and volunteered to pay him. He had spent far less money for his training budget than he originally intended, and was in a generous mood.

He borrowed player-annotated game collections of Kasparov, Topalov, Tal, Alekhine, and Shirov from Garen, and rediscovered the joys of their swashbuckling play. Their dynamic styles were full of kinetic swagger, coupled with phenomenal attention to detail. Axel struggled to follow the variations in their analyses.

He loved how the floor seemed to dip and sway in their wins, with fireballs appearing out of nowhere. The opponents' positions buckled under the relentless pressure, and then broke apart. All the combinations seemed to be conjured out of thin air at will, and calculated down to the last splinter. Axel would have loved to play like that on a regular basis, but the laws of gravity prevented it. With enough immersion though, he could conceivably make Kozlov back down in the chess game with the threat of chaos, the same way he might square him off in the boxing ring.

Axel examined Kozlov's games more closely over the next few days. He looked at the draws that Dima had marked up, and tried to imagine how Kasparov or Tal might have played differently. He looked at the losses that Zoltan had marked up, and came up with moves on his own by imagining moves that Alekhine and Shirov might have chosen. He looked at the wins, and decided what openings would be best to avoid in the bout. Axel went on to look at all the openings that Kozlov played, and brushed up on the latest theory from those openings in the databases.

CHAPTER THIRTY-SIX

Axel studied Kozlov's games on the entire ride towards New York. He arrived at ESPN's studios at two for his interview at three. He was receiving makeup for the cameras when Vyacheslav stopped by to say hello, with a box.

"Hi, Axel. Wow, you look good."

"Thanks, I'm training hard as you requested."

"These haven't been used since your fight with Zolutski." He took out a pair of gloves, and boxing headgear. "We kept them in storage. Are these going to be OK for your fight with Kozlov?"

Axel tried on the gloves and the headgear. "Yes, they're fine."

"Outstanding. They'll be waiting for you ringside." Vyacheslav put them back in the box. "Les will be interviewing you again."

"Any curveballs outside of the questionnaire?"

"You can ask Les yourself. We're not here to make you look bad; we can always film over and splice in your second takes."

"Good. Who is going to be in the main event?"

"A major coup. We convinced the European heavyweight chessboxing champion to fight against the heavyweight from the Moscow chessboxing club. If you can, postpone going to the locker room afterwards to see that bout. It should be amazing."

Before the cameras rolled, Les said he would ask pretty much the same questions as before, with perhaps one additional question about his training methods. The cameras started rolling. Axel talked about his background, his sparring and speed chess training regime, and how seriously he was taking his opponent. Les's final question was how good Axel considered his chances to be.

"I am going to show up in the best physical shape and the sharpest mental acuity I possibly can," Axel replied. "If that's not good enough, then winning the bout was never meant to be. I do promise to all those who show up that I will give it my all."

The interview ended. "No second takes required," Les said. "Great job."

"Great interview," Vyacheslav said. "I'll walk you to your hotel – it's not far from here."

Axel said goodbye to Les, and walked with Vyacheslav to his hotel six blocks away.

"Seriously, Axel. You look fantastic. Are you sure you are going to make cruiserweight?"

"I've been stepping on the scale every week – last Sunday I was a hundred and ninety-four. If I get down below a hundred and ninety-two pounds, I'll step up on the weights."

Vy chuckled. "Kozlov isn't going to know what hit him." He stopped. "Oh, before I forget – here are eight tickets for family and friends."

"Thanks. How far away is the Hofstra Arena?" Axel asked.

"Only thirty miles east of here. Trains from Penn Station can take you there in under an hour."

"I feel ready now, Vy, to tell you the truth. But you can never fully train against the anticipation."

"Most true. But you can always train harder, if only to improve the percentages."

"Even if the percentages are largely in my head?"

"Especially if the percentages are in your head." They had reached the hotel. Vyacheslav looked squarely into Axel's eyes as they shook hands. "Imagine it first, Axel, and then you can make it come true."

Axel again forsook the pleasures of New York City, staying in his room to resume his study of Kozlov. When all the moves in those games started to look the same, he switched to a book of Alekhine's games that he had brought along. The analysis was still buzzing in his head when he hopped on the bus ride back home. Right up to the end of his training, Axel vowed, he would stretch out his mind to its limits, and then simply extend that mindset onto the game during the bout.

In June, Axel turned up the dial of his physical training as close to ten as he could. He ran five days a week, lifted weights three nights a week, and sparred two to three nights a week. He really got his money's worth at the hands of Tim and B. No longer was Axel exhausted when the sessions ended; as the month progressed, the amount of times he was able to drop his sparring partners to the canvas was beginning to equal their dropping him.

Wolfgang could not find any reliable boxing intel on Kozlov; the best he could do was send research on Kozlov's opponents in an email. Those he had won against went on to have mediocre amateur records, while those he had lost to went pro. Based on this history, he looked like as solid a boxer as he did a chess player. The anxiety, Axel realized, was never going to subside.

Ted insisted that the last day of his training was going to be June 23, so that his body could heal in time for the fight. Axel put everything he had into his final week. He finally ditched the leg weights and ran twelve miles a day, put in twenty hours of weightlifting, and extended his two sparring sessions from one hour to two hours. His final day ended with a group hug with Tim, B, and Ted.

"Thanks for your help, guys – I really needed it," Axel said. He was celebrating with his sparring partners and Ted inside the office. They drank beer, while he stuck to grape soda.

"My pleasure, Axel. You're as ready as you can be," Tim said.

"Kick the Russkie's ass," B added.

"Axel, step on the scale please." Ted said. The scale in his office said one hundred and ninety-two pounds. "Perfect. Even if you break training and eat like an idiot the next week – you won't, I know – you have eight pounds of leeway to make cruiserweight. Stop being so anxious. You've put in so much hard work that you couldn't trip yourself up in the boxing ring if you tried."

"I hate equations with two variables, Ted," Axel answered. "I don't have any firsthand knowledge of what to expect with Kozlov, either in chess or boxing. All I know is that the two-headed something I'm going to face in the ring is going to be fast, hard, and heavy."

"You're ready for the boxing," Tim said. "How are you preparing for the chess?"

"I have an Armenian chess guru. He's been organizing speed chess tournaments with his grandmaster friends for me. For the past three months they've been doing to my brain what you've been doing to my face."

"Holistic training. Perfect," Ted said, tongue in cheek.

"Is this event going to be on ESPN again?" B asked.

"Oh, shoot. I was up in New York a few weeks ago, and I forgot to ask the organizer that. The short answer is... yes, probably."

"Let me know, Axel – I will arrange a viewing party for it," Ted said.

"OK, but it's likely to be one of those ESPN2 graveyard times, say Tuesday at one a.m., or Sunday at three thirty a.m."

"Oh, the hell with that – I'll tape it instead, and then we can show it as a training video for the chessboxing classes."

Axel held out the free tickets Vyacheslav had given him to the event. Tim apologized, saying he had other plans; Ted said he'd take two, he could probably find someone he knew in New York who would go; and B accepted two, saying he would take Max and see him there. Ted grabbed the one member still working out in the gym, and asked him to take a picture. The picture was of Axel, Ted, Tim, and B joining fists in a semi-circle as if they were the Musketeers. Ted said: "Give me a minute, I'll print out this picture for you to take. Fight hard, and have fun out there."

Axel had one week to kill before the chessboxing bout on June 30. He told his family where he was going for the weekend, and offered them his remaining tickets. He knew they'd say they had made other plans, and they did. He then asked them to wish him luck, and they did.

Family obligations met, he decided to fill the week with chess while his body recuperated. He called Zoltan, asking if he was available for a couple of weeknights of blitz chess at a local cafe. He would pay for Zoltan's time, and for the coffee too. Zoltan accepted.

Axel planned to leave for Long Island on early Friday morning. He had asked for and received a few days' vacation time before the July 4 weekend holiday. By this point he had so much energy that he jumped out of his cubicle at work every hour to take a run around the building, or do several dozen clap push-ups in the company bathroom. The excitement and the anxiety were making Axel burst out of his skin.

He played Zoltan on Monday night at the cafe, trying to apply as much of his tactically charged chess readings as possible. The games were short: either Axel blew Zoltan off the board in miniatures, or Axel's attacks went down in flames by move twenty. Either way, they were able to get in thirty complete games before the cafe closed.

Zoltan said as they were heading for the door: "I like what you're doing, Axel. However, temper your attitude from hyper-aggressive to moderately aggressive. Kozlov might be gun shy, but he's solid and can make good practical defensive decisions. Make sure you have a solid positional foundation before you launch your attacks."

They played again on Wednesday night. This time Axel took pains to secure equality in the game before he started looking for attacking prospects – he finished plus five. Zoltan smiled, and said to him: "Excellent play. You were a knife with a well-balanced handle. Do exactly what you were doing tonight in your chessboxing game, and you'll be fine."

"Were you channeling Kozlov tonight?" Axel asked.

"I was. You might have noticed I could have counterattacked much more sharply, but didn't. I don't know what sort of boxer you're going to face, but I'm sure that if you shove Kozlov towards a tactical chess fight, he will not shove back."

"Thanks, Zoltan. I don't know what sort of boxer I am going to be facing either. All his fights have been in Russia, and I've yet to see any video of him."

"You are such a kook, Axel. Protect yourself in there, OK?"

CHAPTER THIRTY-SEVEN

Axel offered a ticket to Zoltan, who turned it down because he was going to be playing in the side events of the World Open that weekend. That was OK, he said, and wished him luck in Philadelphia. He was able to give away his four remaining tickets to his chess-playing friend in New York five minutes later on the phone, promising to leave them at the Will Call window.

On Friday, Axel headed out to New York. He arrived in Penn Station by noon, and took the first train out to Hempstead, Long Island within an hour of arriving. The weigh-in was scheduled between four and five p.m. that afternoon. He was anxious, yet buzzed, about laying eyes on Kozlov.

He arrived at the weigh-in with his gym bag at Hofstra University at three forty-five. They weren't ready yet, so Axel had to cool his heels for half an hour. He was the first chessboxer whose information was processed for the event, weighing in at one hundred and ninety-three pounds. He hadn't fasted the whole day like he did last year, so he availed himself to a large glass of water and relaxed in the corner by perusing Topalov's games from the 2005 San Luis World Championship tournament.

The other chessboxers trickled in over the next hour and a half. Most of them predictably wolfed down their first meals of the day. Axel saw a familiar face pulverizing a sandwich in ten seconds. He looked up when he finished, caught Axel's eye, and immediately made his way over to him in the corner.

"Hey, Wojtek."

"Hey, you," Wojtek Zolutski replied cheerfully. They hugged. "You look good, Axel."

"Thanks, you too. Who are you fighting?"

"Some Russian guy named Ivanov, fourth on the card. His FIDE rating is 2000, and his amateur record is six and three. Who do you have?"

"Yuri Kozlov – we're second on the card. He's given me nothing but butterflies for the past three months."

"Ooh, good luck. Yeah, in Vyacheslav's packet I noticed him and that Kuznetsov guy with the 2335 rating. They look really tough."

"I have a game plan for the chess, but just do not have the eighteen amateur fights my opponent has. I've trained for that the only way I know, by having the shit pounded out of me in the sparring ring."

Wojtek laughed. "It does look like they pounded a lot of the shit out of you, as the rest of you looks pretty decent. What was your weigh-in?"

"One ninety-three."

"Same here. This time, they gave me the chance to work off all the beer I drank on Memorial Day." They heard the sound of shuffling feet, and turned around to see a large group of chessboxers enter the room. "The Russians are here," Wojtek said.

Ten chessboxers walked into the room in a collective mass, and occupied an entire wall of the waiting room. They all wore the same matching sweatpants and sweatshirts with the Russian flag emblazoned on their shoulders. Once seated, they talked among themselves and ignored everyone else in the room.

"I see Ivanov," Wojtek said.

"I see Kozlov," Axel said.

Kozlov was seated third from the right. From across the room, he seemed to have the same build as Axel's. He had black hair in a buzzcut, along with piercing blue eyes set in a wide Slavic face.

By five thirty, all the chessboxers had arrived. The heavyweight European chessboxing champion was the last to enter, and Axel was dumbfounded by his size. His name was Todor Mihailov, and he stood six feet eight inches tall with the girth and muscle tone of a WWE wrestler.

"Holy crap, I wouldn't want to meet that guy in a dark alley," Wojtek said.

Vyacheslav stood by the doorway, and announced that it was time for the photoshoot, and would everyone please follow him to the university gym downstairs. Axel noticed the Russian contingent standing up as he made his way to the door. Kozlov, he noted in passing, was his height. But one of the Russians standing up made his eyes pop out – it had to be their heavyweight. He made even Mihailov look small, as he must have been close to seven feet while being just as wide. Yes, Axel was definitely hanging around for the main event after his bout was over.

Axel caught up with Vyacheslav as they walked downstairs.

"What was Kozlov's weigh-in, Vy?"

"One ninety-nine."

"Thanks."

"No problem. Here's your hotel info and voucher. Send me your transportation receipts when you have the chance."

"Sure thing. Can you put these tickets in the Will Call window?" Axel handed him his last complimentary tickets and a slip of paper with the name of his New York chess-player friend.

"You got it. Hey, Axel, you're next to last on the card, so be ready tomorrow night around eleven thirty. Time your biorhythms accordingly."

"OK. Thanks for the countdown, Vy."

"I live to serve. Good luck."

The gym had a boxing ring, and the chessboxers posed there for pictures for the next hour: individual photos, Russian group photos, non-Russian group photos, and paired opponent photos. In his pictures with Kozlov, Axel finally had a chance to directly measure the man.

Kozlov stood half an inch taller than Axel with a slightly thicker neck, with broad shoulders and large calloused hands. He had delineated muscles on his arms and a fully defined six-pack; his legs were a little thinner; and his face had the scar tissue of many hours spent in the ring. They posed half an inch from each other for the obligatory profile shot, and Axel smelled onions on his breath.

When their photos together had ended, Axel said to him in the Russian he had prepared the night before his trip: "Horoshiyi shaunce." Kozlov lifted his head in surprise, and replied "Horoshiyi shaunce vam tozhe." They nodded, touched fists, and separated.

When the photos were over, Vyacheslav announced in English and Russian that the chess clocks in the bouts would have a one second increment per move; there was also a buffet available in the next room. He thanked all of the chessboxers for attending, and told them to be at the arena tomorrow by eight p.m. – the directions and athlete entry passes were available by the exits. It was a good spread, but Axel limited himself to taking a sandwich that he took with him to the hotel. He was going to do very little in his hotel room for the next twenty-four hours, wanting to arrive at the chessboxing ring fully rested and statically charged.

In his room Axel played out the rest of the Topalov games he had brought. Then he did a final review of his repertoire against Kozlov's known openings. Then he played through some of his opponent's losses and draws one more time. At nine p.m. he said aloud: "Oh, to hell with it, I'm ready!" He was in bed and asleep within the hour.

Axel woke up at seven a.m. He aimlessly walked around the streets for most of the morning, coming back to the hotel in time for lunch. Limiting himself to cereal and fruit, he went back up to his room to watch a Rambo movie, and then took a nap. He woke up in the late afternoon, wanting to go straight back to sleep, but turned on the TV instead. He saw two innings of a major league baseball game before turning off the television set, setting an alarm on his phone, and resuming his nap. He finished the boring start to an exciting day by waking up to the alarm, showering, and heading out to the arena with his boxing gear at seven thirty p.m.

All the tension from the training he had put in for the bout came back with a vengeance en route to the arena. By the time he had checked in and changed into the provided trunks inside the locker room, and had his fists wrapped and marked with an 'X', that old feeling of wanting the fight to be over with already was out in full force. Electricity surged through his veins, and he could barely sit still.

He discovered that all the non-Russians were sharing the same locker room, and fighting in the blue corner. "Of course, the Russians are fighting out of the red corner," someone said, which made lots of people laugh.

A closed-circuit TV broadcast covered the event inside the locker room, but Axel purposefully did not look at it – instead he sat in a corner, listening to his iPod. He did get up once to wish Wojtek luck on his way out. "If you haven't been watching, Axel, the Russians are killing us. We've got to turn back this red tide," Wojtek said. They bumped fists, and then he went to the ring. Axel sat back down, and looked at the clock on his iPod: ten thirty. In half an hour he would start moving.

At eleven Axel stood up, and started jumping rope in an open area in the locker room. As the evening went on, the amount of people steadily depleted. When he finished jumping rope, he shadow-boxed near the rest rooms. Eleven fifteen p.m., and there was nothing more to do. Only he, the giant Todor Mihailov, and a few others were still in the locker room.

A boxing official told him ten minutes later to get ready, and after five more minutes the same official beckoned Axel to walk out towards the ring. Mihailov stepped towards Axel and temporarily halted him as he reached the door. He said in broken English: "We beat one Russian tonight at least. Beat him, beat him." Axel nodded, and went through the door.

Axel walked out to the ring. He was relieved that Vy got the right song for his entry music this time. He heard his name called out from the crowd a few times, and he nodded while continuing to look straight ahead – he did not want to look out into the audience, and dissipate his attention. His eyes were only on the chessboard.

Axel showed his mouth guard to the referee, who pointed out his boxing gloves and headgear in the blue corner. Resuming his gaze on the chessboard, he waited for Kozlov to make his entrance. He arrived at the chessboard to Russian rap music. The referee pointed out Kozlov's gear in the red corner, who showed his mouth guard and nodded.

The referee then tossed a coin, asking Kozlov to pick, who chose tails – it was heads. Axel had choice of color, and he picked White. They stood at their respective sides of the board. Only then did Axel look into his opponent's eyes; like his, they contained mayhem ready to explode. They touched fists across the chessboard, sat down, put on their headphones, and the referee started Axel's clock.

CHAPTER THIRTY-EIGHT

Axel opened with 1. e4, meeting the French Defense; he continued with 3. Nd2, the Tarrasch Variation, and Kozlov chose 3...Nf6. Axel pushed the e-pawn, and after Kozlov retreated with the Knight to d7 and started counterattacking the center (4...Nfd7 5. c3 c5), he decided to sacrifice the d4 pawn with 6. Ngf3 Nc6 7. Bd3 Qb6 8. 0-0. Kozlov accepted the pawn and the game reached a gambit position well known to opening theory. After 8...cxd4 9. cxd4 Nxd4 10. Nxd4 Qxd4 11. Nf3 Qb6 12. Qa4 Qb4 13. Qc2 h6 14. Bd2 Qb6 15. Rac1 the referee stopped the clock for the boxing round.

The headphones came off; Axel found his way to the blue corner of the ring through a wall of noise. His gloves and headgear went on. Twenty seconds were left. He looked squarely at Kozlov in the opposite corner, and started jumping high up and down the canvas. As the seconds wore down, the jumps became shorter and faster, and by the time the bell rang the jumps had turned into bounces synchronized to the beat of a hummingbird.

Kozlov came down on him like a hurricane at the sound of the bell, raining heavy combinations while pivoting constantly. Axel took his obligatory first hits to the face, shoulder, and mid-section, wanting to see how he would fare toe to toe with Kozlov. By the second minute Axel had some degree of success by throwing a jab and a straight right, and then moving back diagonally one square to the left, as if he were moving the Bishop on d2 in the game back to its original square on c1. But his opponent moved well. The bell rang. Outside of a few counterpunches that landed, it was Kozlov's round.

Back at the chessboard on went the headphones, and back came on the chess game, front and center. While up a pawn, his opponent was having a hard time castling and coordinating his pieces. In contrast, it was easier for Axel to mobilize his forces. He doubled Rooks on the c-file, and redeployed his Queen to g4 making it dangerous for Black to castle there. Kozlov put his King on f8, leaving a Rook on h8 by the King for defense, and exchanged off one of the Rooks on the c-file. However, it did nothing to alleviate the pressure. When the clock was stopped again, Axel was ready to do damage with his centralized Bishops, and Kozlov was still miles away from converting his extra pawn.

Before the start of the third round in the ring, Axel impulsively decided to do an Irish jig in his corner. What the hell, he thought, the crowd by the extra noise sounded like they loved it. On the walk over, he suddenly saw a way of crisscrossing his attack with the Queen and Bishops in the game that would give Kozlov a lot of problems. The prospect of carrying that out on the chessboard made him feel light and buoyant, and gave him an idea of how to box in the following round.

The bell rang. Kozlov continued to be fast, hard hitting, and elusive. Then in the second minute Axel carried out his idea. He charged forward, causing his opponent to back up, whereupon Axel exploited the temporary lack of mobility to suddenly veer left while bringing up his right arm into a hook. The hook landed into the side of Kozlov's head with a satisfying thud. Before he could react, Axel charged again immediately, only this time veered right and caught him on the other side of the head with an equally thudding left hook. Kozlov backpedaled to recover, but Axel, in a burst of energy, squared off enough of the ring to back him into the ropes, and at last got to see how he fought toe to toe. It turned out his adversary disliked close combat very much; he forced himself back into the center at the expense of a stiff right punch and two hard hooks to the head. Axel continued to pursue, but Kozlov proved fast enough to avoid getting hit again before the bell rang. This round, Axel was sure, belonged to him.

Axel was excited on his way back to the chess game – he couldn't wait to try out his idea, which was putting the Bishop on e7 in an uncomfortable double attack from his Bishop on b4 and Queen on h4. Kozlov could not take the Queen because the Bishop was pinned to the King on f8, and he could not take the Bishop because the same piece was pinned to the undefended Queen on d8. He tried to kick the Queen away from the Kingside by pushing his g-pawn up two squares, but Axel simply captured it with the Knight. Taking the Knight with the pawn on h6 meant losing the Rook on h8, and the Bishop was still pinned to the King and couldn't take the Knight either. If he took the Bishop on b4, Axel would take the pawn on e6 with check, and win the still unprotected Queen next move. Kozlov played his King to e8, breaking the Bishop's pin from b4 and protecting the Queen.

Axel stared hard at the complicated position for a full minute. Finally, the solution hit him like a bolt a lightning. He mentally transferred Kozlov's face onto the Black King, and silently said to it: *Got you!* He checked the King by moving his white-squared Bishop to b5, forcing Kozlov's to d7, and added gasoline to the fire by taking the pawn on e6 with his Knight. Four of Axel's pieces were en prise, and Kozlov could not take any of them with being checkmated or losing a decisive amount of material.

His opponent found the most stubborn defense by taking the Knight on e6 with his f7-pawn, but Axel was ready. He checked the King on e8 by moving the Queen to h5, and after the King was forced back to f8 brought up his final reserves by moving his Rook on the still open c-file to the third rank. Axel was certain that the Rook swinging over to the other side of board, towards Black's exposed King, was going to be deadly, but the referee stopped the clock ending the round before that could happen.

Axel didn't hear a thing when he took off his headphones. He had glanced at the clock before moving back to the ring to put on his gloves, and saw that he had three minutes left to Kozlov's four. All he could think of was finishing off the game in the next round, and that thought surrounded him with white noise.

The bell rang, and Axel deliberately marched straight into a jagged, toothy, and spiky flurry of punches from his opponent. He was going to eat his fill this round. Kozlov was good enough of a chess player to know that his position was critical, and stood his ground as well, steadily turning up the volume and the speed of his volleys as the round went on. Axel then suddenly backed off, deciding to close out the round by sticking and moving. He didn't care if he had lost this round on points, because he believed he could finish the bout in the following round. The time flew by, and the bell rang one more time.

In the break, Kozlov's best defensive chance appeared to him, as well as its refutation. The chess round began. Axel didn't care about how many pieces he was letting his opponent capture on the other side of the board – the Black King was doomed. Kozlov was actually up three pieces on the Queenside, until Axel made a killer move that set up a decisive pin. The pin would either result in checkmate, or force his opponent to give up all but one of his pieces. Kozlov after a minute recognized his hopeless situation, and tipped over his King.

Axel let out a long breath, and bumped fists with Kozlov. The crowd noise was so loud his ears hurt, and he could barely hear Kozlov saying: "Very, very good."

He replied, "Spaseebah," and hoped that his worthy adversary could read lips, as he couldn't hear himself say it.

He had not taken ten steps towards the locker room when B appeared in front and gave him a giant bear hug. No sooner had he been put down than Max appeared and gave him one as well. Axel said thanks, and got their seat numbers, promising to seek them out before he left the arena.

Ten more steps, and his chess-player friend from New York appeared at his side, slapping his shoulder with his congratulations. He introduced Axel to his friend, a fellow chess player from New York. They told him that he was the first (and so far, only) chessboxer that night to win a bout against a Russian. Axel said he would be hanging around New York for a couple of days afterwards, and promised to get together with them for dinner.

He resumed his walk to the locker room, bumping anonymous fists from the left and right, and wondered if he was ever going to arrive at his destination without further interruptions. It was not to be. Vyacheslav appeared five feet from the doorway, beaming at him.

"Just awesome, Axel! – please come with me. We so want to interview you."

Axel sighed happily. "OK, let's go."

As he turned to go with Vy, Mihailov was leaving the locker room towards the ring. Axel caught his eye. The giant Bulgarian flashed him a smile, which Axel returned. "Very good," he said. "I will build on you," he added and turned away to meet the Russian giant in the ring.

"Hope I can see at least one boxing round between those two bull elephants," Axel said to Vyacheslav as they were walking upstairs to the studio.

"Ten minutes tops, Axel," Vy replied. "I want to see it too."

Axel answered short questions in the interview about the crucial moments in the chess game, his chess preparation, his boxing preparation, and why he was so reckless in the last boxing round (answer: he was sure he could close out the fight the following chess round, and because he felt like it). Five minutes in, the interviewer halted the questions and stopped the camera at Vy's request so that they could all see Mihailov and the Russian heavyweight box their first round in the ring.

"They're saving their worst for the later rounds," Axel said.

"Yeah, Mihailov tends to floor it only in the tail end of the fight," Vyacheslav said.

The interview concluded shortly afterwards, with Axel being congratulated on being the only chessboxer so far to make a dent against the Russian team.

"Where did the Russians win? In the ring or on the chessboard?"

"The chessboard," the interviewer and Vyacheslav instantly said at the same time.

"None of your teammates were able to get out of the opening without a serious disadvantage," Vy added.

"The thing about Russians is that even if you can survive their opening preparation, they'll strangle you with their endgame technique," Axel said.

"Not you, Axel. You had the advantage straight out the opening, and never let your opponent reach the ending. Well done!" the interviewer replied.

Axel hurriedly went to the locker room, put on his sweatshirt from his locker, and re-entered the arena in time for the main event's third chess round. He made his way to where Max and B were sitting. They convinced the man in the next seat to move over to an empty one three places over so that Axel could sit next to them. Axel sat down just as the chess round ended, and the next boxing round was to begin.

"I'll say it again and again until you're sick of hearing it. Great job!" Max said.

"Thanks. Wow, I've never seen such big guys box in the ring before. What was the second round like?" Axel asked.

"As boring as the position on the wall," B replied. "It should be heating up soon."

"Ja, and they need a bigger referee. He only comes up to their armpits," Max added.

The bell rang, and the two huge men started boxing more aggressively than before. They really needed more than five rounds to be cut down. The bout went down to the wire, the game ending by the Russian stalemating Mihailov. The judges declared the boxing match a draw – however since the chess game was a draw as well, the match was awarded to Mihailov because he had been playing with the Black pieces.

"I have to change into my street clothes, guys. Thanks for coming out and cheering me on," Axel said, standing up from his seat.

Max said: "Anytime, Axel. It is fun watching you work." He gave Axel a warm embrace.

"Fantastisch, Axel. I'll see you at the next chessboxing class," B said. They shook hands, firm but not bone crushing. "Auf wiedersehn."

"Auf wiedersehn."

Axel finally took a shower, and changed into his normal clothes. After picking up his boxing record book, he entered the street from the arena with the last of the crowds. He was nowhere close to tired when he got back to his room at one thirty a.m., and on impulse resolved to do something that a stranger in a strange land would do.

He turned on his laptop, and web-surfed to a local escort site. After filtering for available escorts who were non-agency, did outcalls, and had listed prices for their time, Axel settled on one whose picture he liked and called the number. He heard an answering service. After leaving his name and number, he hung up. A call came back twenty minutes later.

"Hello?"

"Hello, can I speak to Axel please?"

Her name was Angelina. After Axel gave her the room number of the hotel and the amount of time he wanted, she agreed to come within an hour. *This might be a complete disaster again,* thought Axel, *but the previous day has gone so well for me I don't care.* He heard a knock on the door at two fifteen a.m. To his relief, the pictures on the website matched the person. After taking care of business, they settled on the top of Axel's bed.

Further relief was in store for Axel, as he had no problems performing. She made him change condoms three times, and he finally went fifty minutes later after a variety of missionary, cowgirl, doggie style, and standing positions. He even had enough in the tank for another pop, but his cautious nature to keep something in reserve returned, and he sent Angelina on her way with a tip. He finally went to sleep an hour later, not recognizing himself in his own skin.

He awoke one hour before his mandatory checkout from the hotel. He called Vyacheslav on the trip back to Manhattan, asking if he knew of any inexpensive places to stay in New York – he was not particular about the accommodations, as long as they were clean and safe. Vy recommended St. John's University out in Queens, digging up a number from his contacts list. They sometimes had dormitory rooms available. Axel thanked him and hung up. Upon calling the number he was able to snag the last room, but only for three nights, which he accepted. He had already decided that he wanted to celebrate the Fourth of July back home.

CHAPTER THIRTY-NINE

New York had become brutally hot. He spent the first two days visiting museums on both upper sides of Central Park. After the museums, he splurged on a couple of Broadway shows in Times Square, savoring the air conditioning. On the third day, he finally got together with his New York chess-playing friend, who helped him brave the fearsome crowds at the Statue of Liberty during the morning, and kept him company in Greenwich Village in the afternoon.

Neither was in the mood to play chess in Washington Square nor at the Marshall Chess Club nearby, so they wandered from bookstore to bookstore, and cafe to cafe, as the sun slowly set. Dinner was takeout Chinese, which they took to a bench overlooking the Hudson River.

Axel said: "Someone asked me five years ago – when I was still in a deep funk – what I wanted to do with my life. I'm no closer now to finding that out now as I did then, but at least I know what I don't want to do."

"What's that, Axel?"

"Living in a cubicle forty-nine weeks each year, so that I can enjoy a vacation guilt free for only three weeks."

"How's your money situation?" Axel's friend taught chess in the New York City school system. He liked what he did, but he certainly wasn't becoming rich from it.

"I can almost retire right now. I'm only doing what I'm still doing because I can't think of anything better to do."

"Well, as far as I can see, you've done a great job of ripping out the old transmission that was making you miserable. Actually, you've upgraded it to near turbo status. Decide where you want to go, and don't ask for anyone's blessing. Just go there. I'll still hang out with you." His friend paused a beat. "No matter how weird you are."

Axel smiled so widely his eyes almost vanished, affectionately flashing both his middle fingers. The setting sun finally disappeared over the water.

Axel traveled back on Wednesday, the Fourth of July. The bus was packed, but he was lucky to sit next to an open window. It was amazing that he could still look out a window, even from windows in rooms where he had lived for years, and continue to notice something new. He felt that his life was just beginning, even if parts of his past kept darting into the corners and tamped down the edges. He was back in his apartment by late afternoon.

His sister called to invited him to her town's annual fireworks display, and he accepted. Axel of course had told her over the phone on July 1 how he did, and she said that she was very proud of him. He did not doubt her sister's sincerity, but knew from her pauses that she had no idea why her brother was doing this. Their lives had grown further and further apart, meeting up only a few token occasions per year.

He went to his sister's house one hour before the fireworks were about to begin. She lived a ten-minute walk to the field where the display was, with much easier parking. His nephew and niece were all over him the moment he walked through the door, asking about the bout and when they could see their uncle on TV. Axel answered their questions as best he could, promising to let them know when the DVD and the ESPN special would be available. Together with his brother-in-law, they all walked down to the field.

His sister laid out a large blanket to sit upon. She said hello to her next-door neighbors passing by, who returned the greeting and laid out their blanket next to hers. The people on both blankets introduced themselves, the names promptly forgotten. The night sky was crystal clear, with many more stars visible than from Axel's apartment building.

Since the blankets touched one another, Axel had to be sociable towards the neighbors sitting on the other edge. The neighbors were a husband, wife, ten-year-old boy, teenage girl, and a young woman who looked like she was in her early twenties. The husband and wife chatted between themselves, benignly ignoring the others; the boy was too shy to string more than two sentences together; and the teenage girl texting on her phone couldn't be bothered. That left the young woman.

Axel re-introduced himself, as they sat only a foot apart. Her name was Susan. She was the wife's sister, visiting for the holiday. She had just graduated from a local college with a degree in theater, and was going to perform the following week in a Shakespeare festival on the other side of the state. From there, she said, she was heading out to Los Angeles to try and become a star.

There was still enough light for her to notice the cuts and bruises on Axel's face that had not yet healed from the fight. She asked where they came from, and Axel told her. She laughed in a musical voice that made Axel look straight into her eyes, which were green and extraordinarily beautiful. He smiled, and with great effort looked away lest he be caught staring. Soon the fireworks started.

Axel looked at the fireworks and enjoyed the booming sounds they made, but didn't really see them at all. All he could think about were Susan's eyes. After the show, they talked on the walk back to the houses. She talked about her junior year abroad in Siena, and Axel talked about his recent trip to Berlin. When they arrived, the neighbors invited the adults to come in for a nightcap.

Axel chatted briefly with the husband and wife, thanking them for their hospitality, but then disappeared with Susan into the backyard, where they sat on the lawn chairs and talked about everything and nothing. His sister came out to say goodnight to Axel, kissed him on the cheek, and said not to be a stranger. Later the husband and wife came out, saying that they were going to bed, and told Susan to turn out the lights before she turned in. They talked some more until Axel glanced at his watch and gasped.

"Crap, Susan. It's four in the morning! I have to be back at work in a few hours."

The green eyes sparkled. "What a shame," she said with a Mona-Lisa smile. "I'd like to see you again."

"As would I."

"What do you like to do that doesn't involve checkmate or having your face punched in?"

"Well, I like to eat." Axel finally looked at her as a guy in a bar would. She was five foot six with a slender proportional build, and shoulder-length strawberry blonde hair to go with her green eyes. "In your line of work, are you allowed to eat much?"

"Until the first Academy Award, unfortunately no, not that much."

"Well, I like a good play. Is there anything good in the theaters here you want to see?"

"Yes, there is, this Friday. It's from an experimental company out of Northern England. What they do is take over an old building and put in every floor a – I don't know how else to describe this – an immersive experience that gets rid of the fourth wall between the performers and the audience. You basically go from floor to floor, room to room, and interpret the pieces being performed in your own way. I saw this show at a warehouse in London a year ago, and it's unforgettable – you can't see it the same way twice. They're doing the same thing with an abandoned schoolhouse the next town over, by the river."

"That sounds fascinating. Do they still have tickets?"

Susan reached for her bag, opened it and took out two tickets. "I was going to go with a friend, but she just told me yesterday that she couldn't make it."

"I can make it Friday. If you don't mind going Dutch, I'd love to go with you."

"I'd love to go with you too."

They exchanged numbers and agreed to meet at the entrance of the theater building at eight p.m. They said their goodbyes just inside the front door. Axel confessed he never knew what to say in situations like these. Susan smiled that same mysterious smile, and replied that he didn't need to say anything at all. Axel looked down at the floor, then up at the ceiling, and then moved in close to Susan. They kissed fiercely.

"Go on, get out of here, Axel," she said with a flushed face. "I'll see you again Friday."

"Good night," Axel said with an equally flushed face, opening the door and leaving.

Axel walked to his car parked in his sister's driveway. He could not hear the sound of his own footsteps. The dawn was a few minutes away when he started the car, and on most of the drive back to his apartment the sky was steeped in stars.

CHAPTER FORTY

Axel closed his eyes for a few hours; then he drove to work. His boss was still on vacation for the rest of the week. He did his job with detachment; all he could think of was seeing Susan again.

The workday passed, and the workday after that, and then he found himself in front of the theater on Friday at eight p.m., waiting for time to begin again. He had fussed over his appearance for the first time in ages, settling on pressed blue jeans, black dress shoes, a heavy black T-shirt, and a sports jacket. Susan was wearing a sleeveless floral dress, which somehow made her eyes even greener, and sandals.

"Hi, Axel," she said with a shy smile.

"Hi, Susan," he replied. He gave her a chaste hug, which turned into a PG-rated one, without kissing. "What do I owe you for the ticket?"

Susan told him. After giving her the money, he asked: "How exactly does this show work? I can't see any lobby."

"It's not your typical Broadway show. After going through a tunnel, we arrive at a lounge where you can sit down and order drinks. From the lounge there's another tunnel. Pass through that, and you're in the show. We can explore the show, come back to the lounge, and go back in as many times as we like, until the building shuts down."

"I can't compare that to... well, anything."

"For someone who combines moving chess pieces with hitting an opponent, I think you'll like it."

"There's one way to find out." Axel offered Susan his arm, and she took it. "Let's go."

They gave their tickets at the entrance, passed through the tunnel, and arrived in a strange room adorned with red velvet and rhinestones. A bar occupied the left wall, with tables and chairs in the middle; the tunnel to the show was on the right. A person was handing out masquerade ball masks by the entrance.

A sign above the entrance laid out the rules: never take off the masks, and keep the talking down to an absolute minimum. Axel asked Susan if she wanted anything to drink before going in; she shook her head – their tickets had specific arrival times for visiting the show – and tugged his arm towards the tunnel. Both put on their masks, and in they went.

They came out into a hallway covered with newspaper headlines from the late 1940s and early 1950s. The ceilings were thickly strewn with Christmas lights. A tinkling piano played over the intercom system. Susan turned to face Axel and hooked her right thumb sideways, gesturing if he wanted to go right, and then her left thumb if he wanted to go left. Axel reached out and took her left hand; they went left to the first open door.

They walked through the doorway and found themselves in a ballroom full of Christmas trees. The scent of pine needles was strong. Five couples robotically danced in and out of the trees to swing music in the same distant tinny tone of that in the hallway. The effect was weird, as if the couples were dancing on the Titanic after it had hit an iceberg. Neither Axel nor Susan felt the compulsion to join them on the dance floor, but a few others did.

They left the ballroom through two other open doors on the floor. Each door lead to rooms stuffed with film-noir memorabilia: brass knuckles, period piece clothes, pipes, tarot cards, vacuum-tube radios, vintage TVs, and much more. A soundtrack described a murder mystery, without context and explanation. It would have been compelling to sit in one of the wire-backed chairs by the wall and wait for the tape to loop around, but several other rooms were in the building to explore.

Going up a flight of stairs, they encountered halls and rooms lit by candles, with the heavy smell of incense. The walls were painted black and gave off no reflection. Axel held up his hands palms up to Susan, gesturing where she wanted to go. She chose the second door on the right.

They entered to see an actor taking a bath. He had bloodstained hands. He got up naked, wordlessly shoved two spectators aside to reach his towel, and walked into an adjoining room. Following the actor into the other room, the audience saw a violent wordless argument between the actor and a woman dressed in a British Tudor costume. The woman pulled a knife and stabbed the actor dead. Then she blew out the candle in the room. Both actors must have walked out some hidden exit, for when another actor entered to relight the candle a minute later, they were gone.

Susan must have sensed Axel was becoming bewildered, because she leaned in and whispered if he wanted to take a break back at the lounge. Axel nodded and squeezed her hand. A few minutes later they were sitting back enjoying drinks on a sofa to the left of the bar. Susan had a glass of white wine, while Axel had ginger ale.

"What do you think?" Susan asked.

"I am still trying to make sense of it," Axel replied. "I'm pretty sure the naked guy with the red hands in the bath is Macbeth. I saw the play once, and the phrase 'sore labour's bath' stuck in my head."

"Very good! See that play again, and you'll hear the phrase 'Sleep no more,' in the same scene, which is the title of this show."

"And that is why..." Axel was cogitating. "...that is why I'm seeing film-noir stuff on the first floor? From *The Big Sleep* novel by Raymond Chandler?"

Susan smiled. "You're more than a pretty face, Mr. Axel. You really are."

"Hey, hey, hey, I can lug two-by-fours with the best of them." He added: "I still don't get it. If I remember correctly, Lady Macbeth didn't stab Duncan to death in that scene. And why do you have the period news clippings on the first floor, when you have people acting out the *Sleep No More* stuff on the floor above? And what's with the zombie dancing partners going in and out of the Christmas trees in the ballroom? Is that supposed to be from *The Dead*, the James Joyce short story?" Axel shook his head, trying to jostle in some sense.

Susan rested her face in her hands and grinned affectionately. God, those eyes could start a war. "Enjoy it, Axel, don't overanalyze it."

"For you, I will. Just like that bumper sticker I once saw on a ride home from college: life is a mystery meant to be lived, not solved."

"That fit on a bumper sticker?"

"We were stuck behind that car in a traffic jam for over an hour. I got a good look at it."

Susan laughed. "Want to go back and see the top floor?"

"Sure."

Neither one of them saw much of the third floor, nor did they care. Axel and Susan found a darkened stretch of the hallway on the far wall partially obscured by a pillar. There they made out until an announcement came over the intercom that the show was closing in fifteen minutes.

Axel gave Susan a ride home. In the car, he asked her what her timeline was for next week. She answered that she was going to be in the Shakespeare festival next Monday to Thursday, and then fly to Los Angeles that Friday. She was going to share an apartment with two friends who had already moved there last year.

"What Shakespeare character are you portraying in the festival?"

"Ophelia, in Hamlet."

Axel was silent for a minute. Then he said: "It seems strange to go all the way across the state, only be told onstage to get thee to a nunnery."

Susan shook with laughter. Neither spoke for a few minutes. The car was halfway between her sister's house and Axel's. At a traffic light, she reached over and touched Axel between his legs. She said in a low voice: "I'm not ready for a nunnery. Not even close."

Axel ran out of condoms in his apartment by three in the morning. He left Susan sleeping to slip out and buy more at an all-night pharmacy. He softly shook Susan awake at six, telling her the time and asking if she needed to be anywhere that morning – he didn't, and would be happy to give her a ride. In response, she made Axel reach for his new stash. They both woke up again several hours later.

"Hungry?" he asked. It had to be around noon.

"Starving."

"Don't break discipline, Susan. What do you usually eat for brunch?"

"Cereal with skim milk, but today I feel like a huge omelet with many vegetables. With lots of toast and coffee."

"I can do that. Your timing is excellent; I stocked up at the supermarket yesterday."

After a wonderful shower together, they sat down to consume all those calories they had burned off. Susan said while he was sleeping, she had called her sister to say she was staying with friends for the rest of the weekend.

"Good God, woman, I don't think I'll survive that. You're a love removal machine."

She smiled wickedly. "Everyone dies, honey – it's just a matter of when."

In the late afternoon they finally left the apartment. Susan bought stay-over sundries while Axel bought more condoms. They returned to the apartment for dinner, and then didn't leave his bed again until Sunday afternoon. Sitting together afterwards on the couch, he asked if she wanted him to join her at the Shakespeare festival next week. She kissed him deeply, and said no.

"You're not mad, are you? I don't want this to be complicated."

"How could I possibly be mad at you, Susan? You've charged my battery to the point where I can light up every bulb on this street for the next five years, and you're well on the way to fucking every vindictive bone out my body."

She stood up. "All but one…" she said, pulling him back towards the bed.

Early evening on Sunday, Susan said she had to go back to her sister's house to pack. Axel asked if she wanted a taxi or a ride back in his car, already knowing the answer. As they waited for her taxi to arrive, he said: "If I ever find myself in Los Angeles, can I look you up?"

"Hell yeah." She scribbled down her email address and phone number on a slip of paper. He did the same for her. They went outside and sat on the steps. The taxi arrived ten minutes later, and both stood up. Axel walked down two of the steps and turned around so that they were facing each other at eye level. They exchanged one last long soft kiss before Susan went to the taxi.

"Best Fourth of July ever," Axel said.

"Best Fourth of July ever," Susan replied. She walked down the rest of the stairs, entered the taxi, and left.

CHAPTER FORTY-ONE

The vacation was over. Axel didn't mind that much, because now he knew that life could sometimes be fun. He opened the windows and cleaned his apartment, not because he disliked the smell of Susan, but because he was going back to his normal grind, and that would be easier with the aroma of Comet and Lysol in his nostrils.

He went to work on Monday even more indifferent to his surroundings. At least the office wasn't as dead as it had been last week. His boss had returned, and greatly enjoyed his description of the bout. He made Axel promise to tell him when the ESPN program was going to be broadcast, and to bring in the DVD when it was available.

The numbers Axel had to crunch and the words he had to write calmed him down to some extent. The boring hours at his job helped him appreciate the excitement that he craved but could not live upon all the more. He needed some quiet time.

He couldn't fathom going back to the workouts he had been doing just before his last fight, so he started small. He walked for an hour after work, nothing more. On Thursday Axel dropped by the gym, to find that Ted was out on vacation for the rest of the week— he had posted a notice that chessboxing classes were on hiatus for the summer.

Axel returned to the gym the following Monday. Ted was back, and warmly congratulated him on his accomplishment in New York.

"Thanks, Ted. We never did have a final exhibition fight for the chessboxers this June, did we?"

"Don't worry about that; there never really was much interest in it. Attendance dropped off sharply after Memorial Day. With the students gone for the school year, we were lucky to get six people for any of the classes, so I discontinued them for the summer. The classes should be full again by September. Thanks to you, I've managed to corner the niche for the college crowd, and it should only get bigger through word of mouth."

"I hate to see all the chess equipment you bought go to waste."

"I can always put them in a storage room in the back – it's not like they're perishable produce. We'll use the extra sets and clocks again soon. Willie doesn't mind; he's happy to play all day in the park for the next few months."

"Does any chessboxing still go on here?"

"Yes. A couple of diehards from the classes started a Facebook page, and they meet here once or twice a week. They'd love to have you join them, I'm sure." Ted had a familiar expression in his eyes and was about to say something else, but Axel cut him off.

"No, Ted, don't ask. I do not know when my next chessboxing bout is going to be. Every time you ask that, I get an invitation for another one within the week. I want to enjoy my summer a little while longer."

Ted smirked. "OK, I won't ask, but I know you. You're going to be bored by August, and just twitching to go at it again when the leaves turn. Let me know when you want to start sparring again."

"Will do, Ted, thanks."

After talking to Ted, Axel exercised normally for the first time that month, feeling the gears wrench back into place. He finished two hours later drenched in sweat, and determined to make aching muscles the following morning the new normal into the dog days of summer.

Ted was right. The appeal of taking it slow only lasted until mid-August. By that time Axel had become sick of hitting bags that didn't hit back, and taking long walks that didn't make him feel peaceful. He pursued non-boxing things that made him happy in the past (going to the beach, or playing blitz chess all day in the park), but in the end could find nothing better than what he had been doing the past year, only faster and harder.

Axel's walks turned back into runs. B had moved back in the area to start his new school year, and they resumed sparring once a week. Ted said his next intensive boxing program was starting soon. He stepped up his turnaround time for Garen's homework to one week, and thought about playing in his chess club championship again. He was mulling his short-term options as Labor Day rolled around, when Ted blurted out that fateful question: "So when is your next chessboxing bout?"

He received a call from Vyacheslav two days later. Vy had partnered with the largest chessboxing club in California to stage a night of exhibition bouts later that year on the West Coast, almost certainly in Los Angeles, and with ESPN coverage – would Axel be interested in being on the card?

"Can you cover my transportation and hotel costs?"

"Yes. The fight is going to be on December 30 again."

"You do like to make it a challenge for boxers to make weight, right after Christmas."

"Of course, Axel. It keeps you guys on your toes," Vy responded with amusement. "Actually, the weight classes are going to be relaxed a bit. We are going to have professional referees who will quickly stop the fight if anyone looks like they're being mauled, but this event is going to be private, and not regulated by the U.S. Amateur Boxing Association. That means I can actually pay you; however, there won't be any headgear this time. Is that OK?"

"Sure, that's OK – I wasn't planning to try out for the Olympics any time soon, and I've been hit hard and often enough by now."

"Good. You'd get paid along with incidental health coverage; the flip side is that you might face a heavyweight."

"I've done intense sparring with heavyweights, Vy. But how much heavier are you talking about?"

"Up to two twenty, maybe two forty-five at most, and definitely not above two fifty. I promise, Axel, I'd never make you give up more than fifty pounds in the ring. These are club fighters, like you, with amateur fights under their belts. What they do have is lots of fans, each of whom are willing to shell out $100 and more for a ticket. Only a few of them would be able to give you a serious challenge on the chessboard."

"You must know my decision-making process by now. Can I sleep on it and call you back?"

"Of course. I have to ask right now though, how much money do you want to fight?" Axel gave him a range, and Vyacheslav said that was doable. It would be new territory for both of them, involving contracts and press conferences. "By the way, Axel, the DVDs are being pressed as we speak. A copy will be mailed to you in a couple days. And I have a date and time for the ESPN2 special: Sunday, September 17 at ten thirty p.m. EST."

"Thanks."

"No, Axel, thank you. The bout you just had was so good, you made my organization look good too, and as a result chessboxing is getting more coverage on ESPN. Do a few more of those, and you're going to be a star."

"I'm not a professional boxer, Vy, and I never will be. I started way too late. The only thing I have going for me in chessboxing is the chess. The best I can ever be in the ring is competent."

"As can we all, my friend. As can we all."

Axel thought about Vyacheslav's offer over the next two days. Despite his best efforts at keeping busy the last couple of months, he could not stop thinking about Susan. The bout being held in Los Angeles, where she was now living, was of course the reason why Axel wanted to do it. But he wasn't even sure if Susan would pick up the phone, or answer his emails. In the end, the excitement of the unknown won out over the worrying. He called back Vyacheslav two days later to accept the invitation, pending an acceptable dollar amount in the range they had discussed. So much could go wrong, but on the other hand it could be a whole lot of fun.

Susan gave him more trepidations. She might be out of town. He might chicken out and not call her at all while in L.A; however, he knew deep down that wouldn't happen. If he could take a punch in the face in front of a crowd, he could accept the possibility of being rejected.

CHAPTER FORTY-TWO

Axel told Ted about the new bout without the headgear. Ted said boxing was inherently risky, with or without headgear, and to do this if he really wanted to. He recommended private sparring against the biggest fighters in the gym, and serious weight work for the legs (to improve the chances of standing his ground, and to maximize the strength of his body shots).

Axel signed up for the next intensive boxing program, and asked Ted for a leg workout routine. Ted gave him a printout for the exercises, promising to find him heavyweight sparring partners next month. Axel filled out his plate by agreeing to be the chess trainer for the Friday night advanced chessboxing class, and continuing to solve Garen's problems.

The leg workout consisted of plyometrics, running upstairs, squats, and Nautilus leg stations, all with weights on his ankles. Ted said the workout took one hour to complete, but the first time Axel tried it, he needed two and a half hours. Maybe he could get it down to one hour by the end of his training, but for now it seemed like a sick joke.

A packet from Vyacheslav arrived a week later. The packet contained a DVD of the July event, a copy of the contract, and the requisite clearance form from a doctor. The remuneration was in the upper quartile of the range he wanted, as well as being reimbursed for all travel and lodging expenses. In return, Axel was contractually obligated to pass a drug test, adopt a nickname by October, attend a press conference in November, and do an interview at an L.A. television and/or radio station in December. He had until September 15 to sign and return the contract.

Axel watched the DVD. He occupied ten of the ninety minutes, and didn't look half bad, except for the last boxing round that looked haphazard. The chess was another matter. Under the gun, he had played a really nice game. Future adversaries when looking at this match, he was sure, would try more than ever to take him out in the ring.

The intensive boxing program started a few days later. Axel was fortunate, as this year had a bumper crop of large and experienced fighters to spar against. Having begun his training three weeks earlier, he had a head start against them in reflexes and conditioning that he was going to ride as long as he could. Perhaps he could ride such an advantage all the way towards his opponent in Los Angeles.

The following week the chessboxing classes resumed, all of them full for Monday, Wednesday, and Friday. Willie was back, and fitting in well. The Friday class no longer had B, because he decided to concentrate on boxing by joining the intensive boxing program, yet it still had John, whose sparring skills were becoming better and better, and two super heavyweights from a local college football team who might provide useful training.

Axel obtained the doctor's clearance form with little difficulty. Before he returned the contract, he called Vyacheslav to ask if a clause could be inserted preventing his opponent from weighing more than two hundred and forty pounds. After conferring with the Los Angeles promoter, he called back with a counteroffer of two hundred and fifty pounds. Axel suggested a compromise of two hundred and forty-five pounds, which was accepted, Vy express-mailing a revised contract a day later with the new clause. Axel signed and mailed it back on September 14, and there was no going back.

Axel told his boss, friends, and family about the ESPN special on September 17, and about the bout in Los Angeles. He asked what nickname he should adopt for the event, and received many colorful suggestions, such as Piranha, Zugzwang, and Crimson Bishop. His nephew provided the best one – The Axe – which he passed on to Vy, who loved it and promised to promote it heavily. "Not too heavily, please," Axel said. "If I bomb in L.A., I'll have a hard time living it down."

"I won't promise not to promote that name lightly, Axel," Vy replied. "It's perfect if you're going to be facing a bigger opponent you have to chop down." He said that Axel should know who his opponent was shortly after Halloween.

Axel watched the ESPN special with his mother and his sister's family. They cringed during the boxing rounds (except his nephew – he again thought it was awesome), but were proud when the commentators praised his skill in the chess game. Axel thought they were finally warming up to all the work he had put in, yet sensed a question hanging in the air they were just dying to ask at the right moment.

The moment occurred after the kids had gone to bed. His sister and mother jumped all over him with questions about Susan. They eagerly inquired if there was anything serious going on, and multiple sub inquires of their status thereof. He decided to be coy, and said that he had a very nice time with Susan, and that they had exchanged contact information – nothing more. The questions had no more oxygen, and quickly died out; Axel knew he was going to be grilled again at Christmas.

He brought in the DVD to work, and loaned it to his boss. Axel told him that he was going to do another bout at the end of year, and needed to know if he could use some of his vacation days for the press conference and interviews in California. His boss said no problem.

Ted told everyone in the intensive boxing program about the event in Los Angeles, and those who sparred against Axel were told go full throttle. Ted threw him in all the Saturday inter-team competition bouts. In the individual team training nights, Axel was kept in the ring for ten rounds at a time. Against B, Axel had finally begun to fathom his friend's big bag of tricks, and become able to discern patterns in his ring tactics. In late September, he pulled his first punch against him.

In the chessboxing class, John was learning quickly. He had the same weight and fifteen fewer years, and their sparring was no longer that one-sided. However, Axel could still beat him repeatedly in blitz chess. He told John was to play against several different opponents that were slightly stronger than him, and to learn from the losses.

His boss returned the DVD later in the month. He said it had been viewed by his boss, and his boss's boss. Noticing that Axel was fighting for the Red Cross, they offered to have all the funds he had raised from his next event matched by the company for the charity. Axel thanked his boss for their generosity, but informed him that his next fight was going to be for money. His boss was taken aback, saying HR might not like his possible medical costs from such an event, but added: "Yeah, I guess there's no other way to go if you are going to do this seriously. Please be careful over there, OK?" Axel promised him he would.

It was now October. The boxing was going well, but mentally Axel was becoming weary of the stone he kept having to push up the hill, only to find it at the bottom the following day. The training felt like one self-referencing day after another, with little respite. He asked Ted for advice on how to get rid of the malaise. Ted replied that he should feel more focused once he had a real picture of who his opponent was going to be.

"Why don't you do the exhibition fight that's coming up?" he asked. "Three rounds only, and I'll give you one of the biggest fighters in the intensive boxing program as your opponent. A kind of inoculation of what you're facing in December."

"Sure," Axel replied on the spot.

CHAPTER FORTY-THREE

He had impulse remorse, for he found out that his opponent was going to be Jake. Jake was a mountain of a man, standing six foot four and two hundred and fifty-five pounds. He worked construction, and kept himself in shape on the job by hauling concrete slabs out of the pits by hand. Like most of the people in the boxing program, he was a pussycat outside of the ring. But inside the ring, he looked terrifying. So far, only the college football players in the program had boxed with him.

"Thanks, Ted – you did a great job shaking me out of my funk," Axel said as the clock in the gym ticked down. In thirty seconds, he would be facing Jake for the first time in sparring practice. The exhibition fight was next week.

"Anytime, Axel," he heard from a neutral corner. "Nothing like an espresso shot of terror to get rid of the blahs."

The bell rang. *Where the hell do I start?* Axel asked himself as they met in the middle of the ring. He only came up to Jake's chin, and two Axels fit inside his shadow. He tried to get in close, but Jake stuck out a glancing jab into the region of his thoracic cavity that stopped him cold. He tried moving to the left for a better angle, and almost had his head torn off by a hook that he rolled under in the nick of time. He launched a quick body shot on Jake's unprotected flank, and got away from the danger zone. All danger zones with Jake were jumbo-sized.

He quickly discovered that circling the ring was useless, as Jake was quick enough to cut off the ring with two steps. He alternated the tempo and direction of his gait, which proved successful for most of the round. But with ten seconds left Jake surged forward and clubbed Axel with a pair of jabs that made him see spectrums of the rainbow. He instinctively crouched down and delivered a pair of matching hooks to Jake's ribs and an uppercut at what he hoped was his solar plexus. Unfortunately, Axel missed the last target by a few inches. The bell rang.

Axel decided to start off the second round with a charge of the light brigade. He charged straight into two hard punches, and moved forward enough to be in range to deliver a full jab-straight-hook-straight combination to Jake's head. Axel did not make a clean getaway. Before he could move out of range, Jake tagged him with a savage overhand right. However, to Jake's surprise, Axel instantly moved straight back in and hammered his midsection with hooks. He was waiting in split seconds for Jake to lower his head enough so that he could reach it from his crouched position. When he did, Axel nailed the chin with right and left uppercuts, and delivered four more quick body shots before moving away.

Jake pursued Axel all over the ring for the rest of the round, but more slowly and self-consciously. Axel didn't backpedal the entire round, and met Jake for a few exchanges, which were more evenly distributed. Axel could sense that his opponent was saving up his energy for one last late round surge and strike, and had been thinking of a way to meet it. The solution occurred to him just after the second minute. With fifteen seconds left, Jake surged again. Axel caught a glimpse of the whites of his eyes, and moved to his left while slightly dropping his right arm. Immediately afterwards he leaned forward with his other foot, and launched with all his strength a right hook into Jake's gut. This time he found the solar plexus.

Jake dropped to his knees. Ted jumped in the ring and joined Axel to make sure he was OK. He was, but couldn't do a third round. Ted declared the sparring practice over.

Axel said: "It was a lucky punch, Jake. One of yours equals ten of mine." Jake nodded, wincing, and they touched gloves.

Ted said: "I'm glad you're not complacent, Axel. Jake is getting some training over the next few days to make you dread next week."

"I can't wait. Really."

At the exhibition fight night, Axel's bout drew a lot of attention. Not only he was fighting an outsized opponent, but also because his outsized opponent had an outsized corner person – B, who dwarfed

Jason, his corner person, even more.

"Holy shit, I've been served on a platter to the bears," he said to Jason, stepping into the ring. Ted overheard him, and said from ten feet away that he was good Yogi Bear picnic food. Axel would have flipped him the bird if he wasn't wearing his gloves.

Axel and Jake met in the middle while the referee explained the rules. The overall tone of his instructions was that they should not to try to kill each other. Jake understood, and said in a mock Russian accent while touching gloves: "I must break you," which made both of them, including the referee, burst out laughing.

Axel returned to the basics, bouncing on his toes. He remembered from the sparring session that Jake had been at his most awkward defending against lower side body shots. *How to get there again?* Charging straight in no longer surprised Jake, but coming up briefly into range, temporarily backing off, and then rolling back in during mid-step might. It worked for three times in the first round, allowing a body shot in the same exact spot just above Jake's right hip.

Time to create a second weakness. Axel redirected his aim for the shoulder. He stayed in midrange, blocking Jake's heavy shots with difficulty. He was keeping his eyes peeled to see if his opponent delayed returning his hands after a certain punch.

He saw his opening in the second minute, when he noticed that Jake was not as fast returning his second jab back to his body after a combination as his first. Axel waited for a pair of jabs to be thrown again, and struck. He jerked to the right after the second jab, and fired a straight right hand into Jake's left shoulder. It landed with a solid thud. A few more there, and Jake would consciously cover it. Axel was able to land the punch in the same shoulder twice by alternating it with the body shot above the hip. He was thinking about how a left hook to the head would be a perfect progression from his last two targets when the bell rang.

Ted came by during the break and told Axel to keep his elbows closer together when covering his head. Then he went over to the other corner and said something to Jake. Jason cautioned him not to square up when going from side to side.

The bell rang for the second round. Jake had not been letting the grass grow under his feet. He had managed to land enough solid punches so that both Axel's arms and leading shoulder were bruised. But for the most part, Axel successfully slipped and blocked most of Jake's onslaught, and was executing his strategy unhindered. He managed to tag both the spots above Jake's right side and left shoulder a half dozen times each, and create some bruises of his own. He was still waiting for that opportunity to land the perfect left hook when the bell rang again.

During the break Jason reminded him to keep bouncing on his toes, and not be caught flat-footed. That combined with squaring up, he warned, would be hazardous to his health. Axel nodded, and the bell rang for the final round.

He would thank Jason later for the bouncing toes advice, for it saved his hide when Jake charged straight at him in the opening seconds. Only the quick redistribution of the weight in Axel's feet to his legs allowed him to safely move out of the way, and avoid being shoved into the ropes. He made the fortunate choice of moving to the left, which made Jake's momentum expose his entire right flank as he surged past. Axel was finally able to land the hook he wanted on Jake's jaw, followed by with a straight right to the spot he had previously hit on the lower right side, and another hook to the jaw.

Axel knew that once Jake stopped moving forward, he was going to plant his feet and answer with a left hook that could knock down an elephant. Axel acknowledged a God above, and began to roll in the opposite direction. The force of the missed hook above unleashed a scary current of air. Popping back up, he now found Jake's opposite flank totally open. He concentrated on the bruise he had created on the shoulder, and delivered there three hard rights, a hook, and another hard right before Jake backed off into the middle of the ring.

Axel spent the rest of the fight trying to land a combinational trifecta on the spots above the right hip, the middle of the left shoulder, and the right jaw, but without success. The only way he could pull it off was if he could induce Jake to charge again without sufficient preparation. Jake though kept to the center, while never stopping to try and shove Axel into the corner. Axel's bouncing feet kept him out of danger, and it was a huge relief when he heard the bell that ended the fight.

Jake's hug afterwards lifted Axel half a foot off the ground. He went over to B, and said that for more than one awful moment he was going to be tag-teamed. B looked at him oddly: "You sound punchy, dear friend. We are all armies of one. And you're quite a good field marshal."

Ted caught Axel on his way out the door, carrying a smart phone. Axel looked at the phone, and his eyes widened in a mixture of alarm and consternation.

"Oh, you didn't," Axel said. "Is this going up on YouTube?"

"Why don't you want it there?" Ted asked in return.

"I'm going to find out who my opponent is going to be in a week or two. If the event organizers see this, they'll supersize him."

"Didn't you say you were able to insert a two-hundred-and-forty-five-pound limit clause for your opponent? Jake easily weighs over two hundred and fifty pounds."

Axel sighed. "The waiver allowing you to use my likeness from the last intensive boxing program, is it still in effect?"

"'Fraid so, Axel," Ted replied. "Honestly, the way you described your contract negotiations to me, you're going to get someone much bigger anyway. Don't you want the challenge?"

"Ugh, that's what Evil Knievel kept saying each time before he jumped canyons with his motorcycle and broke yet another cluster of bones in his body. Do what you must, Ted, but life is tough enough without challenges."

In the end, they compromised. Ted would not post the video on YouTube until Axel's opponent had been announced.

On November 1, a package arrived for Axel. His presence was required at a press conference in Los Angeles on November 12 (plane ticket and hotel voucher attached), and a file on his opponent was enclosed. His name was Adam "The Scythe" Brubaker; he was twenty-seven years old from San Francisco, had an amateur boxing record of seven wins and no losses, and a USCF chess rating of 2115. And he was six foot nine, weighing two hundred and forty-three pounds.

CHAPTER FORTY-FOUR

"Are you fracking kidding me?" Axel was taking great pains not to lose his temper with Vyacheslav, whom he had immediately called. "He looks like he should be trying out for the Lakers."

"If Adam makes weight, then sorry, Axel, the contract allows it."

"He's going to turn the boxing ring into a rifle range."

"Sweep the leg – sorry, wrong martial art," Vy said with a laugh. "He's tall and gangly, but if you can get past the arms, his core is vulnerable. Much more vulnerable than yours."

"God, he's built like a Jack-In-The-Box from hell. He's going to make me look like an insect at the press conference."

"He's the one who's like an insect –"

"Yeah, a praying mantis from Madagascar," Axel interjected.

"– whose frame can be broken if hit in the right place."

"Oi. That's all I can say to you. Oi vey, Vy. It should happen to my enemies."

Vy laughed again. "Your sense of humor is your saving grace, Axel. Never lose it."

Axel grunted, and asked: "Are you going to be at the press conference?"

"Yes, along with Dan Prentiss, my counterpart in Los Angeles. He's excited to meet you."

"Great, I can grumble to you both in person, then. See you soon."

"See you soon."

Ted almost fell out of his chair laughing when Axel told him about his opponent.

"I'm posting your fight right now," was the first thing he said. Ted then promised to locate the tallest sparring partners he could find the next few weeks.

"You might have to settle for guys who are only six foot six."

"You are too kind," Axel said. He promised to pay them market rates for sparring.

Axel started wondering if he should contact Susan and tell her that he was going to be in L.A. for the press conference, now less than a week away. The chess player in him wanted to weigh the pros and cons and of possible messages, and analyze as much as possible their hypothetical outcomes, as he did when choosing the best move in a tournament game. Yet his boxing mindset won out over his chess mindset: just send the message out, and deal with the consequences.

In under a minute, Axel composed an email message to Susan. The message read:

"Hi Susan,

I am going to be in Los Angeles on November 12. I'm doing a press conference for a chessboxing bout there later in the year. If you want to get together, let me know.

Hope to hear from you soon,

Axel"

He pressed Enter before any potential regret could set in; he didn't know which would be worse: hearing from her, or not hearing from her at all.

Three days passed with no reply arriving in Axel's inbox. Part of him was relieved. He had said goodbye to her on such a high note; anything more between them would likely be a letdown. Still, he remembered the words of John Ruskin: a man wrapped up in himself made a small package. There had to be so much more to life than chess and boxing.

Axel began to research The Scythe as a chess player. He was able to find twenty games on the online databases. At first glance he had a quiet positional style, with plenty of long drawn-out endgames. Axel asked Garen if he could arrange another gantlet of titled players for a blitz tournament or two in the month of December. Garen agreed; taking the name of Axel's opponent, he promised to pass on preparation tips against him.

Ted called Axel that afternoon to tell him that he found two extra tall sparring opponents. One was six foot seven: his name was Rick, with an angular, wiry build. The other was six foot six: his name was

Thom, and he was just big. Axel met them on Tuesday, three days before he was due to fly to the press conference in Los Angeles. Both promised to train him hard. Axel set up a sparring time next Monday, leaving their money with Ted.

Axel told his family about the event and the press conference, committing a sin of omission by not telling them about the size of his opponent. His sister asked openly if he had any exit strategy for chessboxing. The only answer Axel could give was that he was still trying to work out the tactics.

On Friday he was on a flight to Los Angeles. The press conference was scheduled for Saturday at one p.m. at the Lucha Underground Arena, near his hotel, and then Axel was going to fly back that evening on the red eye. Vyacheslav warned him not to walk there, but take a taxi instead – the neighborhood was rough.

He arrived near midnight, went straight to sleep, and woke up late the following morning leaving him with little more than an hour to make it to the press conference. He arrived out of breath and distracted. Luckily, everyone there was running half an hour behind.

He was given a nametag and a seat at the far left behind a long rectangular table. In the back was a boxing ring with a chess set in the middle – behind that was a large video screen. Twenty-two seats were lined up at the table for the chessboxers and the organizers, which filled up rapidly over the next few minutes. In front was a roomful of chairs.

Brubaker slipped in with a group of shorter people, and sat on the opposite end of the table. Vyacheslav and what looked like his partner Dan sat in the middle two chairs. Axel was surprised how many sports reporters had shown up; more than thirty were there. The rest of the audience was packed with boisterous fans of the chessboxers.

The lights dimmed, and a spotlight fell on Vyacheslav and Dan. Dan introduced the event, Vy described the rules of the sport, and then Dan described the individual matches. As Vy spoke, still shots of all the chessboxers appeared on the video screen. The fans shouted their support when they saw their chessboxers on the screen. There was no mistaking how many fans his opponent had. The cheering for Brubaker grew so loud that Dan had to wait for it to die down before continuing. Axel knew they weren't cheering for him.

Dan and Vy then invited questions from the audience. The first questions were about the rules, and then a reporter asked who was the best pound-for-pound boxer. Dan pointed out a middleweight sitting next to him. This boxer was asked several follow-up questions about his recent experiences at the Olympic team tryouts. Another reporter asked who was the best chess player. Dan and Vy looked at each other, and then pointed out Axel.

Thanks a bunch guys, Axel thought, as he received follow-up questions about how chess helped his boxing. He answered them as best he could, mainly saying that the training to fighting ratio for both chess and boxing was at least one hundred to one, and that the basic chess strategy of creating more than one weakness followed by alternating attacks to the different weaknesses also applied to boxing.

Brubaker was then asked what he thought of Axel's remarks. Axel listened to his opponent speak for the first time with difficulty, as his fans were loud. He heard a strange earnest monotone with little inflection. Brubaker said in a formless mass of words that his reach was longer than Axel's grasp could ever hope to be, and that his puny opponent would be rendered senseless in the first boxing round, drawing a raucous wave of cheers. When asked for an answer, Axel smiled and said that bigger mouths made bigger targets, drawing a cascade of boos.

Dan cut off Brubaker's retort, telling him to save it for the ring. After other fighters exchanged theatrically barbed words, the press conference ended with publicity shots of the chessboxers shirtless and posed staring nose to nose into each other's eyes. It was hard for Axel, who only came up to his adversary's shoulders; he looked up into a platform of elevated contempt. The contempt quickly became mutual. Axel was going to wish him luck, but decided to save his pleasantries for someone who deserved them. This person and his booster squad were self-reinforcing jerks.

After the press conference, Vyacheslav took Axel aside to a table being manned in the corner. The table was covered in boxing gloves. "Try them on, Axel. Pick two pairs you like." After a minute, he chose two pairs of black gloves. "Which pair do you like better?" Vy asked. Axel indicated the pair he had chosen on the left. Vy nodded to the man behind the table, who tied the glove pairs together and took out a small gym bag with Axel's name on the side. He stuffed a small piece of paper with the number '1' inside the glove of his preferred pair, and another with the number '2' inside the other. He put both pairs of gloves in Axel's bag.

"Good, that's settled," Vy said. "You just chose your boxing gloves for the chessboxing bout, along with a reserve pair if necessary. They'll be waiting for you at the ring on December 30. Come on, I want you to meet Dan."

Dan was a burly guy who looked like a rugby player – he was, when asked – and had a friendly, ruddy face. Dan told him his fight would be the eighth fight of the evening, two bouts removed from the main event.

"It's a pleasure to finally meet you, Axel," he said. "Your fights on YouTube and the DVDs are impressive. Unfortunately, you are going to get shredded on social media. A lot of Brubaker's followers are real trolls."

"Sticks and stones, Dan. They can swallow their phones for all I care."

Dan and Vy chuckled. Vy asked: "How are you going to train against such a tall guy?"

"Next week I begin sparring against partners who are six foot six and six foot seven. That and planning to stay within his spider arms."

"You did a great job against a six foot four opponent not so long ago," Dan said. "Your bout will be fun to watch."

"They're all fun, chessboxing bouts, but only in hindsight," Axel replied. "Before then, I have to go through a barrel of rabid monkeys."

Dan and Vy promised to pass on the date of the interview the moment they knew. If they landed a television interview, they would fly Axel out for it and, if necessary, put him up in a hotel again. They warmly wished him a safe flight home, and went on to talk with the other chessboxers. Axel went to the exit. With his hand on the doorknob at the stairwell, he felt a familiar hand on his shoulder.

Axel took his hand off the doorknob and turned around. "Hello, Susan."

CHAPTER FORTY-FIVE

"How did you find me?" Axel asked, after giving Susan a tight hug.

"Your sister called my sister. It's not as if there were other chessboxing conferences today."

"Did you get my email?"

"I did. I'm sorry I didn't reply."

"That's OK. It was also perfectly OK if you chose not to see me. I emailed you to tell you I was in town only because you said it was all right. Thanks for coming here, it's wonderful to see you again."

"It's wonderful to see you too." Susan moved in close enough to share their body heat. "Stop sounding so damn sensible."

Axel knew better not to argue. He pulled her in closer. "OK." They emerged apart a minute later with all their nerves alive. "Everything about you is more than OK."

"You're more than not bad yourself. When are you going home?"

"I'm taking a red eye home at midnight."

"Oh," Susan said. She took his hand and squeezed it. "Come with me."

By late afternoon they were lying on Susan's bed in her apartment. One roommate was out of town on a photo shoot, and the other was at the beach. Susan told Axel about her life in Los Angeles. She was paying the bills by waitressing at a local restaurant, doing occasional commercial work. She had a chance at a regular role in a network TV show – the initial audition was next week.

"Best of luck with that. But I have to ask: is this still a fling? I really like you."

She smiled into his chest. "I really like you too, Axel. But you're flying back so soon. Please don't make me think about this right now."

"Fine. Leave me hanging, then. I'm just as happy to be your boy toy."

Axel felt Susan's elbows on his abdomen. He looked up to see

Susan looking directly into his eyes. She said: "No, no, it's not like that. Listen to me. When we met in July, I had a boyfriend who had just been arrested for drug possession. In September, he was sentenced to six months in jail, but might be released early for good behavior. I still have feelings for him… even if he is a boneheaded idiot. He's an actor and a former classmate of mine. I just don't know how to deal with him when he gets out, while seeing you at the same time."

He looked back at her green eyes, and knew that she was telling the truth. "I'll put this out there, Susan. I really like you, and would love to see you again and again. It's pretty easy to contact me if anything changes. I'll be here on December 29 for a few days for the bout, and possibly one day a few weeks earlier for an interview. I'll send another email, telling you where I'm going to be. You can get in touch with me, or not at all. I'll understand either way. OK?"

Susan put her chin on his chest. "More than OK." They both leaned forward, and met in the middle for a long kiss.

Axel took Susan in his arms and held her tightly. He said: "I need to get out of here by eight so that I can check out of the hotel and catch my flight. What time is it?"

"Too late to stay, and too early to leave."

"Story of my life."

Axel tore himself away at seven thirty, feeling pleased, but not at all content. His goodbye with Susan was all heat and no light, with passionate embraces and words that did not come close to conveying what he truly felt. He had managed to bottle lightning, only to fumble with the bottle opener.

Two days later he was back in Ted's gym, dodging long range bombs from Rick and Thom. He could not land a glove on either of them without eating bushels of punches first. More disheartening, they could elude all his head shots just by leaning back, outside of his reach. And Brubaker was even taller.

Thom provided stiff resistance to Axel's charges. As November progressed, Axel learned how to pivot when the resistance reached an isometric standstill, and get off some good shots. When Axel didn't charge, he was tossed into a corner like a rag doll and had to practice defensive phone-box boxing lest he be pummeled into a grease spot.

Rick – the six foot seven guy with an angular build similar to Brubaker's – forced Axel to spin on a dime to continue pursuit. Rick was fast on his feet, and could use his long legs to slip in and out of range by taking little more than a single step. Axel had to learn to keep his feet no wider than his shoulders while constantly changing direction. If his attention flagged, Rick would repeatedly zing him in his blind spots.

All this time Axel kept up with the running, the weightlifting, and the boxing drills in the intensive boxing program. Ted excused him from the program's fight finale, but gave him more sparring practice than Axel had ever done in all the previous programs combined. Ted did not let up during the Friday chessboxing class, making him do a minimum of twelve rounds in the ring. Axel's skin began to feel like hammered metal.

Just before Thanksgiving, Axel's chess preparation against Brubaker had taken shape. He initially thought that his adversary had a quiet positional style. Upon closer examination, he found that Brubaker liked to induce sacrifices from his opponents. With sticky fingers he then held on to all the sacrificed material, hoping to withstand the attack and win the ending. Seven of his online games followed this pattern. Brubaker seldom lashed out tactically, preferring to let the fight come to him, and then opportunistically pick the attacks apart.

Axel played over games from grandmasters who optimally built up their positions before their attacks spilled over. He studied Paul Morphy and Bobby Fischer. Morphy developed the then radical concept of developing the minor pieces, castling, and connecting the Rooks before launching any major offensive. Fischer embodied pure balanced aggression, and had the great quote: "Tactics flow naturally from a positionally superior position." These champions never attacked prematurely. Neither would he. In Los Angeles, he planned to refrain from sacrificial overtures until the reserves had been brought up, and not put any of his pieces offside.

He continued to plug away at Garen's homework, finishing the homework assignments in two-week intervals.

Thanksgiving arrived. Axel celebrated it again with his mother and friends of his late father. The friends were in their late sixties, yet still looked no older than fifty from all the wine they consumed (two bottles with the aperitifs, and two more bottles for the turkey). He enjoyed the meal and the company, but couldn't help wonder how his health might have turned out twenty years later if he had never stopped drinking. Would he have still been healthy, like his Thanksgiving hosts, or afflicted in a terminal disease spiral like his father? It was a question Axel was glad he would never have to answer.

Two days after Thanksgiving, Vyacheslav sent Axel a packet containing disclosure waivers for a TV interview to be held at a Los Angeles television station on December 15 at three p.m., along with tickets to flights that arrived at nine a.m. and returned on midnight the same day. They would send someone to pick him up at the airport. A reply was requested. Axel secured the time off from work, and then called Vyacheslav to say that he could make it.

Vy replied: "Good. Fax me the waivers as soon as possible. Expect the interview to last twenty minutes. You made so many friends with Brubaker's groupies at the press conference that they might throw open the phone lines for the hell of it."

Garen asked Axel the following day if two tournaments on December 3 and December 17 were doable. He promised to give Axel a dossier on his opponent at the end of the first tournament. Axel said that was fine, and asked in return if Zoltan would be there. He told Garen about Zoltan's chameleonic style abilities, and how he wanted to pay for them again. Zoltan could not make the December 3 tournament, but Garen promised to contact him, and send him the same file.

On December 3 Axel arrived for the first training blitz tournament. Giving Garen the money for the prize fund, he saw three grandmasters, five international masters, and only two national masters (Axel included) on the cross table. Garen said: "The next one on December 17 should be even stronger."

Axel rediscovered the humility of being trivially decapitated on the chessboard by much stronger players. He finished in next to last place with zero wins, four draws, and five losses. Garen said: "Six of these guys are pros, Axel. Nobody here expects you to break even with them." He added: "I have a printout of my analysis on your opponent's style. Sit down, relax, and look it over."

The dossier confirmed that his opponent was a pawn grabber, but went much further with data-driven comparisons of which pawns he liked to take the most. Pawns on the rim he captured the most often, while snatching center pawns made him falter and hesitate in his later moves. He did not like his opponent to have a preponderance of control in the center.

Axel looked up from his printout, and asked what openings he should play. Garen replied: "With White play the English Opening with 1. c4 – develop your pieces and then break in the center, when all of them are connected. With Black play either the Pirc Defense against 1. e4 or the King's Indian Defense against 1. d4. Long pawn chains will drive him nuts; he won't be able to grab any loose pawns. I'll email a copy of this to Zoltan."

"Thanks, Garen."

"You're welcome."

On his way home, Axel suddenly felt weary of all the training. He looked forward to seeing the end of it, and stepping into the ring with Adam Brubaker.

CHAPTER FORTY-SIX

Axel's training found a new gear the next few weeks. He could now curl with the heaviest barbells in the gym, and squat more than six hundred pounds. That would not break records, as he had seen a professional football player squat more than a thousand pounds and an arm wrestler curl three hundred and twenty pounds. Still, it was way past his previous personal bests. This would develop an effective shield from punches delivered from much longer arms, and the stance to keep the shield in place.

Because Axel's legs were shorter, he had to stay within range of his tall sparring partners when they backed off. Ted told Axel to resume interval training, so that he could speed up when his opponents were receding, without any significant loss of balance. He found the time by cutting down on his sparring in the intensive boxing program, which Ted said he could afford to pare back.

In the Friday chessboxing class, John suggested the novel sparring technique of him staying outside the ropes on the ring platform, while Axel stayed a foot below on the gym floor. The novel angle led to useful mid-range adjustments, as from the platform John approximated Brubaker's height. Ted put some speedy lightweights there as well. They had the satisfaction of being able to deliver flurries of head shots to someone in a heavier weight class, and Axel was forced to improve his reflexes.

The weather was becoming bitingly cold. With all the runs he was doing in the frigid mornings, he relished his interview on the warmer West Coast. Ted said that many nasty comments had been posted by his opponent's fans on his YouTube videos. Axel asked if he should look at them in order to get into character for the interview. "No," Ted answered. "Answer in actions, not words. Take the high road straight into his face."

Axel flew to Los Angeles on Saturday morning, December 15. The plane arrived at noon, an intern from KVMD greeting him at the gate with his name on a placard. The intern's name was Jared. He had brought a box lunch to eat with iced coffee while the car weaved slowly through the lunchtime traffic towards the studio in the city.

The car reached the studio parking lot at one thirty. Jared escorted Axel to the makeup room, and said that he would be happy to give him a ride back to the airport that evening – if not, the station would give him a taxi voucher. Afterwards, Jared took him to a waiting room next to the studio, leaving him there with Axel's thanks.

He checked his email for the umpteenth time since arriving in Los Angeles. Axel had emailed Susan on December 13, telling her he was going to be in town. She replied in less than an hour, with news that she had passed many auditions for the TV show role, and had one final reading on Monday. The reading had been postponed many times because of the conflicting schedules of the producers; it might be moved up during the weekend. She hadn't emailed any updates, so Axel surmised that her audition was taking place today, and silently wished her luck.

His interview was scheduled for three. At two thirty Dan walked in, and warned him that the phone lines were going to be thrown open to the viewers.

"Have you seen the comments about you on Brubaker's Facebook page? More than a few are primed to call in for saying God knows what to you."

"I don't even have a Facebook account, Dan. Screw 'em. I'd rather let a forest fire die out on its own than waste any oxygen on it, and make it spread."

"Good attitude, man. These fans would get a bloody nose from a punching bag. Try to imagine them in their jockstraps, with one hand on their nose and the other on their nuts."

Axel snorted. "I'm sure the yahoos farthest from the ring – the ones farthest away from harm's way – are going to shout the worse abuse."

"Yeah, I know they're assholes, but they're paying good money to be there. About the interview: after a few general chess questions, we are going to show footage from your bouts with Zolutski, Kozlov, and that SUV you fought two months ago. And then the questions. Try to answer them good-naturedly, OK? You'll help us sell more tickets."

"Hey, I'll do my bit for the fans, even if they're Brubaker's fans."

The interviewer was a clean-cut recent college graduate, who was more comfortable talking about boxing than chess. The chess questions ranged from perfunctory (When did you start playing chess? How long did it take to become a master? Who is your favorite player?) to the ridiculous (What is your favorite move? How do you manage to stay still for so long?), and Axel answered them easily. He had responded to variations of these questions all his life.

The studio lights suddenly dimmed, and Axel saw footage of his fight against Wojtek Zolutski last year. The interviewer asked why Axel had deliberately seemed to walk into so many punches in rounds six and eight. He replied that he wanted to make sure he could get back to the position at the chessboard, which looked won enough to get through the boxing by losing points.

Then footage was shown of his chessboxing bout with Yuri Kozlov in round six. He was asked again why he had eaten so many punches, as opposed to his more cautious approach in the previous rounds. Axel replied that there too he wanted to get back to the chess round, where he had worked out a win in his head. The best way to close out the bout on the chessboard was to directly power through the last boxing round, and not tread water by waiting passively for a potential thunderbolt from his opponent.

Finally, footage was shown of his YouTube fight with Jake. The interviewer asked him how he had managed to hold his own against a boxer with more than fifty pounds on him. Axel went over the punches that created weaknesses on his adversary's right flank and left shoulder, pointing out the repeated alternating punches to those areas that made the weaknesses feel increasingly sore as the fight went on. He added that he listened to his corner man's advice to keep bouncing on his toes.

The producer indicated to the interviewer that the phone lines were full of questions for Axel. The interviewer pressed a button for line one on the phone by his studio chair. The caller said over the intercom that Axel better checkmate Brubaker in the first ten moves, because he was going down by the end of the first boxing round. Axel asked politely if the caller had a question, which only seemed to make the caller angry. After a string of swear words, the interviewer cut him off, and pressed line two.

This caller started off with the swear words, and asked how Axel felt about being spearfished in the open ring. The interviewer was about to cut this person off as well, but Axel motioned to keep the line open, and answered that 1) he was not a fish and 2) spear guns were not allowed in the ring. More swear words with the word 'mother' in them were shouted over the line, and the interviewer switched to line three.

This caller asked what he thought of his opponent. Axel replied that Brubaker had a large height and reach advantage; to train against him, he was sparring against tall opponents. The caller followed up with a question if Axel was scared. He replied that he was always nervous before every fight, but managed to calm down during the bout by thinking about the chess. Then the caller said that Axel was a geek who should get a life before he got hurt. Axel pleasantly wished him a nice day. The interviewer cut that caller off, and switched to line four.

The producer by this time had managed to screen the calls more constructively. Caller four asked Axel if he had ever knocked out anyone in the ring – he replied that he had a couple of TKOs, where the referee had stopped the bouts before anyone had become seriously injured. Caller five asked about the en passant rule in chess. Caller six asked who was the toughest opponent he had ever boxed – Axel instantly replied that it was the schlub who stared back at him in the mirror.

He was beginning to relax a little, until caller seven came on the line and said that he was going to piss on Axel's shoes as he walked to the ring and leave a bag of excrement in his locker. Axel could only laugh, offering to mail the incontinent caller a roll of toilet paper and an adult diaper if he didn't have them in his parents' basement already. The interviewer immediately cut him off and declared the interview over, repeating the time and place of the event on December 30.

"Wow, tough crowd," Axel told him after the producer declared a wrap. "I hope some of those callers get a big fat lump of coal under their Christmas trees."

The interviewer blew air out of his cheeks. "They'd probably shove the lumps of coal up their butts thinking that they could shit out diamonds on New Year's Day. Thanks for taking it in stride. Our bleeper is going to be very busy."

"Is the interview going be on the news, or part of the DVD?"

"Probably both."

"You could cut out the callers altogether. Not every sport needs input from the fans."

"Your haters are quite entertaining, Axel. The more the merrier."

After the interview Dan said that the weigh-in was scheduled for December 29 at an exhibition hall near the arena – he and Vyacheslav would send the details via registered mail within the week. He added that for the chess game Axel should prepare for a one second increment at most.

After saying goodbye, Axel then turned on his phone in the lobby to his email for the umpteenth and first time. A reply from Susan was in his inbox. She apologized for not getting back to him earlier, and left a phone number for him to call. He promptly called.

"Hello?"

"Hi, Susan, this is Axel. How did your final audition go?"

"URK! This town drives me nuts. I took a day off from work and showed up at one p.m. because one of the producers had to fly out for a conference that evening, but the twit never showed up. It's on for Monday again."

"Sorry. It's true for the army, and it's true for life: hurry up and wait."

"URK and double URK. You are so right. How was the interview?"

"My opponent's fans are a really unpleasant bunch. They called in shit-talking me left and right. They wouldn't dare say such stuff to my face."

"Of course not. Jerks like that always talk with the bravery of being out of range."

Axel laughed. "Do you want to get together for dinner, or a cup of coffee? I fly back home late tonight."

"I'm not really that hungry, but I'd love to see you for coffee. If you don't mind me ranting and bitching."

"I don't mind at all, Susan. Where do you want to meet?"

"I'll email you the address, it's not far from the airport. Is eight OK?"

"Fine with me. I'll see you soon."

"See you soon." Susan emailed him the name and address for the cafe within the minute.

Axel asked for Jared at the reception desk. When he appeared, Axel asked for a taxi voucher. Jared rummaged inside the desk and came up with one for a local taxi company, good for one ride within Los Angeles.

"I saw your interview. I'll try to show up on December 30, and cheer you on."

"Thanks, Jared. I need all the help I can get."

Axel walked out onto the street with no particular destination in mind. He wanted to walk it off, even if he had little idea what the "it" was, and kill time before he met with Susan.

Three blocks from the television station Axel encountered a large black man handing out CDs. He shoved one in Axel's hand and gave him a friendly squeeze on the back of his neck, saying it was a demo album from his band. Axel grunted his thanks, and tried to move on. The man though gripped his shoulder with surprising force, saying that he needed a donation. He was as big as Thom, but flabby. Axel tried to hand back the CD, and that's when the man turned nasty.

"Lemme spell it out for you slow-witted honkeys. I need money for the CD. I knows you got money. What is it about you that's stopping you from giving it to me?"

Axel stared at the guy for a second, broke free of his grip, and then said: "I don't want to give you any money. You want a more direct answer than that?"

The so-called band representative couldn't meet his stare. He recovered quickly though, and came back to defiantly meet Axel's eyes.

"Fuck you, man. Give me back the CD."

Axel took a step back, held out his hand with the CD, and dropped it to the ground. Then he blew the guy an air kiss, and continued walking. He was liking this city less and less.

Axel noticed a police officer on patrol around the corner, and approached him to ask if the address of the cafe was within walking distance. The officer shrugged, and said yes if he didn't mind a distance of forty blocks. When Axel said that he didn't mind, the officer pointed to the left and said twenty blocks that way, take a right on Lincoln Avenue, and then twenty more blocks – the cafe would be on the left. After thanking the officer, he walked on and cogitated.

CHAPTER FORTY-SEVEN

Axel arrived at the cafe at six thirty. He ordered a light dinner, checking his email again. No, Susan had not canceled. He did see that several trolls over the afternoon had managed to get hold of his email address – he could tell from the endearing titles of the subject lines. He opened one for the hell of it, and saw Brubaker's face photoshopped onto a wrecking ball that crushed his head. Axel sighed, sending all the emails to the junk folder.

After dinner, he took a page of Garen's homework problems out of his pocket, and tackled the problems while nursing a glass of water. He was on his fifth problem when Susan's voice sounded inches away.

"Hey, you." She wore stone-washed blue jeans, red sneakers, and a pastel green T-shirt.

"Hey, you, yourself," Axel said, standing up and giving her a hug. Her presence up close instantly made him slam on his inner brakes. "Sorry, I was a space cadet – I was working on some chess problems in my head."

"No problem to me, you nutty man," she said with a wry smile. They both sat down and ordered coffee from the server. "How have you been?"

"I don't think I'd enjoy living in this town." He told her of the guy who tried to sell him a CD.

"Yeah, hustlers don't even pretend here. Everybody acts in L.A., so the only way to get ahead on the street is to be bluntly honest." She winked. "I would have paid money to see him try to mug you."

"Good, because it would have cost me a lot of money. The cockroach would have sued for assault when I defended myself."

"This whole place is a minefield." The coffee arrived. "Unfortunately for me, this is where the work is."

Axel reached over the table and held her hand. She didn't take it away. "You must be more than ready for your final audition by now."

"Am I ever. I've read the words of the audition scene so often they may as well be tattooed on my skull. I just want to know if the answer is 'yes' or 'no', so that I can move on. Have you wanted something so much for so long, that when it finally arrived, it wasn't what you thought it was going to be?"

"All the time. I don't even know what the something is. The only thing I know for sure is that it's where the lights are turned off."

Susan reached over and took his other hand, squeezing both of them. "You are so, so nutty." She smiled brilliantly, and Axel's inner brakes were strained to their limits. They created an electrical circuit so intense that he thought his brain was going to fry. Tears threatened to spill down his face. They released their hands and drank coffee in silence for a few minutes.

Axel said after his cup was drained: "Are you staying here for the holidays?"

Susan looked down. "Yes, and I have to tell you this: my boyfriend is getting out of jail next week. He's been calling me collect every other day, apologizing for what he put me through and begging for another chance. I can't slam the door on him just before Christmas, that would be so cold. And I'm so sorry I am leading you on. You deserve better."

"Susan," Axel said quietly. She looked up at Axel. "Please see me because you want to. I so wish I had met you ten years ago, before I dug this damn hole from which I'm trying to crawl out. I've woken up every morning to train for what feels like forever, and it's gotten to the point where life seems like nothing more than an endless list of drills. You are worth so much more than some stupid chessboxing bout. You always will be."

Susan's eyes shone. "That hole's in your head, dummy. Nowhere else."

Axel looked at the wall clock. "Bugger, I have to go to the airport now if I want to catch my flight. Can you see me off?"

"I'd love to. Tell me more about that hole."

Axel paid the bill, and called the taxi company listed on the voucher. While they waited outside for the taxi to show up, he told her about the last decade of his father's life and how he so did not want to end up like him. The taxi showed up, and they got in – during the ride, he went on to tell her about how the unhealthy amounts of alcohol he had consumed left him nothing but two lost decades, and how he was trying to make up for lost time.

Susan said nothing, and listened. They arrived at the airport, where Axel checked in. They were sitting on adjoining chairs, before the security checkpoints and the departure gates, when Susan finally spoke.

"So, what would be your ideal Christmas present?"

"Hmm... one moment when I could feel good about myself without needing a chessboard or boxing gloves. Just to live one day, instead of always thinking how to make it better, that would be my ideal present."

"You have one pointy head, mister," Susan said, laughing softly. "There's a lot more to you than what you do."

"Maybe someday I'll find that out from the ghost of Christmas future."

Susan leaned in and whispered in his ear: "Or from me."

Axel turned around and kissed her softly. After for a long time, he tore himself away and said: "God, if I start kissing you now, I'm never going to be able to stop. I really, really like you. If you're in town on December 30, you know where I'm going to be. And if you want to get in touch before or after then, you know what to do."

He moved his face in close and rubbed noses with her. "Merry Christmas, Susan. Good luck on your audition next week."

"Merry Christmas, Axel. Punch his mouth shut."

CHAPTER FORTY-EIGHT

Axel disembarked from the plane, quickly returning to his apartment to change, and showed up for the last boxing practice before the program's fight finale, from which he was excused. He was on fire that afternoon. Not one of his sparring partners could punch him more than a few times each round, while he landed combinations at will and darted away easily before his opponents could hit back. After forty-five minutes of taking on all comers, Ted told Axel he was done for the day, and to join him in his office.

"OK, Axel, what's her name?"

He grinned stupidly. "Someone I can neither introduce nor talk about because she isn't currently available. Just being with her though brings everything together without it all becoming too crowded. I don't know if I'll ever see her again, but that would be all right because she was never available to begin with, and I've enjoyed being around her more than I have any right to... I'm not making a friggin' bit of sense, am I?"

Ted laughed. "You got it bad, kid. Did you do the nasty with her? Believe it or not, sex has a detrimental effect on training."

"Earlier this year, yes. It might become serious, but right now it's platonic."

"Well, when the final bell rings on this bout, pursue her. I've never seen you this happy."

"Thanks, Ted."

"Now the bad news, buster. You're getting cocky. On Monday night when you spar with the guys again, the volume will be turned up to eleven. I want you going to L.A. with a healthy dose of fear, because that fear will eliminate over ninety percent of your potential mistakes."

He added: "If you need more motivation, look at the latest batch of comments to your YouTube fights. No joke, you might need a police escort to get to the ring."

"What's the deal with these ass clowns?" Axel asked with dismay. He told Ted about the emails after the interview. "It's only a chess match with boxing on the side."

"I don't know what to tell you, Axel, civility these days is going to shit."

"I'll let the organizers know about those comments, thanks. But I won't look at them. Only on the two gloves bearing down on me, and nothing else."

"Good. Don't forget the chess."

The following Sunday Axel showed up at Garen's second blitz tournament. Five grandmasters, six international masters, and Axel, the lone master, were playing.

"Think I can get a point today?" he asked Garen, handing over the money for the prize fund.

"You are going to have to claw and scrape for them today. Nothing is going to come easily to you," Garen replied.

The first two games his opponents had winning positions straight out of the opening, and converted their advantages with little resistance. During the third game Axel maintained equality all the way into the endgame, only to blunder away a pawn which his opponent used to force him into a painful zugzwang. In the fourth game, he got a draw. His fifth opponent was Zoltan. They played a heavily analyzed opening variation from the Sicilian Defense, which ended in a draw by perpetual check on move twenty.

The sixth game was another blowout loss for Axel. Feelings of rage and helplessness were starting to lap at Axel's feet, but he buckled down, and vowed to make his remaining games less one-sided. In the seventh game, he traded the advantage several times, shaking off an attempted bind with a pawn sacrifice and then meeting a piece sacrifice with a counter sacrifice of a Rook, and finally successfully counting his tempos in an intricate pawn ending to a draw.

In the eighth game, he managed to develop a steady initiative from the opening moves, and intensify the pressure throughout the middlegame to the point where his opponent had to jettison a pawn in order to obtain some breathing room. However, his opponent defended tenaciously, and was able to construct a fortress in a Bishop endgame that Axel was unable to crack, resulting in another draw.

All Axel wanted was one win. In chess, unfortunately, willing something to happen is impossible if the position does not allow it. He did not reach a winning advantage in his last three games, nor in the entire tournament, but he maintained his composure and made the most of his chances against vastly superior opposition.

In the ninth game, he defended valiantly against a scintillating attack from his opponent, yet finally buckled and had to resign on move thirty. In the tenth game, he scored another draw. He dropped a pawn out of the opening, but created enough imbalances in the position so that his opponent became distracted and blundered the pawn back. The eleventh and final game was Axel's best. Despite the sharp tactics, he and his opponent made very few errors and constantly found the best moves, making the draw they agreed to the logical result. It felt great to end such a difficult tournament on a high note.

All of Axel's opponents wished him luck the end of the month. They had looked at the dossier that Garen left on the kitchen table, and said that at the chessboard Brubaker was going to be a cream puff. He would fall like a ripe apple if Axel kept his concentration on building up his position, and not on material equality.

Axel thanked them for giving him back a healthy sense of perspective. The last couple of chessboxing bouts had given him a false sense of security; the beat-downs he received this afternoon had made him see clouds and icebergs again. Before he left, he set aside a couple of nights the week after Christmas with Zoltan for specialized blitz training.

Axel and Garen hugged at the door, wishing each other a Merry Christmas. Garen implored him to make this chessboxing bout one of his last. His parting words were: "I saw some of this tall guy's fights on YouTube. Watch out. He looks vicious."

His brain properly conditioned, Axel showed up at the gym Monday night to complete his treatment. He saw not only Rick and Thom, but B and Jake as well. "Jesus, Ted, do you want me to show up in L.A. in a wheelchair?" he asked in disbelief.

"Consider this your final test, Axel," Ted replied. "Three rounds alternating against each of them for twelve rounds, and I'm off your case the rest of the year. What order do you want?"

Glaring at Ted, Axel asked for five sheets of paper and a pen. He wrote down a number, and placed it face down on the side of the ring. He then gave the pen and the other sheets to his sparring partners; he asked them to write down a number between one and a thousand. Axel then turned over his sheet – he had written down six-six-six ("In honor of you, Ted," drawing guffaws from everyone). The sparring order he picked based on the closest numbers became Rick, Thom, B, and Jake.

As they warmed up, Ted said to the others that Axel was facing a six-foot-nine opponent in a very hostile environment, and that going easy on him tonight was doing him no favors. To Axel, he said to take each round one at a time. He would be in his corner offering advice, and first aid if necessary.

He said to Ted as he gloved up against Rick: "Oh, first aid is probably going to be necessary, because I'm doing all the rounds. I'm going to get to the end of this by imagining Brubaker's trolls looking on, and not give them the satisfaction by stopping early."

"Good, you're motivated."

The bell sounded for Axel's first round against Rick. He was not inclined to chase such a tall opponent all over the ring and wear himself out, so he waited for Rick to come to him. He was content to spend the round blocking, and counterpunch if the opportunity arose. Rick was full of energy, throwing flurries of combinations that Axel for the most part had learned over the last two months to evade by slipping and rolling. Some hard punches landed on the top of the head, but didn't hurt, and Axel managed to land a body shot.

Sixty seconds later the bell sounded for Axel's first round against Thom. He knew better than to go toe to toe, so he moved in an arrhythmic staccato to stay out of range for the first two minutes, then gritted his teeth and started charging. He fatalistically knew that his face was going to be busted up anyway. Axel kept himself covered and tried to get inside his opponent's arms for the last minute, and succeeded, but not before receiving a savage hook to his right shoulder and a sharp jab that snapped his head back.

Sixty seconds later the bell sounded for Axel's first round against B; they knew each other's quirks inside and out. Axel tried to fight conservatively by adopting a classical stance and keeping himself as sideways as possible, yet B in the second minute executed an excellent feint with his jab, and clocked Axel full in the jaw with a straight right. With thirty seconds to go, however, Axel evened the score with a surprise extra hook at the end of a four-punch combination that B did not see coming, and sent him staggering. The bell rang, and the sparring had just turned into boxing.

Sixty seconds later the bell sounded for Axel's first round against Jake. Axel continued his previous strategy against him using pinpointed blows to alternate against, and succeeded in landing three shots in both the left side and right shoulder. Trying to add an area in his opponent's midsection for the later rounds, Axel caught an uppercut over his left eye that was going to leave a mark. However, when the bell rang it was his most successful round so far.

"How you are feeling, Axel?" Ted asked in his corner, before his second round with Rick was about to start.

"The punches they are landing are going to add up in a hurry. Will you please pull the plug if it looks like I'm getting too badly mauled?"

"Of course. With guys this big, err on the side of caution. Conserve your energy when you can, and stay away from brawling."

"Oh, that's so much easier said than done, Ted. But I'll try to do what you say."

"Attaboy."

The second round with Rick started. It was almost a carbon copy of their first round, except that two of Rick's punches clipped his ear and grazed his nose in addition to all the shots tagging the top of his head, while Axel managed to connect with seven clean body shots.

In the second round with Thom, Thom charged within seconds of the opening bell; there was not much Axel could do about being pushed into a corner. While uncomfortable, Axel in cramped quarters managed to land several uppercuts and hooks into the midsection. Thom did connect with some hard punches to his shoulders, but with reduced leverage, and the round was over relatively quickly.

With B during the second round, Axel stuck to the basics, and conducted a brisk stick-and-move strategy. It worked until the last minute, when a ferocious barrage of straight right hands from B yielded pay dirt with a shot straight into Axel's nose, drawing blood. The second round with Jake started late while Ted dammed up the nose.

Jake in the first minute walked into a hook that forced him to clinch; however, during the third minute Axel made a critical error by not covering his rib cage, allowing a powerful uppercut to cause him to lose his breath and take a knee for fifteen seconds. The round ended with Axel backpedaling.

"You're doing great, Axel. Only three minutes left with each of them."

"Damn, Ted – I'm tired. And they look even bigger."

"I know. Think four, three, two, one."

"With ruby slippers, and saying there's no place like home?"

"If that helps."

Fatigue played a factor in Axel's final rounds, though he did his best to keep it at a minimum. He mirrored Rick's footwork, allowing him very few easy openings, and raced in to meet his charges, taking away the thunder of his momentum. Against Thom, he had no objections to being shoved into the corner again to phone box, for he could draft on the opposing energy.

Axel did the opposite against B, expending most of his physical reserves by aggressively chasing his opponent across the ring. The best defense against B was a good offense, not allowing such a skilled adversary the chance to cause mischief.

In the final three minutes against Jake, Axel with ragged breath minimized physical confrontation by bobbing and weaving in the open ring, and resorting to clinches when his reserves dwindled to fumes. He did not escape unscathed: Jake nailed Axel in the other eye during the last ten seconds, giving him a matching set of shiners. He would look like a living Halloween costume by the end of the week, but he heard the bell ring, and it was finally over.

"Ja, I cannot imagine this six-foot-nine dude being any worse than what we put you through tonight," B said to Axel in Ted's office afterwards. All of them were there, drinking beer to Axel's grape soda.

"Neither can I," Axel replied with a mixture of sarcasm and weariness. He was holding an ice pack on the bridge of his nose.

"I've looked at your opponent online. He's even skinnier than Rick," Thom said. "One good shot to the ribs, and he'll sag like an accordion."

"I wish your arms were longer, Axel," added Rick. "His face is so damn punchable."

"I need to make him bend over before I can do that, Rick. I can't just jump up and play Whack-A-Mole with his mug," Axel said. "I really hope Brubaker doesn't fight dirty. He has the range."

Jake said: "If Daddy Long Legs tries to do that, reach over and deliver a rabbit punch. That will make him bend over."

"Axel, trust the referee to stop any street fighting," Ted said. "Rick and Thom, tonight was your last sparring session with Axel – thank you for toughening him up. He told me after the eighth sparring round that he was dog tired, yet he kept going. He grew an extra layer of stubbornness."

"Yes, thanks for everything, guys. If it gets tough over there, I'll remember your treatment tonight to get off my butt and finish what I started."

They clinked bottles, and drank in silence. B said after a minute: "You can also kick the dude in the crotch. That will make him bend over as well."

CHAPTER FORTY-NINE

Axel continued his maniacal training all the way to the end of the week. He threw away his ankle weights, running in the early mornings for an hour and a half, squatted seven hundred and thirty-five pounds, and curled one hundred and twenty pounds. In the last Friday chessboxing class before the holidays, he blocked punches on the floor from John and all the other boxers standing on the ring for twenty rounds. Late Saturday afternoon at the gym, on December 23, he was doing interval training on the bags when he felt a hand on his shoulder.

"Axel, stop. You're ready," Ted said.

"Ready as I'll ever be. It never feels like enough."

"It never does until you throw the first punch in the ring." The gym was about to close. "Come to my office for some final tips."

They were looking at Brubaker's four existing fights on YouTube. "Your opponent is much taller than you, there's no way around that," Ted said. "He has good balance when he moves, along with a solid jab and right, which is going to make him hard to approach without getting thwocked from afar. But he does have some tells." He stopped the video file, and backed it up a few seconds. "Look here. See how he follows through with the right, and his back leg is straight instead of bent? If you can slip that fast enough, you'll have time to deliver some good body shots before he can react. And look here."

Ted closed the file, and opened a new one, speeding and pausing it after three minutes. "He leans in just a little when he delivers that hook after the jab. That lean-in should bring his head just within range to smash him in the chops."

He opened another video, fast forwarding to just after the second round had started. "I do not recommend getting into a corner against him, Axel, because you are going to be strafed, but if you find yourself pinned in do what this fighter does... here." Ted paused the file, rewound it ten seconds, and played it again. "This boxer defended well.

He walked up two steps into heavy punches, then suddenly backed up and darted out to the right. He easily slipped away from Brubaker four more times in the fight this way."

Ted opened the last video file, letting it run for a full round. "Don't do what this opponent did. He got clobbered because he concentrated only on the body, and lost a gazillion points from all the head shots he received." He brought up the previous video. "The boxer who got off the corner well, he had the right idea by trying to alternate his punches to the midsection and upstairs to the head. Unfortunately, his arms were shorter than yours, and he never planted his feet close enough to Brubaker to make his punches count."

"OK, I have some ideas for defense. But how do I mount any sort of offense against this skyscraper?" Axel asked.

"Not without eating a lot of punches from him first, I'm afraid. But if you can digest them without too much pain – and the guys gave you more of a taste of that a few days ago – you can get in close enough to wail away at his torso, and then chop him down to the point where hooks and uppercuts can reach his head. He is going to have a hard time shoving you back with those spindly arms. He'll even have a hard time getting you in a clinch."

Ted stopped talking, and smiled. "You've trained hard and smart for this. You're ready to take abuse, and dish it out."

"How much do I weigh, anyway?" Axel stepped over to the scale in Ted's office, and found that he weighed an even two hundred pounds. Lifting all those weights the past few months had given him more mass. "The weigh-in is on next Friday, and the fun and games begin the night after that. I'm third from the top of the card."

"You're not going to fly out the day of the weigh-in, are you?"

"No, the day before. My office for all practical purposes shut down yesterday, and won't reopen until January 2. I'm on vacation. The organizers gave me a plane ticket with adjustable arrival and departure dates, and will pay for four nights at a local hotel."

"Sweet. Have you chosen your entry music?"

"*Carousellambra* by Led Zeppelin. I've loved the song ever since I was a teenager. The lyrics are really hard to understand, but once the tune gets going, I cannot get it out of my head."

Ted grinned. "The things that the stuff inside our heads makes us do."

At the door, Ted asked Axel to stop by on December 27 for a final session on the pads before going to Los Angeles. After hugging and wishing each other a Merry Christmas, Axel went out to the parking lot to his car. Before putting the gear into drive, he took a cold hard look at his face in the dashboard mirror. The waiting had begun.

Axel celebrated Christmas at his sister's house on a Monday. He received joke presents of a crash helmet, a jumbo jar of Ibuprofen, and an icepack. His nephew and niece were enthralled to hear about his chessboxing training for the bout next week; his mother was too stressed out to ask. His sister tried to sneak in Susan during the conversation at the dinner table, but Axel abruptly changed the subject without making any effort to mask his displeasure.

After dinner he drank a cup of hot chocolate on the porch in the freezing air. Snow was falling again, making strange muted patterns on the screen windows. Axel relished the White Christmas, before he went out to the hostile land of eternal sunshine on the other side of the country.

His brother-in-law joined him outside, carrying a snifter of Tequila. "You do know your sister loves you, right?" he asked.

"Of course, I do. But I don't ask questions about her personal life with you. Why can't she give me the same courtesy?"

"She's family, Axel. Don't hold her to the same standards as strangers."

"I've been adhering to the standards of strangers and family all my life. Being a good son, being a good student, being a good citizen, being a good neighbor, being a good employee, ex-fucking-cetera. It almost made me psychotic, trying to color within the lines written ever more tightly inside everyone else's post cards of what life should look like. I've been making my own standards the last couple of years, and if that includes keeping my private life private at the Christmas table and making her unhappy, too bad."

His brother-in-law was going to say something, but checked himself. He finally said: "Christ, it's cold. Get inside soon, Axel, and let my wife wish you luck before you head out. You don't want to show up in L.A. sneezing your ass off."

Axel stayed outside alone for a few minutes more, letting the cold air clear his mind. He imagined facing his opponent later that week, the noise insanely loud, and also being here, with no noise at all, at the same time. His niece came out to pull him back inside to play a board game with the rest of the family. Two hours later he let his sister wish him luck, and he was on his way towards his apartment to continue the waiting game.

The next two nights he played blitz chess with Zoltan at a local cafe. With Garen's dossier beside them, they played combinations of seven-minute, five-minute, three-minute, two-minute, and one-minute (bullet) games from six thirty in the evening until the place closed. Following Garen's advice, Axel avoided openings where he had to offer material in order to obtain an initiative.

With White, he played instead quiet variations such as the English Opening, the exchange lines of the Queen's Gambit Declined and Caro Kann, the Closed Sicilian, and fianchettoing his King Bishop against all the Indian Defenses. With Black, he played the French Defense and King's Indian Defense where long pawn chains made speculative sacrifices impractical. The pawn-snatching methods Brubaker liked to use had limited effect in these openings.

Few of the games ended under thirty moves. The wins and losses were the results of protracted trench warfare. The deciding factor was pawn storms behind which the pieces rode in and did their damage, not the pieces exploiting open lines from broken pawn structures. More often than not, the most important piece proved to be the clock. Over half the battles between Axel and Zoltan were determined by who ran out of time first.

The first night Axel lost more games on time than by being outplayed. He asked Zoltan if that was a good thing. Zoltan told him:

"Not really. Pick up the pace a little for tomorrow. Running out of time is losing, just like being checkmated. You are holding your own on the chessboard, though. All you have to do is shave off a few seconds by moving quickly in positions where you don't need to think, such as setting up your opening schemes. The extra time window will let you see more tactics that can put the game away."

The following night he made extra allowances to the clock, making sure that he never fell behind in time to Zoltan. He lost more chess games by hasty evaluations of the positions than by hasty tactics from having only seconds left to make a move. More games ended with checkmate or with resignation, but Zoltan emerged again winning most of them. Axel realized with a finality that had eluded him from all his games with Willie: he was not going to play perfect chess next Saturday night. He told Zoltan this, who said that was fine.

"No carbon-based life form can play perfect chess; you should know that by now. I know it's an ideal we all strive for, but really, all we can do is play better chess than our opponents. From Brubaker's games in the dossier, it's obvious that he is going to have to beat you in the ring. If you play the same way you've been playing against me the last two nights, and don't fall behind on the clock, all the pressure in the chess is going to be on him."

"Thanks, Zoltan."

"You're welcome, Axel. Stop overthinking this – you're ready. Just play chess." With a sardonic smile, he added: "Unless you get concussed. Then all bets are off."

On December 27, the day before he was to go to Los Angeles, Axel dropped by to see Ted as he was opening the gym. The bruises from last week had faded away. He expected to emerge dripping with sweat from pad work an hour later, but instead Ted went to his office and came back with a large white envelope.

"For you – open it," Ted said.

Inside the envelope was an oversized card. On the cover was the picture of a lone lumberjack about to deliver the final axe blow that was going to bring down a giant tree. The caption inside said: 'If I had eight hours to chop down a tree, I'd spend six hours sharpening my axe - Abraham Lincoln.' The inside was covered with signatures and upbeat messages of luck from all his sparring partners, all the gym trainers, several members of the chessboxing classes, and the entire intensive boxing program. Axel was speechless.

"You've spent a hell of a lot longer than six hours sharpening your axe for this, Axel. No pads today, you don't need them. When the bell goes off over there, you'll know what to do."

"Thanks for everything, Ted."

"Thank me for what? I just steered you in the right direction; you did all the work."

"I'll do my best to make you proud."

"I already am, no matter what happens." They bumped fists. "Make the bastard afraid to look down."

CHAPTER FIFTY

Axel's plane touched down in L.A. on December 28 in the late evening. He immediately checked into his hotel and went to sleep. The weigh-in was scheduled for the following day at three p.m.

He had sent an email to Susan, informing her of the time and place of the chessboxing bout, but never received a reply. Which was just as well. Axel was so intently concentrating on getting through the next two days that he did not want to walk and chew gum and worry about something else.

Axel woke up at noon, and checked his email. Still no reply from Susan, and the hate emails from his opponent's fans were back. All were promptly flushed into the junk folder. He tried to remember that he was getting paid for this.

Remembering Dan's admonition that the neighborhood around the arena was rough, Axel took a taxi to the weigh-in, even though the building was only a few blocks away. He planned to be one of the first to arrive and take care of business before Brubaker and his posse oozed in. If possible, his exposure to him would only be for the five rounds of boxing; the chess would take care of itself.

He was nevertheless accosted by two lunkheads wearing 'Duke of Brubaker' T-shirts as he entered the building. Luckily, Dan appeared, loudly telling them to fuck off or they would be barred entry to the arena tomorrow. Vyacheslav beckoned Axel to the sign-in desk with an apologetic expression.

"I am sorry about this. If it's any consolation, you are helping us move shitloads of tickets. If we sell out the event tonight, you might just get a little extra under the table."

"I don't even notice them anymore, Vy. What's the deal with Brubaker? Has he gone fully clear in Scientology?"

"No, but he's very popular on Reddit," Dan said from behind. Axel turned around to face him. "Don't follow Reddit? Good. Seriously, don't – ignorance is bliss. The stuff said there is really vile. Both of us talked to Brubaker last week, and we read him the riot act to tone it down. We even threatened to cut his compensation in half. He promised in that weird monotone of his that he would. You haven't been harassed online recently, have you?"

Axel told them about the emails, and said that they were nothing – the junk folder swallowed them painlessly. Vy said: "Good. If it escalates to phone calls or knocks on your hotel room door, let us know immediately. Dan has a LAPD friend on speed dial. We'll also give you a pair of security guys to escort you to and from the locker room."

"Jeez, these people need to lighten up," Axel said. "I've always found chess and boxing together to be fun, at times even funny. The only joy these guys have is pressing the Enter button."

"Sad but true," Dan said. "You've been a trooper about this, Axel. Thanks again."

"No problem. This has been an experience and a half so far. And I haven't even been punched in the face yet."

They all laughed, and Axel went on to process his paperwork. Dan walked back to the door, for he saw four more guys with 'Duke of Brubaker' T-shirts walking through the door. Vyacheslav gave Axel a pass to the athlete's entrance to the arena, asking him to show up at eight p.m.; his fight should be starting around eleven.

"The weigh-in room is down that hall there to the left," he said. "Oh, before I forget: Dan told me to tell you that the time increment for the chess game is going to be one second after each move. Not that I think you'll need it."

On the scale Axel still weighed an even two hundred pounds. His nervous energy that week had managed to metabolize all the food he had eaten at Christmas dinner. After providing his urine for the drug test, he successfully slipped out of the building before Brubaker arrived.

While waiting for the taxi to return him to the hotel room, he noticed a large phalanx of people approaching the front entrance. His extra tall opponent occupied the middle. Dan and Vy would probably be at the door telling them that only Brubaker could come inside, but the taxi arrived and drove Axel away before any such confrontation came into view.

An email shortly arrived from Vy: Brubaker had weighed in at two hundred and forty-two pounds.

His phone had acquired many voice messages in the form of advice. A long-distance conference call from Berlin exhorted him to raise his arms extra higher to cover the top of his head, and Axel recognized the voices of Gunther G., Gunther Z., Wolfgang, and Franz. A call from John told him to move off-balance like a spastic crab. Willie called too, reminding him never to fall behind on the clock. His New York chess friend called to recommend that he should just walk straight up to his opponent with both hands in front of his face, and start wailing away with hooks when he was close enough; that was a decent plan to try tomorrow.

Then there was a message on his phone that had been left only twenty minutes ago, which started with several seconds of silence and ended with a mumbled apology/promise to reach him later. Axel recognized the voice, and immediately called back the number.

"Hello?"

"Hi, Susan, this is Axel. You called?"

"I did. Hi, Axel, how are you?"

"The waiting is almost over. Saturday is going to be six rounds of chess with five rounds of terror, and then I'll work out what I want to tackle next."

"Good luck."

"Thanks. To tell you to truth, I've already put in so much training that I'll be able to live with any result. How did your audition go?"

"Axel, I got the part! I start filming for the show in late January."

"Congratulations, it couldn't happen to a more deserving and talented actress. Can you give up your day job?"

"Not entirely. I only show up in a story arc that lasts five episodes. But I'll have the luxury of working part time for a couple of months if I want to."

"Awesome, Susan. With a bonafide professional credit it's all downhill from here."

"I hope so." After a slight pause she added: "Sorry for the cryptic phone call. I didn't want to distract you. You must have a lot on your mind at the moment."

"Distract me any time you wish. Just thinking about you makes me feel that I can take on King Kong. Maybe we can get together before I fly back home."

"I would love that, Axel. When do you return?"

"My hotel is paid up until the end of the year, and then I have to show up for work on January 2. You know where I'm going to be tomorrow."

"Oh, Axel, I don't think I can bear to see that. But please know I'll be with you in spirit."

"You are, and always have been. If we can't meet, have a Happy New Year. Knock their socks off on the television show."

"Thanks, Axel. I will talk to you again soon, I promise."

"I'll hold you to that. Bye."

"Bye."

He hung up. Catch and release. It had served Axel well so far in his fledgling love life. Only this woman was not a fish, but a nymph, siren, and mermaid goddess all rolled up into one. The thought of her disappearing again into the ocean gave him a twinge.

The next twenty-four hours Axel spent alone in his hotel room. He slept and watched trashy TV movies. He did push-ups and sit-ups. He took lots of showers. He played over chess games. He watched the YouTube fights of his opponent again on the laptop. He re-read Garen's dossier. He ordered room service for his meals. He declined housekeeping for the following day. The closest he ever came to engaging with the outside world was to open all the windows in his room, and then lie on the bed listening to the sounds of traffic.

Axel left the hotel room at five p.m. the following day, his gym bag in tow. He hung around the lobby sitting on one of the sofas staring at CNN on the television there, because he couldn't think of anything else to do. He forced himself to watch two hours of news. The world would go on, as if what Axel was about to do never happened.

Finally, seven p.m. rolled around, and Axel caught a taxi to the arena. No special trunks and shirts had been issued to the fighters, so he had simply brought his usual workout clothes, along with a jump rope and a mouth guard. After showing his pass, he was signed in, and two security personnel appeared to usher him towards the locker rooms. Axel was able to see the ring through a closed-circuit TV above the lockers. The sound was turned off, but the arena looked packed and raucous. He arrived just as the first bout had begun on the card. Seven fights more, and he would be there.

He put his bag in a spare locker, intending to change by the fourth bout, and turned around to see Dan with four burly guys behind him. Dan had a small band-aid on his forehead. "Hey, Axel, these guys are going to make sure you get to and from the ring safely. We had an altercation yesterday. A crowd of Brubaker assholes tried to go in the building with their hero, and didn't like hearing no for an answer."

"Unbelievable," Axel said. "The world would be a better place if they took up video games instead." Dan sighed and nodded.

"I am going to apologize for this in advance again, you are going to face a torrent of shit once you step into the arena. We'll have extra heavy security by the ring so that no one interferes, but please don't poke your head out before then. I've talked this over with Vy, and we are taking half of Brubaker's compensation and giving it to you. He can sue us if he wants, but he's violated the morals clause in the contract and can go have sex with himself."

"Well, he does seem to have helped you sell out the event."

"Yeah, we don't mind the publicity he's brought. His notoriety all but guarantees that we'll be able to organize future events. However, he's forced us to hire more security. The net financial gain he's bringing to the table tonight is zero."

"I honestly don't know what I did to piss him off. Then again, I don't really care."

"Please care while you're here, sir," one of the security personnel said. "Two of us will be escorting you to a taxi afterwards to make sure you leave without incident."

Dan said: "Until then, Axel, chill, and put yourself in that special place that will make you bash the shit out of him. By eight thirty our people will be around to wrap your hands. The gloves you selected at the press conference will be waiting for you in your corner at the ring. Get warmed up and ready to go by the fight before yours, and good luck."

Dan shook hands with Axel, and left to go to the other locker room. Axel turned back to his locker to change before the plaster and the 'X's were on his fists. The fight-or-flight sensations hadn't kicked in yet. The walls of the locker room had excellent soundproofing – not even the vibrations from the crowd noise seeped in. He changed, and was able to get in a full regimen of stretching and a dozen rounds of jump roping before his hands were wrapped. After his hands were wrapped, he sat the same way he had earlier in the hotel lobby, just staring at the wall.

He chatted with the chessboxers on the earlier card as they came back to their lockers, all of whom said the atmosphere was ugly. The fourth bout finished, and then the fifth. Axel found a mirror and shadow boxed in front of it during the sixth bout. He aimed all his punches at the top edge of the mirror. When the seventh bout started, he put in his mouthpiece and sat on a bench next to the arena entrance, nodding to his security detail. He closed his eyes, waiting to hear movement of their feet. He heard it ten minutes later, and opened his eyes to see of one of them pointing to the door.

"Good luck, sir."

"Thanks."

CHAPTER FIFTY-ONE

Axel walked down a twenty-foot hallway, the soundproofed walls of the locker room quickly forgotten. He could barely hear his entry music playing above the din. The closer he approached the arena, the more shockingly loud the noise of the crowd became.

He walked into a maelstrom. The security guys instantly pressed into his left side, right side, and back – the one in front hurriedly told him to place his gloves on his shoulders. A second later, beer cans and toilet paper were being thrown at them. Axel looked briefly to the right and left into a sea of smart phones and distorted illuminated faces.

The colors in the arena were livid and saturated; the phones alone looked like the eyes of vampire bats opening in a dark cave. Axel was transported in an instant back to middle school with all the bullies, and all that retreating his head inside a shell. Infants had better manners than these alleged grown-ups.

Axel kept his head down and briskly walked towards the ring. He saw the display screen of the chessboard above the ring. Twenty security personnel around the referee formed a tight defensive cordon. An opening was made for Axel, allowing him to enter, his escorts joining the group.

The referee checked Axel's mouth guard, and motioned him to stand by the chess table. A coin toss flip would decide where he would sit: by the Black pieces, or the White pieces. His boxing gloves were waiting in his corner of the ring.

The arena somehow became even louder when Brubaker entered, with only two security guys escorting him to the ring. His entry music (some sort of thrash metal), Axel had to admit, cut through the ambient noise better than Led Zeppelin. He stuck out vividly in the crowd, not only because of his height, but also because he had styled his hair into an electric green mohawk. He took his time to arrive, pausing to administer high fives with the audience, his long arms reaching deeply into the rows.

Upon reaching the chessboard, his mouth guard was checked and his security guys joined the others already there. Axel and Brubaker stood next to each other for the first time since the press conference. If anything, Brubaker's contempt for him had only grown. The referee flipped a coin, and told Brubaker to call it. "Tails," he spat out, some of the spittle landing on Axel's forehead. It came up tails to the baying jeers of his supporters, and Brubaker chose White.

They sat down at the chess table. The referee told them to touch their wraps. Brubaker put an extra oomph to the forward direction of his fists, which Axel stopped cold; he then tried to say something before the starting bell rang, but Axel put on his headphones and sat down at the board to await the first move. *Bring it, you goddamn graceless giraffe ear cleaner.* The silence of the headphones brought him back to all the preparation he had put in. The waiting was finally over.

Brubaker opened with 1. a3, a provocative move. It prevented Black from playing Bb4 before such a move was even legally possible, and did nothing to develop White's pieces much less occupy the center. Still, it did not weaken the position, and passed the buck to the opposite side. Squandering the first move like this invited aggression and overextension, which was obviously the intent.

Not rising to the bait, Axel chose a schematic King's Indian Defense setup. The opening moves continued 1...Nf6 2. b4 g6 3. Bb2 Bg7 4. c4 0-0 5. Nf3 d6. It looked more like a Reti Opening than a King's Indian Defense, until Brubaker played 6. d4 committing a pawn in the center. He wanted his advanced Queenside pawns to cramp Black's pieces there, and then stake a claim to the rest of the board with the benefit of his outstretched flank.

The next moves came slowly, eating up the rest of the time in the round. Axel countered in the center by playing 6...e5. He threatened to push the pawn up one square further, creating an advanced central outpost. Brubaker continued 7. e3 (the capture with 7. dxe5 would have won a pawn if not for 7...Ng4, exploiting the pin of the e5 pawn on

White's Bishop on b2). Several seconds later Axel changed his mind about pushing the e-pawn up a square. The resulting position looked better for Brubaker – the Queenside pawns looked faster than any advance Axel could engineer on the Kingside.

Instead, Axel steered the game into a semi-open position with 7...exd4. He thought his opponent was going to recapture with the pawn and keep the elasticity of his advanced pawns intact. Brubaker though recaptured with 8. Nxd4; it improved the position of his Knight, but now the possibility of pawn storms on the Queenside was gone.

Since his opponent no longer threatened a fast pawn advance on the Queenside, Axel played 8...Ng4 to seize the initiative. It threatened to win a piece by pushing up the c-pawn two squares. Brubaker defended by playing 9. Nc3, and Axel developed his other Knight on an active square with 9...Nc6. While Brubaker was thinking about his reply, the referee reached over and stopped the clocks.

Standing up to get ready for the boxing round, Axel saw the mohawk up close for the first time, startled at the green color; it beckoned as a landing strip for head shots. Then he took off the headphones, and the noise of the crowd came back so loudly he jumped. He felt that his nerves had been plunged into an ice bath.

The audience started stomping their feet during the sixty second break. *If you can't beat them, join them*, Axel thought as he put on his gloves, and started bouncing in unison with the rhythm. Brubaker was simply swaying from side to side as if he was uncoiling a whip. Fifteen seconds to go, ten seconds to go, five seconds to go... Axel put down his head when he heard the bell, raised his gloves above his ears, and marched into the center of the ring.

Axel decided to try his New York friend's advice: bounce straight up to Brubaker as far as he allowed, and deliver body shots if within range. He also wanted to take his first hit and get it out of the way. (Then he would get out of the way.)

That was his plan, but he abandoned it quickly. Brubaker established a steady battery of lefts and rights that stopped him from advancing within arm's length. The strength of his opponent's shots did not feel much harder than the ones he had received in Ted's gym a little over a week ago, and all the punches were blocked. However, Axel acquired firsthand knowledge of his opponent's reach. Although quite long – at least six feet – it gave him a metric to work with for the rest of the bout.

Brubaker after a minute switched from defensive punches to offensive punches. Despite all his leg weight work, Axel found himself being pushed into the ropes. He knew the hooks were coming, and would not be pleasant. While slipping a right hand coming straight at his face, he got hit for the first time that evening, a savage left hook that blindsided him in the side of the head, and made his ear ring above the roar of the crowd.

Axel surged forward, and got his range. He landed a left uppercut, right hook, and two jabs into Brubaker's ribs, before he was met with a stinging uppercut that would have broken a tooth had his mouth guard not been in place. His opponent stepped away, but not before flicking off a jab that landed with surprising force on Axel's shoulder and stopped his momentum.

Axel tried circling around Brubaker to the right for an attacking angle, but realized after a few seconds that too was useless. His opponent had excellent balance and much longer legs. Next, he tried to apply his interval training by changing the tempo and gait of his steps around to the left, hoping to see gaps in Brubaker's perimeter, and was almost decapitated by a right hook that seemed to materialize ten feet away and accelerate in under a second. Axel ducked it in the nick of time, the displaced air above his head sending shivers down his spine. He realized now that side to side motion ran the risk of sky hooks in either direction.

In the last minute of the round, Axel chose the safest avenue up the middle. He resumed being repulsed at a distance from Brubaker's lefts and rights, and knew that he was going to have to be more creative. His opponent pushed forward again, but Axel resisted harder, specifically focusing on the all the squats he had done. This time he successfully made a stand a foot from the ropes. The bell rang ending the round.

They were back at the chessboard, the headphones on. After half a minute, Brubaker retreated the Knight by playing 10. Nf3. Axel decided that he was mobilized enough. He played 10...Nce5, intending to invade with his Queen on h4 once the Knight on f3 had been exchanged. Half a minute more thought from Brubaker, and he developed his last minor piece with 11. Be2. Off went the Knight with 11...Nxf3+.

Brubaker surprised Axel by recapturing the Knight with the pawn: 12. gxf3. He wanted the Knight on g4 to go away. However, the move allowed a speculative continuation, which made Axel think for over a minute. It required an upfront investment of material, with no immediate payout, but his opponent's King would be very uncomfortable. It looked promising. He closed his eyes, and ran through the main variations in his head. Reopening his eyes, he saw that neon green mohawk again, and something in the air turned it into a green light. Before Axel could change his mind and lose more time, he sacrificed his Knight with 12...Nxf2.

Brubaker accepted the sacrifice instantly with 13. Kxf2; moving the Queen away lost the Rook. Axel followed up with 13...Qh4+, and again Brubaker replied instantly. 14. Kg1 was practically forced; the f1 square allowed Axel to bring the Bishop from c8 to h3 with check. Despite being a piece down, Axel trusted his gut and continued with the quiet move 14...Re8. The Rook threatened to capture the undefended pawn on e3, and to join the attack on White's King by going to e5 and then the g5 square. Brubaker wanted to transfer his Knight from c3 to defend the boxed in King, but it was pinned to the Bishop on b2. While he thought about his next move, the referee stopped the clocks.

The headphones came off. The partisan cheers for Brubaker did not seem that overwhelming anymore; they must have developed some sort of depth perspective. Axel's brain was firing on all cylinders, developing new avenues of attack in the ring and on the chessboard. He bounced again with the crowd-stomping sound with less self-consciousness. The idea for how to box this round differently came to him after the twelfth bounce.

The bell sounded. Axel resumed the direct approach, pushing hard against Brubaker's long jabs and rights. This time, however, Axel decided after having his punch blocked to hit the glove with an extra, superfluous punch if the glove was still in range. Most of those punches had little physical effect other than to knock the trajectory of the outstretched hand off a few degrees; they did though confuse his opponent. Brubaker was meeting blocked shots with unexpected jolts at the end that were throwing off his rhythm.

As a result, his opponent's hands did not immediately retract to his fighting stance as they normally did. Axel was sure he could engineer new openings from this; it was a new problem to solve. Brubaker quickly grew tired of defensively punching into sand, and switched to offense. These punches were too fast for Axel to add a jolt on the end of a block, but he did see a small tell in Brubaker's posture before he surged forward: he took a quick half step backwards on his rear leg, and swiveled his left shoulder to his right an inch. If he did that again, Axel was prepared.

In the meantime, he had to deal with two long arms attached to a tall body moving forward. Axel again willed himself to stop being pushed back a foot from the ropes, and held his ground. He knew hooks were flying in, and soon. First a right hook to the head, then two left hooks to the shoulder, and another right hook to the head arrived; they were blocked. Then Brubaker tried a left uppercut and a straight right to ribs, but Axel brought down his elbows and prevented those from doing damage as well. He knew his luck would not hold out here for long, so he took one step back and moved to the left, making it to the open ring at the expense of a jab that nailed him in the forehead.

Back in the center, Axel resumed his assault and gave his opponent's extended gloves an extra slap whenever possible. It was clearly irritating Brubaker. He made the telltale sign of another charge, and that's when Axel struck. He saw the front shoulder move slightly to the right, and he knew that his opponent was stepping backwards for a split-second. He took two quick steps in, twisted to the right, and threw a right hook hard into Brubaker's side, knowing already what the next punch was going to be. Without looking, he punched up in a left uppercut, and finally landed a shot into his opponent's supercilious face. Feeling contact, he punched up again with the other hand. The overhead right was a direct hit on Brubaker's nose.

His opponent reacted quickly by firing a jab and right into Axel's chest. The force of those shots made him instinctively duck. He rolled under the hook that followed, but ran sideways into a straight right hand. Axel recovered by retreating quickly and diagonally. He had a ringing in his ears, but noticed with satisfaction that blood was trickling down his opponent's nose. Axel resumed the glove-slapping strategy. Time flew by, and in what felt like seconds later the bell rang, ending the round.

CHAPTER FIFTY-TWO

Back at the chessboard, Brubaker quickly played 15. Qd2. It was not the best move. Better was moving the attacked e3 pawn up one square, when Axel was planning to play a couple of Queen checks, and then plant his Bishops around White's King to continue the attack. The flaw in Brubaker's move was shown up in Axel's reply: 15...Rxe3. White's Queen could take the Rook on e3, but then would be pinned and lost after the Bishop moved from g7 to d4. Axel now had two pawns and an attack for the piece, a decent trade for the sacrificed Knight.

Brubaker transferred his Knight to defend the King with 16. Ne4. Axel exchanged Bishops with 16...Bxb2 17. Qxb2, and then brought his Bishop into the fray with 17...Bh3. White's situation was becoming dicey. The King had no legal moves, and if Brubaker didn't do something soon, would be in trouble once Black put the other Rook on the e-file and kicked the Knight on e4 away by pushing his f-pawn up two squares.

Brubaker played 18. Qd4. It threatened to win the opposing Queen on h4 with a discovered attack by playing the Knight to f6 with check, and also threatened to take the Rook on e3. Axel had seen this possibility earlier, but hadn't fully calculated the ramifications because of the time control. Practically, he was forced to capture the Bishop on e2 and sacrifice the Queen; protecting the Rook with 18...Qh6 would lose decisive material to 19. Kf2.

So, Axel played 18...Rxe2, and Brubaker won the Queen for a Knight after 19. Nf6+ Qxf6 20. Qxf6. Black only had a piece for a Queen, but had the seventh rank for his Rook and a restricted White King that was in serious danger of being checkmated. The next moves had to be played accurately, as checking without thinking would allow the King to get away. After another long think (allowing him only ninety seconds for the rest of the game) he found the most precise continuation. He checked with 20...Rg2+, and after the forced 21. Kf1 played the quiet 21...Re8, keeping the King in a box. He would have liked to play the discovered check by moving the Rook to a2, but the King would have escaped out of the box to the e1 square, and would not have won the Rook on a1 because it was protected by the Queen on f6. Instead, White faced the deadly threat of the Rook on e8 coming to e2, followed by checkmate on the last two ranks.

Brubaker scowled looking for a decent reply. Black had a discovered check hanging in the air, and his King had no legal moves to wriggle out of it. The referee stopped the clocks while he was still thinking. Tearing his eyes away from the chessboard, Axel felt a tingling on the back of his neck; he could feel that White's position was going to fall apart.

The feet stomping was more subdued during the break. Either the audience was becoming tired, or Axel might be winning over some of the fans in the rows. No way the latter, Axel thought – their attention span was fading along with the prospects of a quick Brubaker win, that was all.

When the bell rang his opponent aggressively strode across the ring. When his opponent was a step away of throwing a punch, Axel threw a full combination of jab, right, hook, and straight right into empty air, making him hesitate and slow the advance. Fully warmed up from the combination, Axel exploited Brubaker's reduced speed by lurching to the left, stepped forward with another straight hand into empty space, and then "steplurched" again to the side with a wide left hook that caught his opponent in the gut.

This trick from the Kozlov fight would only work once, so Axel quickly backed out to the open ring and returned to having his straight advance repelled by Brubaker's long jabs and rights. His opponent was clearly becoming pissed by the extra slaps to his extended gloves; a few more might push him over the edge. Brubaker tried a few charges of his own, but they were not of one mind, and Axel after parrying them resumed the slaps to the gloves.

His opponent's patience held out to the second minute. Then the glint in his eyes ignited into rage. He abruptly unloaded a huge right hook when he was seven feet away. It crashed into Axel's shoulder and moved him backwards two feet the moment Brubaker's foot hit the ground. Had Brubaker followed up the punch with a disciplined combination, Axel would have been knocked clean off his feet and listening to a countdown from the referee. However, Brubaker walked in upright, instead of flexibly crouching with the full use of his body's leverage.

Axel remembered to bend. Despite his left shoulder smarting, he saw another right hook coming and reacted in time. He quickly turned himself sideways to the onslaught, and saw Brubaker's hand moving away from the body to begin its arc. Beginning to dip as his opponent committed to the hook, he stepped forward with his left foot and rolled.

When six feet nine of opponent surged past to his right, Axel was ready when he bobbed up again. He saw the exposed flank, drilled a left, right, and left uppercut into Brubaker's open armpit, and then hammered three unanswered left hooks into the ribs. Those punches brought his opponent down to his level, where he continued with a right to the ear, a hook to the nose, and a right uppercut deep into the jaw. Brubaker was forced to clinch to stop Axel from doing more damage.

Fifteen seconds were left in the round when the referee separated them. Axel was content to let it end as it began, advancing against the resistance of the long jabs and rights of his opponent. The bell rang, and Axel felt good despite the pain in his shoulder. For the first time, he felt he might be able to win a chessboxing bout on the basis of the boxing.

It was still Brubaker's move when the clocks were restarted at the chess game. He was in a bind. Despite his material advantage, Black threatened imminent checkmate with his Bishop and two Rooks. The King was stuck on f1, the possibility of a discovered check hanging over its head; neither of the two Rooks on the first rank could move without being lost to various discovered checks; the Queen on f6 had to protect the Rook on a1, and was in danger of being picked off by another discovered check if she moved to the wrong square. The Queen had one check on d8, but after the King moved to g7 had no more checks to give. It was an intolerable situation for White, whose time advantage was slipping away.

After two minutes of thought Brubaker played 22. Qh4, neutralizing the power of the Bishop on h3 behind the Rook on g2. He still had four minutes on his clock to Axel's ninety seconds. At first Axel thought he had a perpetual check with the Rook on the h2 and g2 squares, but belatedly saw that the Queen could just take the Bishop, protecting the Rook on h1. Instead he played 22...Ra2+, giving up the Bishop after 23. Qxh3 in return for picking up a Rook with 23...Rxa1+.

If the King moved to f2, Black would pick up the other Rook on h1 and have a winning advantage of two Rooks and two pawns for the Queen. Brubaker played the forced 24. Kg2, and Axel won the Rook on h1 anyway by playing 24...Re2+, overloading the King's defense to the Rook. His opponent played 25. Kg3, another forced move, and Axel had a large material advantage after 25...Rxh1. If he didn't make any stupid mistakes in time pressure, the game was his.

Brubaker played his lone check 26. Qc8+, and after 26...Kg7 took a pawn with 27. Qxc7, hoping to maintain material parity by winning another pawn or two on the Queenside. Axel stared hard at the position. He knew in his bones a checkmate was there, but didn't see the exact path yet. He was fruitlessly looking at continuations where he captured the h-pawn, when the solution came to him in a flash. With forty seconds left on his clock, he played 27...Rg1+. It was a killer move. If the King went to h4, capturing the h-pawn now was checkmate; if the King went to f4, he would push the g-pawn up with check and after the King had to go to f5 the other Rook would deliver checkmate by moving to e5; and if the King went to h3, the other Rook would go to e5, and the threat of checkmate from that Rook going to h5 would force White to give up the Queen on h4, leaving Black with the decisive advantage of an extra Rook.

Axel looked up and briefly glanced across the board. His opponent knew Black had a win too, from the expression on his face. Brubaker stared at the position, and before Axel could wonder if he would do the classy thing and resign, the referee reached in and stopped the clocks.

Axel didn't even hear the crowd as he went to the ring to put on his gloves. If he got through this round, the bout was his. It took all his self-control to zip up the elation, and concentrate on the next three minutes. He decided to stick to what had been working: attack forward in a straight line, and hold his ground a foot in front of the ropes.

The bell rang, starting a round that Axel's rule-following personality did not see coming.

The first minute started off as that of the first two rounds, with Axel moving forward and Brubaker stopping his approach with jabs and rights. Then suddenly, Brubaker effected a stage stumble. The isometric resistance disappeared, pulling Axel forward, while the opposing head continued to lurch towards him, straight into his nose. Not fooled, the referee angrily told Brubaker that two minutes were going to be taken off his clock at the resumption of the chess game. Copious amounts of blood flowed out of Axel's nose from the head butt, and the bout was halted for a few minutes so that the ring doctor could stanch the bleeding. The comments yelled out from the crowd were mean-spirited and cowardly.

Axel glanced at the clock while his nose was being attended to. Two more minutes. Once the nose was patched up, the referee asked Axel if he was OK to continue, who nodded. He returned to face Brubaker, who didn't show a shred of remorse. Axel approached him cautiously; Brubaker responded aggressively with hard jabs and rights, pushing him back. When Axel felt the ropes at his back, he pushed forward, and prevented his opponent from setting up his hooks.

Brubaker resorted to short uppercuts to slow Axel's counter advance. Axel took two more small steps forward and pressed against his opponent's arms, stopping those as well. He expected a clinch to be called soon. Instead, Axel felt a sudden jerk from the opposite body, and then an excruciating pain above his left brow as if he had been drilled by an errant foul ball at a baseball game.

Axel crumpled to the canvas in agony, clutching the spot above his eye. The referee ordered Brubaker to a neutral corner. He came over to Axel, bent down, and asked to see his forehead. One quick look was all it took to determine what happened. His opponent had shaken himself loose, raised his right arm, and then sent it crashing down elbow-first onto Axel's head. The referee stood up, turned to Brubaker, and signaled that he lost the bout by disqualification.

CHAPTER FIFTY-THREE

The ring quickly filled with people. Eight security personnel encircled Brubaker, and escorted him to the exit; his height allowed him to reach over the escort and high-five fans on the walk back. Dan and a doctor hurried over to Axel. The doctor put a cold compress on Axel's head, saying he was going to have a medical exam in the locker room. Dan asked him how he was.

"Oww... Christ, what an asshole! He is dead lost in the chess game."

"We know. The commentators have chess engines, and they agree – you can stick a fork in his position. You were winning on boxing points, too. Please, let's get you out of here, right now."

Axel was able to get up on his feet. Ten security personnel escorted them back to his locker room. The doctor checked his blood pressure, made him follow his eyes to a moving finger, and administered a whisper speech test. After he successfully walked a straight line forwards and backwards, the doctor left him a bottle of aspirin for the headache, with instructions that Axel if experienced any dizziness or nausea over the night, he was to check into an ER immediately.

The other chessboxers still in the locker room came over to congratulate Axel, and to shit-talk Brubaker. Axel smiled his thanks, and then retreated into a hot shower for the next five minutes. Clean, dry, and changed back into his street clothes, he found Vyacheslav waiting by his locker.

"This is for you, Axel." He handed him a sealed white envelope. "It's half of Brubaker's compensation. That son of a bitch won't be fighting in our next event."

"Thanks, Vy, but I know enough by now to understand how this business works. He put so many buttheads in the seats that he'll be fighting in the event after that. That's all right, I don't take it personally."

Vy smiled ruefully. "You're a class act, Axel. Thanks for a hell of a fight. We're going to edit out the last minute for the DVD. All the rounds before that are nothing less than a work of art."

"Well, thank you in return for giving me the chance to do my thing. Before you called me last year, I had no idea what that thing really was."

"You're welcome, man. Any chance you'll do a chessboxing bout for us again? We'll pay you more."

"I don't know. When it's for charity, that's fine. But when you inject a little bit of money into this, it brings out the crazies. They embody that joke about academic politics: they're vicious precisely because the stakes are so small."

"Seriously, it won't be so nasty again," Vy replied, laughing. "You got the worst of the worst, but came out of it with your head high. Not to mention with a still perfect record."

"My head might be held high, but right now it has a throbbing headache. Can we continue this conversation next year?"

"Of course. Awesome job." They hugged. "These guys –" he motioned to three security personnel by the wall "– will escort you to a taxi. Enjoy your New Year, you've earned it."

Axel heard from behind as he about to go out the door with his protection: "And party the hell out of tomorrow like it's 2999. That's an order from me and Dan."

Axel reached the taxi safely. He thanked the security guys, wishing them a happy New Year. Inside the taxi, he looked at his watch. It was only twelve thirty a.m.

Back in his hotel room he looked at himself in the bathroom mirror. A nasty welt showed above his left eye socket, which wasn't improved by the tissues still stuck up his nose and the purple-black bruises on both his shoulders. He had looked prettier, but never felt so alive, nor so alone.

He checked his email and phone messages again. Axel braced himself to see a burst sewage pipe of sour-grape emails from Brubaker fans, but found none. Apparently, the harassment was meant to throw him off his game before the bout. After the bout, the need to dish out more just evaporated. No phone messages. The time was still evening back on the other coast.

Axel called up Ted and told him what happened. He confessed that he saw no future for himself in the realm of serious boxing, even if it was paired with chess – the vibe stunk. Ted said that was fine: he was proud of what Axel had accomplished, yet told him he had not exhausted his potential and could go still further. If he wanted to improve his boxing, even harder training would be required, but it was up to him how he wanted to spend his time. Ted said he would respect his decision, no matter what he chose. Axel thanked Ted, and rang off with the old joke that he would see him again next year.

Axel then called Garen to rattle off the chess moves in the bout over the phone. Garen was impressed that he had managed to play such a good game while being punched, head-butted, and elbowed, and implored him to stop boxing. It would damage a mind that had produced such wonderful chess that night.

Axel was stuck for a reply. His chess had progressed as far as it could, and he didn't see it ever becoming significantly stronger. The game felt like a dry well for him, and only had become exciting again when he took up boxing. Axel did not have the heart to tell Garen that. He said instead that he appreciated his concern, and would continue to play in tournaments while being his student. He heard a click on the phone, and told Garen that he had another call; they said goodbye to each to other with warm regards.

He checked to see who had called, wishing with all his heart that it was Susan. However, the message was from his sister. She wanted to know how he did. Axel called her back with the result, and how it occurred.

"For God's sake, Axel, stop this!" she exclaimed. "What do you have to prove?"

"That I'm alive."

"Is this about Dad? He loved you. You know that, don't you? He would be horrified today if he could see what you're doing to yourself."

"If he loved me, he never said a word. And if he were breathing today, he'd still be cracking his put-down jokes 24/7. That and guzzling his fucking booze in front of the TV all day, and refining his learned sense of physical helplessness."

"Wait, wait, wait. You're basically living in the gym and getting hit for money because Dad would never think of doing this? That's… so stupid you're going to win the race with him to senility."

"How can drinking yourself to death be any less stupid?"

"That was alcoholism, Axel. He never loved you any less."

"I know you loved him. I loved him too. I just didn't like him one damn bit. He was always pumping me for information, never telling me anything in return. He just wanted me around so that he had a fresh source of material for future teasing. He stopped making me laugh decades ago. The only thing left in the end was tolerating his passive-aggressive bullshit, and filial duty."

"I'm really sorry you two didn't get along." She sighed. "Will you at least please consider stopping for Mom's sake? She comes close to a nervous breakdown when she hears about your fights."

"Unlike Dad, Mom can live her own life without grasping onto her kids for support. She understands, even it makes her anxious."

"Oh, fuck you Axel! You can't keep blaming Dad forever. I'm glad alcohol is out of your life and you're in great shape, but you are still a miserable man with OCD. Please talk to someone and get some help."

"LIKE YOU, PERHAPS?" Axel abruptly screamed. He hung up. He fumed and shouted more things at an empty wall, finally turning in at three a.m.

CHAPTER FIFTY-FOUR

Axel woke up a few hours later, but still muttered dark thoughts at the ceiling, and did not get out of bed for a long time. He was sick of his sister's non-stop suggestions of a well-balanced life. That and his late father's entrenched selfish behavior reinforced Axel's beliefs in erudition and training.

He would call his sister back and patch things up, but not now. This day was for him. Axel suddenly remembered that yesterday was the calendar day when he last had a drink, but the self-congratulations didn't have any wings. He was in a city where he knew no one socially to celebrate the New Year. He would call Susan. No matter what response he received (if he received one at all), he would swallow it whole and digest the consequences. Too many other mountains were out there to climb to be too afraid to ask.

Axel finally roused himself out of bed. He ingested several aspirins, took the tissues out of his nose, and wandered out onto the street by noon. He treated himself to a meal at a diner that all the training this year had been screaming at him to avoid: cheeseburger, fries, milkshake, apple pie with whipped cream, and coffee. Except for the coffee, and he left more than half of it on the table. His whole life for the past two years had rewired him to the point where it couldn't be undone in a day.

He walked around for an hour, until he decided the time had come to bite the bullet. Sitting down at a park bench, he called Susan's number. Something in the dial tone made it feel like a cold call. After a half a dozen rings, voicemail kicked in. He heard two voices in unison, one a man's, the other Susan's: "Hi, we can't come to the phone now. Please leave your name, number, and a brief message, and we'll get back to you as soon as possible. Happy New Year!"

Axel's mouth made the Google 'Aw, Snap' gesture as he listened to the message. The unroyal "we" was being used as the subject. The voice of the person he wanted to hear was of plus-one status. The mouth changed to a sad smile. He left the following message at the beep: "Hi, Susan, it's Axel. Long story short, I won last night. Have a great new year, and I'll see you again when I see you." Then he hung up.

The bullet was bit, and came out bitter. Axel looked around him, searing the images of the park into his brain so that he would never forget this moment, and stood up. He was going to check out of the hotel, fly back home that night, making his resolutions for the next year on the plane.

He was lying down on the bed, on the verge of taking his packed suitcase down to the lobby to check out, when his phone rang.

"Hello?"

"Hey, Axel, it's Susan. Congratulations! Did you kick his ass?"

"Sort of." Axel described the course of the bout, and how it ended.

"Oh my God, are you all right?"

"I did have a bad headache after the fight, but after a long afternoon nap, and not a few aspirins, the headache is gone."

"Good. Is that thyroid turd going to face criminal charges?"

He chuckled at the description of Brubaker. "You can get away with a lot of bad behavior in boxing events where money is involved – it comes close to assault, but that's what boxers sign up for when they step in the ring. The organizers did give me half of his purse as compensation for his violating the morals clause of the contract. The short answer is no. He has too many social media fans for organizers to ignore him. All those followers pay full retail prices for the tickets."

"What a twisted world this is."

"No argument here. All we can do is live in it."

They were silent for half a minute. Then she asked: "So when are you leaving?"

"Well, you didn't call, and all I got was your voicemail. I was about to check out and catch the red eye home tonight."

"Oh good, I got you just in the nick of time. Do you want to get together for a quick bite?"

"Of course. Only I don't want to go very far from my hotel. I just don't feel like dealing with any more of this city today."

"Where's your hotel?" Axel told her. "I know where that is. Does it have a restaurant?"

"I don't think it's open now. There is a cafe is across the street, though. Hold on... I can see the name from the window: The Sunrise Cafe."

"All right, I can be there soon. About an hour?"

"About an hour it is. Don't be too shocked at my appearance – I've looked prettier."

"Well, we actresses have bad hair days. You boxers must have bad face days."

"Bye," he said with an inflection in his voice that had more than one tone.

"Bye," Susan said cheerfully.

Axel had been sitting in a corner booth for fifteen minutes when Susan walked through the door. He held up his hand; upon seeing it, she walked over and kissed him lightly before joining him. He did not think it possible, but she looked even more beautiful than before.

"You're right – you have looked prettier."

"You haven't."

She smiled. "Do you have to go back tonight?"

"No. I have an adjustable return ticket, and can probably conjure up some sort of travel excuse to my boss to come back a day later."

"Good. I've missed you, Axel." She held his hand across the table.

"I've missed you too, Susan." He squeezed her hand. "I really can't say any more until I know what your status is with your boyfriend."

"Oh, yes... that." She did not take her hand away. "He got out on December 23, and I took him back in. We celebrated Christmas together at my apartment when my roommates had gone home for the holidays. The day after Christmas, he was back to using drugs as if his stay in jail never happened. I won't bore you with the fallout that happened this week, but he's no longer in my life."

"I'm sorry it didn't work out."

"Me too." Their breathing made their held hands sway slightly on the table.

Axel said: "So, I'm not really that hungry. Are you?"

Susan looked straight into his eyes. "Nope."

They were later entwined in bed in Axel's hotel room. They had been there for hours. Axel murmured: "Susan, I have to confess, I don't like you anymore."

"Really?"

"Really. I love you."

"Oh, well in that case I don't like you anymore either."

"You don't?"

"No. I love you too."

He took her in his arms, and kissed her tenderly. Suddenly, she turned into a pillow. Axel woke up alone in the hotel room, his still-packed bag on the floor, in the dusk. *This must be the sweet part of what makes love so bittersweet,* he thought, looking at his watch. Seven o'clock. He could still check out and make his plane in plenty of time.

Axel checked his phone messages while he had been dreaming. Susan had not called back at all today. He looked out the window where he had seen the Sunrise Cafe, only to see a brick wall. Just to make sure he was not certifiably insane he checked his phone's call log and yes, he had called Susan's number, and yes, her voice was still on one of the voicemail messages he had saved. Even her emails were there. Everything except the happy ending he wanted.

CHAPTER FIFTY-FIVE

It was over the Rockies when the old year ended and the new year began – the captain said so in an announcement. The passengers spontaneously celebrated, some deciding to buy all their fellow travelers a glass of champagne. Axel politely declined, sticking to orange juice. He had used some of the extra money that Dan and Vy had given him to upgrade himself to business class. The night was clear, with scant clouds obscuring the ground in the moonlight. Looking out the window on the mountains below, he began thinking about resolutions for the coming year.

He thought about doing more chessboxing bouts, or honing his chess and boxing even more. Mostly, he didn't want to feel so alone all the time. If he had an individually fulfilling life first, then sharing it with someone would be icing on the cake. But Axel at that moment didn't think he had anything fulfilling in his life to share. He felt lost in the woods, even though he was tens of thousands of feet above the ground.

By the time the plane flew over Chicago, his list ran out of steam. He saw snow on the ground when it became light. He'd be shoveling his driveway soon, as if all the missed expectations of past years kept piling up, accumulating inches by the hour.

Back at his apartment, Axel on a whim again decided to enter the New Year's Day chess tournament at his local chess club. He could think of nothing better to do. Talking to people at the club's traditional open house was better than brooding and grinding his wheels.

The time control was thirty minutes for the entire game, so that five rounds could be played in one day. Axel stuck to his preference of playing in the unrated section. He always felt freer during a chess game when no rating points were up for grabs, back when the game was fun and had not yet become some involuntary crutch for his ego. He faced two beginners, one charming seventy-something-year-old he had known all his life, one high schooler, and one fellow master in the last round. Axel won all his games, and then donated his prize money to the club.

He still looked like he had just come from a boxing match, and received strange sideways glances throughout the day. The high schooler was bold enough to ask what happened to his face, and Axel told him. Two college students, overhearing his reply, tapped away on their smart phones. As Axel was leaving, the two college students offered to buy him dinner. He agreed.

They took Axel to a Greek restaurant a block away, not far from their college, and pumped him for details. One of them must have been texting under the table, for ten more students materialized after they had been sitting down for no more than a minute, half of them female. Axel answered their questions as best he could, mentioning the chessboxing classes at Ted's gym if any of them were interested. He allowed himself to be pictured in selfies, with some of the coeds pressing themselves quite hard against him. Axel didn't know what was more disturbing: the women being so aggressive, or the fact that he did not feel uncomfortable.

One of them was really cute. She surprised Axel by kissing him full on the lips, and slipping her phone number into his pocket. He was tempted: why couldn't the year begin a different way the previous year had ended? What stopped him was that they were sitting close to the smoking section, and next to a large wall clock. Something in the smell of the cigarettes and the presence of time ticking away turned a switch off inside Axel. It just didn't feel right, so he excused himself. He went home and turned in early, in order to get a good night's sleep for work the next day.

It snowed again that night. Axel showed up for work after several minutes of shoveling snow and scraping ice off his car. It seemed like forever since he last sat behind his desk. His boss came by, supervisors from different departments came by, co-workers came by, and even the cleaners came by, to ask him about his bout in Los Angeles. He didn't need to tell anyone what he did last week; everyone knew already.

After satisfying their curiosity, Axel buckled down and resumed his job. To his disappointment, he found that the work was intolerably boring. He could do the job in his sleep, and for many years that had been the main appeal. Unfortunately, he was now awake. Soon the annual meeting would take place on the factory floor, where long-time employees would be honored for their ten, twenty, thirty, and even forty years of service. The prospect of seeing himself in that company for decades more made him feel like being stuck on Gilligan's Island with the same group of castaways in perpetuity, in a bad dream.

It wasn't the company's fault. A steady job that guaranteed an income for the pursuit of one's hobbies was hard to find. After several years of tenuous positions, Axel appreciated the stability it had provided. Except he didn't need the money that much anymore. His investments were beginning to earn enough dividends for a livable income. Whatever he wanted now, it wasn't this.

Axel finished out the day, and the days after that, knowing that he would be leaving. To where, he did not yet know. He was back in the same boat before he picked up a pair of boxing gloves, only this time he could jump out of the boat and swim before being picked up by another. He was no longer afraid of getting wet.

After a week, the bruises on Axel's face disappeared. He showed up in Ted's gym the following week, and found the place packed with people wanting to lose their post-holiday weight. To his annoyance, he was besieged with requests for shared selfies.

"Well, I guess people know what I did last year," he said to Ted. "What did I do, break the Internet or something?"

"I'd have to say yes, with all the universities here. Who knew?" He added: "I have waiting lists for all levels of the chessboxing classes. They are starting the end of January. Can you help out? Willie is somewhere in Florida for the next few months."

"For the Friday class, sure. Are some of the people who did the classes last year willing to become trainers?"

"Probably. Many of them are starving students who would love to be paid. Oh, in case you didn't know, your sparring buddy Gunther moved back to Berlin. Max called to tell me a couple of days ago."

"I'll miss that panzer tank. Is John around?"

"I was talking to him yesterday. He can't wait to see you again. The boy is walking on air at the moment. He received early admission to his first-choice college (I don't know where). Yeah, John might want to help out with the Monday and Wednesday classes."

"That would be ideal, Ted. Yes, I can help out with the Friday class."

"Great. Have you seen your L.A. bout online, yet? It's there, posted from multiple sources."

"No, and I won't, because I was actually there. Are the comments kind?"

"They're unkind, but for Brubaker, not you. Jesus, what a prick you fought. You should be proud of what you did against such a tall guy – I am. Don't know much about the chess, but you seemed to have kicked his ass there as well. You even shut up your opponent's fans."

Axel grinned: "I managed to shut them up? That's what makes me really proud."

Axel continued to show up for work, but the motivation was gone. His workouts in the gym went back to maintenance mode. Playing in weekend chess tournaments out of town, with slow classical time controls, had predictable results; he held his own against fellow amateurs, and was soundly beaten by professionals, finishing out of the money. Some things never changed. He was waiting for something more exciting to pick him up and sweep him away.

The chessboxing classes started again, and they were packed. Ted needed to order even more chess sets and clocks to handle the overspill. John agreed to coach the chess part for Mondays and Wednesdays; on Fridays, the classes had spectators. Axel suggested to Ted that the gym host an evening of chessboxing bouts for the general public.

Ted thought that was a fantastic idea. Enough people clamored to be in the event that qualifying bouts were necessary to winnow down the number. The bouts would have seven rounds of chess and boxing, the time control for the chess game being six minutes with no increment. Four bouts from the Monday class, four from Wednesday, and five from Friday comprised the card, to be held one week after the end of the classes in April. For the fighters in the beginner classes, the three-punch drill could substitute for sparring.

Ted was less sure how to show the chess games on a screen, and asked Axel for advice. Axel in turn asked Vyacheslav if he knew any tournament organizers who broadcast their games over the Internet. Vy said he knew someone, who he would ask to contact Axel.

Within the hour an IT professional for a chess website called to tell Axel that they needed a sensory game board, compatible chess pieces, and a digital chess clock connected to a host computer with a Bluetooth connection to demonstrate the moves in real time on a wall projector. It sounded like a lot, but the equipment could be rented, and anyone with a network background could set up the graphic user interface easily.

The IT guy told Axel where they could rent the equipment and download the setup instructions. Axel thanked him, obtained a quote for the equipment rental, and passed the information along to Ted. The cost was little more than three months' membership at the gym, and Ted promptly reserved the equipment for the night. One of the students in the chessboxing classes was a computer science major at a local university, who said after looking at the installation and configuration instructions that he would bring a spare laptop from home, and set the whole thing up for free.

Ted asked Axel to participate in the event, who demurred, saying that the students in the classes should be the stars that night. John overheard Axel's answer, and told him he wanted to be his opponent in one of the bouts. With Ted breathing down his neck, Axel accepted the challenge; at last he had an excuse this year to push himself harder.

John did not have Axel's experience in the boxing ring, nor his expertise in chess, and would not be a serious threat in the exhibition bout. However, he was eighteen years old, would never get tired, and be utterly fearless with nothing to lose. Axel trained hard as a sign of respect. He ran several miles a week on a treadmill, and put in three solid workouts a week, sparring at least six rounds every Friday night. For chess training, he confined himself to online blitz games.

For the next two months though Axel was adrift. He had been gripping the steering wheel so tightly for so long that he yearned to let go, and let it spin. Deep down, he knew that he was going to make major changes in his life; however, he didn't yet have the nerve to jump out of the plane, and let gravity take its course. He was still doing what he did out of entropy.

In the meantime, Dan and Vycheslav put on another chessboxing event in March. Brubaker was not invited, but they were going to host another event in June: would Axel be interested in a rematch with him then, for good money? His instant answer was HELL NO. They laughingly replied OK, it was worth a try. They wished Axel the best, and said they would keep in touch.

The chessboxing classes remained full, and fun. Axel liked that complete strangers could get together, compete strenuously against each other, and come out the best of friends. He missed that in school, and in most of his career, where everyone wound up in their own separate worlds, stingily sharing their experiences if at all. Axel hoped that the classes, even if the participants never met each other afterwards, made their world was a less hostile place. The checkmates and landed punches certainly made for a lot of smiling faces.

CHAPTER FIFTY-SIX

At the end of March, B sent an email from Berlin. His club was going to be hosting a series of chessboxing bouts during the summer with fighters from other federations, including those from London and Moscow. The guys had brought Axel's last fight to the attention of the president of their chessboxing federation, who was impressed. He wanted to extend an invitation for Axel to compete for the club. B urged Axel to reply soon. If interested, and if they could work out the paperwork, they could arrange a stipend for him as well.

Axel finally had the nudge he needed to get out of the door. He emailed B the following day, asking what paperwork they needed. Upon receiving an official application packet two days later, he set out in a burst of excited energy to acquire his birth certificate, medical clearance form, criminal background checks, and proof of sufficient financial assets to support himself in Germany should the stipend fall through. By the end of the following week, Axel had managed to assemble the necessary documents, and FedEx'd them.

Axel eventually called his sister, and patched matters up with her over the phone. She knew as well as he that they were family, always would be, and loved each other enough to agree to disagree. She invited Axel to dinner that very night, along with their mother.

At the dinner table, he told his family about the chessboxing exhibition at the gym, and invited them to come and watch. Most of the bouts were going to be between novice boxers, which would be halted immediately if it looked like one of the fighters was going to get hurt. The evening, he stressed, was more about people pushing themselves to see what they could do physically and mentally, rather than injuring another human being. The participants would themselves stop before any of the fights became one-sided.

His niece asked: "Are any women going to fight?"

"Yes, three of the bouts are between women."

"Why?"

"Well, women can get just as angry as men."

"Are you going to be fighting?"

"Yes, against a good friend and fellow trainer. It will be one of the last bouts of the night."

His nephew clamored to go. His sister relented, and promised to come with the kids. "If anyone looks like they're in pain, though, dear brother, we're going home at once," she warned. His mother said she loved Axel, but declined to go. Axel said that was OK; he loved her too.

In the last two weeks of the classes, reporters from a few local colleges showed up to observe the qualification fights for the exhibition. The students were thrilled to be interviewed, many of whom were going to go against each other in front of an audience for the first time. Axel answered some questions about his recent bouts, but insisted that the reporters devote most of their time to the other fighters.

The qualifying bouts were a joy to watch. Axel visited the gym the last Monday and Wednesday of the chessboxing classes to observe. The eight chosen from each of the classes were enthusiastic, respectful, and had lots of friends cheering them on, an excellent sign that the gym was going to be full with spectators on exhibition night.

On Friday, he and John had a practice match. John was still not a threat on the chessboard, but he was rapidly becoming a dangerous boxer. Only Axel's experience kept his energetic opponent from landing many fast combinations. He told Ted afterwards that the bout would be a crowd pleaser. Ted agreed, and said that if John stayed in the area by going to a local university, the gym would train him for a real amateur fight.

An official looking envelope from Berlin was waiting for him in his mailbox when he arrived home that Friday night. Opening it, he found that his application along with a stipend to chessbox in Germany in the summer had been accepted – they needed an answer in the next couple of weeks. His heart was pleased, but his head was lurching all over the place. How would he go about rearranging his life in the months to come? And why couldn't he calculate it all down to the smallest detail right now?

He closed his eyes to do a gedenken experiment. On one hand, he might become injured over there, and would have that much more to do to put his old life back together should he move back home. On the other hand, his old life right now looked like more of the same, of routine and procrastination. The two hands wrestled with each other over the weekend, still fighting to a draw by Sunday night.

Matters came to a head the following day at work. He was writing specifications for his company's contribution to a massive government project that required sign offs from two government agencies and four fellow subcontractors. The specifications came back yet again to be edited due to one bureaucrat who changed his mind for the third time. The experience was Sisyphean. Axel felt his life draining away in a small, enclosed space, getting these lousy ten pages out the door. He was so aggravated that he could not breathe.

He gave two weeks' notice at lunch, with no trepidation in his voice. His boss suggested he take a leave of absence instead. "It might be months before I come back; don't hold the job open for me forever," Axel said to the vice president an hour later.

"We won't. Go on and recharge your batteries. If you return, come back all in," was the reply. It was the most amicable parting Axel had ever had with a job.

It took all of two days to adjust his assets so that he could live off his passive income. Axel had long prepared a spreadsheet for such an occasion. He changed one income cell to zero, added another expense line by purchasing private health insurance, and made arrangements with his brokerage's checking account to make up the difference in another cell. That's all it took. His finances went on as before without a speed bump.

"So, what do you want?" Ted said. They were in his office on Saturday night. The first exhibition chessboxing bout was about go on at the gym in a few minutes. Axel recently told him about the invitation from

Germany, when he had to reply to the offer, and his current leave of absence from work. Garen when told had said go for it; the organized team matches of the Bundesliga there were paradise for a chess player of Axel's level, and would dramatically improve his playing strength within a year.

"My heart of course says yes, and to go, but my home has been here for so long that it's hard to just say 'anchors aweigh' and take off. Nothing's that black and white."

"Of course not. Ask yourself this then, Axel: why are you still here?"

Ted smiled when Axel was silent. "Well, you seem to know what you want over there. Find out what you still want here, and decide whether you still want it or not."

Ted left his office to announce the start of the event. He was in a great mood. The gym was packed with friends and family of the participants, including Axel's sister, niece, and nephew. The rented sensory board and digital clock had arrived that afternoon, which were field tested and ready to go just outside the ring. Axel and John were scheduled to fight around ten thirty p.m. The boxing referee was Jason, with help from the reappeared Willie to consult with the chess positions. Ted took the mike to welcome the attendees at seven p.m.; the first bout started five minutes later.

People were going in and out of the gym constantly throughout the fights to chat on their phones. Reporters from the local colleges were there, as well as a local TV station with a camera crew. Axel looked around. The venue looked just like Dan's and Vyacheslav's in L.A., except the fans were much friendlier. No one booed during the entire night; and the audience was silent enough during the chess rounds that headphones proved to be optional.

At the beginning of the ninth bout, Axel warmed up. While skipping rope and doing pad work with Lou, he realized in an instant what he still wanted here. But that was on a ship which had sailed. Such was life. He needed to stop thinking about what he wanted, and physically meet it more than halfway, if he ever wanted to experience it.

At Axel's request, Ted introduced him as just one of the other chessboxers when his turn came in the ring. He was relieved that the cheering was equally distributed for everyone. With no spotlight on him, Axel was ready with a clear, open mind. He met John at the chessboard, where they firmly touched hand wraps. John won the coin toss, and chose the White pieces.

John opened with 1. d4, and Axel played the Nimzo-Indian Defense. John continued with the Capablanca Variation by playing his Queen out to c2. Axel moved his d-pawn up two squares, and John exchanged it, turning the opening into more of a Queen's Gambit Declined. His opponent played the Bishop to g5; Axel counterattacked by pushing his c-pawn up two squares, threatening the pawn on d4. John captured the pawn on c5. Black kicked the Bishop with the h-pawn, and then with the g-pawn when the Bishop retreated to h4. The pin gone, Axel played his Knight to e4. John instantly captured the Knight on b8 with the kicked Bishop; he was moving quickly because of the absence of a time increment, but Axel thought he was moving too fast.

The clocks were stopped before Axel could consider a reply. It occurred to him as he put on the gloves during the break that capturing the Bishop on b8 was a blunder because the Queen check on a4 would win the Bishop on b4. But he saw a better line for Black as the bell went off; it only needed a few seconds of calculation back at the chessboard to make sure.

The boxing began. Axel was impressed by John's speed and energy. Fortunately, John still had not mastered how to not telegraph his punches, and Axel slipped them fairly easily. A few got through and jolted, but Axel had experienced much worse, and the ones he gave in return made John back off by the closing seconds of the round.

Back at the chessboard, Axel examined the position intently for half a minute, and played his Queen to f6. John could still win the Bishop with the Queen check, but Axel's Queen would do much more damage by capturing the pawn on f2; the Bishop on f1 and then the Rook on a1 would fall. The Bishop thus went back to g3 protecting the pawn, whereupon Axel captured the Knight on c3 with his Knight from e4. Material parity was restored. John could not capture the Knight, because the subsequent recapture with the Bishop on c3 would win the Rook. John tried kicking the Bishop on b4 with his a-pawn, but after

Axel played his Bishop to f5, attacking the Queen, the game was his – Black's pieces were too active, and most of White's were still undeveloped.

John must have sensed he was in trouble, for he continued to play quickly, hoping to catch Axel in time pressure in later rounds. The advantage John held in the clock times, however, came at the expense of his position, which surprisingly collapsed that very chess round.

The attacked Queen moved to d2; Axel moved his attacked Bishop to a5. John impulsively moved the b-pawn up two squares to attack the Bishop again, but he was lost after Axel played his Knight from c3 to e4, attacking the Queen and the Rook on a1. The Queen went to c1, and Axel moved his Rook to c8, which overloaded White's defenses. John instantly played the Rook to a2, whereupon Axel took the c5 pawn with the Rook, attacking the Queen again – the Rook was immune because of the pin from the Bishop on a5. John finally slowed down. He moved his Queen to a1 offering to exchange Queens. After careful thought, Axel moved the Queen to c6, offering his Rook on h8 with check. John took the Rook only to find that he could not avoid checkmate afterwards, which is what occurred four moves later.

Axel and John hugged after the latter tipped his King. He told John to slow down both in his chess and in his boxing; all the time in the world could fit inside a couple of minutes. Then they hastily left the stage so that the next contest could begin.

Everyone at the gym was having a lot of fun, including Axel's family. His nephew enjoyed the boxing; his niece enjoyed cheering on the matches between the women; and his sister saw firsthand the adrenaline and camaraderie he had talked about over the dinner table.

"I finally see why you're into this," she said to Axel as he sat with them after the bout. "It demands so much of the fighters it commands respect, yet is so ridiculous looking that people laugh with instead of at each other."

He laughed and hugged her: "I love you, sis. Thanks for coming out. I want to get some air; I'll be right back."

Axel nodded to Ted as he stepped out into the parking lot. It was a beautiful starlit night. People continued to mill in and out of the building, devices clutched in their hands and pressed to their ears. He looked back into the building, and considered Ted's questions again: *What did he want here, and did he still want it or not?*

Axel realized that he was looking into the crowded gym with contentment. He had helped start something inside that made a lot of people happy, had paid for itself, and would continue perfectly well without him. He hung his head and said to his Dad silently (wherever he was): *If that doesn't make you proud, then to hell with you.*

He wasn't that angry anymore.

He looked back up at the stars and asked aloud to no one in particular: "Have you ever felt that you were sleepwalking through life, and had to be punched awake?"

"Yes."

Startled, Axel turned around. "Hello, there," he said. "I just had a very nice dream about you recently."